Pouring from the fortress gate was a rag-tag army of heavily armed soldiers waving swords and screaming like banshees.

The koala wizard steeled himself. "They think they've got us outnumbered, but I've handled nearly that many by myself. One thing I don't understand, though. Why would an evil sorcerer send only females against us, and only human ones at that?"

Jon-Tom might have ventured a guess, but he couldn't speak. An arrow whizzed past his head. He blinked but could not bring himself to move, to dodge.

He couldn't do anything because each of the onrushing valkyries looked exactly like her sister, and that meant all of them looked like his beloved Talea...

D0456438

Also by
Alan Dean Foster

THE SPELLSINGER SERIES
Spellsinger
The Hour of the Gate
The Day of the Dissonance
The Moment of the Magician

The I Inside
The Man Who Used the Universe
Alien
Clash of the Titans
Krull
Outland
Shadowkeep
Starman

Published by
WARNER BOOKS

ATTENTION: SCHOOLS AND CORPORATIONS

WARNER books are available at quantity discounts with bulk purchase for educational, business, or sales promotional use. For information, please write to: SPECIAL SALES DEPARTMENT, WARNER BOOKS, 666 FIFTH AVENUE, NEW YORK, N.Y. 10103.

ARE THERE WARNER BOOKS
YOU WANT BUT CANNOT FIND IN YOUR LOCAL STORES?

You can get any WARNER BOOKS title in print. Simply send title and retail price, plus 50¢ per order and 50¢ per copy to cover mailing and handling costs for each book desired. New York State and California residents add applicable sales tax. Enclose check or money order only, no cash please, to: WARNER BOOKS, P.O. BOX 690, NEW YORK, N.Y. 10019.

ALAN DEAN FOSTER
THE PATHS OF
THE PERAMBULATOR

WARNER BOOKS

A Warner Communications Company

WARNER BOOKS EDITION

Copyright © 1985 by Thranx, Inc.
All rights reserved.

Hardcover edition published by Phantasia Press

Cover art by Carl Lundgren

Warner Books, Inc.
666 Fifth Avenue
New York, N.Y. 10103

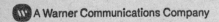 A Warner Communications Company

Printed in the United States of America

First Printing: February, 1986

10 9 8 7 6 5 4 3 2 1

Here's one for Alex Berman and Sid,
who had confidence and who print 'em pretty.

I

For once all seemed right with the world, even if the world in question happened to be the one to which he had been unwillingly transported, Jon-Tom reflected with a resigned sigh. It was a perfectly gorgeous autumn morning. Bright sunshine warmed his face, his stomach was giving him no trouble, and there was a delicious bite to the air.

Not only did all seem right with the world, he was also feeling especially good about himself. His studies had progressed to the point where even the wizard Clothahump was willing to concede, albeit reluctantly, that with continued practice and attention to detail Jon-Tom might actually be worthy of the sobriquet of Spellsinger. The wizard had been in a particularly good mood lately. Some of that could be attributed to the fact that his apprentice, the owl Sorbl, had sworn off liquor after coming out of a three-day drunk. While he was lying unconscious on the floor of a tavern, the owl's drinking buddies had amused themselves by pulling out most of his tail feathers. The result left the apprentice sufficiently mortified to embark on a return to the long-forgotten state known as sobriety, of which he had not been an inhabitant for some time.

Even the wizard's bowels were behaving, for which Jon-Tom was equally grateful. There is no more pitiful sight than a turtle with the trots.

There was only one problem. His fine morning mood notwithstanding, Jon-Tom couldn't shake a vague feeling of unease. It wasn't anything specific, nothing he could put a claw on, but it had been nagging at him most of the morning. It was unconscionable for something so intangible to spoil his mood.

Nothing like a good breakfast to banish lingering sensations of discontent, he mused as he bent over his tray. But though the annelids were fresh and the dried anemone crunchy and well seasoned, the food failed to alleviate his discomfort.

He turned toward the single window that let light into the cave, his eyestalks twisting for a better view. Beyond and below, the waves smashed energetically against the sheer granite cliff. The damp air of his cavern was perfumed with the sharp smell of salt and seawater. Dried algae and kelp decorated the floor and walls.

Both suns were already high in the sky. The largest gleamed deep purple through the clouds, while its smaller companion shed its normal pale green light on the coastline. The purple clouds reflected his mood but were not responsible for it.

Turning away from the feeding tray, he used a lesser claw to wipe edible tidbits into his mouth. The tension caused his eyestalks to clench, and he made a deliberate effort to relax.

Nerves, he told himself firmly. Nothing but nerves. Except that he had no reason to be nervous. If all was right with the world, what was there to be nervous about? He sighed deeply, shook himself, preened his eyestalks. Nothing helped. Something, somewhere, was seriously wrong.

A hiss behind him made him shift from contemplation of his continued unease to the passageway that led out of his cave. The hiss was followed by a rasping noise and a formal greeting. Moving lithely on six chitinous legs, Clothahump shuffled into the chamber. As befitted his age, his shell was twice the diameter of Jon-Tom's, though Jon-Tom was more intimidated by the wizard's intellect than by his size.

His mentor's eyes bobbed and danced on the ends of foot-long stalks that, like Jon-Tom's, were a pale turquoise blue. Upon entering sideways, the wizard assumed a stance next to the window where he could inhale the full rush of salt-stained air. Settling his legs beneath him, he gestured with his primary claw.

"A question for you, my boy. How are you feeling this morning? Anything troubling you? Headache, nausea perhaps?"

"Nothing." Jon-Tom's eyestalks dipped and bobbed eloquently. "I feel great. It's a beautiful day." He hesitated. "Except . . ."

"Except what?" the wizard prompted him.

"Nothing, really. It's only that since I woke up this morning, well—it's hard to define. I don't feel a hundred percent, and I should. There's something, a funny feeling of—I don't know. I just don't feel *right*."

"You feel that something is not as it should be, but you are unable to define what it is?"

"Yes, exactly! You've been feeling the same thing?"

"Yes, indeed. I believe it woke me up."

Jon-Tom nodded excitedly. "Me too. But I can't pin it down."

"Really? I should think you would have been able to by this time."

Before Jon-Tom could respond, a three-foot-long centipede wandered into the chamber. It peered mournfully up at Clothahump before glancing over at Jon-Tom. He recognized the famulus immediately.

"Sorbl. You've been drinking again. I thought you'd sworn off the stuff."

"Sorry." The centipede staggered toward the depression in the middle of the chamber. "But when I got a look at myself in the mirror this morning, well, you can imagine."

"I can? Imagine what?"

The centipede returned its sorrowful stare to its master. "Hasn't he figured it out yet?"

"Figured what out yet?"

"You don't notice anything unusual?" the famulus asked in disbelief.

"Unusual? No, I don't . . ." And then it hit him as sharply as if he'd stuck his finger in an electric socket. That was his problem: he wasn't noticing. Noticing, for example, what was wrong with the wizard's assistant. Sorbl was an owl, approximately three feet in height, with wings to match and vast yellow eyes, usually bloodshot. What he was *not* was a three-foot-long centipede.

"Holy shit, Sorbl—what happened to you?"

The centipede gaped at him. "What happened to *me*? How about what's happened to you? Or haven't you taken a look at yourself yet this morning?"

Not possessing the right equipment for frowning, Jon-Tom settled for clicking his lesser claw several times to indicate the extent of his confusion. Then he took the time to inspect himself.

Nothing out of the ordinary. Everything was in its proper place. His six legs were folded neatly beneath him, his primary and lesser claws held out in front. His eyestalks enabled him to study every part of his body. Oh, his palps were still a mite grungy from breakfast, and his shell could use a cleaning, but other than that, everything appeared to be in good working order.

"You still don't know what's wrong, do you?" Clothahump sounded more curious than accusatory.

"No, I don't." Jon-Tom was growing irritated by the repeated question. "I don't know what happened to transform Sorbl, but I can't be expected to . . ."

Transform. The word meant something important in the context of this morning's unease. Change. Alter. Different.

Something went click inside his head. It was as if his eyes were lenses in a camera belonging to another individual entirely and that individual had just released the shutter.

He took another look at himself; a good look, a long look. Then he started to tremble, which is not easy to do when one is mounted on six legs and is sitting down besides. The internal vibrations were impressive. Nausea? Clothahump had inquired about it upon entering. He was in the process of having his question fulfilled.

Wishing for a sudden onset of blindness, Jon-Tom stared around the chamber. Sorbl was not all that had been transformed. For openers, the wizard Clothahump did not live in a rocky, moisture-drenched cave that looked out over an ocean. He lived in a giant oak tree whose interior had been dimensionally enlarged by one of the sorcerer's spells. The oak grew in the middle of a forest called the Bellwoods, not by the shore of some unknown sea that foamed red instead of white against the rocks.

There was also the matter of the sun's absence and its replacement by two unhealthy-looking orbs of green and purple. Clothahump himself was a turtle many hundreds of years old, not an arthropod of unknown origin. For that matter, he himself, Jon-Tom, née Jonathan Thomas Meriweather, was a young man six feet two inches tall, a bit on the slim side, with shoulder-length brown hair and a thoughtful expression. He looked weakly down at himself for a second time. Nothing had changed since this revelation had struck him.

He was still a giant blue crab.

"You would think, my boy," declared Clothahump in that

sometimes maddeningly condescending tone of his, "that you would have noticed the change before this, but I suppose readjustment takes more time when it occurs immediately upon awakening."

"Readjustment?" He was very near panicking. "What the hell's going on? What's happened to you? What happened to Sorbl? What . . ." He started to gesture with a claw, and as soon as he saw it hovering in front of him, he quickly drew it back against his body as if the very movement might make it disappear. "What's happened to *everything*?"

"Well, my boy." The wizard spoke while nonchalantly preening one eyestalk with his secondary claw, acting as though it were a task he performed regularly every morning. "It would appear that we are confronted by a problem of grave dimensions."

"Oh, no," Jon-Tom moaned. At least, he thought he moaned. It emerged as a kind of sibilant hiss. "Why must it always be a problem of grave dimensions? Can't we ever be confronted by a problem of lighthearted dimensions? A problem of mild dimensions? A problem requiring only simple, straightforward solutions?"

"You are becoming hysterical, my boy."

"I am not becoming hysterical," Jon-Tom snapped. "Sarcastic and mad and maybe a little crazy, but not hysterical."

At that moment the enormous blue crab, which had been listening patiently to him, vanished. So did the algae- and kelp-strewn wall of the cave, and the roar of the ocean outside, and the thick tangy odor of salt spray. The purple and green light that had illuminated the chamber was replaced with a warm, indistinct transparency. Clothahump the wizard, the real Clothahump, was sitting facing him on a stool not six feet away and regarding his young guest calmly.

Behind the wizard was the soft blond-brown wood that formed the interior walls of the great tree. The cave, too, had gone, to be replaced by the familiar surroundings of his own room. There was his bed, there his desk and chair, over in the corner the simple washbasin and spigots. Rising on shaky legs, he crossed to the basin, turned the cold water tap on full, and splashed it freely over his face and arms. As he dried himself he felt with relief the soft smooth skin that covered his arms. The hard chitinous shell was gone. He touched his head, felt the recently washed shoulder-length hair.

I am me again, he thought with exquisite relief.

The world was normal once more. Or was it? What of the problem the wizard had alluded to? Jon-Tom knew that the turtle did not refer to such matters lightly, and he'd already been subjected to an intimate illustration of the seriousness of the problem.

Well, no matter. They would handle it, as they had handled such matters before. Clothahump would know how to cope, what to do. Oh, he would moan and groan and gripe about the loss of his precious time, but he would take care of things, and Jon-Tom, as always, would learn from the experience. Surely any sorcerer who could conceive a strategy for defeating the Plated Folk at the Jo-Troom Gate and who could provide hot and cold running water in the heart of an oak tree could cope with this small matter of waking up in another world in the body of a giant blue crab?

Only—what if it happened again?

With some amazement he saw that his hands were trembling.

"Hey," he said, trying to sound cool and failing because his voice was also shaking, "look at my hands. How about that? Maybe I am a little hysterical."

Clothahump responded with a disapproving clucking sound, though his expression was full of sympathy. "Delayed reaction." He reached into one of the drawers built into his plastron, spent a moment searching, and removed a small foil packet. He tossed the contents into the air while reciting a spell new to Jon-Tom.

"Suffer the shakes to cease and desist,
Soothe the disquiet and stir.
The neural pathways now should consist
Of quiet not unlike a cat's purr
Tallium, condralium
Come forth endorphins and valium!"

Immediately a feeling of great contentment and well-being spread through Jon-Tom's entire body. The relief was so sudden and complete that he didn't mind the fact he could no longer stand erect. Sorbl caught him just in time, helped him over to his bed.

"I may have overdone it a bit," Clothahump muttered.

"No, no, I feel fine," Jon-Tom assured him. "Just—fi-ine."

The wizard was nodding to himself. "Definitely overdid it. You are enjoying yourself too much." And he made some signs in the air while Jon-Tom struggled to protest.

His head cleared and his hands remained steady. He tried not to show his disappointment.

"Uh, what was that stuff, sir?"

The turtle wagged a warning finger at him. "This is no time for pharmacological experimentation, my boy. You are not mature enough to utilize such spells in proper moderation. Your head needs to be clear, and what brain you have to be functioning optimally. Or have you forgotten already what I just told you?"

"Yeah, yeah." Unable to conceal his boredom, he sat up on the bed, put his hands on his knees. "Another serious problem. Big deal."

Clothahump eyed him carefully. "I definitely should have used a less powerful spell. Well, any remaining aftereffects will wear off quickly enough."

"Too bad," Jon-Tom muttered. "Look, I've heard it all before, sir. But I just can't get excited anymore. Especially since you're obviously capable of handling this particular problem.''

"Is that so?" Clothahump peered at him through six-sided glasses. "What makes you think I will be able to handle it?"

"You already have." Jon-Tom blandly waved a hand at his room. "You put everything right again. I mean, I'm myself again, and you're you, and the world is what it ought to be. Everything is as it should be."

"Indeed that is so," the wizard conceded, "except that I am distressed to admit that none of it was my doing."

Jon-Tom blinked at him. "You mean you didn't bring things back to normal?"

"Absolutely not, my boy, any more than I bent them askew in the first place."

"Then," Jon-Tom said, much more slowly, "it could happen again? I could turn back into a giant blue crab?"

"Oh, yes, most certainly. At any moment. And myself also, just as Sorbl could turn back into that crawly thing he was, and this comfortable tree back into a damp cave, and—"

"All right, all right." The thought of returning to that skittering crablike shape, smelling of alienness and sea-stink, was enough to shock Jon-Tom out of his boredom. "But I don't understand. Things like that don't just 'happen.' "

"Ah, but we have indisputable evidence that it did, my boy. Furthermore, should it happen again, the effects could be quite different."

'What do you mean 'different'?" Jon-Tom asked uneasily, inspecting his room as though signs and portents of any impending change might be lying there on his chair or hanging from his clothes rack next to his extra shirt.

"I mean that next time the world might become less recognizable still. At any moment, without warning of any kind."

Jon-Tom considered this. "It wasn't an illusion, then? I actually changed. You and Sorbl actually changed."

"Quite so. The entire world was transformed. You did not imagine that you were a large blue crab. You *became* a large blue crab."

"I wasn't sure. I thought that maybe—" He broke off.

"Maybe what, my boy?"

Jon-Tom found it difficult to meet the wizard's gaze. "That you were playing some kind of elaborate joke. You're always testing me."

"A not unreasonable assumption on your part, save for the fact that I never engage in anything as juvenile as practical jokes. This was no test. I wish it were so."

Jon-Tom nodded thoughtfully, then reached for the duar, which was hanging by its shoulder strap from one of his bed's corner posts. He slipped the strap over his shoulder, cradled the instrument against his ribs.

Now it was the wizard's turn to look discomforted. "What are you going to do with that, my boy?" While Jon-Tom's control over his spellsinging had improved dramatically under the turtle's tutelage, it was still far from precise. His ability to evoke marvelous things with his music was still matched only by his inability to control them.

"I'm just holding it," Jon-Tom replied irritably. Did Clothahump still regard him as nothing more than an amateur? "Do you think that after all my practicing I still don't know what I'm doing?"

"I could not have put it better myself."

Jon-Tom was ready with a sharp retort, but he never voiced it. He was too busy staring at the little finger of his left hand. It had grown six inches and turned into a bobbing, weaving worm. It curled back over his palm and glared up at him out of tiny glittering gold eyes.

As quickly as it had appeared, it vanished. He wiggled the small finger again, swallowed.

"Yes, I saw it," said Clothahump in response to Jon-Tom's unasked question. "The changes vary in degree. Not all need be as drastic and complete as the one we awoke to. The whole world and everything in it can change, or only a small part can shift. One finger, for example. Our reactions to such changes depend on what we happen to be doing at the time the change occurs. We were fortunate that we were engaged in nothing more complex than eating breakfast when the first perturbation struck. The damage, not to mention the psychic shock, would have been much more severe had, for example, you been spellsinging or sitting on the john."

"I get the idea," Jon-Tom shook his head. "I've been exposed to a lot of magic since you brought me here, but I've never heard of anything half so powerful as this."

"It has nothing to do with magic," said the wizard firmly. "What has happened, what is happening, is the result of natural law."

"Whatever." Jon-Tom waved the comment off and took a second to make sure the object doing the waving was a normal five-fingered hand. "You call it natural law, I call it magic, somebody else calls it physics. The result is the same. Structures and functions are being altered against the will of those involved." He let the fingers of his right hand strum lightly over the duar's strings. A mellow, soft tone filled the room. Fortunately that was all, but Clothahump checked the corners of the chamber just to be certain.

"Yes. And there is no way of predicting when the changes will occur or how severe will be their effects. But it must be stopped. If nothing is done, the changes will continue with greater and greater frequency. They will also become more extreme."

"How could I turn into anything weirder than a giant blue crab?"

"Look at yourself and reconsider that question," said the

wizard dryly. "I would rather live as a blue crab than as a tall mammal devoid of pigment."

Jon-Tom had become inured to comments about his species defects and continued to lightly strum the duar. "So who's out to get us, then?"

"No one is out to get us."

"There's no vast evil behind what's happening? That's a switch."

"Not on the part of the cause of the disturbances, no," Clothahump told him. "It is a natural phenomenon, like an earthquake."

Jon-Tom knew better where earthquakes were concerned but decided not to interrupt the wizard with a digression. "You say 'it.' Everything that's happened has a single cause?" His little finger tried to turn back into the worm again, but a sharp glance seemed to put a halt to the incipient transformation.

"That is correct." Clothahump began to pace the bedroom. "It is producing blurs, alterations, changes in the composition of existence by inducing shifts in the atomic substructure of matter. It does this by emitting destabilizing bursts of energy of unbelievable intensity. The degree of change our universe experiences varies proportionately to the strength of each burst."

"Our universe?" Jon-Tom swallowed.

Clothahump nodded somberly. "Did I not say it was a large problem? Fortunately such occurrences are as rare as they are serious. There are not that many perambulators around. And that, my boy, is the source of these unsettling alterations we are experiencing." He squinted through his glasses. "You comprehend my meaning?"

"Oh, sure, absolutely. Uh, what's a perambulator?"

"Well, it is one of two things. It is either a baby carriage or a perambulating prime. I believe we can safely exclude the first as the cause of what is happening. The other is difficult to define. It is reputed to be a part organic, part inorganic, part orgasmic creature that's neither here nor there, only in this instance it's both here and there. It drifts around, cavorting between an infinite number of possible universes as well as the impossible ones, inducing changes wherever it goes."

"I see," murmured Jon-Tom as he frantically tried to sort some sense out of the bits and pieces of seemingly contradictory nonsense the wizard had been spouting.

"There aren't many of them," Clothahump continued. "Normally they pass through our universe so quickly that the few disruptions they cause occur without attracting attention. Although it has never been done, it is theoretically possible to capture a perambulator, to restrain it, and to hold it in one place. As you can imagine, this would be very unsettling to something that is used to traveling freely between entire universes. Our theoretically restrained perambulator would be likely to respond by throwing off more frequent bursts of perturbating energy. This is what I believe has happened."

"So what you're saying," Jon-Tom replied slowly, "is that we are in trouble because something that is capable of disturbing the entire fabric of existence is suffering the equivalent of an interdimensional attack of claustrophobia."

"Your analysis is unnecessarily verbose, as usual, but you are essentially correct."

"Wish I wasn't. How do you stop something like that?" He was aware that his skin had suddenly turned a delicate shade of puce. Clothahump had gone bright pink. It only lasted a moment, and then his normal healthy skin color returned. "I understand the need for urgency. The world's a tough enough place to try to make a go of it in without having to worry about its changing from day to day."

"The solution is simple, though accomplishing it may prove otherwise. We must find the place where the perambulator has been frozen in space-time and free it to go on its way."

Jon-Tom shook his head. "I still don't understand how

something that's capable of traveling from one dimension or universe to another can be restrained. It's not like catching a butterfly.''

Clothahump spread his hands. ''I don't know how it can be done, either, my boy. But something has done it. Or someone.''

The tall youth essayed a nervous grin. ''Come on. Surely you don't think someone like you or me is capable of doing something like that?''

''Anyone is capable of anything,'' Clothahump informed him sternly. ''There is nothing that can be imagined that cannot be done given enough time, devotion, intelligence, and blind luck.''

''So somebody has to find this thing, cope with whatever has it trapped, and free it before we all go nuts. Swell.'' Again his fingers caressed the duar's strings. ''So why can't somebody else do it for a change? Why not send a whole coterie of wizards after this thing?''

''Because, as you well know,'' Clothahump said in his best lecturing tone, ''I am the most powerful and important wizard there is, so it behooves me to act for the common good in instances where others would have not the slightest inkling how to proceed.''

Jon-Tom's expression turned sour. ''Uh-huh. And, of course, I have to go along with you because I'm sharing your house and your food and you're the only chance I have of ever returning home.''

''And because you have a good heart, value my counsel, and suffer from an irresistible urge to help others who are in trouble,'' the wizard added. ''You also are an incorrigible show-off.''

''Thanks, I think. Well, at least all we'll have to deal with are these damn changes. They're disconcerting, but it's not like they put us in any danger of bodily harm.''

''That remains to be seen,'' said the wizard unencouragingly.

"Look, can't you manage without me? Just this one time? On your own?"

Clothahump steepled his fingers and looked blandly skyward. "If the perambulator is not freed and the world changes too many times, the local structure of matter could become permanently distorted. We might lose a thing or two."

"Like, for instance?"

"Like gravity."

Jon-Tom took a deep breath. "Okay, I'll come. You've made it pretty clear that there's no place to hide from this thing."

"No place at all, my boy, any more than there is a place where you can hide from my criticisms."

"You sure you want me along, what with my inaccurate spellsinging and all?"

"Do not take my little jibes to heart. You have accomplished some wonders with that instrument, and your voice and you may yet have the chance to do so again in the course of our journey. Besides, I'm getting on, and I need someone young and strong . . ."

"To help you over the rough spots, I know," said Jon-Tom, having listened to the wizard's lament many times before. "I said I'd come, didn't I? Not that I have any choice. Not that any of us have any choice, I guess, with the stability of the world at stake. What's this perambulator thing look like, anyway?"

Clothahump shrugged. "No one knows. It is said that it can look like anything, or nothing. A tree, a stone, a wisp of air. You and I define what we see in terms of what we are familiar with. We compare new sights to the nature we know. The perambulator is not a freak of nature; it is a freak of supernature.

"It is said that in shape and composition, structure, and outline it is like many individuals I know: unstable. There are ancient lines that insist it is pleasant to look upon. Nor is its character malign. It does not disturb from purpose or evil design. The perturbations are an unavoidable consequence of itself. It would be a very nice thing to encounter, I suspect, if it did not have this unfortunate habit of causing the universe in which it happens to be residing to go completely haywire."

"And you're sure that's what we're dealing with here?"

"Nothing else but a perambulator could perturb the world in such a fashion," Clothahump assured him. The wizard had assumed the shape of an elderly moose with bright yellow wings. It needed the wings because he was sitting atop a hundred-foot-tall spruce. Jon-Tom looked at the dizzying drop beneath his own dangling, furry legs, and fought to hold on to the crown of his own tree. He saw no reason to disagree with the wizard's assessment.

The perturbation lasted longer this time, almost three minutes, before the world snapped back to reality. Jon-Tom breathed a sigh of relief when it became clear that they had returned to the reality of Clothahump's tree once again. Of course, in reality they had not moved, had never left it. Only reality had moved.

"You're *sure* these are real changes we're experiencing and not just some kind of clever mass delusions?"

"You would have found out had you fallen from that tree in which you had been squatting a moment ago," Clothahump assured him. "You would have changed back, of course, except that you would now be lying spread all over this floor. You had been given wings, but could you have determined how to use them in the brief moment of falling?"

"I'm beginning to see why we have to find this perambulator and free it fast." He walked over the washbasin and poured himself a glass of water from the jug standing on the shelf nearby. Except that instead of water, the glass filled with an alarmingly noisy bright blue liquid that fizzed and bubbled. He had the distinct impression that his drink was angry at him.

The glass slipped from his fingers. As it tumbled, the fizzing reached epic proportions. He dove for the far side of his bed while Clothahump retreated inside his shell. Propelled by the explosive blue fizz, the glass rocketed around the room, bouncing off suddenly rubbery walls and hunting furiously for the creature that had dared try to drink it. It barely missed Jon-Tom's head as he scrambled beneath the bed.

Lacking either a butterfly net or a shotgun, they could only wait until the fizz lost its zip. This occurred at almost exactly the same moment when they slipped back to reality and the perturbation ceased. Occupied once more by ordinary water, the glass lost momentum in midair and shattered wetly against the footboard of the bed. Clothahump emerged from his shell while Jon-Tom warily crawled out from beneath the bed, keeping a watchful eye on the liquid debris lest the puddle try to bite him.

"Try the sink again, my boy. It should be all right now."

Jon-Tom straightened. "Never mind. Suddenly I'm not thirsty anymore."

"You're going to have to keep your nerves under control. We all are. Why, we haven't so much as begun, and things can only get worse before they get better."

"That's what I enjoy about assisting you, Clothahump. You're always so reassuring about the outcome."

"Tut, my boy," the wizard chided him sternly, "you must remain calm in the face of chaos. If for no other reason than to maintain control over your spellsinging."

" 'Keep control.' 'Stay calm' Easy for you to say. You have some idea of what we're up against, and you're the world's greatest sorcerer. Of course, you can keep your reactions under control. You're sure of your abilities. I'm not. You know that you'll be okay.''

Clothahump's reply did nothing to boost Jon-Tom's confidence.

"Are you kidding, my boy? I'm scared shitless.''

II

Jon-Tom had to bend his head to avoid bumping it on the ceiling. Clothahump had proven himself an accommodating host where his ungainly young human guest was concerned, but such accommodations did not extend to altering the tree-home spell to provide the dimensionally expanded interior with higher ceilings and doorways. Such spells were time-consuming and expensive, the wizard had informed him, and one did not mess with the details unless something happened to go wrong with the plumbing.

So he was compelled to bend low whenever moving from room to room. It wasn't all bad, though. There were beneficial side effects. During the months of residing in the tree he'd become quite agile, and he could now take a blow to the forehead without so much as wincing.

He thought he was intimately familiar with every chamber and cubbyhole the tree possessed, but the tunnel Clothahump was presently leading him down was new to him. Not only

19

was it alien in appearance, it seemed to be leading them downward.

Sorbl appeared, waiting for them. The famulus held a glowing bulb on the end of a stick. The light flickered unevenly, a clear sign that Sorbl had put the illumination spell on the bulb by himself.

"Here I am, Master."

"Drunk again," snapped the wizard accusingly. Sorbl drew himself up straight.

"No, Master. See, I am not swaying." Indeed, Sorbl looked rock-steady. "I see you and Jon-Tom clearly."

Jon-Tom looked at the famulus. Yes, the great yellow eyes were much less bloodshot than usual.

Clothahump nodded brusquely toward the glow bulb. "We won't be neding that."

"You are going down into the cellar, Master?"

"Cellar?" Jon-Tom let his gaze travel upward. "I didn't know the tree had a cellar. How come you never showed it to me before, sir?"

"It is not a place that is used for storage. It is a place used only for certain things. There was no reason to use it—until now."

The famulus extended the glow-bulb pole. "Here you are, Master. I'll be going now."

"Going? Going where? You're coming with me, Sorbl. How do you ever expect to learn anything if you keep running off?"

"From books, Master."

"Books are not enough. One must also gain experience."

"But, Master, I don't *like* the cellar."

Clothahump looked disgusted and put his hands on his hips—well, on the sides of his shell, anyway. Being a member of the turtle persuasion, his hips were not visible.

"Sometimes I think you'll never progress beyond famulus. But I am bound by our contract to try to hammer some knowledge into you. Keep the light if it reassures you." He shook his head. "An owl that's afraid of the dark."

"I am not afraid of the dark, Master," Sorbl replied quickly, seeming to gather some of his self-respect around him. "I'm just afraid of what's down in the cellar."

"Wait a minute," said Jon-Tom, "is this something I ought to know about? What's this all about? What are you so frightened of, Sorbl?"

The owlet gazed up at him out of vast yellow eyes. "Nothing."

"Well, then," asked a thoroughly confused Jon-Tom, "what's there to be afraid of?"

"I told you," the famulus reiterated, "nothing."

"We're not making a connection here," said the exasperated Jon-Tom. He glanced at Clothahump. "What's he so scared of?"

"Nothing," the wizard informed him solemnly.

Jon-Tom nodded sardonically. "Right. I'm glad that's cleared up."

The wizard glared at his assistant. "Sorbl, you must stay with me. I may require your aid. We have to do this because it is the only way I can divine the location of the perambulator. That should be obvious to anyone." He eyed Jon-Tom expectantly. "Shouldn't it?"

"Absolutely," said Jon-Tom without hesitation, simultaneously wondering what he was concurring with.

"Furthermore," Clothahump went on, turning his attention back to Sorbl, "you will be accompanying me on the journey to come."

"Me?" Sorbl squeaked. "But I'm still just a famulus, a lowly apprentice. And besides, someone will have to stay to look after the tree, pay the bills, take out the—"

"The tree can look after itself. I'm ashamed of you, Sorbl." He gestured at Jon-Tom. "This lad is coming with me, so how can you think of staying behind?"

"It's easy if I put my mind to it."

"He comes from another world entirely and has no desire to apprentice in wizardly matters, yet by persevering he has developed into something not unlike a spellsinger. He should be an example to you. What happened to your ambition, your drive, your desire to experience and learn about the mysteries of the universe?"

"Can't I just stay and take care of the laundry?" Sorbl pleaded hopefully.

"You are my apprentice, not my housekeeper," Clothahump reminded him sternly. "If I'd wanted just a housekeeper, I would have contracted with someone far more comely and of the opposite sex. As my apprentice, you will follow and learn whether you like it or not. You signed the contract. At the time I thought you were doing so with half a brain. I did not realize you were in the afterthroes of a drunken stupor, nor did I know that was your preferred state of consciousness. But a contract is a contract. I will make a wizard of you even if it kills both of us in the process."

"How about just one of us?" Sorbl muttered, but to himself.

"Besides," Clothahump continued in a more conciliatory tone, "on this particular journey you can be especially useful."

"I can? I mean, I can."

"Indeed. During the perturbation we experienced this morning, you displayed none of the panic one would have expected from one of your intellectual temperament."

"Perturbation? What's that?" Sorbl appeared genuinely bemused.

"Don't you remember?" Jon-Tom stared at the owl. "The change. The tree turned into a cave, the forest outside into an ocean. Clothahump and I became giant blue crabs and you turned into some kind of squiggly centipede thing."

"Oh, *that*." Sorbl looked relieved. "For a moment I

thought I'd missed something. You mean you saw it too? That's a switch."

"Sorbl," Jon-Tom explained patiently, "the change was for real. The perturbation actually happened."

"No kidding?" He glanced from wizard to spellsinger. "Really?" Both man and turtle nodded somberly. "Well, so what? I mean, what's to get excited about?"

"You see?" Clothahump continued talking to Jon-Tom while examining his innocent-eyed famulus the way he would a new metal or something interesting found beneath a stump. "We are witness to the single beneficial effect of the long-term consumption of alcohol. Sorbl was not fazed by the perturbation because he exists in a state of perpetual perturbation already—though perhaps perpetual inebriation would be more accurate."

"I get it," Jon-Tom said. "You mean that since he lives with the D.T.'s every day, the sudden transformation of the world around him isn't any more upsetting than anything he experiences during his regular binges?"

"I do not have regular binges," protested Sorbl indignantly. "Each one is the result of glorious spontaneity."

"And that is why, my good famulus," Clothahump informed him, "you will be of such help on this journey, for nothing that overtakes us will faze you, since you are used to such transformations. So that you may remain in this benign state I will even permit you to bring along a supply of liquor, which I myself will allocate to you on a liberal daily basis. A cart runs best when properly lubricated, and so, it would appear, does a certain famulus."

Sorbl couldn't believe what he was hearing. His beak all but fell to his foot feathers.

"I will come, Master—since I have no choice in the matter, anyway." He hesitated. "Did you really mean it when you said I would be allowed to bring along, ah, liquid refreshment?"

Clothahump nodded. "Much as the idea distresses me, it is important that you remain in the state to which you would like to become permanently accustomed. Your intake will be carefully moderated. You will be kept 'happy' but not unconscious."

"No need to worry about that, Master!" The owl all but saluted. "I shall follow your instructions to the letter."

"Hmmmm. We'll see. And now that we have settled the matter of who is going where, let us continue on our way downward. We have little time to waste. If the perambulator is not freed as soon as possible, the frequency of the resultant perturbations will increase and we run the risk of becoming encased in permanent change."

"I know, Master," murmured Sorbl as he led the way down, "but the *cellar.*"

Clothahump gave him a shove. "I said there was no other way. And pick up your feet or I'll set fire to your feathers and use *you* for light."

Sorbl's pace increased markedly.

The tunnel walls were composed of nothing more elaborate than packed earth. There was nothing in the way of visible support: no wooden beams, no concrete pillars, no metal flanges or masonry. Only the damp, thick-smelling soil. It muddied his boots. Tiny crawling things retreated from their advancing light, burrowing hastily into walls or floor. Maybe they didn't need the light, as Clothahump had insisted, but Jon-Tom was very glad of its presence nonetheless.

Perhaps the tunnel's stability was maintained by another of Clothahump's complex dimensional spells, or perhaps this was merely part and parcel of the tree-home spell itself. The notion of a tree with a cellar was even more outré than the reality of one that had been dimensionally expanded.

Sorbl was several paces ahead of them now, so he was able to lean forward and whisper to the wizard. "He can't hear us, so maybe now you can tell me what there is to be afraid of down here?''

"Sorbl already informed you: nothing."

"Look, sir, I don't want to appear dense, but could you be a little more specific?"

"Specificity is the soul of every explanation, my boy. A question: What is the shortest distance between two points?"

"A straight line, of course. I mean, I'm prelaw, and math was never my best subject, but I know that much."

"Then you know nothing, or rather, you don't know about nothing, which is, of course, the shortest distance between any two points."

Jon-Tom frowned. He was growing more confused, not less. "Nothing is the shortest distance between two points?"

"Ah!" The wizard looked pleased. "Now you have it. Of course, the shortest distance between two points is nothing. Obviously, if there is nothing between two points, then they must coexist side by side."

Jon-Tom considered this. "I'm not sure that makes sense."

"Does the logic follow?"

"Semantically speaking, yes, but mathematically speaking . . ."

"Pay attention. If there is nothing between two points, then there is nothing preventing them from being tangent to one another, is there? If the only thing that lies between us and the location of the unperambulating perambulator is nothing, then we should be able to find it quite easily."

"But there is something between the perambulator and us: a great deal of distance. You said so yourself."

"That's right, I did."

"Then how the blazes do you expect to find it by going down into this cellar?" an exasperated Jon-Tom demanded to know.

"Because if we go into the cellar, we will find there is nothing there. And on the other side of that nothing lies the perambulator. And everything else that is. But our concern at the moment is with the perambulator only."

"I see," said Jon-Tom, deciding to give up and wait to see what might actually await them down in the cellar.

They walked for what seemed like another hour but in reality was only another few minutes before the tunnel bent sharply to the left. It opened onto a small domed chamber which, as nearly as Jon-Tom could calculate, lay directly beneath the center of the great oak tree in which the wizard made his home. The floor of packed earth was smooth and clean. Something froze for an instant, momentarily stunned by Sorbl's light. Then it scurried across the floor to vanish in a small hole in the opposite wall.

Thick gnarled branches protruded from the ceiling, twisting and curling overhead. Though entirely natural, they gave the dome the appearance of a room with a latticework ceiling. Small fibers protruded from the larger wooden coils, probing the air in search of nutrients and moisture.

Roots, Jon-Tom mused. A root cellar. Of course. *I should have thought of that,* he told himself. He said as much to Clothahump.

The wizard had settled himself in the chamber's single piece of furniture. The sturdy chair occupied the exact center of the room.

"A root cellar, yes, and a very particular one." He searched the ceiling a moment before pointing. "Up there is the root of envy. Over there the root of inspiration." He turned slightly in his chair. "And up in that corner, that slightly golden-hued wood? That's the root of all evil."

Jon-Tom stared. Was that particular branch composed of golden-hued wood or wood-hued gold? Clothahump noticed the intensity of his stare and smiled.

"Don't let it affect you so. It's not all it's cracked up to be." He turned back around to face the center of the room once more. "Sorbl, since we have the globe, put it here."

The famulus approached, jammed the light-supporting pole into the earth, and retreated back against a wall without Clothahump having to prompt him to do so. Jon-Tom moved to stand next to the apprentice. Clothahump crossed both arms over his plastron and closed his eyes, a sure sign that he was about to embark on a most powerful spell indeed. As further proof of the seriousness of his intentions, he muttered a few phrases, then removed his glasses and slipped them into their protective case in one of the uppermost drawers of his chest.

"What now?" Jon-Tom whispered to the owl. "What's he going to call forth?"

Sorbl was standing as close to the wall as possible, heedless of dirtying his vest or feathers. He was staring wide-eyed at the wizard, who had entered into his preevoking trance.

"You already know. He's going to call up nothing."

"Oh, right, I forgot. Well, then, there's 'nothing' to be afraid of, is there?" He meant it as a joke, but there was no suggestion of humor in the famulus's reply.

"That's right, that's right! You *do* understand."

Clothahump turned slowly to face them, his eyes still shut tight. From another drawer in his plastron he brought forth a small, tightly rolled scroll of paper. "Sorbl."

"Y-yes, Master?" The famulus approached hesitantly.

"It is for you to read." Jon-Tom noted with awe that the wizard's voice had changed. It was slightly louder and a good deal more powerful, as though its owner had grown two hundred years younger in the space of a few moments of silent contemplation. There was much he wanted to know, but this was neither the time nor place to ask questions.

In any event, he suspected that Clothahump would soon show, if not describe, his intentions.

Sorbl carefully unrolled the top portion of the scroll, squinted at the lines thereon. "I don't know if I can read it, Master. The print is very fine."

"Of course you can read it," Clothahump rumbled in his youthful voice. "Your other qualities require much work, but your natural vision is superior. Return to your wall if you wish, but when I raise my arm, you must begin."

"As you say, Master." Sorbl retreated until he stood very close to Jon-Tom once more. Man and owl waited to see what would happen next.

Clothahump slowly lifted both hands until his arms were pointing straight up into the dark air. To Jon-Tom's amazement the arm continued to rise, pulling the wizard's body with it until he was sitting in emptiness several inches above the seat of his chair. He drew his legs into his shell, pulled in his head until only the eyes were visible above the upper edge of his carapace. For protection? Jon-Tom wondered. His eyes darted around the chamber, found only dirt and emerging roots. There was nothing there to threaten them.

Exactly what the terrified Sorbl had been trying to tell him.

Clothahump began to speak, reciting in a peculiarly monotonous singsong. As he spoke, the blackness seemed to press tighter around them. It shoved and pushed and bullied the single light of the glow bulb until it was no more than a pinpoint of light struggling to hold back the encroaching darkness.

In that near total blackness sounds were amplified. Jon-Tom could hear the pounding of his own heart. His breathing grew shallow. The darkness that surrounded them was no normal dark. It did not have even the comfort of a moonless night about it, for there were no stars. It was a solid blackness, not merely an absence of light but a thing with weight and mass that pressed heavy on his throat and belly.

He found himself on the verge of panic, felt he was choking, suffocating, when a second light appeared and pushed aside the cloak of obsidian air just enough for him to breathe again. It came from the scroll that Clothahump had handed to his famulus. As Sorbl read the minuscule print, hesitantly at first, and then with increasing confidence, the light from the paper brightened.

"My friends," the owl recited, "I come to you on this day seeking nothing but your votes. If elected, I promise to serve long and faithfully. I will endeavor to be the best governor Cascery Province has ever had. I will cut taxes and increase public spending. I will increase aid to the aged and strengthen our defenses. I will . . . I will . . ."

A puzzled Jon-Tom listened to the familiar litany of endless promises as Sorbl read on. The words the owl was reciting were not the ones he'd expected to hear. It sounded like nothing more than your standard political campaign promises. The same old assertions, the same old claims, no different in this world than in his own. Just so much political hot air, amounting, as it always did, to a lot of . . .

Nothing.

Clothahump was calling it up, invoking it, bringing it to this place of power. He was seeking the nothing that lay between them and the perambulator, so that he could pinpoint its location. That was what was closing in around them, trying to snuff them out with the full force of its awesome nothing self. He could feel it, a dry, cottony taste in his mouth. It crawled over him like a living blanket, trying to plug up his nostrils and force its way down his throat. Only the feeble light of the glow bulb and the stronger one emanating from the scroll kept it at bay.

There was one other possibility: he still carried his duar. For a moment he thought to sing something bright and cheery. Common sense told him to hold his silence. If his spellsinging could have been of any use, the wizard would have mentioned it. If he launched into a song now, unbidden, at what was obviously a crucial moment, the nothingness might overwhelm the wizard's spell. And if nothing didn't kill him, Clothahump surely would. So he stood quietly and watched, and tried to learn.

How could there be nothing in the room when there was obviously something? There was Clothahump's chair, and the glow bulb on its staff, and the scroll, not to mention the three of them. It troubled him for a few moments, until Sorbl's drone provided him with the answer.

It was a typical campaign speech, as boastful as any and stuffed to bursting with the usual lies and falsehoods. It was not merely nothing, it amounted to *less* than nothing, thereby canceling out those few somethings that occupied the cellar.

Not all the somethings, apparently. He stared hard into the darkness. There the glow bulb, there Sorbl and his scroll, in the center of the chamber the floating Clothahump and his earthbound chair—and suddenly, something more. Shapes. Formless, faint of silhouette and shifting of outline, but definitely there. Indistinct grayness swimming slowly through black jelly. They did not have color so much as they were slightly less black than their surroundings. Anthracite ghosts.

As he stared they became slightly less nebulous. Charcoal-gray heads held gray faces. Gray tongues expectantly licked black teeth. Nor were they silent, for they moaned softly, almost imperceptibly, to one another. Whether the sounds were the components of words or music or cries of pain, he couldn't tell. They were the nothings that inhabited the Darkness.

Sorbl's voice rose a little higher. He was straining to keep reading, from tension as well as fear, but he did not break. Clothahump continued his own recitation, his indecipherable words rising and falling in regular cadence.

The glow bulb brightened. Or perhaps the air around them merely became a little less stygian. The cellar had vanished. The roots, the moist dirt that had encased them so claustrophobically an instant before, was gone. He desperately wished for their return.

Because now they were surrounded by nothing.

They seemed to be drifting in a universe without boundaries, without definition. There was no warm earth walling them in, no sense of a great oak tree hugging the ground above. Nothing but distant lonely stars that beckoned forlornly to him, and few enough they were. He wished for sight of a nebula or two, but no great splashes of red and purple greeted his searching eyes. This was a region from which even the dust fled.

Somehow he managed to speak and was startled by the soft sound of his own voice. "Where are we? What is this place?"

"I told you, it is nothing," Sorbl explained, interrupting his reading long enough to reply. "An instant, a passing thought, something imagined made real. We are beyond nothing now. This is the backside of chaos. Not a nice place to visit and you wouldn't want to live here." They were beginning to tilt, and he resumed his recitation quickly, reading twice as fast as before until they were facing upright again. Except that *upright* was only the vaguest of terms. You couldn't stand straight relative to nothing.

Suddenly the glow bulb was joined by something new. It drew Jon-Tom's attention immediately. In that place of floating nowhere it was vibrant with life and energy, spinning and twisting and changing with such dazzling speed, it made him blink as he tried to focus on it. With each blink it had assumed an entirely different appearance. It was alive, but not in the sense that he was. It lived but was not organic. Nor was it rock or metal. It was something else from somewhere else, and it obeyed no natural laws but its own.

He tried to define it, could not. It was a Klein bottle running the inside of a Mobius strip balanced on the head of a Schwarzchild Discontinuity. It danced and mutated, metamorphosed and slid from one unreality to another. It spun through nothingness at a billion miles a second and was brighter than a red giant. And there was something else, something he could not see that stayed in the background but very close by.

Something far more ordinary and yet touched by a tremendous energy and power.

It saw them.

Jon-Tom didn't know how it saw them or with what. He sensed only the presence of unseen eyes, but he felt their touch as though he'd been struck by a pair of hammers.

The unseen observer let out an outraged howl. It must have done something, because that magnificent, indescribable, undefinable shape that was the perambulator suddenly twisted violently in on itself. The chaos around them crystalized. There was an explosive shattering sound, which threatened to implode Jon-Tom's skull. His hands went to his outraged ears and his teeth ground against each other. Someone was pounding a crescendo on the kettledrum in which he'd suddenly taken up residence. He staggered and would have fallen except that there was nothing to fall onto.

Sorbl was picked up and thrown against a wall of emptiness. The scroll came apart in his wingtips, the fragments flying off in all directions. He tried desperately to hang on to a few scraps, to keep reading, but it was impossible. The nearest was a thousand parsecs away in seconds.

He hit the floor with a *whump*, landing hard on his tail feathers.

They were back.

Back in the cellar. Back among roots and dampness and dirt. Jon-Tom inhaled deeply, sucking in the thick humidity. It tasted of soil and water and living things. The cellar was rich with the perfume of life, the dirt of the wall he was clinging to, thick with the texture of reality.

In the center of the room the glow bulb was at full intensity. Clothahump was no longer floating inches above his chair but was seated firmly on the hard wood. He was holding tightly to the arms with both hands and breathing hard. When he was convinced it wasn't going to disappear on him, Jon-Tom let go of the wall and stumbled toward the wizard to see if he could be of any help. He was sweating profusely in the heat of the cellar. Except that it wasn't hot. It was the same temperature that it had been when they'd arrived.

He was sweating from the cold, the cold of where they'd been. That's why it seemed hot to him now. He hadn't been aware of the cold at the time. You didn't feel hot and cold on the far side of nothing. You didn't feel anything at all.

He shivered.

"How are you doing, sir?"

The wizard glanced up at him, gathered himself, and let out a long sigh. Then he smiled reassuringly. "All right. Right as can be expected. I don't travel as well as I used to. Did you see it?"

"I saw something. I don't know what." He stared at the glow bulb sitting atop its staff, drinking in the pale, reassuring luminescence. Never had he been so grateful to be in a hole in the ground. "I think it might have been the perambulator."

"What else could it have been?" Clothahump's strength was returning and, with it, his enthusiasm. He pushed back the chair, stood next to the light, and stretched. "Consider yourself privileged, my boy. I don't believe anyone has seen a perambulator in living memory. They don't hang around long enough to be seen, and even when they do, you might not realize what it is you're looking at. I confess it's appearance surprised me."

"The way it kept changing, you mean?"

"Oh, no. Change is the very soul of a perambulator. What I did not expect was for it to be so beautiful." He glanced past the tall young human. "Sorbl? You still with us?"

The famulus was standing and rubbing his backside. He grimaced at the wizard. "Unfortunately yes, Master."

"Good. Get your feathers in gear. We're going back upstairs."

"I lost the scroll, Master. It was torn from my feathers. There was nothing I could do."

"It matters not. I can replace it at any time. I have access to an endless supply. Now, quickly, I need for you to begin packing for our journey."

The famulus staggered toward the glow bulb and pulled the staff out of the ground. "You don't need to convince me, Master. Anything to get out of this place." He started for the tunnel that led upward.

Clothahump extended an arm. "A little support if you please, my boy. I am feeling a mite queasy."

"I'm not surprised. I don't feel too steady myself." He put his right arm around the back of the wizard's shell, steadying him as they followed in Sorbl's wake.

As soon as they were in the tunnel proper and climbing, Clothahump called a halt while he recovered his glasses from the uppermost drawer of his plastron. He studied the six-sided lenses at arm's length. "Fogged up, my boy." He produced a cloth and began to clean them. "That was quite a transposition."

Jon-Tom found himself gazing worriedly back down the tunnel. Nothing was coming after them, nothing pursued them from the depths of the cellar. How could it? They had been alone down there. There had been nothing with them.

"I know where we must go now, my boy." The wizard tapped the side of his head. It made a loud clicking sound, shell on shell. "A long ways but not a difficult one."

I've heard that before, Jon-Tom muttered, but only to himself. What he said was, "Anyplace I'd know?"

"I think not. It lies far to the north, north of the Bellwoods, past Ospenspri and Kreshfarm-in-the-Keegs, farther north than you have ever been. Farther north than civilized people care to travel. We will have to hurry. In another month winter will be upon us, and travel in such country will become impossible. We must free the perambulator before the snows begin. And there is a new problem."

"Another one?"

"I fear it is so. I had thought the perambulator frozen by some freak of nature, trapped here by some crack or fallen into some hole in the interdimensional fabric of existence. Such is not the case."

Jon-Tom felt the coldness returning. He remembered the pressure of those unseen eyes, heard again that singular wild howl.

"Its presence here isn't an accident, then."

"No, my boy," the wizard said somberly. "It has been stopped here intentionally, deliberately, with purpose aforethought. It seems incredible, but the truth often is. I can scarce believe it myself."

"I can't believe it at all. From everything you've told me about it I don't see how anyone could catch it, much less restrain it."

"Nor do I, yet it is clear to me that this is what has happened. There is a formidable and sinister power at work here. I could not do such a thing. Something, someone, has caught the perambulator and is holding it prisoner in this time-space frame. If it is not freed, it could not only alter our world permanently, it could eventually destroy it in its attempts to get free."

"Then whoever is restraining it could also be destroyed."

"Just so," agreed the wizard, nodding.

"That's crazy," Jon-Tom said firmly.

"Ah. Now you begin to have some understanding of what we are up against."

Jon-Tom said nothing for the remainder of their climb back to the surface.

III

It didn't take long for him to finish packing. A very good friend of his had told him that he who travels light travels best, and Jon-Tom had adhered to that advice ever since. On this world speed was more important than comfort, flexibility a better companion than a spare pair of pants.

He found Sorbl in the wizard's study, packing vials and packets under Clothahump's supervision.

"I'm all set," he told his mentor.

"Good, my boy, good." He was showing mild frustration as he pawed through a cabinet. "Where did I put those measuring spoons? We will be ready to depart as soon as I'm finished here."

Jon-Tom leaned against the wall nearby. "I've been thinking about what you said yesterday as we were leaving the cellar. About what we're 'up against'? If I'm following what you said correctly, whoever or whatever has trapped the perambulator is not stable."

"You're almost right." He unearthed a set of tiny spoons

36

bound together by a bright golden ring, looked pleased with himself, and passed it to Sorbl. "Whoever it is, is not unstable; they are crackers, crazy, nuts, bonkers, looney tunes, living in cloud-cuckoo land. Do I make myself clear or do you require further elaboration?"

"No, I think I get the point," Jon-Tom said dryly.

"It is important that you do. It is important that we all do. Because it is highly unlikely that we will be able to reason with this whatever-it-is. It is difficult to fight someone who may not even be conscious of the fact that they are engaged in a fight." He pulled a tall metal box from another drawer and opened the lid with unusual care. Straining, Jon-Tom could see that it was filled with padding.

Clothahump extracted a single small wooden box, opened it to inspect the contents, which consisted of one glass vial full of oily green fluid. Satisfied, he closed the box and secured the lid, handed it with both hands to Sorbl.

"Place this in the center of your backpack, and whatever you do, don't drop it."

Sorbl gingerly accepted the box, cradling it in both flexible wingtips. "What would happen if I did drop it, Master?"

Clothahump leaned toward his apprentice. "Something so horrible, so vile, so unimaginably awful that in more than two hundred years I have not acquired sufficient vocabulary to describe it."

"Oh." Sorbl turned to place the box in his open pack. "I will be very careful with it, Master."

Clothahump moved toward Jon-Tom and began selecting volumes from a long shelf of mini-books nearby. The much taller human spoke while watching Sorbl pack. "What's in the vial you gave Sorbl, sir? Some kind of acid or explosive?"

"Of course not," the wizard replied softly. "Do you think I'd be fool enough to travel with dangerous liquids? It's lime fizz."

Jon-Tom's brows drew together. "I guess I don't understand."

"You say that far too often, but your ignorance is mitigated by your honesty. Won't you ever learn that to handle magic effectively you must learn to manipulate people as well as formulae? Without anything to worry about Sorbl will find ways to overindulge himself in the liquor I am permitting him to bring along—would that his deviousness extended to his studies. This will give him something to worry about."

"I thought we had plenty to worry about already, but I see your point." He watched while the wizard thumbed through tome after tome, replacing the majority in their places on the shelf, setting the rare selection aside for packing.

"What do you think our opponent is like? Besides dangerous, I mean."

Clothahump considered. "If you're out of your mind, there are two things that can be done to make you feel better. You can get yourself cured, or you can make everyone and everything else you have to deal with crazy. This is the first instance I can think of where a psychotic has attempted the latter course.

"It is clear that whoever is restraining the perambulator is doing so for a purpose, with a definite end in mind. That end appears to be turning the world upside down and inside out. For to an insane individual, an insane world might be quite comfortable. No one can accuse you of being mad if they're mad too. No one can say that you've retreated into a world made up out of your own mental fabrications if they're living in the same world. That is what we are going to have to deal with, my boy. The logic of the mad."

As he concluded on the word *mad*, the wizard began to change. His body attenuated and lengthened. In seconds Jon-Tom found himself conversing with a large, furry yellow caterpillar. Nor was he leaning against the wall of the wizard's study. The oak tree had been displaced by a giant silken globe within which hung strange objects of unknown origin and uncertain purpose.

All this he took in through two pairs of compound eyes. He felt uneasy, and from the waist down he had begun to itch. Using several legs operating in tandem, he began to scratch himself, digging for mites in his orange-and-brown fur. Over in the corner of the globe a small blue moth fluttered anxiously back and forth.

"So strange," said the moth. "In this world, Master, you are larger than Jon-Tom. Here size must be a reflection of one's age, for I am the smallest of all."

"Reflection of intelligence, more likely," snapped the wizard. "This is inconvenient. You are not alarmed by your new form?"

"Oh, no. I believe I have taken this shape before."

"Well, I don't like it," muttered Jon-Tom, "and I hope we change back soon." His stomachs were doing flip-flops, and the absence of a skeleton made him fearful of taking so much as a step, even though he knew that his squishy, soft body was unlikely to collapse around him. He was determined not to throw up, not only in order to save face before Clothahump but also because he had not the slightest interest in seeing what a four-foot-long orange-and-brown caterpillar might regurgitate.

So he sat there and scratched. Several minutes slid past. Five more. Now he was itching from nervousness and not mites. "What do we do?"

"There is nothing we can do." Clothahump was preening multiple antennae. "We can only keep calm and wait it out."

"It's held a lot longer this time," an uneasy Jon-Tom observed.

"Considerably. I have already pointed out that the duration of each perturbation might increase."

"I don't like this one. I like it even less than I did being a blue crab." He tried to shift his position to a more comfortable one, with little success. "I think I'm going to throw up."

"Try not to, my boy. I expected side effects to begin appearing, but we can do without that particular one. Though it might be interesting."

"Like hell!" Jon-Tom bawled. He started to bend over.

Only to find himself back in the familiar oak-lined study again. He was himself again, tall and human and in possession of a solid internal superstructure. The interior of that superstructure, however, was still queasy, uncomfortable assurance that the transformation hadn't been a dream. He rushed to the sink and ran cold water over his face and hands, sipping at it when he felt able to keep it down. It stayed down, as did his breakfast. He was pale when he looked up from the basin, gripping the rim with both hands for support.

"I can see where these perturbations can be more than just awkward."

"Quite so." Jon-Tom couldn't tell if the wizard was disappointed that he hadn't thrown up or not. "For example, if you were crossing a bridge and that bridge abruptly became a thin rope, you would have only an instant to assess your new status and adapt to it by balancing yourself or grabbing tight to the rope. Otherwise you would fall, and when the world snapped back to normal, you would find yourself in pieces, no less deceased for having perished during the perturbation. That would be awkward indeed."

Sorbl joined them. "All is in readiness, Master."

The wizard nodded. "About time. You have your pack, my boy, and I have mine." He trundled over to the study exit and prepared to shoulder one of the two heavy packs the famulus had prepared. Jon-Tom wrestled his own onto his back and followed his mentor into the front hall.

He halted there, wondering why the thought hadn't occurred to him earlier. "Wait a minute. Why are we walking? Surely we're not going to foot it all the way to the Northern Plateau?"

"Of course not," Clothahump assured him. "Once we get to Lynchbany we'll rent ourselves a wagon or coach."

"But that's a pretty good hike in itself. Why walk even that far"—he swung his duar around in front of him—"when we can ride?"

"Uh-oh." Sorbl's eyes sought a discreet hiding place.

"Boy." Clothahump harrumphed, "I'm not much in the mood to try any transportation spells. I've too many other things on my mind. Besides, there are one or two bits of sorceral knowledge I've managed to forget over the past two hundred years, and we've no time to waste looking up the necessary formulae."

"I know you're not being modest." Jon-Tom was smiling fondly down at the old conjurer. "So I have to assume that you're worn-out from dealing with the nothing."

"I will not deny that the effort was fatiguing." He was eyeing the duar uneasily. "I sense what you have in mind, but I am not certain you are up to it. I know that you have had a great deal of practice lo these past many months. Despite this, the precision of your spellsinging still leaves much to be desired."

Jon-Tom felt himself flush. "I don't claim to be perfect. I never did. But I'm a hell of a lot sharper than I was when I first picked up this duar and started playing. And I have conjured up transportation before. Boats and rafts and one time M'nemaxa himself."

Clothahump was nodding slowly. "I am aware of what you have accomplished, my boy, and you have much to be proud of, but the ability of calling up simple land transportation is a talent that seems to have escaped you."

"You're forgetting, sir. Remember when we first journeyed south to the Tailaroam River to seek transport upstream to Polastrindu? So that we could all travel together in ease and comfort, I called forth a fine L'borian riding snake."

"You're right. I had forgotten. I remember now, though—

just as I remember that you were trying to conjure up something entirely different. You were as startled by the snake's appearance as the rest of us.''

Jon-Tom looked away and coughed slightly. "So I was. But at least I produced something, and it turned out to be perfectly serviceable. This time I'm going to *try* for a L'borian riding snake. Having already conjured one previously, I ought to be able to produce it on demand.''

The wizard considered, said reluctantly, "I admit I was not looking forward to the long tramp into Lynchbany. I am of a mind to give my blessings to your attempts. If you are confident . . .''

"Of course, I'm confident.''

Clothahump sighed. "My legs feel older even than my head. We could avoid the sordid haggling that would surely ensue over the hiring of a coach. Very well, then. Let us see what you can produce. But let us move outside first. Some of this furniture is old.''

Jon-Tom followed, feeling several inches taller. Not literally this time, but emotionally, for no perturbation was affecting the world. This was the first time he had actually been requested to spellsing by the wizard, and he was determined not to let his benefactor and teacher down.

The morning was crisp and clear, with the first bite of fall in the air. Clothahump's anxiety to hurry on their way was caused by the nearness of winter, when the paths to the Northern Plateau could become clogged with early snows. It was difficult to imagine everything cloaked in white, so brilliant were the red and gold hues of the forest.

They set their packs aside. Jon-Tom prepared himself while Clothahump placed a simple but effective lockspell on his front door. Then he and Sorbl stood off to one side while Jon-Tom walked out into the taller grass, away from the shade of the enormous old oak tree.

He let his fingers strum the duar's double set of strings,

adjusted the mass and tremble controls, and cleared his throat. Sorbl left his master's side and tried to edge inconspicuously around behind the bulk of the tree. Clothahump was made of sterner stuff. He sympathized with his apprentice's apprehension but held his ground.

Jon-Tom stood off by himself and let individual chords and notes tumble from the duar. This was not the first time he'd had to hesitate. The problem was that while he knew exactly what he wanted to bring forth, he didn't know what song to employ. Snakes were not a popular subject of popular music.

There was a group that called itself Whitesnake, however. One of their tunes, anything related to transportation, might do it. He couldn't think of anything more appropriate, and he was acutely conscious of an increasingly impatient Clothahump standing nearby and staring at him. Better to sing something, if only to loosen up, than to continue standing there looking like a complete fool. He closed his eyes, remembered the words, began tapping his right foot in time to the beat, and started to sing.

A slight fluttering in the air, more perceived than seen, caused him to open his eyes. One or two gneechees, those harbingers of magic, were teasing the fringes of his vision. They always appeared when his spellsinging was working. It was a good sign and spurred him to greater efforts with the duar. But while the gneechees remained, darting and dancing around the edge of reality, they did not appear in the hoped-for numbers. Neither did the long, scaly shape of the riding snake.

He sang harder still, peeling the riffs off the duar as smoothly as any Richie Blackmore might have wished. He strained and sang, and finally something did begin to materialize; a twisting, coiled form on the ground in front of him.

He would have smiled and called out to Clothahump and Sorbl but the spell was far from complete, and it was evident he still had a lot of singing to do. The famulus was confident enough to edge back around from behind the tree, since it appeared nothing was going to blast the earth out from beneath his feathers. Jon-Tom sang on and on. He was beginning to worry.

Not that anything remotely dangerous had appeared, but no matter how many verses he recited, the shape on the ground refused to expand. It was a beginning only. It remained nothing more than a beginning. He kept playing until both the song and his throat were worn-out. The last chord faded away into the trees. The pair of gneechees lit out for more congenial climes.

He approached what he had conjured. It was little more than a few feet long, only a thin shadow of the massive, powerful shape of a L'borian riding snake. But he *had* brought forth something. He hesitated, then reached down to pick it up. It was a snake, all right, but not one that would call L'bor home. Not only was it far too small, it was made of rubber.

Clothahump had walked up to join him, stared thoughtfully at the object over the top of his glasses. "It is well known among wizards, my boy, that even the fates have a sense of humor."

"Son of a bitch." Jon-Tom threw the rubber snake as far into the brush as he could. Anxiety had been replaced by anger. Not only had he failed in his declared intention, he'd gone and made a first-class fool of himself in front of his mentor. All those weeks of practice, all that careful studying of fingering methods and positions and sonic adjustments so he could call up something from an interdimensional novelty shop. Maybe the fates weren't laughing at him, but something surely was, somewhere.

Clothahump sighed and called out to Sorbl, "Pick up your pack, famulus. Lynchbany has come no closer, and I don't want to spend more than one night in these woods."

"Wait—wait a minute. I'm not through."

"You may not be through, my boy, but it appears that you are finished."

"Just be patient, sir. One more attempt is all I ask." So they wanted to see some spellsinging, did they? Spellsinging they were going to see! He was going to conjure up a L'borian riding snake or a reasonable facsimile, or bust a gut trying. Grim-faced, he turned away from both wizard and apprentice and settled on another song. His frustration and embarrassment gave added emphasis to each phrase he sang.

Both were powerful forces, though not the ones he would have chosen to fuel his magic, but there was no question about their efficacy. Instantly the transparent autumn morning seemed to darken around them. In the dim light the gneechees that had materialized stood out sharply. Not a couple this time but hundreds, enveloping singer and companions in a cloud of iridescent light. As usual, not one of the minuscule apparitions could be seen straight on. They could be perceived only out of the corner of one's eye.

Jon-Tom wailed and twisted, sang and played. The fingers of his left hand danced a saraband over the upper strings while his right hand was a blur in front of the duar's body. As he played, something new was taking shape and form in front of him, something substantial, something worthy of a spellsinger's best efforts.

Sorbl retreated behind the tree again, and even Clothahump took an unwilling step backward. A foul-smelling wind blew outward from the solidifying manifestation. Its outlines did not flutter and break this time but grew steadily more visible. It grew and added weight and reality.

But the shape was still wrong. He hurried to bring the song to a conclusion, trying to see through the glowing mist that enveloped the object. It was not the object of his desires. It certainly was nothing like a L'borian riding snake. But neither was it a cosmic joke akin to the toy he had conjured up previously.

In shape it was more than recognizable; it was quite familiar. Certainly he had not expected to see anything like it. His throat was sore and his fingers numb from the effort he'd put into the song. Carefully, painfully, he slid the duar back around his shoulders so that the instrument rested against his back. Then he approached the product of his spellsinging. The lingering glow that attended to it was fading rapidly.

Sorbl flew out from behind the tree, circled the manifestation a couple of times, and then landed next to Jon-Tom. "What in the name of the seven aerial demons is it?"

Jon-Tom ignored him as he touched it. There was no burning sensation. Neither was it dangerously cold to the touch. The surface was smooth and shiny, like the skin of a L'borian riding snake. He walked completely around it, inspecting it from every possible angle as Clothahump joined them.

"As I feared, not what you wished for, my boy, but an interesting piece of work nonetheless. Though I recognize neither its origin nor composition, it is clear that it is a vehicle of some kind. For one thing it has wheels." He tapped one. "They appear to be fashioned not of wood or metal but of some flexible alien substance." He wrinkled his nose as best he was able. "It possesses a most disagreeable smell."

"I know what it is, though," Jon-Tom told him. "I didn't think anything like it actually existed. I should say it's considerably rarer than a L'borian riding snake. But it looks like we'll be riding to Lynchbany and beyond, after all. Not in style and I agree that it stinks, but at least we won't have to walk.

"Where I come from there are books, magazines, other cheap publications, and they all have advertisements for this thing in them, but I never believed they actually existed, and I never heard of anyone actually obtaining one of them. The ads are for army surplus materials."

"I do know what an army is," said Clothahump thoughtfully, "but I have yet to encounter one that boasted a surplus of anything."

"In my world," Jon-Tom informed him, "armies exist for the sole purpose of acquiring the taxpayers' money so they can spend it on things they don't need and then turn around and sell the stuff to these surplus stores. The armies have less material and need more money than ever, and there are also more surplus stores each year than before. It's a miraculous cycle that bears no relationship to anything else in nature.

"These publications I mentioned are always carrying ads for many things that are quite useful. In addition to what they actually have for sale, they also try to get your attention with items that I'm sure have never existed. The most famous of these is the army surplus jeep for twenty-five dollars.

"It's impossible to sell a jeep for twenty-five dollars, but despite post office regulations, ads like that have been appearing for decades. But not one of those twenty-five-dollar jeeps ever existed. And now I know why. The only way to actually get one is by using magic. The wonderful aroma you're inhaling, by the way, is the delightful fragrance of leaded gas. One of the more common smells on my world."

"My profoundest sympathies," said Clothahump, sniffing ostentatiously.

"I still can't believe it," Jon-Tom murmured as he stared at the uncovered, olive-drab, open-bodied stripped-down, but nonetheless serviceable twenty-five-dollar genuine army surplus jeep. His wonder was not misplaced, for true to his suspicions he was actually the first person in history to set eyes on one of those fantastic, mythical machines. There must be a special place for such things, he told himself. A special, near-impossible-to-locate corner of the cosmos where hundreds of twenty-five-dollar army surplus jeeps were arraigned side by side with such other imaginary beasts as vegetable choppers that worked with the lightest of pressures, bust-developing creams, two-dollar X-ray tubes that enabled adolescent boys to see through walls, and income tax forms that could be comprehended and filled out by human beings who had not yet obtained their Ph.D.'s in accounting.

He hefted his backpack and plopped it down in the backseat. "What are we waiting for? Let's go."

Clothahump eyed the alien manifestation warily. "Are you sure this thing is safe?"

"We're not likely to run the risk of meeting another one in a blind intersection," Jon-Tom told him, "so I imagine it's safe enough."

"I would have preferred a snake." Grumbling, the wizard clambered in on the passenger side, tried to make himself comfortable. "Odd sort of seat, but I expect it will have to do."

Sorbl lifted himself off the ground and settled down on the back of the rear bench seat, which made a convenient and stable perch. He would probably be more comfortable bouncing over the rough terrain ahead, Jon-Tom reflected, than either of his flightless companions.

"Let's see." The dash was less than basic. The keys dangled from the ignition. He turned them, stomped the gas a couple of times, and waited. The engine turned over smoothly. He raced it a couple of times, enjoying the look of surprise on Clothahump's face, then depressed the clutch and put it in gear. They started off fast, got approximately halfway around the tree, and stopped. The engine died. He frowned, wrenched the key a couple of times. The battery jolted the engine, but it refused to catch.

There was nothing magical about the reason. His gaze dropped to the ancient gas gauge. The needle was over past the _E_, as motionless as a corpse.

He took a deep breath. "Well, we *almost* got to ride. I came as close as I could, but even a L'borian riding snake needs fuel."

Clothahump considered the mysterious gauge and the motionless needle contained therein. "I see. What does this thing eat?"

"Gasoline, like I told you." Jon-Tom wore a sour expression. "What we're smelling is the bottom of the tank."

"Where do you get this gasoline stuff?" Sorbl asked him.

"Oh, anywhere," he replied bitterly. "Hey, I'll just walk up to the nearest Shell station and fill up a can."

"You are not thinking, my boy." Clothahump was shaking a stern finger at him. "You are feeling sorry for yourself. Wizards are not permitted the luxury of feeling sorry for themselves. An occasional pout, yes, but nothing more. It is bad for appearances. Now *think*. This gasoline: what does it consist of?"

"It's a refined fuel." Jon-Tom wondered even as he explained why he was taking the time. "It's reduced from oil. You know, oil. Petroleum. A thick black liquid that oozes out of the ground. So what? Even if we could find some oil, it wouldn't do us any good. I don't happen to have a refinery in my pocket."

"Speak for your own pockets, my boy." There was a twinkle in the wizard's eye. Reaching into one of the lower drawers in his plastron, he produced a single marble-sized black pill.

"Where is the ingestion point, the mouth?"

Frowning, Jon-Tom climbed out and moved to the rear of the motionless vehicle. "Over here, on the side."

"Deposit this within." Clothahump handed him the black pill. Jon-Tom took it, rolled it between his fingers. It had the consistency of rubber and the luster of a black pearl.

Well, why not? It couldn't damage what they didn't have. Wondering why he was bothering but having learned to trust the wizard's abilities, he dropped the pill in the gas tank. There was a faint thunk as it struck bottom.

Clothahump raised his right hand and muttered to the sky.

Then he spat over the side. Jon-Tom thought, but couldn't be sure, that the wizard's sputum was distinctly black.

"Now try it, my boy."

Shrugging, Jon-Tom slipped back behind the wheel and dubiously cranked the ignition. The engine rumbled a couple of times, caught weakly. He pumped the gas pedal, and the rumble became a steady roar. When he lifted his heel off the pedal, the jeep was idling smoothly. The needle on the gas gauge had swung over to "full."

"What did you do—no, *how* did you do it? What was in that pill?"

"Petroleum, as you call it, is a common ingredient in many important potions," the wizard informed him. "I merely utilized some concentrates and catalyzed them with an old spell used for adapting hydrocarbons. Nothing complicated. I have no idea how long the combination will suffice to power this machine, but it would appear that at least for now we shall indeed have transportation, thanks to your spellsinging and my magic."

"If I ever find a way back home," he told Clothahump, "I'd be much obliged for a sample of that pill and a transcription of the accompanying spell." He put the jeep in gear again, sent it rolling toward the nearby trade road that led into Lynchbany. "Ride we shall—unless there's something else as yet undetected missing from this relic's chassis."

But as they bounced over the rocks and dirt toward the main wagon road, he realized he couldn't be too severe with his creation.

After all, they'd gotten it for a song.

IV

The stripped-down jeep banged and rattled its way northward. Jon-Tom was convinced it had no suspension at all: just wheels attached to an axle that was directly bolted to the underbody. He wondered which would come apart first: the underside of the jeep or his own.

Clothahump was of two minds concerning Jon-Tom's otherworldly procuration. While considerably less comfortable and reassuring than a L'borian riding snake, he had to admit that the jeep was faster. And it had no will of its own. When they startled a fifteen-foot-tall trouk lizard sunning itself in the road, the jeep did absolutely nothing to defend them. A L'borian snake would have quickly driven the monster away.

Instead they had to settle for an inglorious end-run around the awakened carnivore. The concomitant jolting nearly bounced the wizard out of his shell. In addition to these unexpected drawbacks, the hydrocarbon spell that kept the metal box's belly sated was continuously running down and

51

had to be periodically renewed. He reminded Jon-Tom that his resources were not unlimited. Before long they would reach the point where the machine would become useless because they could no longer fuel it.

The bone-jarring ride affected Sorbl least of all. When the bouncing and jouncing began to bother him, he simply spread his great wings, released his grip on the backseat, and took to the air, soaring effortlessly above the treetops while keeping track of his unfortunate companions below.

They encountered no more dozing carnivores, however, and the road began to smooth out as they drew nearer to Lynchbany. The autumn Bellwoods were beautiful to look upon, with many leaves still clinging to the trees and the ground between carpeted with umber and gold.

They were less pleasing to listen to, since the dying leaves that still hugged the branches sang out of tune when the wind blew through them. As Clothahump explained, the music of the bell leaves was a direct function of the seasons. An experienced woodsman could forecast the weather by listening to the music the trees played. The tree songs were sweet and melodious in springtime, languorous in the summer, and harsh and atonal as they dropped from their limbs in the fall. They struggled to blot out the discordant chorus from Lynchbany all the way past Oglagia Towne, until they left the woods just south of Ospenspri.

"Not as fine a sight as grand Polastrindu," Clothahump told him, "but an attractive little city in its own right, sequestered among rolling hills at the northernmost fringes of civilization." He was leaning forward expectantly, scanning the terrain ahead for their first sight of that lovely metropolis.

They were driving through herds of fat abismo lizards let out to graze on the last of summer's grass. Off in the distance the landscape lifted toward the sky, the distant slopes the first manifestation of the high Northern Plateau. It struck Jon-Tom as strange that no herdsfolk were visible among the abismos, but perhaps they were trained to return to their barns at nightfall by themselves.

"Ospenspri is particularly famed for its orchards," Clothahump was telling him. "Up here they grow the best apples and toklas in the warmlands."

Jon-Tom kept both hands locked on the wheel. The long drive north from Lynchbany had been harder on the jeep than on any of them. While never exactly responding like a Porsche, its handling had become worse than ever. He'd driven the last couple of days haunted by visions of the wheel coming off in his hands just when they were attempting to round a sharp bend in the road. But the wheel stayed on the steering column.

Just get us into town, he whispered silently at the straining machine, *and I'll see that you get a formal funeral.*

They swung around a hill crowned with pines and saw the cloud first. A massive black cloud. It was not moving. It just hung there in one place like a lump of sooty cotton that had been pinned to the sky. Directly above Ospenspri. Jon-Tom slowed but didn't stop.

As for beautiful Ospenspri, the Ospenspri that Clothahump had never ceased describing to him ever since they'd left home, Ospenspri of the numerous streams and delicately arched bridges and many fountains, Ospenspri the flower of the north, it bore little relationship to the wizard's word pictures.

Instead of tall, graceful buildings with fluted walls, the valley that lay beneath the black cloud was occupied by a succession of mud and adobe huts. Dirty water flowed down a few central canals. These joined together below the city to form a single river. What beggared comprehension was not the fact that the water above the city flowed clear and pure, but that it appeared to become fresh again the instant it left behind the city limits. It was as though the pollution it acquired within the city was unable to depart with the current.

Yet there was no sign of any kind of filtering or treatment system where the canals became river.

There were plenty of trees among the houses, as Clothahump had predicted. Every one of them was dead, and not from the onset of winter. They had been blighted by something far worse than inclement weather. On the slopes north of the city where grew the famed apple and tokla orchards there was nothing but twisted, spiny lumps of brown bark huddled together against the wind. No neatly tended rows of healthy trees with busy citizens working among them.

And hovering over it all, that single, ominous, unmoving black cloud.

Sorbl fluttered down to resume his perch on the frame of the backseat. "Are you sure we didn't take a wrong turn somewhere, Master?"

"No, we did not take a wrong turn, you feathered twit." But there was little venom in the wizard's retort. He was staring in disbelief at the city spread out before them. "This *is* Ospenspri. There's the Acomarry Hill, and there the three springs, each winding its own way into town." He rose, leaning on the windshield for support. It groaned.

Behind them stood the autumnal forest of the Bellwoods, shedding its leaves to the accompaniment of mournful but hardly malign notes. Ahead was once-beautiful Ospenspri, with its polluted waterways, devastated architecture, and clear air, dominated by that unnatural mass of cumulonimbus. When he spoke again, his tone was subdued.

"Drive on, lad. Something dreadful has overtaken this place and the people who make their home here. Perhaps we can do something to help. We are honor-bound to try."

Jon-Tom nodded, took the jeep out of neutral. The tenuous transmission made gargling noises, and they lurched forward.

"What's a tokla?"

"You never had a tokla, my boy?"

"I don't think so." He kept his eyes on the road as he

spoke. "It doesn't sound like anything that grows where I come from."

"That is your loss, then, for it is a most delightful fruit. You can eat all you want because it shrinks inside your stomach."

"You mean it shrivels up?"

"No. It shrinks before it is digested. In shape it is like this." His hands described an outline in the air that reminded Jon-Tom of two pears joined together at their tops. "Each bite starts shrinking on its way down. By the time it hits your belly, it's barely as big as a fingernail, but you're sure you've eaten something as big as a loaf of bread."

"Would that ever be a hit on the shelves back home," Jon-Tom murmured. "The tokla fruit diet."

"Diet? What's a diet?" Sorbl asked.

"You don't know what a diet is?"

"You always repeat questions, Jon-Tom. I don't know why humans waste so much of their talking time. If I knew what a diet was, I wouldn't have to ask you what a diet was, would I?"

"I think I like you better when you're drunk, Sorbl."

The owl shrugged. "I'm not surprised. I like me better when I'm drunk too."

"A diet is when people intentionally restrict their intake of food in order to lose weight."

The famulus twitched his beak. He was a little shaky on his unsteady backseat perch, but not so shaky that he couldn't recognize an absurdity when he heard one.

"Why would anyone want to lose weight, when nearly everyone is working hard to put it on? Are you saying that among your people there are those who intentionally starve themselves?"

"To a certain degree, yes. They do so in order to make themselves look better. See, among the humans where I come from, the thinner you are, the more attractive you're considered to be.''

Sorbl wiped at his mouth with a flexible wingtip. "Weird."

"The multiplicity of peculiar notions your world is infected with never ceases to amaze me," Clothahump put in. "I am glad I am exposed to them only through you. I do not think I could cope in person."

Sorbl interrupted long enough to point. "Look. It's not deserted."

They were passing through the first buildings now, though the mud and wattle structures were hardly worthy of the term. Staggering listlessly through the filthy alleys were the citizens of Ospenspri. It was evident that whatever catastrophe had blasted their community had affected them personally.

As with all large cities, the population was a mixture of species, and all had been equally devastated. Felines and lupines, quadrupeds and bipeds, all wore the same dazed expressions. They shared something else besides a communal aura of hopelessness, a singular physical deformity that owed its presence to something other than defective genetics. Difficult to accept at first, the evidence overwhelmed the visitors as they drove on toward the main square.

Every inhabitant of Ospenspri, every citizen irrespective of age or species or sex, from the youngest cub to the eldest patriarch, had become a hunchback.

Clothahump adjusted his glasses, his expression solemn. "Whatever has happened here has crippled the people as well as their land. Turn right at this corner, my boy."

Jon-Tom complied, and the jeep slowed as it entered an open circular courtyard. In its center stood a thirty-foot-high pile of mud and gravel. Water trickled forlornly down its flanks. It was surrounded by a fence fashioned of rotted wood and a few lumps of granite.

"Stop here." Jon-Tom brought the jeep to a halt, watched as Clothahump climbed out to stare at the pitiful structure.

"What is it, sir?"

"The Peridot Fountain. Three years in the designing, twenty years in the construction. Fashioned by the Master Artisan's Guild of Ospenspri. I've read of it all my life. This is where it should be, and this patently is not it. It is built of marble and copper tubing, of sculptured alabaster and peridots the size of my shell. Whatever has infected this place breaks beauty as well as backs."

Many dispirited citizens had seen the strangers drive into the square, but only one retained enough curiosity and spirit to seek them out. The fox was old and bent like the rest of the populace. He had to lean hard on the cane he carried to support himself. The fur of his face was white with age and he was missing all the whiskers on the right side of his muzzle. A few of the others tried to hold him back, but he shook them off and advanced. The thought of death no longer frightened him. There are some older folks who are never touched by that particular fear, and the fox was one of them.

"Strangers, where do you come from? By your posture as well as your faces I know you are not from the city or its immediate environs."

"We're up from the south," Jon-Tom told him. "From just south of Lynchbany."

"A long way." The fox was nodding to himself. He turned his attention to the jeep, walked slowly around it, felt of the metal with an unsteady hand. "A most peculiar method of transportation. I have never seen the like. I should like to compliment the blacksmith who fashioned it."

"We make do with what we have." Clothahump waddled around to confront him. "I am more concerned with what has happened here. I have never visited your city, but I feel as though I know it from all that I have read about it and been told by other travelers. The last description I was given was not so very long ago. Surely Ospenspri cannot have changed so much in such a short time." He gestured at the sagging edifices surrounding the square, the dead or dying vegetation. "This has all the hallmarks of a sudden disaster, not one long in the making."

The fox was eyeing him with interest. "You are perceptive, hard-shell. In truth, we lost everything in an instant. There was no warning. One moment all was well with our city and selves. The next—there was the cloud." He jabbed skyward with his cane.

"See the evil thing hanging there? It does not drop rain and move on. It does not thunder or hail. No wind blows out of it save an ill one. It is as motionless as stone."

"You have been unable to influence it?" Clothahump had his head tilted back and was studying the black mass.

"All the efforts of our best magicians have failed. Their spells either have no effect on it at all or else they pass right through it. It is only vapor, after all. How does one threaten vapor? We have invoked every agent in the meteorological pantheon, all to no avail."

"It is not a climatic phenomenon that hangs over your city and your lives but a pall of supernature. Weather spells will have no effect on something like this."

"The perambulator," said Jon-Tom, with a sudden realization of what the wizard was getting at.

"Quite so, my boy."

"But we're inside the city now, and we haven't changed." He found himself straightening his back reflexively. "And the forest beyond the city limits wasn't affected."

"Not all the effects of the perambulator are global in scope, lad. Many perturbations, of varying degree, are highly localized. It is shifting and spinning and throwing off, upsetting energy all the time. Sometimes nothing larger than a plot of land a foot square is affected. Sometimes a grove of trees. Or, in this case, an entire community.

"But this is the severest perturbation we have yet encountered. Remember what I told you, that unless it is freed, the perambulator's perturbations will grow steadily more intense, until we run the risk of being locked in permanent change. That is what has happened here in Ospenspri. The perturbation, of which I believe that cloud to be an indication, has settled in permanently. This part of the world has been damaged for good. Unless . . ."

"Unless you can do something about it—Master," Jon-Tom finished respectfully.

The wizard nodded. "We must certainly give it our best effort."

" 'Our' best effort." Jon-Tom moved to the back of the jeep and began unpacking his duar. Clothahump moved over to put a hand on the young man's wrist.

"No, my boy. Leave this one to me. The citizens of this poor community have suffered enough."

Jon-Tom swallowed his hurt. He knew nothing of the mechanism that had devastated Ospenspri, and he'd had many occasions on which to learn the error of false pride. It was time to abide by the turtle's wish.

The fox watched them intently as Sorbl aided Clothahump in his preparations. A second distorted figure came hobbling over the dirt to join them. It made for Jon-Tom.

He turned to the newcomer as the bent shape drew close. "We're friends. We're going to try to help you. But my mentor there needs plenty of room to work his magic and—" He stopped in mid-sentence, staring. Despite the hunchback, there was something almost familiar about the oncoming figure. That was absurd, of course, but still, that outline, those eyes, those whiskers . . .

"Don't tell me to get lost, you 'airy son of an ape!"

"Mudge?" Jon-Tom couldn't take his eyes off the figure. It was nearer now, and he could see the speaker more clearly. Bent, dirty, undistinguished—and unmistakable. "Mudge, it *is* you!"

"O' course it's me, you bloody oversized naked monkey!

'Ave you gone blind? Me 'ead 'appens to be a mite nearer the ground at the moment, but it ain't by choice, wot? Me face is still the same, though. So's yours, I see. As ugly as ever.''

A warm feeling spread throughout Jon-Tom's body. "Mudge, it's good to see you again. Even under these circumstances.''

"Circumstances ain't the 'alf of it, mate.'' The otter nodded toward the jeep. "There's 'is sorcerership, senile as ever, and 'is sot of an apprentice. Would 'e 'ave any booze with 'im, do you know? I could use a good stiff one, if 'e ain't drunk all the liquor betwixt 'ere an' the southern ocean. I never could understand those people wot drinks to excess.''

"That sounds pretty funny coming from you, Mudge.''

"Why? I never drink to excess, mate. Me body don't know the meanin' of the word. I just drink till I'm full. Then I piss it out and start over. So I never reach excess, wot? Tell me, wot are you and 'is nibs doin' so far from 'is tree? I'd think you'd be hunkered down south, warm an' cozy an' waiting for winter.''

"Perhaps you've noticed something a bit out of the ordinary in the world these past few weeks?''

The otter chuckled, shook his head. "You always did 'ave the gift of understatement, mate. Aye, you could say that, if you'd call the world goin' totally mad a bit out o' the ordinary.''

"How'd you get all the way up here, Mudge? Why are you in the same sorry state as the Ospensprites? Not that your usual state isn't sorry, but this is different.''

"Just lucky, I guess, mate. Well, I 'appened to be doin' some work down in Malderpot—it ain't such a bad place anymore since they 'ad that recent change o' government—and I 'ad occasion to depart the vicinity in a bit of a 'urry.''

"Who'd you cheat this time?''

"Wot, me cheat someone, mate? You sting me to the quick, you does.''

"Forget it," Jon-Tom said dryly. They were both watching the jeep. Clothahump was assembling something out of pieces of wood salvaged from the crude fence enclosing the mud fountain, adding unrecognizable devices from his pack and what looked like a few kitchen utensils.

" 'Tis been an interestin' month for old Mudge," the otter went on. "Ever since this out-o'-the-ordinary's took hold of us. You never know wot you're goin' to wake up facin' in the mirror, much less wot you're liable to find yourself in bed with. Why, there was the night in Okot I was dallyin' with the most luscious capybara lady you ever set eyes on—you know I like 'em big, mate."

"You like anything that walks, talks, and is a member of the opposite sex, Mudge."

"So I'm enthusiastic instead o' discriminatin'. Anyways, there we were, just about to consummate the evenin', when suddenly, right before me very eyes, not to mention beneath me chest, she turns into somethin' with 'alf a dozen extra see-alls, two 'eads, and all the rest o' the critical body parts badly out o' place as well. O' course I looked just about the same, but I tell you, mate, the damage to our respective libidos was nothin' short o' devastating."

"I can imagine. Spare me the sordid aftermath."

"That was the trouble, mate. Weren't no sordid aftermath. Weren't much foremath, either." He sighed with the remembrance. "Anyways, was after that that I 'ad me little difficulty in Malderpot and decided that wot with winter comin' on an' all, it was time for me to 'ead south again. Fast. But I thought to take some time to linger up 'ere in be-ooti-ful Ospenspri— and it were beautiful, you can take me word on that, mate."

"So Clothahump has told me."

"Right. So I'm doin' a little sight-seein', takin' in the air and the good food and an occasional compliant an' 'opefully drunk lady or two, when all of a sudden another one o' those bleedin' suddenlike changes comes over me. An' the 'hole bloomin' city and everyone in it as well. Only this time, a couple o' minutes go by, and then a couple o' 'ours, and suddenly we're realizin' that the change is 'ere to stay. First off everyone goes a little crazy, not that I blames 'em. I went a mite bonkers meself. Then the panic goes away and this permanent depression kind o' takes 'old of you. Like wakin' up one mornin' to find someone's stolen your balls while you were asleep.'' He jabbed a thumb skyward.

"An' over it all, that bloody stinkin' black cloud, sneerin' down at us an' mockin' the memories o' our former lives. Pretty pitiful, mate. So that's 'ow I come to be 'ere talkin' to you like this, all bent over and stove up like everyone else. I 'ope 'is wizardness can do somethin' about it, because most o' these folks are just about at the end o' their rope.''

"If anyone can do anything, Clothahump can,'' Jon-Tom replied with pride.

"Aye, if 'e 'asn't forgotten 'alf o' wotever spell 'e's a mind to try. Two 'undred years ago I wouldn't worry, but 'e ain't the wizard 'e used to be, you know.''

"None of us are what we used to be, Mudge.''

The otter spat sideways. "If you're goin' to go an' get profound on me, lad, I'm goin' to leave. I've 'ad about enough solemn pronouncements this past week to last me a lifetime. Say''—he squinted sharply up at his old friend— "wot brings you up from the wizard's cozy 'ome to this cold part o' the world, anyways?''

"The very thing that's ruined this town. The same thing that's causing similar changes all over the world. Unless something's done to stop it, these perturbations, as Clothahump calls them, will keep getting worse.''

"I see. An' you and mister Clothyrump aim to try and do something about 'em? Wot's behind it, lad? Some kind o' runaway natural condition?''

"Yes and no. These kinds of changes happen all the time but usually on a much smaller scale and always with far less frequency. The problem is that someone or something is making sure that the cause of all the changes sticks around. Clothahump thinks whoever's doing it is completely mad.'' He nodded in the direction of the mountainous slope with its blighted orchards. ''Whoever's responsible is holed up with the perambulator, the change-inducer, somewhere north of here. That's where we're headed.''

Mudge eyed him in disbelief. ''*North* of here? You can't mean that, mate. You know wot the Plateau country can be like this time o' year, wot with winter fixin' to settle in? 'Tis not a comfortin' place to be, especially for a poor 'uman like yourself wot 'as no fur of 'is own to protect 'im from the cold winds and snows.''

''My comfort matters little when considered in the greater context. If this perambulator isn't freed and its captor challenged, then the world risks permanent perturbation. A little cold will be a trivial danger by comparison. You know how serious it is, because Clothahump's come all this way.''

''Instead of sendin' just you, for a change, 'is magicship 'is riskin' 'is own precious arse, wot? I admit that's a point, lad.'' The stooped otter considered. ''A perambulator, eh? So that's wot's causin' all the trouble. And you call wot it's doin' 'perturbing' things.''

Jon-Tom nodded. ''That's right.''

''Then it's only right an' proper that you and 'is sorcererness be the ones to be 'untin' it. I've always known old Clothybump to be more than a little permanently perturbed, and I've never been too sure o' you, neither. Well, I expect that you're doin' wot 'as to be done.'' He tried to straighten, but his distorted spine fought against the effort. ''I'm comin' along, o' course.''

''What?'' Jon-Tom stared hard at the twisted, furry figure. He must be wrong. This couldn't be Mudge.

''Aye. As you say, someone 'as to stop this bleedin' switchin' and changin' from gettin' any worse. You can use all the 'elp you can get, especially where you're goin'.

Besides, mate, wot would you do without me to bail you out of a tough spot?''

Jon-Tom had no ready reply. Nor could he mouth one upon a moment's reflection. The otter's words were as much of a shock to his system as the sight of the perturbed city. Mudge possessed an extensive and colorful vocabulary, but to the best of Jon-Tom's knowledge, the word *volunteer* was as alien to the otter as celibacy.

"I'm not sure," he finally said slowly. "Are you actually offering to help? Of your own free will? Without having to be coerced by Clothahump or myself?"

"Well, o' course I am, lad." Mudge looked hurt, a specialty among his vast repertoire of expressions. "Wot do you take me for?"

"Let's see." Jon-Tom ticked them off on his fingers as he recited. "A thief, a wencher, a coward, a scoundrel, a—"

Mudge hastened to interrupt the steady flow of derogatory appellations. "Let's not be overenthusiastic, mate. O' course I'm volunterin'. You're goin' to need me 'elp. Neither you nor 'is wizardship is wot you'd call a master at scoutin' or fightin', and that flyin' bag of feathery booze old hard-shell calls 'is famulus ain't much better."

"We've managed to make it this far." It was Jon-Tom's turn to be insulted.

"Luck always travels in the company o' fools, wot? Nonetheless, I'll come along if you'll 'ave me. Wot's left o' me, that is."

The combination of the once vibrant otter's wrenched appearance coupled with his apparently selfless eagerness to be of assistance caused moisture to begin forming at the corners of Jon-Tom's eyes. He had to struggle to keep his voice from breaking as he replied.

"Of course, we'll be glad of your company and your help, Mudge."

The otter appeared both pleased and relieved. "That's

settled, then." He nodded toward the mud fountain where Clothahump was engaged in the erection of his sorcerous apparatus, mixing the steady litany of a long spell with selected curses that he heaped on the bumbling, unsteady Sorbl. "Wot's 'e up to?"

"I don't know," Jon-Tom confessed. "He said that he was going to try to help these people, but he didn't go into details. You know Clothahump: he'd rather show than tell."

"Aye. That's so innocent bystanders like you an' me don't 'ave a chance to get out of the way."

A few of the blasted inhabitants of Ospenspri had gathered to watch, but all remained on the fringe of the square. Only the aged fox was daring enough to stay and chat with them. Jon-Tom left him conversing animatedly with Mudge and walked over to see if he could help the wizard in his work.

"You certainly can, my boy," the old turtle told him as he adjusted his glasses on his beak. Jon-Tom started to swing his duar off his back, and the wizard hastened to forestall him. "No, no, I do not have need of your singing. Could you hold this up here?"

Mildly mortified, Jon-Tom bit back the response he wanted to make and took hold of the folding wooden platform, steadying it on the cracked surface of the square. Mudge did not comment on this demotion with the expected flurry of jeers. Perhaps the otter's disfigurement had sobered him.

He tried to make some sense out of the interlocking platform and failed. "What's this setup for, anyway?"

Instead of answering, the sorcerer was walking a slow circle around the enigmatic apparatus, studying it intently from every angle, occasionally bending over or kneeling to check its position relative to the hills on the north side of the city. From time to time he would interrupt his circumnavigation to adjust this or that piece of metal or wood, then step back to resume his journey.

Having returned to the precise spot where he'd begun, he

turned and marched over to his supply pack. A large box had been removed and now stood next to it. It contained half a dozen drawers. As Jon-Tom watched and struggled to contain his curiosity, the wizard began to mix powders taken from the six drawers in a small bowl. It took only a few minutes. Then he dumped the contents of the bowl into a small, deep metal goblet that hung suspended in the center of the structure Jon-Tom was steadying against the breeze.

"That cloud overhead," the wizard explained, as though no time at all had elapsed since Jon-Tom had first asked his question, "is the localized center of the disturbance that continues to hold Ospenspri and its population fast in its perturbing grasp. If we can change its composition, not to mention its disposition, back to that of a normal cloud, I believe this also will result in a shift in the perturbation."

Jon-Tom tilted his head back to gaze up at the threatening mass of black moisture billowing overhead. "How are you going to do that, sir?"

"The best way I know how, my boy, the best way I know how. Hold the platform firmly now."

Jon-Tom tightened his grip on two of the wooden legs, at the same time frowning at his mentor. "This isn't going to be dangerous, is it?"

"My boy, would I ever involve you in anything dangerous?" Before Jon-Tom had an opportunity to offer the self-evident reply, the wizard had launched into a most impressive and forceful incantation, simultaneously passing his hands rapidly over the central goblet as he traced intricate geometric shapes in the empty air.

> Harken to me, affronting front.
> Winds that linger, false winter solstice.
> Prepare to flee, to leave, to shunt
> Aside thy paralyzed coriolis.

  Disintegrate and break apart the lattice
  That maintains thy present cumulostratus status!

  As the wizard recited, the goblet began to jiggle and
bounce. Then it broke free of its leather bindings, and instead
of falling to the hard ground below, it remained in place,
dancing and spinning and beginning to glow. Jon-Tom could
feel the powerful vibrations through the supporting sticks.
The apparatus seemed far too fragile to contain the rapidly
intensifying rumble that was emanating from the base of the
goblet, but somehow the aracane concatenation held together.
  The goblet was glowing white-hot. The ground began to
tremble. He held his position as the few observers who had
clumped on the outskirts of the square scattered into the mud
huts. The rumble became a deafening roar in his ears. He felt
as if he were standing under a waterfall. Clothahump's words
faded into inaudibility.
  The wizard abruptly brought both hands together over his
head. A small thunderclap rolled across the square. Sorbl was
knocked from his perch atop the jeep's windshield. Jon-Tom
gritted his teeth and held on, the concussion making his ears
ring, his fingers beginning to go numb.
  Through half-closed eyes he saw something bright and
shiny rocket skyward from the mouth of the goblet. The
whistling sound of the miniature comet's ascension was
quickly swallowed up by the roiling blackness above.
Clothahump was shading his eyes with one hand. He spoke
absently, clearly concentrating on the place where the shiny
object had vanished into the bottom of the great cloud.
  "You can let go now, my boy."
  With relief Jon-Tom did so, joining the wizard in gazing skyward while he tried to rub some feeling back into his hands.
  The cloud let out a rumble that was a vaster echo of the
one the goblet had generated. It was less explosive, more
natural, and the sound of it lingered not unpleasantly in the

ear. It was preceded by something akin to lightning but not of
it, a more benign electrical relative. The pale white pulsation
that lit the underside of the cloud spread quickly to its edges.
A second rumble came from the far side. It sounded like a
question.

"What did you do, sir?"

"The only thing I knew how, my boy, the only thing I
knew how."

"What happens now? Something wondrous and magical?"

"If we're lucky, yes."

Unable to keep his head tilted back any longer, Jon-Tom
turned his attention to the now-silent jumble of wooden poles
and metal strips that had been used to precipitate the glittering
whatever-it-had-been into the sky. The leather strips that had
originally supported the metal goblet had been vaporized. The
goblet itself now lay on the ground, a blob of half-melted
pewter. In contravention of every law of physics, the fragile
wooden apparatus remained standing. The explosion that had
flung the shiny object skyward should have blown the collage
of dowels to bits; the heat that had melted the goblet should
have fired it like kindling. Jon-Tom shook his head in
amazement. Truly Clothahump was a master of elegant super-
natural forces.

Mudge, who had limped over to join him, nodded at the
construction. "Weird, ain't it?" His black nose twitched as
he leaned toward it. "One o' these days I 'ave to ask 'is
conjureness why magic always stinks."

"Mudge, you could steal the wonder from a fairy castle."

"Castles stink too; marble floors soak up odors. An' I've
met some pretty slovenly fairies."

Trying to ignore him, Jon-Tom bent over and reached for
the goblet. Thunder· continued its querulous exhortations
overhead, and a prickly dampness could be felt in the air. He
touched the melted metal carefully. It was cool against his
palm.

Removing it, he turned the barely recognizable lump over in his hands. Not just cool but ice-cold, despite the intense heat it had recently endured. And Mudge was right; there was a peculiar smell attending to the metal. He stuck a finger inside, rubbed it against the bottom of the curve. When he removed it, it was smeared with black and glittering sparkles. He held it to his nose and sniffed.

Mudge made a face. "Wot is it, guv'nor?"

"I'm not sure." He eyed the sky again. "It smells and looks something like silver iodide. Where I come from, something similar is used for seeding clouds."

The otter gave him a sideways look. "We seed the ground 'ere, mate, not the clouds. You're not makin' any sense."

But Jon-Tom knew better. He looked over to where the patiently waiting Clothahump stood motionless, still shading his eyes and inspecting the sky. You clever, sharp old codger you, he thought, and found that he was smiling.

Then something wondrous and magical began to happen, exactly as the wizard had indicated it should, and Jon-Tom found that he was not just smiling, he was laughing. Laughing, and feeling good enough to kick up his feet in a celebratory jig.

It began to rain.

The rumbling from the cloud had sounded querulous at first, then confused, but now it was booming and roaring with unperturbed assurance. He stood there with the rain pelting his upturned face, luxuriating in the clean, pure, undistorted moisture.

Well, maybe just a little distorted.

Mudge grabbed the goblet. " 'Ere now, let me 'ave a sniff o' that, you dancin' ape. Something's not right 'ere." He inhaled deeply. Then his eyes grew wide. "Bugger me for a wayward clergyman! That's brandy, mate, and top-quality stuff too! Maybe there's a drop or two left in the bottom to whet old Mudge's whistle, wot?'' He started to tilt the melted goblet to his lips.

Jon-Tom quickly snatched it back. "Whoa! Silver iodide's a strong poison, Mudge. Or maybe it was silver chloride? No matter.'' He sniffed himself, looked puzzled. "It's not brandy, anyway. It's bourbon.''

The otter leaned forward, and now he looked equally confused. "Peculiar, mate. I get chocolate liqueur this time.''

And Jon-Tom again, "Sour mash—or vodka. Say, what's going on here?''

Clothahump was trying to keep his glasses dry against the downpour that was soaking them. "It's none of those, my boy. The particular ingredient to which you refer and which you are having such difficulty identifying is far more basic, not to mention expensive. I would never utilize it so freely were it not for the seriousness of this moment of mercy. It is very scarce, very hard to come by, and very much in demand, and not only by those of us who dabble in the sorcerous arts. We call it Essoob.'' He glanced upward again, studying the storm with a critical eye.

It was raining steadily. The thunder had worked itself out, and now there was only the steady patter of rain against the ground. There was no wind and the big drops came straight down.

"Never heard of it,'' Jon-Tom confessed.

"Essence of Booze. I determined that we needed not only to prime this particular cloud but to shock it back to normality. I also had to utilize something that would mix well with water.''

Mudge was standing with his head back and his mouth open, swallowing and smacking his lips. "Well, I'll be a shrew with a migraine! Drink up, mate! We'll likely never stand in a storm the likes o' this ever again!'' Sorbl, too, was partaking of the alcoholic rain, had been since the descent of the first drops. That explained the owl's unusual silence,

Jon-Tom mused. The famulus was drifting peacefully in some imbiber's heaven.

Cautiously he parted his lips and sucked in the moisture that was running off his nose. Crème de ménthe. A second slurp brought home the taste of Galliano, a third of Midori, or something like it.

Enough, he told himself firmly. He was not thirsty and had no desire to be unconscious.

"Oasafin!" Mudge was babbling. "Terraquin. Coosage, guinal, essark, goodmage, sankerberry wine!" The otter was lying on his back in the mud, his arms and legs spread wide but not as wide as his mouth.

And he wasn't the only one, for the unique properties of the downpour Clothahump had induced had not passed unnoticed among the other inhabitants of Ospenspri. They came stumbling out of their mud and wattle houses, in pairs and trios at first, then in a delighted, exuberant rush. Even those citizens who considered themselves teetotalers participated, for they could hardly pass on such a wonderful piece of sorcerous business and leave it to their less inhibited neighbors to tell them all about it when it was over.

As the aromatic rain continued to fall it began to have an affect on the desiccated trees and shriveled plants. Flowers bloomed from seemingly dead stalks. Bushes put out new, fresh green growth. Up in the ruined orchards the apple and tokla trees straightened; their limbs lifted and erupted in a burst of green. They did not put forth fruit, for it was too late in the season, but next year's harvest would surely be spectacular.

The rain worked its most wondrous transformation out in the fields of late autumn wheat. The flattened, burned stalks lifted skyward, and the dry heads grew swollen with golden kernels. Not merely gold in color but in promise. Because for months thereafter, any bread baked from that season's threshing was famed throughout the Bellwoods and even beyond.

Renowned and marveled at, bread and long rolls alike, for their texture and color and most especially of all, the faintly alcoholic flavor each bite imparted to the palate.

Through the rain and the fog that accompanied it, Jon-Tom could witness the transformation of Ospenspri and its inhabitants. The city itself seemed to straighten as it returned to health, buildings and citizens alike drawing strength from the rain and the concomitant metamorphosis of the cloud. As that black mass of moisture lightened, so did the mood of the city and the lands surrounding it. As he stared, Ospenspri changed from an island of devastation and despair to the jewel of the north.

The mud huts vanished, to be replaced by finely wrought structures of hardwood and dressed stone. The mud seemed to dissolve beneath his feet, leaving behind yard-square paving blocks of ocher-streaked white marble. Close by, the mud spring was transformed into a graceful spire of filagreed arches. Water spurted or trickled from dozens of nozzles. Set among the marble sculptures that comprised the fountain were hundreds of the brilliant green garnets called peridots, which gave the square its name.

The storm was beginning to abate, the black cloud to break up. Once the dissolution had begun, it proceeded rapidly. For the first time in weeks the sun shone brightly on the tormented city. The thirsty earth soaked up what precipitation managed to escape the tubs and rain barrels of the inhabitants. Having spent its force, the cloud and the perturbation it had sheltered faded away with equal alacrity.

Nor was the city all that returned to normal. Mudge had straightened and now danced a wild saraband on the marble edge of the towering fountain. But Jon-Tom found his attention drawn to the one citizen of Ospenspri who had greeted them.

No longer crooked and bent, the old fox stood tall and proud before Clothahump. He was bigger than Mudge, and his silver-streaked ears were on a level with Jon-Tom's shoulders. As both wizard and spellsinger looked on, he performed a deep, profound bow. In place of the dirty rags he'd been wearing when he'd initially approached the visitors, he now wore a splendid suit of dark brown edged with green velvet and fastened with hardwood buttons inlaid with brass. A peculiarly narrow hat of green felt and leather rested between his ears.

"I am Sorenset," he informed them, "a senior member of the ruling council of Ospenspri." Another bow toward Clothahump. "We are laid low by the weight of your genius, sir, and raised up again through your timely assistance. I am honored to reflect the glory of the greatest of wizards."

"The people of Ospenspri have always been famed for the accuracy of their observations," Clothahump said blithely. "I only did what any traveler of my stature would have done."

"But which none could do until now." Sorenset closed his eyes and stared at the sun, luxuriating in its feel against his face. "The curse has been lifted. Ospenspri has suffered before, but such calamities have wrought their damage and then moved on. We began to fear that the black cloud was destined to stay with us forever."

"It could return, in the same guise or another."

Sorenset dropped his face and stared at the wizard. "Do not say such things. Have you not banished the cloud?"

"Yes, but not its cause. Until we can do that, no morning will be the same as the one that has preceded it, and none of us can go to sleep with any assurance that we will wake up recognizing what we are. It is to remedy this matter that the three of us have undertaken this journey from our home in the South."

Sorenset nodded somberly. "Anything that you require that can be found in Ospenspri will be provided. We will help in any way that we can. You have restored our bodies, our city, and our souls."

He turned toward the beautiful homes and apartments, no longer poor structures of mud and wattle, which fronted on the central square. Laughter, shouts of relief, and other sounds of merriment poured from open windows and doors. The cries might have been deafening except that many of Ospenspri's restored citizens had ingested too much of the flavorful downpour and now lay savoring their restoration in stuporous slumber on porches and doorsteps, streets and benches.

Mudge leapt off the fountain enclosure and wrapped his arms around Jon-Tom, hooting and barking with delight. Jon-Tom staggered under the weight and collapsed to the ground with the otter on top of him. He wasn't angry. He could only grin. The otter's high spirits were infectious. Besides, he'd done more than taste of the alcoholic precipitation himself. He was feeling pleasantly giddy.

As for the wizard's famulus, Sorbl was flying in tighter and tighter circles around the spire of the fountain, until his wings and coordination finally gave out. Mudge and Jon-Tom had to drag him from the pool.

As befitted their station, Sorenset and Clothahump observed this display of youthful celebration with a tolerant eye. "It appears that it is left to us to proceed with practical matters."

"I am not displeased," Clothahump told the fox. "We will not be interrupted with foolish questions. I will lay out our needs for you. They are modest in scope. We will also require proper lodging for the night, assuming any innkeeper has recovered sufficiently to serve us."

"I know just the place," Sorenset replied. "The finest establishment in the city. When the owners learn who their guests will be, they will be even more effusive in their praise than I. This I will attend to myself, in the name of the council and the people of a grateful Ospenspri."

The music that the orchestra was playing for the enjoyment

of the diners was soft and light, all flutes and strings. Such sounds ordinarily would have driven a hard-rock guitarist like Jon-Tom from the building. But after all they'd been through on the long journey northward, he found he was glad of the respite from anything harsh, including sounds. He was particularly fascinated by the multireeded flute the bobcat was tootling on and the thirty-stringed lyre the well-dressed gibbon was stroking. The latter made the double strings of his duar seem simple by comparison. But then, the gibbon had arms that trailed on the ground when he walked. No human could match his reach.

On the other hand, he told himself as he regarded his duar fondly, it wasn't an easy matter to bring forth chords from strings that tended to blur into another dimension when you were playing on them, either.

It seemed that everyone in Ospenspri wanted to thank the city's saviors personally. Sorenset politely but firmly warded off the multitude of well-wishers, explaining that their visitors were exhausted and still had many leagues to travel.

The deluge of hosannas was mitigated more than a little by the perturbation that struck later that afternoon. It was not as damaging to the spirit as the black cloud and it lasted less than ten minutes, but it was a sobering reminder to all that the world was still a long way from returning to a state of normalcy. Everyone became a multihued butterfly, each building a cocoon of varying size and shape. There was much nervous flapping of brilliantly colored wings before the perturbation ended and the real world returned with a snap.

It certainly took the edge off Clothahump's achievement. Sorenset no longer had to fend off citizens who wanted to kiss the wizard's feet.

"Ungrateful wretches." The turtle sipped his soup. "It's not enough that for them I turn their town right side up. They want me to tip the world for them."

"Don't be too hard on them." Jon-Tom was finishing his

own meal, savoring the subtle spices and the tender meat that now rested comfortably in his belly. After weeks of hasty meals followed by continuous jouncing in the old jeep, the meal at the inn had reminded him that eating could be a delight as well as a necessity. "They don't understand what's going on. We're probably the only ones in the world who do—along with whoever's restraining the perambulator, of course."

"Ignorance is no excuse for bad manners," grumped the wizard. But Jon-Tom had managed to soothe him somewhat.

Sorenset and several other members of the city council joined them at the oval table. A pouty Clothahump allowed Jon-Tom to tell their story and explain what they intended to try. The rulers of Ospenspri listened politely.

"One thing is certain." The flying squirrel, Talla, was president of the council and wore his medals on the flaps of skin that connected his wrists to his ribs. "The vehicle in which you arrived will not take you where you wish to go. Between here and the northern reaches you will have to climb."

"What about riding snakes?" Jon-Tom asked.

The squirrel shook his head. "No L'borian could survive the conditions on the Plateau. It's far too cold."

"Then we will have to continue on foot." Clothahump was tapping the table with the fingers of both hands. "A daunting prospect, yet one that does not concern me a tenth so much as whatever we will encounter at the end of our journey."

"What do you suggest?" Jon-Tom asked again.

Sorenset considered. "Ospenspri is home to many independent transporters. But to go north of the Plateau at this time of year, I don't know. All we can do is inquire if any quadruped is willing to undertake such a journey. You will have all the supplies you need, but we cannot compel a citizen to risk a life against his will."

"Of course not," said Clothahump.

"I will go and make inquiries right now." A nervous bandicoot excused himself from the gathering and hurried toward the door.

"Even a single horse willing to carry our supplies would be a great help," Clothahump said, "though I am not sanguine about one volunteering."

"What, after you saved the whole city?" Jon-Tom observed.

The wizard gave him a knowing look. "My boy, when you have lived as long as I have, you come to learn that among the virtues, altruism is not the most common."

The contemplative silence that followed this wise observation was interrupted by a loud smacking sound from the table behind the conference oval. Jon-Tom turned a disapproving eye on Mudge. Only the top of the otter's head was visible. His face was buried in the midsection of a two-foot-long broiled fish. Jon-Tom tilted back in his chair and whispered.

"Do you have to eat with your mouth open?"

Mudge promptly stopped munching to squint at his friend. Bits of meat and skin hung from his teeth and jaws, and his face was shiny with oil. "Well now, guv'nor, if you can show me 'ow to eat with me mouth closed, I'll 'ave a shot at it. Otherwise, be a good chap and bugger off." He plunged his face back into the hollowed-out fish and took an enormous bite, loudly crunching up meat, skin, and bones.

"That's not what I meant." Jon-Tom struggled to remain patient. "It's the noise you're making."

Again the otter glanced up. "Wot of it?"

"It's disconcerting. You should eat quietly and chew with your mouth closed."

Mudge sighed in amazement. "You 'umans. The notions you come up with. Mate, I couldn't eat like that even if I wanted to."

"Why not?"

"Because me mouth ain't flat against me face like an ape's, that's why. 'Tis easy for you to keep your cud restrained behind your cheeks, but my jaws protrude. See?'' He stuck his face close to Jon-Tom's, and the spellsinger recoiled from the overpowering odor of fish. ''The sound comes out both sides o' me face. 'Tis a matter o' design, not preference.''

''Oh. I hadn't thought of that.'' He sat silently for a moment while the otter resumed gorging himself. His forehead twisted in contemplation, and then he spoke sharply. ''Hey, now wait a minute—'' He didn't get the chance to finish the thought. Clothahump was speaking again.

Only, this time the wizard's words were directed not to the attentive members of Ospenspri's ruling council but to the newest member of the expedition.

''You.''

Silence. It finally penetrated Mudge's food-sodden consciousness that everyone was looking at him. He turned, managed to mumble around a mouthful of food.

''Who, me?''

''Yes, you, river rat.'' Behind the six-sided glasses the wizard's gaze was intense. Jon-Tom watched with interest. Something serious was up.

Mudge could sense it too. Carefully he positioned the remainder of his fish on its plate and commenced an ostentatious licking of his fingers. ''What can I do for your magicness?''

''Jon-Tom tells me that you have volunteered to accompany us northward to aid us in our endeavor.''

''Um. Well, if Jonny-Tom says that's wot I said, then I guess I said it.''

Clothahump leaned forward. ''I am curious to know why. It is uncharacteristic of you.''

''I'll let that one by, guv'nor.'' He began to preen his whiskers. ''It's like I told Jon-Tom. You 'elped me like you 'elped everyone else. I'm meself again. I'd 'ave 'ated to 'ave gone through life bent over under that bloody cloud. You saved me. So I figure I owes you. I couldn't very well 'ave continued in me profession all twisted and gnarled like I was."

"Your profession?" The wizard's eyebrows would have lifted if he'd had any. "Are you referring to your practice of pickpocketing and general thievery?"

" 'Ere now, sir, is that any way to treat an old friend who volunteers 'is 'elp out o' the goodness of 'is 'eart to accompany you on a journey no doubt as dangerous as your usual travels? If all you can do is sit there and insult me, maybe I—"

"I do not mean to belittle your generous offer. I merely am trying to define your motives. I suspect you are in this because you sense the scope of the danger and, possessing a crude sort of native intelligence, realize that the safest place to be is as close as possible to me."

Jon-Tom spoke softly to his friend. "Is he right, Mudge?"

"Mate, you do me a disservice. You both do me a disservice. Seems like every time I volunteers to 'elp you blokes without regard for the safety of me own person, all you can do is question me motivation. I can't tell you 'ow much it 'urts me."

"It will hurt you a great deal more if you insinuate yourself into our company only for your own selfish reasons. My concern, however, is not so much with your motivations as with your allegiance once we have reached our destination. I cannot afford to have you running off at a critical moment. I must be able to rely on *all* my companions." Before Mudge could profer the inevitable protest, Clothahump was pointing a heavy finger at him. Behind those thick glasses the wizard's eyes seemed to have darkened from their natural brown to a deep, glowing crimson.

"Swear, son-of-a-stream, miscreant offspring of a midden maiden, that you come on this journey of your own free will, that you will do what is required of you as a companion in peril, and that you will do so without thought or regard for your own safety, for the good of all the inhabitants of the warmlands." A red haze had enveloped the table and the awed patrons of the inn. Everyone had turned to watch.

"Swear this to me now, by the blood that flows in your veins, by the intellgence that may hide in your brain, and by the desire that rules your loins."

"Okay, okay," said Mudge disgustedly, putting up both paws defensively. "Take it easy! Jump me tail if I don't think you like overdoin' these things, Your Wizardship. Be that as it may, I swear."

The red haze dissipated into the walls of the inn, and Clothahump's eyes regained their normal placid hue. Satisfied, he settled back into his chair. It was higher than most in order to raise his midsection to table level. He picked up a fork and jabbed at the soggy mass of colorful river-bottom greens that had been served earlier.

"Very well. I accept your oath and your company. Needless to say, the consequences of reneging on your agreement are too horrible to mention."

"I know." Mudge sighed. He did not appear in the least upset or, for that matter, impressed. "All that fuss over nothing." He picked up his fish, was about to bite into it again when Jon-Tom leaned close.

"That's the first time Clothahump's made you swear an oath."

"Wot of it, mate?"

"It doesn't give you much leeway for slinking off on side trips the way you like to when we're traveling. You'll have to toe the line pretty tightly or something dreadful's likely to happen to you."

"I know that, lad. 'Tis no big deal." He chomped down on the fish. Bones splintered under his sharp teeth.

Still Jon-Tom was not satisfied. "Mudge, this isn't like you. You've changed."

"Who, me? I 'aven't changed a bit, mate. The truth o' the

matter is that I'm bein' agreeable because it suits me, not old armor-britches over there. I've 'ad a taste or two o' these perambulations and wot 'is wizardship says about the safest place in the world bein' close to 'is arse is mighty near the truth."

"I can't argue with that myself," Jon-Tom admitted. "It'll be good to have you with us, especially when we have to confront whoever's trapped it."

Mudge paused, the fish halfway to his mouth. "Wot are you babblin' on about, mate? Once His Magicsty once there frees this perbambulator or wotever the 'ell it is, we can all come a-skippin' 'ome safe an' clear, right?"

"Maybe not. We still have to deal with the instigator of this crisis, and there's no telling what he, or it, is like or how it'll react to our attempts to intervene. Freeing the perambulator will assure that the world is saved, but it won't do anything for us. We still have to get away from whoever's restrained it. I imagine that psychotic will be more than a little upset when his plans are ruined."

"I see now." The otter carefully returned the remnants of the fish to his plate. "I think I've 'ad enough. Nothin' was said about dealin' with no psychotic monster once this 'ere peramutraitor was freed to go on its way." He started to rise.

Jon-Tom put a hand on one furry shoulder. "Your oath, Mudge."

"Oath? I don't recall anything in me oath that says I 'ave to stay at this table. So if you'll all excuse me." He pushed his chair back quickly and made a dignified dash for the bathroom.

Sorbl was sitting on a perch behind the oval conference table. "What's wrong with the water rat?" He plucked another fried lizard from the brochette stuck into one end of the perch and gulped it down. "Did he eat too fast? He certainly ate enough."

"I've never known Mudge to get sick from overeating,"

Jon-Tom told the owl. "I think he's just realized what he's gotten himself into, and he's choking on his oath."

Sorbl nodded sadly. "Those can be hard to swallow. Few of us truly have the foresight to consider all the consequences of our actions. My signing on as wizard's famulus, for example."

"What was that? Did you say something, Sorbl?" Clothahump was glaring up at his apprentice.

"I said that Jon-Tom's singing was an example to us all, Master." The owl belched politely and smiled.

V

The inn's beds were as well prepared as the food, and they all enjoyed their soundest sleep in weeks. As usual, Clothahump was awake and making notes before Jon-Tom arose. Sorenset met them for breakfast. The fox looked tired.

"There is much to be done in the city. Some people are still suffering from the aftereffects of the perturbation, as you call it. Not to mention the aftereffects of that remarkable rainstorm. I have some good news for you. When you have finished your meal, I am to escort you to the transport barracks."

"You found us a volunteer, then?" Sorenset nodded and Clothahump looked satisfied. "Good. That will speed us up considerably."

"Not quite a volunteer, exactly." The fox looked apologetic.

"What do you mean 'not quite'? Did you find us someone willing to haul our supplies or not?"

"It's likely. The problem is, I'm not sure you'll find this particular transporter to your taste. She's something of an iconoclast, very strong-willed, and apt to cancel a contract at the smell of the slightest ill wind.''

"She?" Clothahump grunted. "No matter. As long as she has a strong back and legs. As for the possibility of some imagined personality conflict, that does not concern me. I am the most agreeable person in the world, quite able to get along with anyone I have to work with.''

A strange noise came from the far side of the table. Clothahump's gaze narrowed as he eyed his apprentice. "Something in your breakfast not to your liking, Sorbl?''

"Gnuf—no, Master," the owl managed to choke out. He was holding a thick napkin over his face, though whether to shield his mouth or hide his expression, no one could tell.

"Fine. We must meet this sturdy transporter and settle upon a contract immediately. We've no time to waste.''

"But, guv'nor," Mudge protested, "I 'aven't finished me breakfast yet.''

Jon-Tom rose and pulled the otter's chair away from the table. "Come on, Mudge. You heard Clothahump. The way you're gorging yourself this morning, you'd think you hadn't had supper last night.''

The otter wiped at his whiskers. '' 'Ardly enough to keep a shrew alive. One little fish and I didn't 'ave time to finish that proper.''

"The fish was nearly as big as you. Let's go.''

"Right then, 'ave it your way." Grumbling, the otter jumped out of his chair. "But wait until I catch you 'ungry someday." He slipped his arrow quiver and bow over his back while Jon-Tom picked up his duar and ramwood staff. Together they followed Clothahump and Sorenset out into the street while Sorbl glided along overhead.

The fox led them past the central square, now restored to its original beauteous state, through busy commercial streets, and into the industrial end of Ospenspri. It took that long for Mudge to cease complaining.

The stables that comprised the transportation barracks were spacious and well maintained, with ample roads between them to allow for the movement of cleaning crews and feed delivery wagons. The buildings were owned, Sorenset told them, by an old and revered family of heavy horses, one of whom sat (or rather stood) on the city council. There were triple-sized stalls available for married teams and families, with quarters to either side for studs and mares.

At the head of each line of stalls was an office where the inhabitants' business was transacted by hired help. This necessary arrangement was common to the warmlands, for while a percheron could do heavy work all day, managing a ledger with hooves was a next-to-impossible task. So capuchins and baboons and similarly dexterous individuals did the paperwork for them.

Sorenset led them past the fancier accommodations toward the back where a number of less elaborate but still spotlessly clean stalls faced a small stream. Such stable space was usually occupied by free-lancers: those haulers and packers who preferred to work alone rather than in teams. Here hay was more in evidence in the feed delivery bays than oats or alfalfa.

Around a corner and down a pathway shaded by ancient woolwood trees, they found themselves facing a shuttered stall front and door. To the left of the double door was an oversize mailbox, a large round depository whose contents could be removed with equal ease by hands or lips. Above the box was a brass nameplate on which a single name was engraved in incongruously elegant script: DORMAS.

Sorenset smiled at them before pushing the door-bell button. Something clanged inside, was followed by a deep yet unmistakably feminine voice. It sounded slightly irritated.

"Get lost! I ain't in the mood."

Mudge was nodding approvingly. "Ah, a lady after me own 'eart."

Sorenset looked embarrassed as he cleared his throat. "It's me, Sorenset of the council, acting the part of guide."

"I don't care if it's the Grand Randury of the Moshen Theatre Ensemble acting the part of the spasmed duck! I'm not interested in company." A pause, then, "Oh—wait a minute. I do know you. You're the one who told me about the southerners trekking north who needed someone to haul for them up onto the Plateau?"

Sorenset fought to retain his dignity as he replied. "I am. Of the city council. Could we come in, please?"

"Suit yourself. Door's open."

Sorenset pulled on the latch and swung the heavy wooden barrier aside, held it open while his charges filed through.

Wearing a beige blanket and standing before them was their volunteer. Jon-Tom's eyebrows drew together as he frowned at the animal.

"You're not a horse."

Dormas immediately cocked a jaundiced eye at the fox. "Who's this fountain of wit?"

"Oh, indeedy, my kind of lady," said Mudge with a delighted chuckle as he crossed his legs and leaned back against the wall. Sorbl closed the door behind him.

"You're a mule," Jon-Tom added.

She turned her gaze from their guide back to him. "You don't know much of anything, do you, human?" She went on to explain as if to an idiot. "For your information I am not a mule. I am a hinny."

"I beg your pardon?"

"And about time too." She looked back to Sorenset. "You told me I'd be traveling in the company of wizards and warriors, not idiot children."

"Now look," Jon-Tom began, "I don't think—"

"A mule," she explained, interrupting him, "is the off-spring of a donkey and a horse, or more specifically, of a jackass and a mare. Whereas a hinny is the offspring of a stallion and a female donkey. Either of which is preferable to being the fruit of the union of a couple of hairless apes. The wonder of it is," she added, looking him up and down, "is that so much could spring from so little effort."

He made hurried placating gestures. "Hey, I'm sorry, I didn't know. Quadrupedal biology isn't one of my specialties."

"Nor is diplomacy, apparently."

"I *said* I was sorry. My name's Jon-Tom. This is the great wizard Clothahump, his famulus Sorbl, and my friend and traveling companion, Mudge. We're delighted that you've volunteered to help us."

"Help you, hell." She snorted once, glanced over at Clothahump. "It's pretty clear that you're the leader of this lot of mental defectives, hard-shell or not. The man's too green, the owl too tipsy, and the water rat has shifty eyes. You're acclaimed by default."

"De fault of an unfair fate, I calls it," murmured Mudge, low enough so that Clothahump couldn't hear him.

"The fox told me I'd be paid in accordance with the danger involved. With winter threatening to bust open over our heads any day now, that's danger enough."

"I concur, and your recompense shall reflect that," Clothahump told her.

She appeared somewhat mollified by this ready agreement. "Well, that's better. Didn't mean to appear contrary."

"Nice to meet you," said Sorbl, fluttering his wings. He'd found a proper perch on a crossbeam."

"Me too," added Jon-Tom. "I apologize for any offense I may have caused. I assure you it was unintentional. I still have a lot to learn about this world."

"Um. I'm Dormas. None of us can help what we are."

"How's tricks, good-looking? I'm Mudge." The otter added a cheery whistle.

"Shifty eyes, but I like you, otter. You don't walk two inches above the ground." She shifted her attention back to the council fox. "Get lost, Sorenset. I've got dealings to quantify. And thanks for the business. You'll get your cut later."

"My cut?" The fox was already retreating toward the door. "Why, I don't know what you're talking about!" He bestowed a wan smile on the saviors of the city. "I really do have to run anyway. Good-bye and good luck." He departed with unseemly haste.

"And now it's time to settle on a few details," Dormas said brightly.

"Details? I thought Sorenset had taken care of those," Clothahump said.

"Naw. Just brought us together, he did. Come in back and let's sit a spell."

The back room was a revelation. There was a finely worked straw bed whose contents were obviously changed and scented daily, a gilded water trough, and the usual assortment of equine-type accoutrements. There was also a large amount of artwork, much of it consisting of finely wrought renderings of rolling hills and lush meadows, but also several paintings of mountain scenery. Jon-Tom was particularly taken by one that showed their hostess flanked by a pair of mountain goats. All three had a hoof raised to wave at the recording artist.

"Speed painter did that one for me. What do you think? Not a bad likeness."

Mudge had strolled over to join Jon-Tom in inspecting the picture. "Looks like it were painted quite a few years ago."

"Hmph." Another snort as she turned and walked over to an oversize filing cabinet. Using lips and teeth, she opened the second drawer, sorted through the material inside, and pulled out a sheet of paper as thick as cardboard. This was placed on a nearby desk, between four raised pieces of wood that served to hold it in position.

"I can do moderately well with a toothpen, but anyone

with hands and fingers can do better. It's my standard contract. I've already had it modified to reflect our destination. Check it out.''

Clothahump waddled over, adjusted his glasses, and began to read. ''I would think, madam, that judging from your age and circumstances, you are hardly in a position to dictate terms.''

''Is that a fact? Now let me tell you something, double-breather. I don't need this job. I like living back here because this is where my friends are, because I like to look out at the creek, and because I can't stand the way the swells in the high-rent district put on like their shoes are hammered out of gold. I've no need of external ornamentation, either on my body or in my home, to justify my competence to others. I've got plenty in the barracks bank, and I don't ever have to work again unless it suits me. If you think you can do better, go up and down the lines and try to find somebody else to pack your junk up onto the Plateau this time of year.''

''If you're so well-off,'' Jon-Tom asked her, ''why'd you volunteer to take us on in the first place?''

''Because, my dough-faced young human, I appreciate what you did in raising the curse from our city, and I believe in what you're trying to do, according to what Sorenset told me. And unlike most of my colleagues, I have a broad mind as well as a broad back, not to mention a modicum of ethics. I think you deserve help—albeit at a fair price.

''Besides, I can always use some petty cash.'' Jon-Tom felt as though he were being lectured by a maiden aunt. ''And there's nothing to hold me here. I like to travel for my own entertainment and elucidation, not just on business. There's nothing to draw me back here, if this should turn out to be my last gallop. I'm between books.''

''Books? You read a lot, huh?'' Jon-Tom asked.

She shook her head. ''You have a fine facility for seeking out the inaccurate. I am a writer, and one with quite a reputation. Though you don't strike me as the type to delve into a heavy romance, especially one featuring four-legged protagonists—though you never can tell about an individual's reading preferences. I take it you haven't heard of the authoress Shiraz Sassway?''

"I'm afraid not, though I haven't had a chance to do much light reading lately," Jon-Tom told her. "I've been studying hard."

"Shame." She looked wistful. "I'll have to give you a copy of my latest when we return. *Long-legged Love's Lust Lost.* I'm told it's very big in the south."

"Maybe you and I could do some research some time, luv—with other company, o' course." Mudge gave her a lecherous wink.

"I don't do much research anymore, water rat. I draw instead upon previous experiences. I had an industrious youth. It's all behind me now."

"I'll bet it was behind you most of the time," Mudge put in, making sure he was out of biting range.

It was Clothahump who spoke next, however. "There are more clauses in this one document than in a binding between a witch and its familiar."

"I've been cheated once or twice. Nothing personal, wiz. Don't you read your contracts?" She looked thoughtful as she enumerated a few favorite phrases. "Packs to be arranged and bound according to my design, not yours. Weight to be predetermined—no last-minute additions, not even a sandwich. The usual hazardous-duty bonus clauses. In return, you get everything I can give. I can carry more than any horse and move faster than any donkey. I can climb grades that would give your average packhorse a stroke on the spot, and I can do it blindfolded if necessary. I can do all that on less food, which I'm not as particular about. Plain wild grains and grasses suit me when I'm packing. I'm a good scavenger, and I can survive on stuff you'd use to brace your house with.

"You're going north. I can handle the cold better than any horse except maybe a Pryzwalski, and there ain't any in this neck of the woods. Plus you get the benefit of all my experience. I've been around. I'm not citified like some of these tenderfoots who haul produce from door to door out in the suburbs."

"W're not exactly innocents abroad ourselves," Jon-Tom told her.

"Glad to hear it. I'm not in the nursing business, colt. Oh, and one more thing. Absolutely *no* riding unless someone gets hurt too bad to hoof it. I'm a packer, not personal transport, and I don't intend to change my ways now. If that's what you have in mind, you need to move upstall and talk to the Appaloosas and pintos."

"We'll walk," Clothahump declared. "We've done so before and we can do so now. There is nothing wrong with our feet, albeit that we are reduced to traveling on two instead of four. I promise you that you will only be required to haul our supplies. We will haul ourselves." He indicated the contract.

"But before I put my name to this, I must in turn be certain of your commitment. We may well find ourselves in mortal danger at the hands of an opponent whose face and name remain a mystery to us and whose motivation is driven by an unknown madness. In addition we must somehow deal with an incredibly powerful and dangerous phenomenon that is not of this universe. Issues of great gravity are at stake here. We will in all likelihood have to face dangerous moments together, and at such times we must stand as one. I cannot have any member of our small party backing out at such times, whether for personal reasons or because of some footnote on a piece of paper."

Dormas drew herself up until she looked every bit as proud as an Arabian. "I won't be the one to break when push comes to pull and the Black Wind threatens to sweep us away. You can rest assured on that." Her dark eyes swept over them to settle on Mudge. "What about you, otter? You're not afraid?"

Mudge had resumed his place against the wall. He'd appropriated a sliver of straw from the hinny's bed and was chewing on it as he examined the claws of his right paw.

"Well now, lass, actually I'm terrified out o' me gourd. But I've seen wot 'Is Socerership can do, as well as me not-too-bright but well-meanin' spellsinger friend 'ere, and I 'ave confidence in the both o' them. This perambulator's perturbin' strikes me as a worldwide problem. Since there ain't no runnin' aways from it, I figure we might as well 'ave a try at puttin' it right. I've been through this sort o' thing with this one"—and he jerked a thumb in Jon-Tom's direction—"a couple o' times previous. Not that I'm gettin' used to 'avin' me precious self regularly threatened with dismemberment, but I ain't surprised when somethin' takes a try at it.

"See, I'm beginnin' to feel that me fate is some'ow bound up with this 'ere spellsinger chap and that I might as well trot along with 'im. You know, sort of like bein' in an accident where two wagons smash into one another at this intersection, and the owners can't get themselves untangled?"

"That's not a very sweet metaphor, Mudge," Jon-Tom groused.

"It ain't a very sweet relationship, mate." He turned back to Dormas. "Anyways, seein' as 'ow there ain't no place to run to for gettin' away from the effects o' this perambudiscombobulator, I figure I might as well tag along. Maybe there'll be some profit in it, wot?"

"I see. Strong feelings are involved as well as strong reasons. I like that. Hand me that pen there, in the wall holder."

Clothahump passed it over. Taking it in her teeth, she signed the contract with an unexpected flourish. The wizard nodded approvingly. Then he touched his signet ring to the blank place below her name, leaving behind the imprint of a turtle shell cut by a large letter *C*.

Dormas studied the signet admiringly. "A neat trick."

"Cheaper than buying new pens," the wizard told her. "I'd have one made up for you and sell you the necessary permanent ink spell, but your hoofprint would cover half the page. Your solicitor wouldn't like that. He'd have less room to complain in the margins."

She smiled, deposited the contract in a drawer, and closed it with a nudge of her muzzle. "Really, I'm not as cantankerous as I seem. On the trail you'll find me an agreeable and pleasant companion."

"Another one like 'Is Magicness," Mudge whispered to Jon-Tom. "Spirits preserve us!"

"When do we start climbing?"

"Tomorrow morning, if you are amenable."

"Fine. I'll be up with the sun. We can pack and be off fast."

"Another go-getter," Mudge muttered glumly. "Won't I ever fall in with sensible folks wot knows 'ow to take their time and their lives easy?"

"It's pretty hard to relax when the stability of the entire world is at stake, Mudge."

The otter stretched and yawned. "I don't know as 'ow it's all that stable now, mate. Not that it matters very much. You know what they say: 'Everyone's crazy but me and thee, and I ain't so sure about thee.' "

Jon-Tom studied him with a shrewd and familiar eye. "All that blather about your duty to Clothahump and your fellow beings—you're really coming along to protect youself, aren't you?"

"I never denied that were part o' the reason behind me decision, guv. Anyways, things are slow 'ere in Ospenspri, especially since that cloud come over the city, and you know 'ow quickly yours truly can get dead-bored. Leavin' aside 'ow 'ard it is to 'old a set o' dice properly when your back's all bent out o' shape.''

"I might have guessed. You wouldn't be coming along if you weren't broke as well as worried about your own skin.''

Mudge winked at him. "Mate, I wouldn't go to a friend's funeral if I didn't think I'd 'ave a shot at the 'ankerchief concession. You know me that well, at least.''

"I guess I should be relieved. For a while there I wondered if the perturbation had affected your brain as well as your body.''

"Wot, me? Why, lad, old Mudge is as sturdy as the mountains, as free-runnin' as the river Tailaroam, and as steady as the ground under our feet.''

At that moment the ground beneath their feet vanished. So did the sky above. Jon-Tom observed that he was floating in slighty murky blue-green water, staring at something that looked like a small barracuda. Off to his right was a bloated sunfish. Next to it drifted an armored throwback to the time when fish comprised the planet's dominant life-form.

For a moment he struggled to catch his balance. He relaxed when it became clear that he was neither sinking nor drowning. He flexed his fins experimentally; first the dorsal, then the lateral, ventral last of all. The piscean analogs of Mudge, Dormas, and Clothahump stared back at him.

A new arrival zipped past his face. It was small, brightly colored, and fast. It began swimming rapid circles around Clothahump. "This is a bit much," said the Sorbl-fish.

"Try to be calm," Jon-Tom advised him. "We've been through worse.''

"Easy for you to say," Sorbl shot back. "The master spends much time in water, and likewise your otterish friend, but I'm used to spending my time above the surface, not beneath it.''

"You think you're the only one who's stuck with a difficult

psychological adjustment? I'm not exactly aquatic by nature, let alone by design, and Dormas even less so."

"But you have been in water before," the blue-striped darter protested. "I have cousins who have—cormorants and ducks and such—but I've never been beneath the waves in my life. I find it exceedingly distressing."

"Oh, don't put on such a show, you feathered twit!" This from the immediately recognizable floating version of Mudge. "Y' think I'm comfortable with fins instead o' feet? Besides, if this 'ere ocean were colored amber instead o' blue-green, you'd probably feel right at 'ome since you spend 'alf your time moonin' about near the bottom o' a bottle, anyways."

"I'm on the verge of a nervous breakdown and he adds insults," grumbled the apprentice.

"Take it easy." Jon-Tom spoke absently, fascinated by the alien environment in which he found himself. "The perturbation will end soon enough."

"Oh, it will, will it? You're certain of that, are you? Are you going to spellsing it back to reality with that fine instrument you're carrying?"

Jon-Tom noted that where his duar ought to have hung there was only a broad strip of olive-green seaweed.

"Or," Sorbl continued, "is the Master going to return the world to normal again by means of his potions and spells? Remember what happened to Ospenspri. If it has happened again, but differently this time, we will remain in this wet, stifling water world forever, locked into the forms we presently are inhabiting." He darted through the water, zipping around Clothahump, then Mudge and Dormas.

"I don't care what anyone says. It's not like flying. It's like—"

Before Sorbl had a chance to explain what it was like, a by now familiar snap took place somewhere in the vicinity of Jon-Tom's optic nerves. His fins were gone and he was standing, as before, on the floor of Dormas's stall. The hinny blinked at him, then at Clothahump. Mudge stumbled but caught himself before he fell. Sorbl was not so fortunate. He'd been racing wildly through the water when the perturbation ceased and had crashed headfirst into the wall. Now he sat on the floor, his great golden eyes half closed, holding the top of his head with the tips of both wings. But he was smiling through the pain. He had wings again, and the only water in sight occupied the lower portion of Dormas's drinking basin.

"I warned you," said Clothahump evenly. "These perturbations can be dangerous even when they do not become permanent. During a change it is important not to make any sudden moves or take any risks. I think you will all agree that the reason for demonstrating such caution is self-explanatory." He gestured to where Sorbl was climbing unsteadily to his feet. "Thank you for the example, famulus."

"You can take your example," Sorbl started to say, but wisely chose not to finish the suggestion.

"We have been further enlightened, and everything is settled," the wizard concluded. He extended a thick hand. Dormas nudged it, and the bargain was sealed.

"Tomorrow morning, early," she reminded them. "Where're you staying?"

Clothahump gave her the name of the inn. "We will want to pack and be on our way immediately after breakfast."

"Suits me fine, hard-shell."

"I am looking forward to a fruitful collaboration and the eventual success of our mutual enterprise."

"And I'm looking forward to using the john," she replied. "So if you boys will excuse me?" She turned and moved toward a curtained partition near the back of the room.

Thus dismissed, they left to return to their own accommodations, to prepare themselves for the long, difficult climb that would begin when they bade farewell to Ospenspri on the morrow. By now the descriptions of the city's saviors had been widely circulated among the citizenry, and they found that they were the center of polite attention as they strolled up the busy streets.

Most of it was focused on Clothahump, whose shell seemed to swell as he soaked up the stares and the occasional mild applause. The wizard wasn't one to shrink from the opportunity to bask in the glow of his own radiance. Sorbl drifted along overhead, flying a straighter course than usual, sobered by his recent brief incarnation as a subsurface water dweller. So Mudge was able to sidle up close to Jon-Tom to chat without fear of being overheard.

"Tell me true, mate; wot do you think our chances are?"

"Chances of wot—I mean, of what, Mudge?"

"Don't play games with me, lad. We've been through too much together. You know wot I means. Our chances o' goosin' this perbabuter, or wotever it turns out to be, back to where it belongs?"

"According to Clothahump it will leave of its own accord once the restraints restricting its movement have been removed. The danger we face is from whoever is keeping it trapped in our world. Since I've no idea what we're up against there, I can't very well tell you what the odds are of our defeating it."

Mudge looked crestfallen. "I can always depend on you for encouragement and succor, mate."

"We'll make out all right, Mudge. We always have."

"That's wot worries me. I keep worryin' that the police are goin' to catch up with me one o' these days. Or an old lover. Or someone who lost to me at cards. But the thing I worry most about catchin' up with old Mudge is the bloody law o' averages, and I fear that on this trip it may be dogging me tail a mite too near for comfort."

"Come on. Where's the optimistic, always cheerful Mudge I know best?"

"Back down the road to Lynchbany about a hundred leagues or so."

"Consider this: On our previous journeys we've had to deal with whatever danger threatened us by ourselves. Clothahump's with us this time. Between his knowledge and my spellsinging we can handle anything that's thrown against us."

"Some'ow that don't inspire me confidence, mate." Mudge was silent for a long moment, then jerked a thumb back over his shoulder. "Wot about our ladyship back there? She appears to 'ave as strong a back as she does a tongue, but she's gettin' on in years. We'll find ourselves in a fine pickle if the old tart ups and quits on us in the middle o' the back o' beyond. I'm not one for haulin' a pile o' supplies up a steep grade."

"Dormas will be fine. And we're all getting on in years, Mudge." Jon-Tom spoke from the rarefied heights of one who has yet to turn twenty-five. "I've found that this world tends to age you rapidly."

"It does if you lead the kind o' life we've led this past year or so," Mudge readily agreed. "I expect you're right about the old darlin', but I can't 'elp wishin' we 'ad a bit more o' the mundane 'elp o' extra arms and fighters. Pity you can't run out and find that dragon friend o' yours."

"What, Falameezar? The last time I saw him he was swimming steadily southward from Quasequa. You know how far that is from here. And he wouldn't do too well up in the Plateau country. He likes warm water and warmer air, and from what Clothahump's told me of where we're headed, we're going to find precious little of either."

"Cold won't bother me. We otters are as at 'ome in cold temperatures as hot. 'Tis you I worry about, lad."

"Why, Mudge? I appreciate the concern."

"Concern, 'ell. If your buns freeze to the ground, that's one less sword arm I've got standin' at my side, not to mention the loss o' your spellsingin', which some'ow does seem to work from time to time. You 'aven't a bit o' decent fur on you to protect you from the cold."

Jon-Tom stared straight ahead. "I'll be okay as long as we beat the onset of winter in the mountains."

"And if we don't?"

"Then you can haul my frozen carcass back here, dump it in a hundred-gallon martini, and drink to my demise. You worry too much. I feel as strong as an ox."

"Aye, and with a brain to match. I wish I were feelin' as well meself."

"What's wrong?"

"I'm just not feelin' meself is all."

"It couldn't have anything to do with your life-style by any chance?"

"I admit that 'as occurred to me, mate. So I've decided to cut down on wenchin', eatin', and drinkin'."

"Your timing's good. You won't have the chance to indulge to excess on any of those on this trip."

"Aye, that's me point. That's why I don't feel well. Because I'm goin' to 'ave to cut down on wenchin', and eatin'—"

"And drinking," Jon-Tom finished for him, shaking his head. "And I thought there might be something seriously wrong with you." Disgusted, he increased his stride.

"Why, mate," Mudge asked, looking honestly puzzled as he hurried to keep up with his tall friend, "wot could be worse than that?"

"Than what?" Jon-Tom snapped at him.

"Than moderation o' course."

VI

_____

True to her word, Dormas not only kept up with them as they left Ospenspri behind the following morning but, despite her heavy load, was impatient to take the lead. So frequently did she make the request that Clothahump had to remind her of his own advanced age and of the fact that two legs, no matter how strong, could never keep pace with four.

Jon-Tom was sure she was showing what she could do if she wanted to, in order to establish herself as a qualified member of the expedition right from the start. In any case, after the first long, hard day of walking, there were no more comments about her age or hauling ability from Mudge or anyone else. Jon-Tom recalled her initial reaction when they'd finished loading her outside the inn.

"Is that all? Hell, you boys don't need a hinny to haul this stuff for you. A couple of pack rats would've done as well."

Despite her admonition against riding, she did allow Sorbl to rest from time to time atop the uppermost sack. Resting, she explained, was not riding. Jon-Tom got a kick out of watching the owl bob back and forth atop the mountain of supplies, clinging to a strap with his clawed feet and looking like nothing else but a feathered hood ornament. He would ride that way for a moment or two before rising toward the clouds to resume his aerial patrol of the terrain below.

Dormas's endurance had a salutary effect on Clothahump's companions as well. They were spared the usual unending litany of complaints about the wizard's sore feet, his rheumatism, and the weight of his shell. Instead, he held his peace, ground his beak in silence, and said nothing as they traversed the difficult places. Jon-Tom was glad of his long legs. Mudge possessed neither long legs, wizardly determination, wings, or an extra pair of walking limbs. He compensated for these deficiencies with typically unflagging otterish energy.

North of Ospenspri the woods were mostly uninhabited. As they climbed higher they began to lose the Belltrees themselves, along with the more familiar oaks and sycamores. Evergreens took their place. Jon-Tom thought he recognized sugar and piñon pine as well as blue spruce. There were also more exotic varieties, including one stalwart growth whose three-inch-long needles were as sharp as a porcupine's quills. Mudge identified the most dangerous growths and led his companions carefully around them. They couldn't harm the armored Clothahump, but a casual misstep could turn any of the rest of the marchers into green pincushions.

With Sorbl scouting overhead and Clothahump relentless in his examination of the forest floor, Jon-Tom found he was able to relax and enjoy the hike. The evergreens, the bare rock, the pinecones that littered the ground reminded him of Oregon or Montana.

As they climbed out of the lowland forest onto the Plateau, he amused himself by kicking twigs and pinecones out of their path. He was about to boot aside a particularly large cone when he found himself knocked to the ground. He rolled over, furious and confused.

"What's the big idea, Mudge?" The otter had tackled him from behind. Carefully he checked his precious duar, let out a sigh of relief when he'd concluded his anxious inspection. "You could have busted this!"

"Better it than you, mate." The otter nudged the feather that adorned his cap back over his head. It had fallen forward over one eye when he'd jumped at Jon-Tom's legs. Clothahump, Sorbl, and Dormas stood nearby, watching.

Mudge indicated the huge pinecone, careful not to touch it. "Wot about you, Your Wizardship? You recognize this charmin' little gift o' the forest primeval?"

Clothahump squinted through his glasses at the seemingly innocent cone that lay in the middle of the path. "Your eyes are as sharp as your tongue, river rat." He lifted his gaze to Jon-Tom. "You should be thanking your friend instead of shouting at him."

"For what?" Jon-Tom was still irritated, still saw no reason for the abruptness of the otter's action. After all, it was only an ordinary—

He halted in mid-thought. He'd learned little enough of this world in the time he'd been marooned in it, but one thing he had learned early on was that there was little in it that could be defined as ordinary.

"Everybody loves pine nuts. Some o' me near relations will do just about anything for a handful." Mudge stood surveying the cone. "I've been nibblin' on 'em meself as the occasion permitted. 'Tis a fine and 'andy snack for travelers in a 'urry like ourselves."

Jon-Tom was brushing dirt from the sleeves of his indigo shirt. "What's so special about this one?"

"The trees 'ave their ways o' makin' sure that at least some of the seeds they scatter aren't disturbed by 'ungry passersby, mate, be they intelligent like meself or dumb like the forest browsers and yourself." Leaning forward, he slowly inspected the cone from every conceivable angle before gingerly picking it up in both hands. Turning, he showed it to the others, handling it as delicately as a hollow egg.

Jon-Tom leaned close. "Looks like a normal pinecone to me."

"O' course it does, lad. 'Tis supposed to. But look 'ere." He pointed with a finger, not touching the cone. "See there? The top ring o' seed covers is missin', wot? It didn't get knocked off in the fall, and it weren't eaten by some traveler. The tree pulled it out when it dropped the cone."

"I still don't understand. So what?"

"So this is wot, mate. Wot 'appens if you picks it up and tries to make a meal o' its seeds or kicks it playful like." He turned, drew back his arm, and threw the cone as far as he could over a pile of boulders.

There was a second of silence followed by a substantial explosion. Jon-Tom flinched. Orange flame seared the sky, shadowed by black smoke. As the smoke began to dissipate Mudge turned to face him, paws on hips.

"Just a discouragin' shock to the would-be seed-eater. It would've blown your bloomin' leg off, mate."

"I—I didn't know, Mudge." His throat was dry as he stared at the fading smoke. "It's a damn good thing the pinecones on my world aren't like that."

Mudge resumed the march, falling in step behind Clothahump and Dormas. "Oh, I expect there're some like that everywhere, lad."

"No, you're wrong about that. I've never heard of anyone being killed by an exploding pinecone."

The otter cocked a challenging eye at him. "Don't you 'ave curious folk wot goes a-travelin' through woods like these and never comes out again?"

"Of course we do. But they perish from hunger or thirst or snakebite or something like that. Not from stepping on exploding pinecones."

" 'Ow do you know, mate, if you never find 'em?"

"We find most of them."

The otter was persistent. "But wot about those who just up an' disappear?"

"Well, they're presumed to have fallen off a mountainside or died in a cave or something."

"Ha! 'Ow does you find the pieces o' someone who's been blown to bits in a heavily wooded area? The scavengers would clean up wot didn't get vaporized."

Jon-Tom lifted his eyes to stare resolutely straight ahead. "This is a ridiculous conversation, and I refuse to continue with it."

"Are there lots o' pine trees in your world, mate? Trees like this?"

"Mudge"—Jon-Tom sighed—"there are millions of them, and many of them have been cut down en masse for lumber and such. I never heard of anyone being blown up while working as a logger."

"D'you think the trees are bleedin' stupid? They know they can't stop a whole lot o' folks workin' in unison. So they tries to pick 'em off one at a time when nobody else is around to see."

"I'm not listening to this anymore!" So saying, he stepped off to one side and began picking the occasional ripe redberry, popping it angrily into his mouth. The tart juice did nothing to sweeten his disposition. A quick glance showed Clothahump smiling at him, and that made him even angrier.

Exploding pinecones! Inimical pine trees! The whole business was absurd. Clothahump and Mudge were having fun at his expense. There were no such mutated monstrosities on *his* world. Of course people disappeared in the forest, in places like Oregon and Montana. People who were stupid enough to go tramping through the wilderness all by their lonesome. They deserved to stumble over a cliff, or into an unswimmable river, or . . .

To trip over an explosive pinecone?

It was too bizarre a notion to countenance.

Nonetheless, this was not his world, and he refrained from kicking any more fallen cones as they trudged onward. One fell from an overhanging branch, making him jump. Mudge started to giggle, stifled it, and hid his face when Jon-Tom threw him a murderous look. He picked the cone up and turned it over. The top ring of seed shells was present. Fortunately.

He tossed it angrily aside. When he got home, he'd dispose of this stupid theory during his first visit to the mountains.

He just wouldn't kick any cones first, he told himself thoughtfully.

Evening revealed an unexpected talent on the part of their tireless packer. In addition to an acerbic wit and strong back, it also developed that Dormas was the owner of a superb, lilting soprano voice. Not to mention a lifetime of songs and ballads, which she proceeded to deliver to them while seated around the fire. Enthusiastic applause punctuated the conclusion of the impromptu recital. The hinny looked away, unexpectedly embarrassed.

"I don't do it often," she told them, "but frankly, you lot bore me, and I'd rather hear myself sing than listen to you babble."

"I'd rather listen to you sing too," Jon-Tom told her. Then he frowned. Something was not right. Not radically wrong but not right, either. "Odd. I feel peculiar all of a sudden." He held up a hand. His hand, definitely, and yet—somehow changed.

"Another perturbation." Sorbl spoke from his evening perch in a nearby tree and he, too, did not sound quite right. Jon-Tom let his gaze wander around the firelit circle.

There was Sorbl, the same and yet not. There Mudge, also somehow subtly different. What kind of perturbation was this? And still the peculiar softness that had come over him.

Not quite like an upset stomach. Something more complete, less transitory. He couldn't quite put his finger on it.

Then he did put his finger on it, in several places.

"Oh, my God." He looked anxiously up at Clothahump. "This is one change that better not last too long."

"I have been taking note of the most recent alteration with a great deal of interest." The wizard's appearance had changed only slightly. His voice, however, had undergone the same kind of shift as Jon-Tom's. It was still penetrating, still authoritative, but an octave higher.

Moans came from Mudge and then Sorbl as they discovered the nature of the latest outrage perpetrated by the perambulator upon their personal reality.

"It is not nearly as radical a change as many we have previously experienced," Clothahump calmly pointed out. "Some perturbations result in changes far more subtle than others."

Dormas was studying her altered physiognomy intently. "Fascinating. I always wondered what it would be like. Seems kind of clumsy, though. I wouldn't want it to be permanent, either."

"The degree of change varies according to the species, of course," the wizard reminded them all.

"This is what you call a 'subtle' perturbation?" Jon-Tom barely recognized the voice that spoke as his own.

There was nothing complex or indeterminate about this latest perturbation. The effects were quite clear. Each and every one of them had shifted sex. Without warning the hopeful expedition had become a quartet of ladies accompanied by a single male.

"When's it goin' to change back?" Mudge was moaning. Squeaking, rather, in his new, high voice. " 'Tis only another temporary change. Ain't that right, Your Sorcerership?"

"There is no way of telling how long this particular perturbation will last, Mudge. No way at all." Jon-Tom noted that the pattern of red on his shell had changed to a distinctive mauve.

"It bloody well better not last long. Damn lucky we ain't in Ospenspri. I couldn't show me face, I couldn't."

"Something wrong with being female, water rat?" said Dormas in a tone that was all stallion.

Jon-Tom tried to ignore his own voice as he explained. "You'd have to know Mudge better to understand what he's going through right now, Dormas. I'm afraid this particular metamorphosis has hit him harder than any of us."

"Come on, Your Lordship." The otter was pleading with Clothahump. "We saw wot you did back in Ospenspri, changin' that black cloud an' all. Couldn't you work just a wee bit o' magic and put us right? I don't know as 'ow I can 'andle this for very long. I've a weak constitution, I do."

"It is not a life- or even situation-threatening perturbation," Clothahump declared formally. "Hardly worth the danger entailed by a serious conjuration. You will just have to be patient, like the rest of us, and wait for the change back to occur naturally."

"Aye, but wot if it don't? Wot if it takes days, or even weeks? Cor, I can't stay like this for weeks." He turned on Jon-Tom. "Wot say, mate? Use your duar there to sing us a change-back song, will you? Just one little ditty?"

"I'm no more comfortable in this guise than you are, Mudge, but I agree with Clothahump. It's not worth chancing any dangerous spells." A sudden thought had him grinning. "Just sit back and enjoy the fire—beautiful."

Mudge didn't find the suggestion funny. "Look, mate, a joke's a joke, but this ain't amusin'."

"Amusing? I'd say it's more like poetic justice. Who says fate has no sense of humor?"

"I'm warning you, you skinny ape. Watch it or I'll—"

"Or you'll what? Scratch my eyes out?"

The otter growled and yanked his hat down sharply over his

ears (or was it her ears?). His hat had changed along with his more personal accessories. Just as Jon-Tom's had. Actually, he thought the dress he was now clad in rather attractive.

It is truly astonishing, he told himself, the situations that a sense of humor can carry one through.

The effects of the perturbation were most obvious in Mudge and himself, for in Clothahump, Sorbl, and Dormas's species, the differences in appearance between male and female were not nearly so striking. Mudge continued to try to retreat into his hat, which had turned into a frilly broad-brimmed chapeau that might have been borrowed from some petite southern belle.

"Please do somethin'," the otter whined, in a tone so pitiful Jon-Tom was moved to look hopefully at Clothahump.

"I could try, sir. It might be a good idea for me to make a stab at reversing the effects of one of these shifts when the change involved isn't quite as severe as it might be."

The wizard looked thoughtful. "Very well, my boy. But do be careful. It is not inconceivable that a badly thrown spell might make things worse."

"'Ow could things be any worse?" Mudge wanted to know. "Wot could be worse than this?"

"You really can be extraordinarily insulting, you know," Dormas told him.

"Right now I'm just extraordinarily miserable, lass—or is it to be sir?"

"I don't know myself," she murmured. "Let's see what your spellsinger can do about it."

Jon-Tom took his time preparing and choosing, keeping Clothahump's warning in mind. He tried to use songs by both the most masculine and feminine performers he could think of, ended up alternating lyrics by good old Elvis P. with some hot flashes by Tina Turner. The result left something to be desired musically but apparently not magically.

"There," he said with a sigh, as he cleared his throat and

put his duar aside. It had been fun to sing soprano for a
while, but he was glad to have his own voice back, though
not as glad as Mudge. Once the otter discovered that he was
indeed himself again, he bounded from his position by
Sorbl's tree and danced frenziedly around the fire. Only
exhaustion finally brought him to a halt.

" 'Tis a true abomination wot's forcin' this poor perambulator to wreak such obscene havoc. I'll personally put 'im out
of 'is misery when I see 'is rotten face, I will."

"I personally hope it is that easy," Clothahump commented
quietly. "Now I suggest that we retire, early as it may be. We
will need all our reserves in the event the morrow brings fresh
surprises. The next perturbation may require even stronger
magic to counter."

As close as the wizard ever came to complimenting him,
Jon-Tom thought sourly. He'd expected nothing more. He
was right about getting some serious sleep, though. Jon-Tom
put his duar aside, wrapped himself up in his lizard-skin
cape, and rolled over. Mudge was laying out his own bedroll.
Jon-Tom smiled at him.

"Good night, you cute little pinch of fluff, you."

The otter glanced at him sharply. " 'Ow'd you like to try
singin' without your front teeth, mate?" He flopped down in
a huff, turned away from the tall young human.

Morning provided a powerful reminder that serious perturbations could take place as dramatically while they slept as
while they were awake. The indifference of sleep offered no
escape.

Instinctively he reached for his duar. Not only was the
instrument missing, he discovered that he had nothing to
reach with. He tried to sit up and found to his considerable
confusion that he had nothing to sit up with, either.

No amount of bewilderment could mask the fact that this
was the most radical perturbation they'd yet suffered.

Around him the air was murky, thick, and cloying. He tried

to see through it and felt his vision slide. It was as if his eyes were rattling around loose inside his head. Shoving down the panic he felt, he struggled to get hold of himself. At least he could still see, even if only in shades of black and white. He could not make out any colors. Or perhaps, he told himself, he *could* make out colors and there were none to see.

The sky overhead was a pale, reflective white. Surrounding him were dark gray trees. That was when he saw the monster and recoiled from it. At the same time the monster shrank back from something unseen, and Jon-Tom realized it was cowering away from him.

There were other monsters around, and every one of them appeared petrified by the sight of its neighbor. Jon-Tom began to wonder what he looked like.

Along with color vision he'd lost any sense of smell. He could still hear clearly, though. Just as he could hear the sound of his own body moving forward. The sound was not pleasant. It implied a means of locomotion involving something far less sophisticated than legs.

This time the perturbation had not merely knocked reality askew, it had turned it inside out. Heretofore the perambulator's changes had made some sense, but this current transformation made no sense at all. Had it begun to draw upon its captor's insanity?

He struggled to form words. "Can anyone understand me?"

"I can." The gross form that replied was more incongruous than repugnant in appearance. It did not seem an appropriate home for someone as lithe and swift as Mudge, but it was Mudge's voice that spoke to him. Directly, through some unknown variety of thought transference. Neither the Mudgeshape nor Jon-Tom nor any of the other monsters possessed anything recognizable as a mouth.

Clothahump spoke up, and then Sorbl and Dormas. Transformed as they were by the unaccountable, all were accounted for. Dormas was the biggest of the five, Sorbl the smallest. The perturbation had stuck to the laws for transformation of mass. It seemed that some rules still applied.

Excepting differences in size, they all looked pretty much like each other: bloated, colorless blobs of gelatinous protoplasm drifting in a slightly less dense fluid. Smaller shapes and outlines were visible within their own bodies. Their shiny epidermi were in constant motion.

Giant single-celled entities, mutated amoebas—Jon-Tom didn't know enough to be certain exactly what they'd become, but he was glad of what little biology he'd been forced to take.

"This is most disconcerting," murmured Clothahump voicelessly. "I wonder how limited our present range of movement is." He extruded a pseudopod and tried to grip something floating through the liquid. This led to the discovery that they could change their positions by shifting their internal mass. It would have upset Jon-Tom's stomach if he'd had one. Instead he suffered a faint mental nausea.

"What is this? What've we turned into?" the Dormas-shape wanted to know.

"My experience does not extend to acquaintance with such shapelessness," Clothahump told her.

"Well, mine does." All light-sensing organelles turned to Jon-Tom. "We've been turned into something like amoebas, only much larger and far more complex. Just as an example, we're still capable of higher thought."

"That's all right, mate," said the Mudge-mass. "We'll all shift back to ourselves in a minute or two. Ain't that right, Your Blobship?"

"I certainly hope so." He glanced around. "Our supplies appear to have vanished. This has not happened during any of the previous perturbations."

It struck Jon-Tom then that his appraisal of their current situation was more accurate than he'd first imagined.

"Our supplies haven't disappeared. They're right here, all around us. We just can't see them in our present states. See, we don't resemble microscopic organisms. We've *become* microscopic organisms. We've shrunk." He gestured with a pseudopod. "Those boulders over there are probably nothing more than grains of sand, those trees microscopic lichen or something. A light breeze could scatter us, blow us away. It's a good thing we decided to sleep in a protected glade."

"How can something so small be capable of thought and speech?" Dormas asked him.

"How should I know? I'm no expert on the ramifications of perturbations. Who says they have to be logical, anyway?"

"The danger is apparent," said Clothahump grimly. "We cannot wait passively for our return. We must try to do something. But my potions are elsewhere, and I have not the faintest notion of how to begin."

"How about a spellsong, Jon-Tom?" Sorbl asked him.

"I need my duar, Sorbl. You know that."

"Can't you just try without it?"

He sighed, and it washed through his entire body. "It'd just be a waste of time and energy."

"Perhaps not." Jon-Tom could feel the wizard's attention on him. "Since you have no duar on which to accompany yourself, you must try to fashion one."

Jon-Tom let his simplified gaze roam through their oleaginous surroundings. "Out of what? There's no wood here, nothing to fashion strings from. Even if I could rig a crude sort of duar, I couldn't play it."

"Why not?" Sorbl wondered.

"Because 'e ain't got no fingers, featherbrain," Mudge told him.

"That need not hold him back," said Clothahump thoughtfully.

"You could spellsing up a duar, mate, if you 'ad a duar."

"What do you mean, it needn't hold me back, sir?"

By way of reply Clothahump twisted a section of himself into an intricate figure eight. "Our present bodies are extraordinarily flexible. They can be stretched into any possible shape."

"Oh, I see. Even into fingers."

"No, my boy. Not only into fingers. Into a duar itself."

"That's impossible."

"That word is an obsession with you. Try."

Jon-Tom shrugged, felt a portion of himself ripple. "Why not? It's better than sitting here waiting to be blown or washed away."

How does one go about becoming the instrument one is used to playing? He fought to conjure up a concrete image in his mind. Strings like *so,* resonance chamber *so,* measurements such and such—just thinking about it hurt his mind. When he had the mental picture refined to his satisfaction, he began to twist, to contort, to strain.

It was not only difficult, it was painful. But he kept at it, readjusting his tissues, polishing his exterior, until to his very considerable surprise he had molded himself into a familiar shape composed of gleaming gelatinous material.

A song now, he mused. Something appropriate to their situation, something suitable for changing shape and volume. Yes, Paul Williams should work. He began to sing, and to play himself.

The notes didn't sound quite right, nor did his voice, but he persisted. Distortion was only to be expected under the circumstances. It still seemed a waste of time, until something vast and glowing could be seen coming toward them. It was an enormous lambent shape, like a small sun, though within the light he thought he could make out the dim outline of something almost familiar.

Dormas shrank away from it, and Mudge and Sorbl tried to flee. As Jon-Tom played on, only Clothahump held his position. For he recognized it immediately. Its appearance was not only proof that Jon-Tom's spellsinging was working, but of the true size to which they'd been reduced.

"Stay," he ordered the others. "It is quite harmless. It is only a gneechee."

A single gneechee, those can't-be-seen specks of light that were so much more. They were attracted to active magic, and this one had sought them out to cavort in the echoes of Jon-Tom's spellsinging.

As he played himself on, the eerie wail became real music. He found that regardless of the results, he was enjoying himself. It is one thing to play an instrument well enough to feel it is a part of you. It's quite another to make it all of you.

As he sang on, played on, the sky began to lighten. From a liquid translucence it brightened to yellow, the first true color he'd been able to perceive since the perturbation. The yellow intensified to gold. The sun seemed to be coming straight toward them. Not the gneechee this time but the bright, glowing orb that warmed the world: the true sun.

The by-now familiar mental snap, a moment of complete disorientation, and he staggered momentarily as he fought for balance, clutching with one hand at the duar hanging from his neck and at a rock with the other.

Back again.

A single bright spot of light vanished from the corner of his vision. He bid a silent farewell to the gneechee, hoping it had enjoyed the concert. Music rang through his brain, reverberated the length and breadth of his body. These aftereffects of the perturbation and his time as an instrument did not linger long, for which he was sorry. Not every perturbation made you feel lost or ill. He had been granted a few moments to live the musician's dream. From now on he would only be able to live up to those moments of musical epiphany in his memory.

Around them the forest stood silent sentinel, seemingly unchanged. Before him he saw their campsite and supplies.

Clothahump lay on his back, kicking violently and attempting to right himself. Mudge sat on a rock, grasping at various parts of his body as if to reassure himself of his restored solidity. Dormas lay prone on the far side of the fire. She quickly rolled onto her knees and stood. Once more capable of flight, a relieved Sorbl took to the air to scan the woods surrounding them, darting in tight, happy circles overhead, whistling the defiant cry of his clan.

Clothahump barked an order at Jon-Tom, snapping him out of his rapidly fading chordal reverie. "Don't just stand there gaping, my boy! Give me a hand. I'd turn myself, but I fear the transformation has weakened me more than I first thought."

Lazy, Jon-Tom thought. The turtle was perfectly capable of standing by himself. But he put his duar aside and, together, he and Mudge stood the wizard back on his feet.

"A bad one, that," Clothahump commented. "I should not have enjoyed continuing through life without a skeleton."

Mudge settled himself back on his tree. "You're right. There's worse things than goin' through a change o' sex. At least you look like somethin'. Me, I could use a good stiff one."

"Under the circumstances, I believe we could all do with a drink." He waddled toward their packs. "Will you join us, Dormas?"

"Under the circumstances, you bet your shell-shocked ass I will."

The bottle was passed around, and when each of them had sipped from the same opening, shared the same liquor, the feeling of a real bond between them was stronger than ever.

"I'll just repack it for you, Master." Sorbl tried hard but failed to completely mask the eagerness in his voice.

"I will manage." The wizard fumbled with the carton from which he'd extracted the bottle. "Otherwise we will not have the advantage of your excellent eyesight for very long. We may need it the next time this happens."

"You're sure there'll be a next time soon?" Jon-Tom inquired.

"I did not mention a frequency. There is no way of predicting the perambulator's perturbations. We could suffer three or four in a single day and then go for weeks without incurring anything more upsetting than momentarily blurred vision. One of the few certainties about a perambulator is its uncertainty. One can no more predict the frequency of occurrence than one can the severity. Truly it is most unsettling."

"'Tis freakin' weird is wot it is, guv'nor!" Mudge slid down atop his bedroll and put a paw to his forehead. "All of a sudden I feel like I ate somethin' with little green things growin' out of it."

Jon-Tom would have grinned, except for the discovery that his own stomach was doing flip-flops. Sure enough, all of his companions were suffering similar dysenteric effects. Dormas was trembling on her feet.

Looking none too healthy himself, Clothahump was studying each of them in turn. "Yes, I, too, am experiencing the symptoms of an unpleasant internal disorder." He winced, closing his eyes briefly. "It appears to be developing with extraordinary rapidity, for which we may find reason to be grateful."

"Another—perturbation already?" Jon-Tom groaned.

"No, I think not. Rather, the aftereffects. The minuscule creatures we became, it seems, were not entirely harmless. As you may recall, each was slightly different in size and appearance from the other."

"You think they're causing the pains we're feeling now? That they were disease-causing organisms?" Jon-Tom wondered aloud.

The wizard sat down very carefully. "We did not notice this at the time because a disease is most unlikely to generate its own symptoms within itself. Now it is different. We have each of us become the disease that we were."

Jon-Tom's stomach settled even as he felt beads of sweat start from his forehead. First upset, then fever. At least whatever it was they had contracted was moving through their bodies with unnatural speed. He glanced over at Mudge.

"How about you? My stomach's okay now, but I'm burning up."

"No fever in me, I thinks, mate," replied the otter. "Trouble is, I've developed this bloody itch."

"That's too bad. Where?"

"I'd rather not get too specific, mate." He looked to his left, to where Sorbl was landing unceremoniously in the bushes. Unpleasant bodily noises soon reached them.

Emulating Clothahump, Jon-Tom took a seat. Since this wasn't a perturbation but merely the aftereffects of one, it should pass soon enough. He might have tried to spellsing them back to health, but he didn't want to push his luck. Besides which, he didn't feel very much like singing just then.

From what little he could tell, Dormas appeared to be suffering from an unbelievably accelerated case of hoof-in-mouth. Clothahump was now blowing his nose nonstop and giving every indication of trying to ride out a severe cold. He stared across at Jon-Tom through suddenly swollen eyes.

"How interesting. Red blotches are beginning to appear on your—on your—*achoo!*—face."

"Measles." Jon-Tom swallowed, wiping sweat from his brow. "I never had the measles. This isn't so bad after all. I'll have them and be done with them permanently in a day or so instead of a couple of weeks. How about that? We finally get something beneficial out of a perturbation."

"Don't try to tell that to Sorbl." The wizard nodded toward the trees behind Jon-Tom. From within the brush pitiful retching sounds alternated with less pleasant ones.

"Too bad." Of them all, Mudge appeared the least affected

by his personal infection. "Needs to lead a 'ealthier life, the poor sod."

"I have not had a cold in some time," observed Clothahump. "And you say you have never had these measles before?" Jon-Tom nodded. "It appears then that each of us has contracted something new to our systems, or at the very least something which we have have not experienced in some time."

"Blimey, you'd think you were all dyin', wot with all this sneezin' and sweatin' and pukin' an' all. Wot you chaps need is—" He halted in mid-sentence and his eyes got very wide. Abruptly he bent over and grabbed his crotch with both paws. The reason for his earlier reluctance to identify the location of his itch was now apparent.

Clothahump studied the bent-over otter studiously as he blew his nostrils for the fortieth time. "A new and particularly virulent strain, I should say."

"Of what?" Jon-Tom touched his cheek with one hand, felt the heat.

"Difficult to say. Gonorrhea, perhaps, or something even less comfiting." The otter was rolling around on the ground and moaning while he clutched at his privates. Since the diseases they had contracted were moving with exceptional rapidity through their bodies, each of them was suffering the cumulative effects of his or her respective infection. None was more discomforting than the otter's.

"It ain't fair," he was shouting at a vicious fate, "it ain't fair!"

"Nothing the perambulator does is fair, Mudge."

"It can't be. I mean, everyone's been clean wot I've been with the 'ole bloomin' year."

"Doesn't mean anything to a perturbation," Jon-Tom told him sympathetically.

Breathing hard, the otter at last rolled to a stop. Sitting up, he pulled down his shorts and commenced to examine himself in detail. "Blimey, you don't think there'll be any permanent effects, do you, mate?"

"Mudge, I have no idea. I hope that I'm going to be immune to measles from now on, but I've no way of knowing for sure. None of us do."

Clothahump adjusted his glasses, blew his nose yet again, and murmured, "Poetic justice."

Mudge's head snapped around, and he glared at the turtle, barely suppressing the frustration and fury he felt. "If we didn't absolutely need you to straighten out this rotten mess the world 'as got itself into, Your Wizardshit, it would give me the greatest pleasure to knock your bloody smug face down into your bloody arse."

"I did not make the comment out of a casual desire to provoke." Clothahump was not in the least concerned with the otter's threat. "I have had occasion to notice, water rat, that you are a great one for laughing at the misfortunes of others. But when it is your own person that is involved in disquieting circumstances, your sense of humor absents itself."

"Don't be too hard on him," Jon-Tom requested. "Really, sir. There's nothing funny about venereal disease. Why, it could cause shriveling and complete ruination of his—"

Mudge let out a cry of despair and fell over on his side.

VII

They recovered from their assorted infections by the following midday. Jon-Tom had suffered and been done with a severe case of measles in less than twenty-four hours. Clothahump's cold had left him, and Sorbl no longer had to vanish into the bushes every five minutes. Having contracted the most serious disease of all, Dormas was the last to recover. None of them had any permanent damage to show for their respective bouts.

Mudge was as fit as any of them, having been fully restored to health. That didn't keep him from taking occasional peeks at himself when he thought no one was looking.

"Relax, Mudge," Jon-Tom told him. "It's all over. Pretend it never happened. We're as healthy as we were the day before last. There are no aftereffects."

"Bloody well better not be." He was helping Dormas adjust her load. "If that blasted perambulator baiter's 'urt me love life, I'll dice 'im for a stew."

"I'm sure you're none the worse for wear, Mudge. Everyone else is healthy again. You must be too."

"Well—on close inspection she all appears to be in workin' order, but I ain't really in a position to find out for sure. One thing's certain: I'm goin' to take 'er slow an' easy at first."

Jon-Tom nodded approvingly. "Thataboy. It wouldn't hurt you to rein in your profligate life-style a little, anyway."

"You may be right, mate." Mudge slipped his longbow over his shoulders. Then he raised one paw, put the other one over his heart, and solemnly intoned, "No more orgies. No more a different lady every night. By the digger of dens, I swear this. I'm goin' to cut down."

"It was worth the trouble if it made a new otter out of you. There's nothing wrong with seeking pleasure in moderation for a change, you know."

"Aye, mate. It made me see the light, that bloomin' infection did. I've done wot I pleased lo these many years without 'avin' a care to wot I might be doin' to me body. 'Tis time for a bit more maturity. If I start watchin' meself, maybe I'll never 'ave to suffer with that kind o' sickness for real." He shouldered his own small backpack and started briskly up the narrow game trail they'd been following.

"Much as it's goin' to 'urt," he muttered. "I guess I'll 'ave to restrict meself to a different lady every *other* night."

Clothahump was shaking his head as he waddled off in the otter's wake. "Incorrigible, as are most of his kind. You can try your best, my boy, but water rats are unreformable."

Jon-Tom fell into step alongside him, keeping his strides short to match the wizard's. "You can't expect him to turn into a church mouse overnight, sir."

"I expect him to turn into a desiccated corpse one night is what I expect. But keep trying. Far be it from me to dampen your enthusiasm."

"You may be right, sir, but keep trying I will." He let his eyes shift forward. Mudge was leading the way, those bright black eyes darting left and right, missing nothing. He was whistling cheerfully.

At least he'll die happy, Jon-Tom mused. And who was he, unwilling visitor from another place and time, to criticize? This world had already forced him to relinquish many long-held moral precepts. He would never degenerate to the otter's level, of course, but neither was he the same person he'd been when Clothahump had mistakenly brought him over. Nor could he exactly be called pure, having enjoyed a joint on occasion and spent more than his fair share of study time trying to focus his roommate's binoculars on the girls' dormitory across the way from their apartment.

So who was he to judge Mudge? At least the otter knew how to have fun. Jon-Tom had to work at it. It was the lawyer in him. He was too restrained, too much in control of himself. Maybe one day Mudge would be able to show him how to really let *go*.

You worry too much, that's one of your problems, he told himself. *Like right now, you're worrying about worrying too much.*

Angrily he kicked at a rock (making certain it was not a pinecone) and tried to think of something else. Nothing was more frustrating than arguing with yourself and losing.

As if doing penance for all the trouble it had caused recently, the perambulator did not trouble them for some time. They marched on, climbing steadily across the plateau, unaffected by discombobulating dislocations, save for a few minor ones. Jon-Tom spent one morning trying to adjust to being suddenly left-handed, while one evening Mudge's fur turned pure silver. Not silver-colored, but solid strands of metallic silver. He was bitterly disappointed when he changed back before he could give himself a shave.

At the same time Dormas was transformed into a gloriously hued palomino, Jon-Tom acquired the skin tone of a Polynesian, and Sorbl's brown-and-gray feathers all turned to gold. It was a reminder, Clothahump declared, that not all the perambulator's perturbations need necessarily have harmful consequences. Jon-Tom was disappointed when his artificial tan vanished along with the rest of the changes. It would have stood him in good stead at the beach.

He'd managed to use his spellsinging to help relieve the discomforts of certain perturbations. What he needed now was a song that would enable him to make the effects of selected perturbations permanent. Like his briefly acquired tan, for example. It would be nice if he could figure out how to freeze a perturbation that added forty pounds of muscle to his upper body or raised his IQ a hundred points.

It gave him something to concentrate on as they continued their climb. Eventually he broached the idea to Clothahump.

"A dangerous proposition, my boy. Particularly when one takes into account the notorious inaccuracy of your spellsinging."

"You'll have to come up with something besides that if you're going to stop me from trying, sir."

The wizard sighed. "I do not doubt it. Consider this, then: Instead of perpetuating a benign perturbation—you could not merely alter its effect with your spellsinging—you could transform it into something terrible and uncontrolled."

"But think of the possibilities, sir, if it could be done right! For example, suppose we were to be struck by a perturbation that took a hundred years off your life? You could be young again, physically as well as mentally vigorous."

"To be granted another hundred years of activity, that is tempting, my boy. Yes, tempting. To a certain extent we can prolong life, but we cannot restore what has already been used. But a perturbation—yes, a perturbation *could* possibly accomplish that." It appeared to Jon-Tom as if the wizard was growing slightly misty-eyed behind his six-sided spectacles.

"Certainly it would be worth considering. Sadly, you youngsters tend not to take the time to balance possible gains

with probable risks. Think about it, though, if it pleases
you.''

Jon-Tom did so, enthusiastically at first and then with more
and more caution. There was only one problem with a
perturbation that would take a hundred years off the wizard's
life. It would also make Jon-Tom seventy-four years less than
being born, a difficult position from which to rescue oneself.
Maybe trying to make the effects of a perturbation permanent
wasn't such a good idea after all. It wasn't long before he
dropped the once-promising idea completely. The perambulator was dangerous because it monkeyed with reality. Monkeying
with the monkey, he decided, could be more dangerous still.

Thoughts of freezing the perambulator's effects were soon
replaced by thoughts of freezing things closer to home. They
were well to the north of even Ospenspri by now. The nights
had become very cold, but the sunlit days were still quite
tolerable. Winter was still several weeks away from wrapping
the northern portions of the warmlands in a blanket of white.

The chill did not trouble the thickly furred Mudge or the
heavily feathered (and well-lubricated) Sorbl. Nor did it
appear to bother Dormas. But both Jon-Tom and Clothahump
were warm-weather types. They could cope with the late fall
weather but not with snow and ice.

The extent of Clothahump's concern for the weather was
indicated by the fact that he alluded to it at least once a day.
''We must find and release the perambulator soon, or winter
will trap us here on the plateau. I am not anxious to save the
world, only to freeze to death as a result of doing so.''

''We'll make it,'' Jon-Tom assured him confidently. ''If we
run into any serious weather on the way out, Dormas can
carry us. Remember, her contract stipulates that her ban
against riders doesn't include the injured or incapacitated.''

''She would still require assistance in finding her way back
down the plateau.''

''Sorbl can guide her.''

The wizard let out a snort of derision. "I would not trust my famulus to guide me to the bathroom."

"All right, then, Mudge could do it."

Clothahump glanced at Mudge, who was blissfully whistling away, cracking nuts on a flat boulder with a fist-sized chunk of granite. Then he looked back at Jon-Tom.

"I am glad that after all you have been through these past months, you still retain your unique sense of humor."

"I know that sometimes Mudge acts like less than the ideal companion, but if it came down to a real life-or-death situation, I'm sure he'd be there to help me. He's demonstrated that he's prepared to do that on several previous occasions."

"Which is no indication that he hasn't experienced a change of heart," the wizard argued. "I think your confidence is badly misplaced, my boy."

"Well, I disagree. Mudge and I understand each other." He turned and raised his voice. "Don't we, Mudge?"

The otter looked up, ostentatiously chewing the fruits of his labors, and eyed the tall young man quizzically. "Don't we wot, mate?"

"Understand one another. I was just telling Clothahump that if I fell down to die in the snow, you'd drag or carry me to safety."

"Why, o' course I would! Wot are mates for if they can't depend on one another? I'd pull you until the soles wore out o' me boots an' me 'ands were raw an' bleedin' from the effort o' draggin' your oversize skinny carcass back to civilization. I'd get you to warmth and nursin' at the risk o' me own life. I'd haul and haul until—"

"Don't overdo it, Mudge."

"Right, mate." The otter turned back to his remaining unopened victuals.

"You see?" Jon-Tom told the wizard. Clothahump smiled back at him.

"And, of course, the otter has never lied to you."

"Oh, he's fudged the truth a little now and then, but when the chips are down, Mudge is up."

"Hmph! Up and away, I should say."

Silence took up a stance between them. Just as well, or Jon-Tom might have said something disrespectful to the old magic-maker. Of course, Mudge meant what he said! He was a faithful companion and good friend. He found himself glancing ever so surreptitiously in the otter's direction and was ashamed to confess that Clothahump's pessimism had started him to thinking unflattering thoughts about the otter.

He finished his cup of tea angrily.

The following morning revealed a northern landscape filled with towering, snow-clad peaks. Jon-Tom stared at the precipitous crags, asked dubiously, "We're not going to have to go up into that, are we?"

Clothahump shaded his eyes as he considered the terrain confronting them. "I don't know, my boy. I have traced the perambulator this far, but it is difficult to ascertain its location with absolute precision. We can only continue to follow the line that lies between it and the home tree. I only hope its prison is accessible to us."

"And wot if she ain't, guv'nor?" Mudge was more surefooted than any of them, but even he had no stomach for challenging the mountains that lay in front of them. "We turn back for 'ome an' 'ope that everything turns out for the best?"

"Nothing turns out for the best, my furry friend, unless you strive to make it do so. Hope is no substitution for hard work. Wherever the perambulator is being held, that is where we must go. Somehow." He led them onward.

Those towering peaks and sheer granite walls still lay a long way ahead of them. It was possible that they would encounter the perambulator and its captor long before any real climbing was necessary. Everyone hoped so. Jon-Tom could only gaze on the wizard with new admiration. While everyone was complaining about the possibility that they might have to do some difficult climbing, no one had remarked on the fact that of them all, Clothahump was the least equipped to do so.

Several days more brought no sign that they were any closer to their goal, but it did present them with a new challenge: fog. No more than ever they had to rely on Clothahump to guide them, for in the thick, cloying grayness Sorbl could not fly and scout out the easiest path ahead.

Mudge sniffed endlessly, nervously, at the damp, moist air. "Never did care much for this stuff. There's them that think it romantic. Me, I says that's tallywabble. 'Ow's a person supposed to watch out for 'imself in this gray crap?"

"Reminds me of movies I've seen of the Golden Gate, in San Francisco."

That piqued the otter's interest and raised his spirits as well. "A gate made out o' gold! That's the first reference you've made to your world that interests me, mate. Maybe she ain't as bad a place to live as you make it out to be."

"Sorry to disappoint you, but the gate I'm referring to isn't made out of gold. That's just a name given to it because of how it looks at certain times of day."

"Oh, that's the case, is it? Doesn't compare to the jeweled gate of Motaria, then? Pity. As for Motaria, I've 'eard tales that say . . ." And he proceeded to spin the story without having to be prompted by Jon-Tom. When he finally ran out of words, the fog was thicker than ever.

They walked on in silence. Mudge kept sniffing the air, searching the dampness for suggestions of possible danger, when the discordant mumbling from off to his right finally made him search out his tall friend once more.

"Look, mate, I don't mind you practicin' your spellsingin', but I'd be obliged if you could do it a mite more quietly."

Jon-Tom didn't look at him. He was scanning the forest,

what he could see of it through the fog. "I haven't been spellsinging, Mudge. In fact, I was just going to ask you to be quiet."

"Me? I 'aven't so much as—"

"Nobody can hear themselves think over all that damned sniffing of yours. But I think I hear something else."

Mudge frowned but stood quietly, save for one involuntary sniff. His gaze narrowed slightly. "Blimey, you're right, mate. I 'eard bad singin' for sure, but it weren't you." Dormas had trotted over to join them. She stood next to Jon-Tom, her nose held high to sample the air, her ears cocked alertly forward.

"I hear it, too, boys. Some kind of singing or chanting. Think I can smell something also."

"What species?" Clothahump's eyes and ears were neither as sharp as Mudge's nor as sensitive as Dormas's. Besides which, he was fully occupied with trying to keep moisture from congealing on his glasses. He wiped them with a cloth as he stared into the fog.

"Rodentia, I think." Dormas inhaled deeply. "There's so much water in the air, it's tough to say."

"Right about that, lass. Take a deep whiff and 'tis like blowin' your nose backwards."

Jon-Tom made a face. "Your gift for metaphor is as effervescent as ever, Mudge."

"I 'ope that's as dirty as it sounds, mate."

"More than one of them, whoever they are." The hinny's nostrils flexed. Jon-Tom was acutely conscious of his olfactory inadequacies. Compared to any one of his companions, he was virtually scent-blind.

"Any idea how many of them there might be?" Clothahump asked her.

"Can't say. Don't matter, anyways, does it?" She glanced down at him. "We're not headed in that direction."

"We cannot be certain which route we will employ to

return." The wizard considered the tantalizing fog thoughtfully. "I confess to curiosity. I should like to know through
whose territory we have been traveling." Behind him, Sorbl
let out a groan.

"Me too," avowed Dormas.

Mudge eyed first the hinny, then Clothahump in disbelief.
"Wot's with you two? Remember, curiosity killed the cat."

"Not anybody I know." Dormas started into the trees,
dropped her head to sniff the damp ground ahead of them.

"We are far from Ospenspri, far north of any civilized
town." Clothahump put his glasses back on his beak. They
immediately began to fog up again. "There can, however, be
habitation without civilization. I have heard many tales of the
wild tribes that are said to infest these infrequently visited
north woods. It would be useful to obtain some firsthand
knowledge of their ways."

"Why don't you just read a bleedin' book about 'em,
guv'nor?"

"There is little to read, my water-loving fuzz-brain." The
wizard moved to follow in Dormas's wake. "Few explorers
come this way. They prefer the warmlands or the tropics. We
have a unique opportunity here."

"Aye, to become some shithead rat's dinner." Mudge
looked up at Jon-Tom. "You see the wisdom in me words,
don't you, lad?"

"I see that wisdom is not gained without risks." Clothahump
smiled approvingly at him. "Sorry, Mudge." He stepped
forward to join the other two.

"You're all bloody fools—not that that's the surprise o' the
year." The frustrated otter folded his arms and held his
ground. What really made him angry was that they were
ignoring him. He didn't mind being screamed at, yelled at, or
insulted, but when those whose opinion differed from his
acted as though he didn't exist, he wanted to stab something.
Given his present company, however, even that release was

denied to him. His knife couldn't dent Clothahump's shell, Jon-Tom would sense him coming, and Dormas's arse was too high.

So he drew his short sword and relieved some of his frustration by hacking a nearby bush to pieces.

Jon-Tom, Dormas, and Clothahump continued to ignore their apoplectic companion. They were too busy trying to identify the source of the mysterious, eerie chanting that floated through the woods. It seemed as if it were being carried along by the fog itself, rising and falling, the cadence distinctive, the words unrecognizable.

"An ancient language," the wizard commented, "doubtless handed down from chanter to chanter. It may be that those who sing no longer know the meaning of the words but continue to recite them because they believe they have power."

Jon-Tom was no linguist, but even he could sense the age of the chants. They seemed to consist largely of grunts and groans, of the kinds of sounds animals would make: animals incapable of reason and speech and higher thought. A tribal legacy retained from a precivilized past. No wonder Clothahump was interested in the people who would make such sounds. He glanced back over a shoulder.

"Mudge, you're the best stalker among us. Why don't you lead the way?"

Having demolished the bush and returned his sap-stained sword to its scabbard, the otter resolutely turned his back on them. "Not me, guv'nor. Go stick your neck into the pot if you want to, but I'm stayin' 'ere."

"Leave the water rat be," Clothahump told his tall human charge. "We shall advance without him. If naught else, our approach will be quieter. Dormas, can you still smell them?"

"Faintly. It'll get stronger as we get closer. Maybe this damn fog will lift a little too."

They started forward. Sorbl rose from his perch to settle on the top of Dormas's pack. Mudge looked at the owl in surprise.

"Sorbl? You're not goin', too, mate?"

"I have no choice." The apprentice looked back at him. "I must go where my master goes."

"Don't worry, Mudge," Jon-Tom told him. "We'll be back in a little while. You can stay here and guard the campsite."

"Wot? All by meself?" The otter gazed warily into the impenetrable, claustrophobic fog. He made a growling sound in his throat as he spoke to Jon-Tom. "You think you're bloomin' clever, don't you, you 'airless son of an ape? You know I ain't likely to squat 'ere on me fundament in this stinkin' fog without anyone to watch me back."

"Frankly I don't care what you do, you spineless offspring of a cottonmouth, but if you're coming with us, get up here and make yourself useful."

Having concluded this exchange of pleasantries and having reavowed their undying friendship, Mudge joined Jon-Tom in leading the way. In fact, the otter took the lead, professing a desire to keep as far from his tall friend as possible.

Clothahump looked approvingly at his guest. "You are learning, my boy, that words are more useful than weapons."

"What do you expect from somebody in law school? I've known Mudge long enough to know what buttons to push. He would've come along, anyway. He just likes to make it look like he's been forced."

"Don't be too sure of your ability to manipulate him. Otters are an unpredictable lot. One thing I would never count on is for him to act in a predictable fashion."

"Overconfidence on my part where Mudge is concerned isn't something you need to worry yourself about, sir."

They ascended a gentle slope, crossed a ravine, and climbed the heavily wooded far side. As they neared the crest of the ridge the chanting grew much louder. In addition to the voices they could now make out the sounds produced by individual drums, reed flutes, and something that sounded like an acerbic tambourine. Mudge motioned for silence, unnecessarily. It was clear they were very near the source of the singing. The time for conversation was past. It was time to listen and to observe.

Then they were able to see over the ridge. They found themselves looking down into a small valley. Set among the trees were semipermanent angular huts fashioned of twigs, branches, and mud. Fires danced in rock pits in front of two or three of the buildings. Laboriously gathered vegetation had been laid out to dry next to the flames. Berries of many kinds, nuts, and the thin, tender heart of some unknown plant were constantly being turned and patted clean by the females of several species.

"I see some ground squirrels," Jon-Tom whispered. "I don't recognize the ones with the small round ears."

"Pikas." Clothahump was squinting through his glasses. "The big fat ones are marmots. Notice their attire."

Regardless of species, all were scantily clad in primitive garments. With their thick coats of fur, none required heavy outer clothing to protect them from the cold. Decorative skirts had been fashioned of tree bark pounded thin and softened with water. There was an extraordinary variety of headgear, ranging from simple headbands to elaborate tiaras of dried seeds and animal bones.

Away from the transitory village and off to the right, a group of musicians sat in a semicircle pounding or tootling or rattling their instruments. Seated in the semicircle opposing them were the chanters. These included all the senior males. They were dressed like warriors. In addition to their decorative necklaces and rings they wore headpieces made from the bleached, hollowed-out skulls of other creatures. Nor were all the gruesome chapeaus fashioned from the bones of prey animals.

"Crikey," Mudge murmured in realization, "they're a bloody lot o' cannibals."

In the center of the two semicircles was a wooden platform surmounted by a single post. A trio of barbarically clad pikas tended a fire beneath it. They were careful not to let the flames rise high enough to threaten the wood. The purpose of the blaze was to produce as much smoke as possible in order to make life as difficult as possible for the single leather-clad individual who was tied to the pole above. This the pikas achieved by feeding the flames a steady diet of damp leaves and bark.

The unfortunate prisoner was wearing snakeskin pants and shirt, leather boots, and fingerless leather gloves. Brass spikes studded his clothing from the top of the short boots to the broad shoulders. Jon-Tom was unable to tell just from looking whether these bits of metal were designed to serve for decoration or defense. Among some warlike people they did double duty.

Around a considerable waist the prisoner wore a brass-studded belt. A matching collar girdled his neck. He was about four and a half feet tall, though he appeared shorter because he was bent over as much as his bonds would permit, coughing and wheezing, unable to avoid inhaling the thick black smoke that rose from beneath him.

A hook hammered into one corner of the platform supported a large knapsack fashioned of the same black leather the prisoner wore. It bulged with unseen objects. Tied to it was a thin saber that was nearly as tall as the prisoner himself.

From time to time a light breeze would disturb the fog long enough for the hidden spectators to get a decent view of the prisoner. His face and large furry ears were instantly recognizable. Species identification was as easy as it was surprising.

"What's he doing here?" Jon-Tom asked of no one in particular. "I thought koalas preferred tropical climes. I haven't encountered one anywhere in the Bellwoods."

"They are not frequent visitors to our part of the world, it is true." Clothahump was straining for a better view of the prisoner. "Certainly this one is a long way from his home, though he is not dressed improperly for this climate."

"The poor slob." Dormas sniffed sympathetically. "Wonder what he did to get himself taken prisoner and subjected to such treatment?"

"Probably just trespassing." Mudge started to inch his way backward. "Right. We've seen enough to satisfy any aberrant biological curiosity. Now 'tis time to leave, right?"

"Wrong. Their intentions are pretty damn clear. They're going to slowly suffocate him. No one deserves that kind of death."

" 'Ow do you know that, mate? Maybe this one's committed some kind o' heinous crime against this lot o' savages. Maybe 'e's been fairly judged and condemned. Wot 'ave I told you about tryin' to foist your moral precepts on other folk?" He nodded toward the encampment. "Look at 'ow 'e's dressed, will you? A rough bloke for sure. Me, I says they deserve each other."

"If he's guilty of some crime, I'd like to know about it," Jon-Tom responded. "If not, we'd be morally derelict to let him die slowly like that. I'd like to think a passing traveler might do as much for me someday."

"Not bloody likely," the otter grumbled. "I thought you'd been 'ere long enough to know better than that, mate."

"I would very much like to know his story," Clothahump declared. "Not only how he comes to find himself in this dangerous situation but also how he comes to be in this lonely part of the world in the first place."

"That's fine, that is! I should've stayed back at the camp."

"Mudge, where's your concern for your fellow being?"

"In me left 'ip pocket, where it belongs. As for that, those 'appy dirge drippers down there are as much me fellows as that armored fat bear. I ain't enamored o' their table manners, but that doesn't mean I'm about to risk me own arse to try and rescue some other fool's.''

Jon-Tom turned his attention back to the encampment. It was clear that the prisoner was rapidly becoming too weak even to cough. ''We have to do something.''

''Swell, guv. You an' old rockback 'ere 'ave a stroll on in, untie the object o' your pity, an' announce to that angelic choir that you're sorry but the party's over and you're all leavin' together. I'm certain they'll understand. They'll be delighted—that they 'ave three carcasses for the smoker.''

''Much as my curiosity—and my sense of justice, of course—draws me toward that poor unfortunate,'' Clothahump said, ''the water rat does have a point. We have a much greater responsibility. I do not see how we can risk everything to rescue this one individual.''

Jon-Tom considered a long moment before replying. ''You're right, sir. So is Mudge.''

The otter looked surprised but pleased. ''About time you started showin' some o' the sense I've spent a year poundin' into you, mate.''

''We can free him without risking a thing.'' He started to unlimber his duar.

It did not take a wizard to divine Jon-Tom's intentions. ''Are you sure you want to try this, my boy? While it is true that this will not expose us to retaliation at first, it will not take long for those forest-dwellers below to locate us if you fail.''

''Don't worry, sir. This one's going to be a cinch.'' He started tuning the instrument immediately. ''I've got it all figured out. Most of the problems I have with my spellsinging come from my usually being rushed to come up with an appropriate song and then having to perform it before I'm completely ready. But I've had a chance to listen to these people and to observe them. I know just what I'm going to do, and I don't see how I can fail.''

"Your confidence is reassuring and, I hope, not misplaced. Why are you so sure of yourself, my boy?"

Jon-Tom grinned at him. "Because I'm going to use their own music against them. I've got the basic rhythm of that chanting down pat. I'm going to do a rock version of their own hymn and add my own words." He let his fingers fall across the familiar strings. "It's pretty much all two-four time. I can play riffs off that in my sleep."

"A fine idea, lad," said Mudge. "I'll just meet the lot o' you back in camp, wot?" He turned and started back the way they'd come.

"Don't mind him," Dormas said, smiling at Jon-Tom. "I have confidence in you. Go on—blow the furry little shitheads back into the trees."

"Well, I hope the results aren't *that* severe." He cleared his throat. He wanted only to free the prisoner, not perpetrate a massacre. He launched into his own interpretation of the mass chanting below, utilizing the duar at maximum volume and trying to sing the improvised song with as much grace and clarity as an Ozzy Osbourne.

The reaction was instantaneous. Sticks froze in the air halfway to drums. The hooting of flutes and the rattle of tambourines ceased. The chanting stopped as every eye in the valley below turned to stare up at the twisting, gyrating figure atop the ridge.

Jon-Tom had hoped that his version of the chant would paralyze the heavily armed warriors below. It did nothing of the kind. But while the tribefolk were not mesmerized by the heavy metal chords emanating from Jon-Tom's instrument, neither did they come charging up the hill brandishing their spears and clubs.

Instead they started running. Not toward the singer but away from him. In every direction. As they ran they cast aside what weapons they held. The females joined them, kicking over cookpots and piles of laboriously gathered food.

Even the cubs scampered off in full retreat. Their wailing and crying was pitiful to hear. The warriors threw away their weapons because they needed their hands—to clasp over their ears or to fold them flat against the tops of their heads. Within a very short time the last inhabitant of the village had vanished among the trees. That was when a new voice rose above the silence below.

"For sanity's sake stop that horrible noise and come and untie me! Or else put a spear through my heart and put me out of my suffering now!" The koala tried to add something more but broke down in a fit of coughing. The fire beneath him was still smoldering.

Abashed, Jon-Tom halted in mid-phrase and turned to regard his companions. Apparently the prisoner was not alone in his agony. Mudge had fallen against a tree and was only now removing his paws from his ears. Sorbl still had the tips of his wings pressed to his, while poor Dormas was gritting her teeth in pain. Somehow she had managed to fold the ends of her own ears in on themselves. Clothahump had retreated completely into the relative safety of his shell.

Now he emerged, popping legs and arms out first and his head last of all. His glasses hung askew from his beak. He straightened them as he walked up to Jon-Tom and put a hand on the spellsinger's arm. The fingers were shaking slightly.

"Do as he says, my boy."

Jon-Tom looked out into the fog. "What if they're trying to sneak around behind us?"

"I do not believe they wish to remain anywhere in the immediate vicinity."

"Then my spellsinging worked?"

The wizard cleared his throat delicately. "Let us just say that they did not find your interpretation of their ancient ceremonial to their liking."

"Oh." He paused thoughtfully, then added, "Neither did the rest of you, huh?"

"It held our attention. Let us leave it at that."

"Aye," said Mudge loudly, "like 'avin' an anvil dropped on your 'ead."

"The combination of an extremely primitive rhythmic line combined with what you refer to as your variety of contemporary music as rendered on the duar apparently possesses unexpected strengths."

"Are you saying, sir, that no magic was involved? That it was my singing alone that made them want to flee?"

"No, mate. What 'Is Sorcererness is sayin' is that your singin' o' that old music and your new music made 'em an' the rest of us as well want to run screamin' an' pukin' through the bloody forest."

"I see." He shrugged, took a deep breath. "Well, anyway, it worked."

"Are you up there going to untie me or not?" The koala's voice was surprisingly deep and resonant. It made him sound much more massive than he was.

"Bleedin' impatient sort o' chap, ain't 'e?" Mudge and Sorbl started down the hill. Jon-Tom waited until Mudge was out of earshot before turning to Clothahump again.

"What you're really trying to say, sir, is that my singing hasn't improved any."

"I suppose it would not be terribly undiplomatic of me to admit that I do not think it has kept pace with your playing, my boy. There is, sadly, a quality, a timbre if you will, which renders your voice somewhat less than sweet-sounding to a sensitive ear. The native chant was not exactly melodious to begin with. Your singing backed by the playing of the duar did not exactly enhance what slight harmonious overtones it possessed."

"That bad, huh?"

"I believe that for once the otter did not exaggerate in his description. Do not look so downcast. It is the results that matter. You are a spellsinger, not a bard."

"I know, but I *want* to be a bard! I can't help it if I don't sound like Lionel Richie or Daltrey."

"I am sorry, my boy, but it appears that you may have to settle for being a spellsinger."

He ought to be pleased, he told himself as they waited for Mudge and Sorbl to return with the freed prisoner. He could do things no other musician could do. He could send his enemies fleeing in panic, could conjure up wonders, could move small mountains. The trouble was, what he wanted more than anything else was to be able to sing.

And he tried so hard to sound like a McCartney or Waite, only to end up producing a noise that must have resembled a cross between AC/DC's Angus McKie and a sex-starved moose. Come to think of it, McKie and the moose didn't sound all that different from one another.

He kept his eyes on the forest and fog enclosing them, his hands on the duar. Despite Clothahump's reassurances, he wanted to be ready in the event that some brave warrior did try to slip in behind them.

Before he sang that chant again, though, he'd have to remember to warn his companions.

VIII

Mudge's knife made short work of the ropes that secured the prisoner to the pole, while Sorbl used his beak on the smaller bonds that bound the koala's wrists. Mudge had to catch him once he was freed, so cramped had his muscles become from disuse and the severe restraints. While the otter helped him up the slope, Sorbl plucked his knapsack from the corner platform post and flew back toward his master.

Eventually otter and koala reached the top of the ridge. The former prisoner was still coughing, though neither as violently nor as frequently as when he'd been tied to the post. It would take awhile before his lungs were completely cleared. His eyes were badly bloodshot and he wiped at them repeatedly. Mudge eased him over to a fallen log and gently sat him down.

He sat silently for a while, catching his breath and letting his lungs clear, only his large furry ears moving. The black nose was wet and running from having inhaled too much

soot. Eventually he looked up at them and spoke again in that
unexpectedly profound, deep voice.

"Thanks, friends. Not everyone would go out of their way
like that to save a stranger, though I had a pretty good idea
something like this was going to happen. Darned if I wasn't
starting to get a little worried, though. I'm obliged."

"What do you mean you 'had an idea something like this
was going to happen'?" Jon-Tom said.

"We can talk about it later. Right now we're still a mite
too close to that fire for my comfort. Let's walk the walk and
I'll talk the talk." He rose, tilted his head back to gaze up at
Jon-Tom. "You're a prime specimen, aren't you? Thanks for
your musical aid. You won't be insulted if I don't ask for an
encore."

"If my music doesn't please you, you can always go back
down there and talk over your problems with your friends."
He smiled to show the koala that he was only responding in
kind.

Their new acquaintance grinned back up at him. "No
friends of mine down there. Heathens and barbarians, the
cowardly sons of lizards. Hope they run off the end of the
world. My name's Colin. You can introduce yourselves later." He took a step, stumbled. Mudge hastened to lend him a
shoulder, but the koala waved him off.

" 'Preciate the offer, otter, but I'll make it on my own.
You've risked enough on my behalf already. I'll not be a
burden to you." He retrieved his knapsack and saber from
Sorbl, shouldered the pack after sliding the saber into a
special scabbard sewn to its back. Despite his short, thick
arms he managed to slide the blade straight in without
looking over his shoulder. Whoever this Colin was, Jon-Tom
decided, he was no stranger to weaponry. If Jon-Tom had
tried the same trick, he would have sliced himself from neck
to coccyx.

Mudge led them back toward the campsite. "You know

more about your 'appy companions than we do,'' he said to the koala. "Think they'll try an' follow us? The wizard 'imself 'ere says no."

"Wizard, huh?" Colin gave Clothahump a perfunctory nod, polite but in no way condescending, respectful without being obsequious. "I think he's right. Heck, it'll take the bravest among them half a day just to decide to slow down." Everyone laughed but Jon-Tom. He managed a weak smile.

They were halfway back to the camp when Colin called a halt. "We'll take a minute here to make sure they don't follow us." He turned his back to Jon-Tom. "Upper compartment, left side. A small green bottle. Take care. They threw my kit around quite a bit, and I don't know what's broke and what's intact."

An uncertain Jon-Tom unsnapped the pack, located the bottle in question, and handed it to its owner. The stopper was loose but still in place. Colin held it up to the fog-diffused light, examined it critically for a moment, then grunted and began searching the ground around them.

"We need some good-sized branches with the needles still on them." Jon-Tom bristled at being ordered around by someone they'd just had to rescue, but he kept silent as he helped the koala and Mudge collect several healthy evergreen boughs.

"Now what? They're hardly big enough to hide behind," he snapped.

There was a jauntiness to the koala's manner and a twinkle in his eye that defused any real anger on Jon-Tom's part. "That's what you think, man."

After sprinkling a few drops of the colorless liquid on each branch, he had Jon-Tom replace it in his knapsack. The powerful odor made Jon-Tom's nostrils flare, even at a distance.

"Do like so," Colin instructed them. Jon-Tom and Dormas brought up the rear, the three of them sweeping up their footsteps with the branches. Eventually they tossed the boughs aside.

Mudge's sensitive nose was running, and he wiped at it continuously. "Blimey, mate, wot were in that bottle, anyway?"

"Intensely concentrated oil of eucalyptus," Colin informed him. "If they do try to track us, they'll sniff up a nice healthy whiff of that stuff and spend the rest of the day sneezing themselves silly." He grinned first at Mudge, then up at Jon-Tom.

An interesting character, and that was an understatement, Jon-Tom told himself as he considered their stocky new companion. Not gruff exactly but not given to small talk, either. Straightforward and no-nonsense. He'd be able to find his own way back to civilization without much trouble.

As it turned out, however, that parting of the ways was not to take place for some time yet. As they paused in the shelter of a rake tree later that day, they discovered that they shared something in common with the koala besides a dislike of barbaric hospitality.

He was sitting against the thick, deeply scarred bole, chatting with Sorbl and Dormas. Clothahump was off by himself, meditating within his shell, visiting that sorcerous never-never land that only he could enter. It reminded Jon-Tom of hibernation. The wizard called it taking a metaphysical sighting. He was, he had explained on more than one such occasion, checking their position by judging his relationship to certain stars. When Jon-Tom had protested that it was absurd to imagine one small individual having a personal relationship with several incredibly distant suns, Clothahump had informed him that it depended upon the mental size of the individual in question, not his physical stature. As a result, Jon-Tom was half convinced that the turtle was bluffing him. But it did not make him feel any bigger.

He was sitting slightly away from the tree, using the usually concealed blade of his ramwood staff to whittle at a chunk of dead pine. Wood and grain fascinated him. Maybe he ought to give up the idea of being either a lawyer *or* a rock guitarist and settle for a contemplative life of carving. Not a very practical vocation to try to make a living at where he came from, he reflected. If he'd lived in greater Los Angeles, Gepetto would doubtless have been forced to go on welfare.

Footsteps sounded nearby. He looked up to see Mudge approaching. The otter wore his usual expression of concern.

"Wot say you, mate?"

Jon-Tom glanced skyward. They had long since climbed out of the fog, and the sky overhead was a brilliant, pristine blue. "Everything seems to be going pretty good, Mudge. We're not being followed, we've managed to rescue a fellow traveler in need, and we haven't suffered a perturbation in days."

"Aye, seems as though our luck 'as changed, wot? That's just wot I were wonderin' about." As he spoke he kept glancing back toward the tree, to where Colin was laughing and joking with Sorbl and Dormas. " 'Asn't the coincidence struck you?"

"To what coincidence do you refer?" He sighed. The otter's capacity for paranoia was exceeded only by his capacity for drinking, eating, and wenching.

"You just think on it a minute, mate. I'll spell it out for you. Don't want you to think I'm jumpin' to conclusions or nothin'."

"What, you, jump to conclusions? Why would I ever think that?"

"Try an' stifle the sarcasm a moment and look at this thing objectively, mate. 'Ere we are trippin' merrily along, lookin' like ourselves for a change instead o' a bunch o' purple bugs or somethin', when we 'ear this chantin' and follow it to find this Colin chap all bound up an' in the process o' bein' smoked for a holiday roast by a bunch o' savages. Wot does that suggest to you?"

"That we did our good deed for the day and that I don't have the faintest idea what you're getting at."

"I'll try an' be more specific. We've no way of knowin' for 'ow long this Colin was a prisoner. Might've been for an hour, might maybe 'ave been for a day. But just suppose 'e'd been stuck down there for several days. 'Tis been several days exactly since the last bad perturbation. Maybe whoever or wotever 'as imprisoned this 'ere perambulator can't use it on us anymore. Maybe we're too close to 'ome or somethin'. So wot might 'e do, especially if 'e's gettin' worried about us? Mightn't 'e look for some other, subtler way o' stoppin' us? Maybe by gettin' us off our guard first?"

It didn't take a two-hundred-year-old wizard to see what the otter was hinting at. "You're reaching, Mudge. In the first place, there was no guarantee that we would have taken the risk of rescuing Colin. In the second, distance has no effect on the perambulator's perturbing effects. You can't be too close to be affected, and you can't get far enough away to escape it. And lastly, Colin just doesn't seem the type an insane sorcerer would choose for a servant. He's too independent. That's not a put-on. It's the soul of his personality."

"Then it don't strike you as suspicious that in this dangerous and cold northern land where we ain't encountered so much as a decent restaurant for days, we suddenly 'ave a run-in with someone whose species prefers much warmer country? Not to mention that 'e's runnin' around 'ere all by 'is lonesome."

"Of course, I'm curious as to what he's doing up here. He's probably just as curious about us."

"Then why ain't 'e asked about it? And why ain't he told us what 'e's doin' 'ere?"

"Maybe," Jon-Tom suggested, "it's none of our business."

"Cor, don't 'and me that one, mate! We saved 'im from the cook fire, if 'e is as independent as you think. 'E owes us an explanation."

"What if he's on some kind of private pilgrimage, something religious, say?"

"Wot, 'im? The wanderin' preacher o' the Church o'
Leather and Studs? Now who's reachin', mate?"

"I think you're way off base, Mudge. But if it's troubling
you that much, why don't *you* ask him what he's doing
here?"

"Uh, well, you see, lad, you're so much better versed in
the diplomatic arts that I, I was kind o' 'opin' that you'd put
the question to 'im."

"I see. Because I'm more diplomatic, is that it?" The otter
nodded. "Not because if he takes offense, it'll be me he runs
through with that saber of his?"

The otter looked outraged. " 'Ow could you think such a
thing o' me, mate?"

"I don't know." Jon-Tom put his whittling aside as he
rose. "Repeated experience, maybe."

Mudge sidled up close. " 'E's not wearin' that long sword
just now, but we'd best keep an eye on that pack o' 'is."

Jon-Tom frowned. "The knapsack? Why?"

"You just 'aven't learned much about observation, 'ave
you? 'Aven't you noticed 'ow protective 'e is of it? No tellin'
wot 'e's got inside besides a bottle full o' stink-oil."

That much was true. Colin had been excessively protective
of the pack, to the point of refusing to let Dormas carry it for
him until he'd fully recovered from the effects of his near
suffocation. He insisted on carrying it himself, despite the
fact that he was still coughing and choking from time to time.
The more Jon-Tom thought about it, the more peculiar the
koala's presence and actions seemed. He broke off that
unpleasant train of thought abruptly.

"There you go, making me paranoid like you."

"A little 'ealthy paranoia can add ten years to your life,
mate. You can 'andle it. I've seen you in action. 'Tis your
solicitor's training. Me, I'd just make 'im mad, most likely.

But not you. Don't go accusin' 'im o' nothin', or challengin' 'im. Just work it into the conversation, like. I'll be right behind you if 'e takes offense."

"You're such a comfort to me, Mudge."

"Wot are friends for, lad?"

With Mudge sauntering along beside him Jon-Tom strode into the shade of the tree. The otter bent to inspect the grass, then turned to work his way behind the seated koala, trying to render his movements as inconspicuous as possible.

Not inconspicuously enough, apparently, for as experienced a fighter as Colin to let it pass without notice. He said nothing, but he put down the cup he'd been sipping from so he would have both hands free. He did not turn to look at Mudge but remained aware of the otter's position nonetheless.

Dormas was talking while Sorbl listened from his perch on a low-hanging branch. The owl was standing on one leg. Now he shifted to the other, a habit he'd picked up from a friend of his, a member of the stork family.

Dormas looked over at Jon-Tom. "We were just talking about the country to the east of here. Colin tells me there are high mountains, then open plains before you get to his home, which lies farther south."

Mudge picked up a seed cone, inspected it with apparent indifference. "You've come quite a distance, then."

"A long ways, yes," Colin replied. "Considerably farther than the rest of you."

Jon-Tom rubbed his chin. "You know, we don't mean to pry, but it wouldn't be natural for us not to wonder what someone like you is doing up in country like this, so far from the kind of terrain you'd be likely to find agreeable, and traveling by yourself as well."

"I like to travel," Colin told him. "Since not many of my fellows like to, I'm forced to travel alone."

"I see." Silence.

Mudge looked over at Jon-Tom and, when nothing else was forthcoming, said exasperatedly, "Well, go on, mate!"

"Go on where, Mudge?"

The otter spat into the grass, moved to confront the koala. "So you like to travel, wot? Funny sort o' country to be travelin' in. This ain't exactly a tourist mecca up 'ere, and the local yokels not wot I'd call 'ospitable. You couldn't 'ave any other business 'ere besides just travelin', now could you?"

"What sort of business could one have in this empty land?"

"Couldn't o' put it better meself." Mudge's fingers felt for the hilt of his short sword. "Come on now, mate. You don't expect us to believe you've come to this part o' the world just to 'ave a look-see at the scenery?"

"Why not? Isn't that what you're doing? You don't seem equipped for anything else."

"Now 'ow would you know wot sort o' equipment we might be carryin'?"

A slight smile creased the koala's broad face. "I make it my business to notice such things."

"Do you, now? That brings us back to the nature o' your mysterious business again. We can't seem to get away from that, can we?" His fingers locked around the sword hilt.

Colin let his eyes drop to Mudge's waist. "No need to get excited, pilgrim." He let his gaze flick over the otter's face, then Jon-Tom's and Dormas's. "Right. I'll tell you, but you aren't going to believe me."

"Try us." Mudge smiled wolfishly at him.

The koala's voice grew reminiscent. "This all started many months ago. Longer than I care to think. I was hard at work at my true profession—"

Jon-Tom interrupted him. "You have more than one profession?"

"Two, yes. The first is"—and here he stared hard at Mudge—"that of bodyguard. That's how I support myself.

I'm pretty good at it.'' The otter's hand moved away from the handle of his sword. "But it's not my true profession, my real calling. Go ahead and laugh if you will, but I am a caster of runes.''

"What's that?'' said a new voice, sounding surprised. Everyone looked to their left. Clothahump had emerged from the isolation of his self-imposed trance. Now he blinked, stretching and yawning as he came out of his shell. He stuck out his legs, stood, and walked over to join the rest of them, wiping at his eyes with one hand. "A rune-caster, you say?''

"I say." Colin turned and reached for his knapsack. Jon-Tom and Mudge tensed, but all the koala extracted was a small sack of brown leather secured at the top with an intricate knot. Several arcane symbols decorated the sides of the sack, having been stitched in with heavy silver thread. Jon-Tom recognized none of them.

"The tools of the trade,'' the koala explained.

"I can see why you'd chose work as a bodyguard.'' Mudge sniffed derisively. "Throwin' runes ain't much of a profession. Some would say 'tis more in the nature of a con game.''

The koala stiffened slightly, and when he next spoke, there was an edge to his voice. "There are more charlatans than truth-speakers who throw, that much is true. I am no charlatan. Anyone can cast. It's the reading that requires skill. I have practiced for many years, have thrown thousands of times. I was apprentice to Solace Longrush the quokka.''

"I know that name. I thought he was dead,'' Clothahump murmured.

"He is. Died ten years ago. Was casting one day, saw his own death in the runes, gathered everything up, put his house in order, walked to the cemetery he'd chosen, and fell right over into an open grave. Damnedest thing you ever saw.'' He jiggled the leather bag. Faint clinking noises could be heard as small objects within bounced off one another. "His runes. He left them to me.''

"That's why you're so protective of your gear," Jon-Tom said, and was rewarded with a nod. "I've never met a rune-caster before. What do you cast for?"

"Whether someone should make a left turn or go right, whether or not a marriage is likely to succeed, when and where to plant what kinds of crops, that sort of thing. Pays the bills." He leaned forward. "But what Solace Longrush did that no other rune-caster could do, and what I've tried to learn from him, is how to predict the future."

Mudge laughed without shame: a brisk, sharp, barking sound. Dormas let out a loud snort. Sorbl fought back a smile of his own.

"Told you that you wouldn't believe me." The koala did not appear miffed by their reaction. Undoubtedly he was used to skepticism.

As soon as Colin had made his confession Jon-Tom had turned to look at Clothahump. The wizard was neither laughing nor smiling. Instead he was studying their guest with utter seriousness.

"And how," he inquired, "does practicing your true profession bring you to this isolated part of the world?"

"Like I said, I've been traveling for many, many months. What started me on my journey was a cast I was making for a local farmer. He wanted me to find the best place on his land to dig a new well. I had thrown six times and thought I had a pretty good spot picked out for him, but I pride myself on being thorough and giving value for money. So I threw a seventh and last time." He swallowed. "Ten runes lined up in a pattern I'd never seen before. I gave the farmer his location and rushed off to the local Sorceror's Guild library, spent hours trying to find a schematic that resembled the pattern I'd thrown. Finally did."

"And?" Jon-Tom prompted him anxiously, by now thoroughly engrossed in the koala's tale.

"The pattern signified an imminent world change. But not

an immediate one. The change indicated was the kind that takes place in stages, each one more severe than the next. It was also clear that if these gradual changes were not stopped, they were going to culminate in a final change of apocalyptic proportions.''

''The pattern did not by any chance happen to suggest the nature of this final change?'' Clothahump asked him.

''I'm not sure. Patterns are precise, but reading is not an exact science. As near as I could tell, though, it had something to do with the size of the sun.''

''Size?'' Mudge squeaked.

Colin nodded somberly. ''The pattern suggested intensifying local changes, ending in an abrupt expansion of the sun to many times its present size. I think a change like that would make us long to stand above something as chilly as the savage's fire.''

''Nova.'' Jon-Tom squinted through the branches at the placid midday sun above. ''A perturbation strong enough to affect the helium-fusion cycle. It would make the sun go nova. I wonder if the sun in my own world would be affected?''

''Wot's all this rot?'' Mudge muttered. ''Wot's a bloomin' nova and wot's it 'ave to do with the sun, and wotever it is, we've only this chap's word for it, anyways. And wot's it got to do with the question?''

''That's why I'm here. To see if I can't prevent that cataclysmic change. The runes didn't tell me how it could be done, but they showed me where it would have to be accomplished. I'm on my way there.'' He mistook their silence for disbelief. ''I told you you wouldn't believe me.''

''On the contrary,'' Clothahump told him quietly, ''we believe you more than you believe yourself. Because, you see, the answer to our question is also the answer to yours. We are bent on the same task. By different methods we come to this place, intent upon achieving the same end.''

Colin regarded each of them in turn, silently, seeing the truth in their faces. "So that's it. The runes were more thorough than I thought. I did not expect the help they predicted to appear so soon."

"Now 'old on a minimum, mate," Mudge urged him. "If anyone's goin' to 'elp anyone 'ere, 'tis you who are bound to 'elp us."

"It doesn't matter, Mudge," Jon-Tom told him irritably. "We're all here for the same reason."

"True." The koala sounded disappointed. "The runes were thorough but not accurate. As I read them they spoke of aid in the form of an army of several thousand seasoned warriors." He shook off his disappointment. "But if I'm to have the company of a quintet of oddities instead, so be it."

Mudge made a sound low in his throat. "Just who are you callin' an oddity, fat face?"

"Quiet, river rat." Clothahump turned back to Colin. "Then your reading of the runes is not always precise?"

"I'm afraid not. It's the nature of runes. You can't make perfect predictions with imperfect materials, and there's no such thing as a perfect rune. Half a year back I lost two months traveling in the wrong direction before I knew I was off on the wrong track."

"That's all right." Jon-Tom was naturally sympathetic. "I'm a spellsinger myself, and there've been one or two occasions when the results of my spellsinging were other than what I intended." He immediately turned a warning look on Mudge, but the otter's thoughts were elsewhere, and he missed the opportunity to insert the expected sarcastic comment.

"We shall help one another," Clothahump announced firmly. "Your company and what assistance you can provide will be welcome. I know what is causing these changes and approximately where it is located. By cooperating we may define our approach more accurately."

It was clear that Colin was impressed. He glanced up at Jon-Tom. "Tell me, tall man, does he speak the truth?"

"Most of the time. This time."

"Casting is something I have never practiced," the wizard was saying, "because of its notorious inaccuracy. But it may be that you will have the chance to supplement our collective abilities when such aid is needed most. In any event, a strong sword arm is always welcome in such an enterprise as this. We will seek to resolve this danger together."

"I'll be glad of the company. We koalas are sociable types. Traveling solo hasn't been easy." He hesitated. "Not appearing to contradict you, old one, but by the reading, we haven't much time left. We may not get there in time."

"We may not get there at all," Clothahump admitted, "but it is a waste of time to wonder about time. With due respect to your talent, where a perambulator is involved, time itself is mutable. We may have more time left to us than your reading would lead you to believe."

"I hope you're right and I'm wrong."

Clothahump lifted his gaze past them, toward the lower slopes of the mountains that defined the northern horizon. "My greatest fear at this moment is that despite his madness, whoever has trapped the perambulator in this world is beginning to learn how to manipulate those perturbations."

"That might not be all bad," Jon-Tom commented. "If he learns how to do that, maybe he can keep the sun from going nova."

"Should he want to."

"But if that happens, then he'll be killed along with everyone else. That's—"

"Crazy. Precisely, my boy. If the imprisoner is both mad and unhappy, what better solution than suicide on a grandiose scale? My immediate concern is that we may see perturbations directed at us specifically. It seems incredible but it cannot be ruled out."

"You're not bein' very reassurin, Your Masterness."

"The truth rarely is, Mudge."

"Truth. Bleedin' slippery stuff. We still ain't 'ad no proof that you're anything more than a sack o' 'ot air, big-ears."

Colin's eyes narrowed, and he put his hand on his sword. "You calling me a liar, pilgrim?"

"Don't try that shit on me, mate. I believe you can 'andle that sword. That ain't wot we need proof of." He eyed his companions. "Listen, you gulliable lot, don't you want some proof this bloke ain't workin' for the one whose arse we're after before we invite 'im to share our camp?"

"Mudge, sometimes you—" Jon-Tom started to say, but Colin raised a hand to cut him off.

"No. The otter's right. Impolite, but right. You deserve more conclusive proof than fast talk." He placed the leather sack on the ground in front of him and knelt. Jon-Tom paid close attention but for the life of him couldn't discern how the koala unfastened the incredibly complex series of knots so quickly. Making certain the drawstrings were stretched out straight, Colin carefully unfolded the leathern square.

The resultant revelation was something of a disappointment. Jon-Tom didn't know what to expect: brilliantly faceted gemstones perhaps or eerily glowing bits of metal. What the pouch contained was a few pieces of wood, some colored stones and old bones, and a few strips of dyed cloth.

"That's it?" Mudge wanted to know.

"Have you ever seen a set of runes before, otter? Not imitations or fakes, but the real things? Some of these have been handed down from caster to caster." He leaned forward to nudge a few of the pieces with a finger. "These here are hundreds of years old."

"I can smell the power." Clothahump waddled over and asked Colin to identify each rune in detail. Meanwhile Mudge eased over next to Jon-Tom.

"You know, mate, this 'ere meetin' may turn out to 'ave beneficial consequences after all."

"It certainly will, if Colin's telling the truth about his abilities."

"No, no, not that." The otter looked exasperated, then excited. "I mean, 'ave a look at that junk! I can see meself now." The otter's mental wheels were spinning fast. "All I've got to do when we gets back to civilization is trip on down to the local dump and fill me up a little leather bag with the first interestin' crap I stumble over. Then I can go around predictin' the future. The only thing wot puzzles me is 'ow I never thought of it before."

"Mudge, this isn't a scam. This is for real."

"Scam, reality, wot's the difference? The whole universe is a scam, perpetrated by some supreme deity, maybe. 'Tis one's perception of it that matters. Anyway, if a lot o' soft-'eaded twits take me for a rune-caster, who am I to dispute their opinions? I'd 'urt their feelin's by confessing, I would. Folks don't care whether a prediction of the future is accurate or not. They just want someone to tell 'em wot to do so they won't 'ave to think. Besides, I'll only make predictions about wot I'm expert at: sex an' money."

"Sex and money, sex and money. What are you going to think about when you reach a ripe old age, Mudge? Assuming you ever do reach a ripe old age, about which achievement I have serious doubts."

The otter solemnly raised one paw. "I'll change me ways then, mate. Despite wot you might think, I've given that day plenty o' thought. You'll see. When I'm bent over an' white-whiskered, with a streak o' silver down me back, it'll be different. I'll spend all me time thinkin' about *money* an' sex."

"I don't know why, but that confession doesn't surprise me." He motioned for the otter to be quiet. Colin had finished talking to Clothahump. Now it was the koala's turn to raise a commanding paw.

"Silence, please."

"Cheeky bugger, I'll give 'im that," Mudge whispered. Jon-Tom made shushing motions.

Colin had closed his eyes and was mumbling something under his breath. Abruptly a breeze sprang up where there had been no breeze. It whistled in from the east, swirling around them, ruffling Dormas's mane and Jon-Tom's long hair. The wind changed direction repeatedly, as though confused and nervous, a zephyr that had lost its way.

Still murmuring in a guttural singsong, Colin leaned forward to pick up the unimpressive fragments of stone and leather and wood in both paws. Jon-Tom noticed his impressive claws. Keeping the runes cupped in his hands, the koala continued his indecipherable chant. Clothahump was looking on and nodding slowly, though whether he recognized some of what the koala was saying or was merely offering him encouragement, Jon-Tom could not say.

No glowing points of light, no gneechees appeared. This was a different kind of magic, ancient and simple, as alien to Jon-Tom as Republican economic policy. Going by Colin's own description, it was as much luck as magic.

The fur rose on the back of the koala's head. The fringe lining those oversize ears seemed to quiver as if with an electric charge. Colin concluded his incantation. Then he simply held his paws out over the leather square and opened them. There was no skill involved that Jon-Tom could see. The koala simply opened his paws and let the double handful drop.

The stones and bones bounced a couple of times before coming to rest on the leather, which Jon-Tom could now see was crisscrossed with a network of fine lines that had been etched into the fabric by some kind of needle-tipped awl or knife.

Colin inhaled deeply, opened his eyes, and leaned forward to scrutinize the results of his casting. He did not take his eyes from the runes, did not even blink. Such concentration was frightening. Though he tried not to show it, it was evident that even Mudge was impressed.

Colin took another deep breath, then several short ones. Sitting back on his haunches, he put both paws on his leather-covered knees.

"What're you trying to find out?" Dormas finally asked him.

"I wasn't casting for anything particular. Many times the throw is uninformative. Other times it results in a pattern you can't trust. I hope that's the case with this one."

"Why?" Jon-Tom was suddenly concerned. "What does it say?"

There was a genuine sadness in the koala's eyes. They shifted from Jon-Tom to the otter standing next to him. "My good friend Mudge, if this pattern is accurate, you have less than thirty seconds to live."

IX

There was dead silence from the little cluster of onlookers. Mudge could only gape at the stranger in their midst. How did one react to a pronouncement like that? Finally the otter tried to smile. He worked at it as hard as he could, but for once that ready grin failed to materialize.

"You're tryin' to scare me, you sorry sod. You're tryin' to scare all of us so we won't find you out for the rhummy-mugger you are. Well, you can't fool me. I don't believe in your bag o' bones for a minute, I don't." He spat at the ground, barely missing the leather and its mute contents. Looking around warily, he began backing away from the silent, sorrowful Colin.

"I wish it might've been otherwise," the koala apologized. "There's no predicting what the runes will say."

"Say? That pile o' shit can't say boo. 'Tis a lot o' garbage, Jon-Tom." Jon-Tom was staring wordlessly at his friend. "Wot 'e says as well as wot 'e's tossin' around. Just garbage. Tell me 'tis garbage, Your Wizardship."

158

Clothahump watched the retreating otter with a maddeningly clinical eye, then spoke to the caster. "By what means?"

Colin looked back at the motionless runes. "Doesn't say, old one."

" 'Tis garbage, it is!" The otter's voice rose uncontrollably. "Garbage and a bloody lie!" He was glancing around nervously, as though he expected to be attacked at any moment. "Fakery and trickery, I ought to know. The fat bear's a con artist. There's more snow in 'is spiel than crowns those mountains up ahead. Oh, you're slick, you bloated fuzzball" —he sneered at Colin—"real slick. But you can't fool old Mudge. No one can predict the future. No one! And if anyone could, they wouldn't do it by dumpin' a pawful o' junk on the ground an' starin' at it while belching!" He rapped his fist against his chest.

"I'm as 'ealthy as ever me was, surrounded by me good friends, an' there's nothin' in the world I'm afraid of, nothin' that can touch me, nothin' that can—"

He was interrupted by a loud cracking sound. Jon-Tom jumped involuntarily while Dormas backed up fast. Clothahump and Colin did not move. Only Sorbl's marvelous eyes and reflexes, even though slightly numbed by his daily intake of alcohol, enabled him to react fast enough to shout a warning. He gestured with a wing and yelled, "Look out!"

Mudge whirled, eyes wide. Very few creatures can move as fast as an otter. Even so, he wasn't fast enough.

The huge, rotten branch fell from near the top of the big fir he'd backed beneath, striking him on the back of the head and landing with a tremendous crash. Broken sub-branches, leaves, and dead twigs went flying in all directions. The fall was loud enough to echo several times off the surrounding hillsides. Everyone rushed toward the fallen otter except Clothahump. The wizard stood close by the rune-caster's tools and looked on curiously.

"Most interesting," he murmured to no one in particular.

"I was half inclined to agree with the otter's charges of fakery, having known a multitude of witches and warlocks, sorcerers and spellsingers, and so-called casters but never one who actually *could* predict the future."

"You still don't!" Jon-Tom yelled joyfully back to him as he bent over the otter's prone form. Mudge's feathered cap had been knocked off by the impact. It lay several feet away. Blood stained the fur on the back of the otter's skull. But appearances, to Jon-Tom's great relief, were deceiving.

"He's breathing. Sorbl, your hearing's better than any of ours."

The owl nodded and put a pointed ear against the otter's chest. When he looked up at the rest of them, he was smiling knowingly. "Beating like a celibate's after a four-day orgy. He's no more dead than I am."

"Let me have a look." Colin slipped both arms under Mudge. Showing off the considerable strength in his compact body, he easily carried the unconscious otter back to where they'd been sitting when the branch had fallen. Jon-Tom hunted through the medicine pack on Dormas's back and brought out a narrow bottle full of golden liquid.

"Really," said a distressed Sorbl, smacking his beak, "couldn't you make do with some of the cheaper brand, Jon-Tom?"

"Sorbl! I'm surprised at you!"

"I mean," the owl muttered, "it's not as if he's dead or anything."

What a crew, Jon-Tom mused as he bent over the motionless otter and let a few potent drops tumble into the open mouth. Mudge coughed, his body spasmed, a second cough, and he was sitting up sputtering. Jon-Tom was the first thing he saw.

"Wot are you tryin' to do, mate, drown me? Ohhhh." Gingerly he touched the back of his head. "Crikey! It feels like somebody dropped a bloomin' tree on me."

"Close enough, even if it wasn't blooming," Jon-Tom told him. Indeed, the branch that had struck the otter only a glancing blow was bigger in circumference than many of the smaller trees surrounding them.

"Just nicked you, pilgrim." Colin was inspecting the back of the otter's head. "Fortunately. Like I said, rune reading's not a precise art."

"I'll give you a dose o' precise, you walkin' 'airball." He tried to lunge at the koala. The pain in his head held him back. When he touched himself again, his hand came away covered in crimson. "I'm bleedin' to death while you sit there and lecture me."

"Quit whining," Dormas snapped. "Jon-Tom, there are bandages in the bottom of the medicine kit." He nodded, rummaged around until he located a roll of sterilized linen, then began wrapping it around the otter's head.

"Ow! Take it easy back there, mate. That's no steak you're wrappin', you know."

"I'm being as gentle as I can, Mudge."

"Likely, that is." He glared at Colin. "I ain't sure if I buy your whole story, guv'nor, but you've scored a point or two in its favor, that's certain."

Colin sniffed. "You could have been killed, you poor excuse for a coat. I'd think you'd be giving thanks."

"You do, do you? If you're such a hotsy-totsy reader o' the future, 'ow come you didn't see that branch fixin' to break? 'Ow do we know you didn't plan it that way?"

"I don't care for your implications, pilgrim. That blow's affected your reasoning. Or maybe it hasn't. In any case, how could I have known that you'd react to my prediction by retreating right underneath that tree?"

"Use your head, Mudge," Jon-Tom admonished him.

"Not right now, mate, if you don't mind. I admit I ain't figured that one out yet."

"That's about enough, water rat," said Dormas firmly.

"You're pissing in the wind. Mr. Colin strikes me as a perfect gentleman. We should be glad to have him along."

"Speak for yourself, four-legs."

"Mudge, think a minute." Jon-Tom split the end of the bandage and began knotting it around the otter's forehead. "If Colin wanted to kill you, he could have laughed at you when the branch hit you on the head. He didn't. His first reaction was identical to ours: He ran to try to help you."

"You bloody solicitors are all alike, just stinkin' of logic an' reasonableness. I've about 'ad me fill of it—ouch, damn it!"

"If you'd give your mouth a rest, your jaw muscles wouldn't put so much of a strain on the back of your head." He tied the knot firmly. "There. I thought that branch might've knocked some sense into you. I guess it would take a giant sequoia."

"What might that be?" Clothahump inquired.

"An extremely large tree that comes from my world. Bigger than anything you've ever seen."

"Oh, I don't know. Once, in my younger days when I was traveling in southern lands, I—"

"If you don't mind," said Mudge, "could we drop the botanical travelogue until we see if me 'ead's goin' to fall off?"

"I do not think we need fear for the integrity of your skull, Mudge, as opposed to, say, its contents." Clothahump was regarding the injured otter benignly. "As has been demonstrated on more than one occasion, it is unquestionably the strongest part of your anatomy, having both the impermeability and density of solid lead."

"Right. 'Ere I lie, wounded near to death, an' instead o' sympathy an' compassion, I get insults."

"You could be dead, Mudge," Jon-Tom told him again. "Colin's reading might have been completely, instead of partially, accurate."

"Like your spellsingin'. Much more o' that kind o' good fortune an' I'll save the gods the trouble by cuttin' me own throat."

Colin was recovering his runes, packing them just so in the center of the leather square. "Maybe I was wrong. Maybe I shouldn't have cast and, having cast, should have said nothing."

"No. It wouldn't have mattered," Jon-Tom told him. "And I guess we *were* all a little bit suspicous of you."

Colin pulled the four corners of the leather together and secured them with his intricate series of knots. "It's a sad day when a koala's word is no longer believed."

"With the fate of an unknown portion of the cosmos at stake," Clothahump said, "you must concede a little caution on our part."

"Your caution? What about me? What proof do I have that you're a wizard or that the tall, bald body is a spellsinger?"

"I drove off your captors, remember?"

"I remember hearing a sound so awful, it made me wish for the fire at the time. That's not magic, that's torture."

It was worth the bruise to Jon-Tom's ego to hear Mudge laugh again.

"So I don't sound like Nat King Cole, but I'm not *that* bad."

Clothahump frowned. "I do not recognize the line. What kingdom does he reign over?"

"The kingdom of scat," Jon-Tom replied impatiently. "Look, are we in a hurry or not?"

"We are indeed. We should move."

"Sure, why not?" groused Mudge. "The sooner we get there, the sooner we'll all be lyin' quiet in our graves. Fine bunch to be off tryin' to save the world! A wizard who knows where the enemy lies, more or less. A reader o' the future who knows wot's goin' to 'appen, more or less. An' let's not forget a spellsinger who can conjure up the means to defend us from wotever we may face—more or less. 'Ow could a poor tagalong like me be anything but confident about the outcome?''

"That's the spirit, Mudge," Jon-Tom told him. "It's good to know that if we get overconfident about anything, you'll be right there with your undying pessimism to get us back on track."

"You can be sure o' that, mate." He scanned the ground nearby. "Hey, where's me cap?"

"I'll get it." Sorbl half flew, half hopped over to the giant fir, hunted around the sides of the fallen branch for a moment, then returned with something limp and green in his beak. This he passed to Mudge.

"Sorry. I'm afraid it was partly under the branch. Better it than you."

Mudge held the smashed fragment of green felt out in front of him. "Now, ain't that a sorry sight?" He ran two fingers along the sides of the single feather, trying to fluff it out. "A quetzal tail plume, bought at the top o' the matin' season too. Do you 'ave any idea 'ow much a quetzal charges for one o' its mating plumes?''

"I'm surprised he would sell one," Colin commented.

" 'E were broker than 'e were 'orny," Mudge explained. "Wearin' one's supposed to confer exceptional virility and stamina on the part o' the wearer—not that I believe in any o' those primitive arboreal's superstitions, o' course."

"Then why are you crying?" Jon-Tom asked him.

"Cryin'? Wot, me? Cor, I'm just washin' out me eyes. 'Tis just that if one did 'appen to believe in those superstitions, well, the condition o' one's works is supposedly dependent on the condition o' the feather."

"Oh. Well, there aren't any ladies around here to court in any event."

"And a damn good thing too." Sadly the otter plucked the demolished feather from his cap and tossed it aside. "Maybe 'tis for the best. I'm not likely to be distracted along the way—not that we're likely to encounter any worthwhile distractions.''

"So that's settled." Jon-Tom hefted his pack. "Let's be going. Now, Mudge. Mudge? Come *on*."

But the otter was holding back, sampling the air.

"I smell it, too, otter," said Dormas. She had her head tilted back and her muzzle high in the air.

"Smell what?" Jon-Tom asked.

"Something burning, mate."

"I do not smell it yet," said Clothahump, "but the air is decidedly warmer, and I fear not from the sudden onset of an early spring, Sorbl, have a look."

"Yes, Master." Spreading his great wings, the owl rose from his perch on Dormas's back and climbed rapidly.

The rest of them stood and waited, watching the only airborne member of their little party as he circled higher and higher above them.

"I can smell it now too," Jon-Tom murmured. "It's strong, but there's something else about it. I can't say what."

"Maybe Sorbl can tell us," Dormas ventured. The wizard's famulus had folded his wings and was dropping like a stone toward them. At the last possible instant he spread his wings, braked, and landed on the hinny's back. He did not look worried; he looked terrified.

"We're trapped," he informed them in a shaky voice, "doomed. This time there is no way out."

"Come now," Clothahump prompted him, unperturbed, "there is always a way out. We have proven that in the past, and we shall prove it as often as necessary in the future. What did you see?"

"F-fire," the owl stammered.

"Fine. Fire. From which direction is it advancing?"

"From everywhere, Master. From all directions."

Something wasn't kosher here, Jon-Tom told himself. Even if they were completely surrounded by a forest fire of as yet unknown dimensions, Sorbl ought not to be concerned for himself. Surely he could soar to safety.

"What was burning?" he asked the famulus. "The woods?"

"The woods, the ground, everything but the air itself," the owl told him. "The whole world is on fire."

"You are not making sense, apprentice," Clothahump snapped at him. "It is not the first time."

"Truly, Master, everything burns."

Jon-Tom was standing on tiptoes, turning a slow circle and scanning the various horizons. The air temperature continued to rise. But there was no smoke to be seen in any direction. Even if Sorbl was greatly exaggerating and only a small grove was ablaze, they should still be able to see some smoke.

And why should he exaggerate?

"Somebody's eyes are deceiving them," Dormas muttered. "How can the world burn without sending up smoke?"

"A perturbation." Clothahump was fumbling through the drawers in his plastron, searching for a particular vial. He was sure he'd stored it securely in the compartment closest to his left armpit—maybe down nearer knee level. "I suspect it approaches from the south. The all-encompassing perturbations usually begin quite far from the perambulator itself."

"So we're to be incinerated." Mudge sat down heavily. "A short reprieve, that."

"I can see it now." Jon-Tom pointed toward the southwest, and all eyes turned in that direction.

The flames came marching over the line of trees, engulfing everything in their path. The fire was like a moving wall. There were no gaps, no cool spaces where a desperate runner might slip through to freedom. Above the advancing wall the sky was alive with darting, dancing fireballs. They could hear the crackle and roar clearly, the rising susurration of a combustible choir. And still there was not a puff of smoke to be seen.

"Far out," Jon-Tom whispered. He was starting to sweat.

Now the conflagration was close enough for them to see that the rocks themselves were burning. Each bit of gravel, each smooth-shouldered boulder burst forth with orange-red streamers. Jon-Tom was dimly aware that behind them Clothahump was holding both hands in the air and reciting a rapid-fire sequence of ancient words.

Moving with preternatural speed, the flames swept down on them. The heat was intense but not volcanic. No one's clothes burst into flames on his body. No one collapsed from sucking in a single hot, suffocating breath. No natural blaze this, Jon-Tom told himself wonderingly. Sorbl was right about that.

Suddenly the onrushing wall of flame split as though cleft with an ax. It swung around them, consuming the land on either side. The air remained breathable. They were completely surrounded by a towering wall of fire.

"Great light show." Jon-Tom mopped at his face. The perspiration was pouring off him, but it was not intolerable. He tried to pretend he was lying on the beach at Redondo with the Santa Ana bringing in air from off the Mojave. "What do we do now?"

"To think that not long ago I was worried about getting too cold," Colin commented, displaying a fine sense of koalaish irony. He'd instinctively drawn his sword as the fire had approached, holding it tightly in both hands, the long claws interlocked to intensify his grip. But there was no enemy to stab at here, no flesh to cleave. He slipped the saber neatly into his back scabbard.

Dormas was more uneasy than any of the them, a characteristic of her kind. "We can't go forward and we can't go back. Wizard?"

"I have preserved us. That was all I had time to do," Clothahump told them. "We can do naught but wait for the perturbation to end and pray it is not a lengthy one. I should not like to have to chance changing it by force. Natural fires are difficult enough to spell, and this blaze is anything but natural. The problem is that it is exceedingly difficult to convince a flame to hold still for anything, much less a decombustion spell.''

"What happens when it ends?" Dormas wanted to know.

"Everything snaps back, as with any perturbation—unless the effect is permanent, as was the case with Ospenspri.''

"You mean, trees become trees again, rocks turn back to rock, and anyone caught in the blaze is restored to normal?''

Clothahump nodded. "There is no limit to the tricks a perambulator can play with the laws of nature. Do not attempt to apply logic to its actions; you will go mad. It must be defined and dealt with on its own terms.''

"Maybe you're not ready to deal with it, sir, but I can't take much more of this heat." Jon-Tom was already unslinging his duar. He eyed Colin. "You wanted proof that I was a spellsinger? You're going to get it.''

"But, my boy, the risk," Clothahump said earnestly. "One wrong word, one wrong note, and you could cancel out the protective spell I put in place around us. We could be swallowed up by this fiery perturbation of unknown duration, never to become ourselves again until it is too late.''

Jon-Tom nodded toward the sun. "The greater fire or the lesser, what's the difference? We might as well be swallowed up. We're not getting any nearer the perambulator by sitting here and sweating. He who hesitates is lost." He thumbed a few chords, the notes clearly audible above the rumble of the imprisoning flame.

" 'E who plays the wrong song is screwed," Mudge warned him.

"Work your magic if you can, man," said Colin. "I am not afraid.''

"That's because you 'aven't seen wot shit-for-brains 'ere can sing up," Mudge told him as he backed as far away from his tall friend as the fire would permit.

Jon-Tom considered. There were plenty of fire songs in his repertoire. Trouble was, most of them, such as the old "Fire—you're gonna burn" or "Come on baby, light my fire" were pro-conflagration rather than anti. It took him several minutes to recall the lyrics to a suitably dousing ditty. Then he began to sing and to play.

The sound of the duar had an immediate effect on the crackling, twisting ocean of heat surrounding them. Flames big and small shuddered and shrank in time to his beat. But when the song had done and he'd mouthed the final stanza, the fire was still there.

Closer than there, in fact, for part of the blaze appeared to jump toward him. He'd finally gone and done it, then. Not only had he failed to make the perturbation snap back to normal, he'd canceled Clothahump's protective spell exactly as the wizard had feared. He spread his arms and prepared himself as best as he could to accept the embrace of the flames.

The red-orange tongue of destruction halted a yard in front of him. "Don't be so melodramatic," it hissed.

"We only want you to join us," crackled another, moving in from the right.

Jon-Tom opened one eye, his arms still spread wide, and squinted at Clothahump. "This is part of the perturbation?"

"Most extraordinary." The wizard was studying the dancing flames. "It would appear that the fire has released the spirits of land and forest, of individual trees and stones. They have taken up residence in the blaze itself. Have a care, lest they induce you to join them. If they are attempting to convince you to do so voluntarily, it must mean that they cannot overcome us by force."

"Don't worry." A relieved Jon-Tom held his ground against the tempting flame and let his arms drop to his sides. "I don't even like to hold a match."

"Join us, join us! Come and play and burn. Cast off your

solid raiment and feel the pleasure of weightlessness! Run before the wind and devour the world anew! Don't try to beat the heat—join it!'' the blaze chorused.

"No, thanks," Jon-Tom told them firmly. "I never was big on conspicuous consumption.''

"Well, then, sing us another song. Another melody of searing affection, of rampant incineration and fickle combustibility.''

"And if I'm so inclined?'' He held his breath. So did his companions.

"Why, then, if you please us, we'll pass on by and not trouble you any more. Sing to us again and we will not disturb your rest, much less consume you.''

Jon-Tom thought of challenging them to do their worst, since it was Clothahump's opinion that the fire couldn't touch him without his willing acquiescence, but it seemed prudent not to force a confrontation with a forest fire of major and unnatural proportions. Easier to sing all the songs he'd thought of at first. If there was such a thing as an intelligent blaze, better to be on its good side, he told himself.

So he sang, smoothly and skillfully but without putting any more energy into it than was necessary in case they were trying to pull a fast one on him. He'd sung better but never hotter, leading off with Kiss's ''Heaven's on Fire'' and concluding with half the songs from Def Lepard's *Pyromaniac* album. The flames appeared to appreciate his efforts, jumping and prancing, throwing off bits and pieces of themselves into the sky.

By now the heat had become truly oppressive. He would have disrobed, save that he didn't dare take his hands off the duar or his eyes off the intelligent flames dancing before him. At the moment they were enjoying themselves, but he didn't doubt that their attitude could change quickly. And he was running out of stamina as well as songs.

"I'm getting tired," he told them. "Couldn't we take a break for a little while?''

"Oh, no, play on, burn on, dance on!" A thin tongue of flame reached out from the fiery wall and came within inches of caressing his right palm. It scorched the small hairs on the back of his hand. He jumped back a step and kept playing. Clearly Clothahump's spell was weakening. Their continued survival might depend on his continued singing.

He was beginning to despair and his throat was getting sore when the flames vanished. Instantly and without warning they were gone, down to the last smouldering ember. Trees were trees again, and the rocks no longer burned. Once more they found themselves standing amid the cool confines of the coniferous north woods.

"Sorbl, get up there and let us know if you can see any flames, anywhere at all."

Obediently the owl took wing. He did not stay up very long.

"Nothing, Master. The world is as it was before the fire. We have snapped back. Nothing burns, except—" He pointed in alarm to his left.

The duar was glowing. Jon-Tom did a hysterical little dance as he fought to disengage himself from the instrument and toss it to the ground. It lay there glowing white-hot but did not burst into flame. Everyone waited and watched until it had cooled off enough for its owner to pick it up again. The strings were still warm.

Jon-Tom inspected it thoroughly. "Looks okay."

"That's a sight," Mudge commented. "I know you can overheat an engine, an' a draft animal, an' a party or a lady, but I never saw anyone overheat an instrument before."

"Too much singing about fire and burning and flames." He caressed the precious instrument lovingly, then turned to face Clothahump. "Sir, you spoke of perturbations that might be aimed at us specifically. Do you think this was one of those?"

The wizard considered. "Difficult to say. I could not sense

any unusual malignity, but that is proof of nothing except how much age has affected my sensitivity. One thing is certain, though. Regardless of whether or not this was intended to stop us or was one more in the series of general perturbations, it was more serious than most. As the perambulator's frustration and agitation grows, its perturbations are likely to become more and more dangerous.

"From now on we must mount a night watch, lest some life-threatening perturbation catch us unawares in our sleep."

"I'll take the first watch tonight," Colin volunteered. "I like the night."

"I'll 'ave the second," said Mudge hurriedly. "I'd rather stand early than late."

Jon-Tom sighed. "I guess I'm stuck with the graveyard shift. Dormas, I'll wake you when my shift's done." She nodded agreeably.

It wasn't often that Sorbl had a chance to show off. This was one time when he did. "And I, naturally, shall stand watch last and longest. Being a Buboninae, I can tolerate the night better than any of you."

"Provided Dormas keeps a sharp eye on the liquor supply," Mudge murmured to Jon-Tom. "Wot about you, Your Brilliantship?"

Clothahump's manner was ever so condescending. "I am the most powerful wizard in the world, not to mention the brains of this little troop. I do not stand guard over myself."

"That's about wot I thought."

"Watch your tongue, water rat. If you would like to bid to take the leadership of our group, I will—"

"No, no, not me, Your Conjurerness." The otter was grinning. "Far be it from me to dispute the fairness o' your awesome decisions."

"When you're going on three hundred years old"—the wizard harrumphed—"you find you require the maximum amount of sleep."

The next morning dawned clear and cold. Colin yawned, stretched, and spoke to his companions, who were still wrapped in their blankets and bedrolls.

"I'll see to the fire."

"You couldn't make a fire if somebody doused you in oil and stuck a torch between your teeth!"

"What?" The koala rose quickly, turned a fast circle. The only other member of the party who was on his feet was Mudge. The otter was standing on the far side of the central campfire, surveying the forest.

Colin glowered at him. "I'll let that one pass. It's too early for this."

"Wot?" Mudge turned and eyed him curiously.

"Nothing." Colin bent over the pile of dead wood that remained from their scavenging of the previous night, began to stack several fragments in the center of the pile of gray ash.

Mudge shrugged. "Wot would you like to 'ave with your meal? Berries, perbits, nuts?"

"Doesn't matter" came the quick reply. "We have the biggest nut of all in camp already. Or maybe it's a fruit."

The otter whirled. "Now see 'ere, guv'nor, there's such a thing as stretchin' 'ospitality too far."

At first Colin didn't appear to hear him. Then he looked up to see Mudge staring at him, and his gaze narrowed dangerously. He paused in the middle of lighting the fire. "Are you talking to me, pilgrim?"

"Yeah, I'm talking to you, cookie-ears. Just what did you mean by that?"

"What did I mean by what?" Colin was as confused as he was upset.

Dormas lifted her head from beneath her blanket, sleepily peered out at the world. "If you two kids are going to argue, I'd appreciate it if you'd do it somewhere else. I'm still working on my beauty sleep."

"And everyone knows how badly you need it, too, nag-hag."

The hinny was instantly awake. She rolled over onto her knees and glared around the campsite. "Who said that? Where's the bastard who said that?"

Mudge and Colin were too busy trying to stare each other down to pay any attention to her. "If you don't find our company to your likin' anymore, mate," the otter growled, "we'll be 'appy to do without you."

"Actually I could do without your face. Also your neck, paws, and the rest of your degenerate body. In fact, the world could do without you altogether."

"Is that a fact?" The otter reached for his sword.

"Wait a minute." Colin's anger had given way to genuine puzzlement.

"That's all it'll take to teach you some manners, you—" But Colin cut him off.

"No, think a minute, pilgrim. I didn't say anything a moment ago."

"The pudgy one is correct." Both of them turned to see Clothahump standing and scanning the air around them. "Restrain your natural impulses, you two. There is mischief afoot this morning. Up, everyone, wake up!"

"Huh, wha—" Jon-Tom rolled out from beneath his blanket. "What's going on?"

"Get up, Jon-Tom."

Their confrontation already forgotten, Mudge and Colin were staring down at the spellsinger. "Is he always like this?" Colin inquired.

Mudge sighed. "I'm afraid so. 'E's good to 'ave around, as he showed durin' yesterday's 'ot spell, even if 'e is a bit of a prude an' lazy to boot. But 'e's a spellsinger o' the first water when 'e's on, which ain't always."

"I heard that, Mudge." Jon-Tom sat up and fought with his shirt. "Where do you get off calling anybody else lazy?"

"Silence, all of you," ordered Clothahump in a commanding voice. He turned away from them and strolled softly over to the small tree where a wary Sorbl still stood watch. "What have you seen approach the camp?"

"Nothing, Master. Nothing has come and gone, not so much as a lizard. But—I sense something. I did not think it worth waking anyone. It has been present only since sunrise."

Clothahump nodded approvingly. "Good. You are learning suspicion. All those lessons may not have been in vain. I sense it also."

Jon-Tom climbed to his feet, trying to clear his mind and his eyes, which were both still foggy with sleep. "Sense what? I don't see anything."

The wizard started back toward his sleeping basin, was brought up short by a challenging, sneering voice. "Where do you think you're going, you senile old fart? You think you're tough because of that shell. Well, it is hard, except for your head, which is soft like a ripe tomato."

"Who said that?" Jon-Tom looked at Mudge. Mudge looked cautiously at Colin, who returned the stare.

"You didn't insult my fire-making, did you?"

"Of course not, mate. I did nothin' o' the sort. An' you didn't snap at me when I were about to set out on the mornin's foragin'?"

"No. Why would I do that?"

Clothahump had proceeded on to the far side of the camp when the voice sounded again. "Can't even walk in a straight line anymore, can you? Advanced decrepitude's definitely set it. Wonder which'll go first? The brain or the body?"

The wizard took a couple of steps backward and the voice ceased. "It is a wall," he announced confidently. The others gaped at him.

"A wall?" Jon-Tom muttered. He looked in front of the wizard, saw nothing but clear air. "But everything's normal, everything and everybody are normal. The world's unaltered."

"It is definitely a designed perturbation," Clothahump

went on, "sent here to stop us. Truly the individual we seek is one of power and talent, though his thoughts are distorted and his methods unorthodox. We are in a cage."

"I don't see any bars, Master." Sorbl spread his wings and lifted off. He was ten feet off the ground when that by-now familiar voice boomed at him.

"Looks like a pie plate with wings."

"No," declared a second voice, at least as nasty as the first, "it's a flying feather duster."

Sorbl was brought up as short, as if he'd smacked into a glass ceiling. He barely had time to right himself as he tumbled groundward, landing hard on his left side. Pushing himself upright with a wing, he hopped onto his feet and studied the seemingly empty air overhead.

"I am sorry I doubted you, Master. It was just like hitting a roof."

"I still don't see any bars or anything," a thoroughly confused Jon-Tom muttered.

"This is not your ordinary sort of cage, my boy. I have seen cages fashioned of wood and cages made of steel. I have heard of cages built of clay and delicate cages woven of silk. I have even heard of cages built with the bodies of living creatures. But I have never heard of, read of, or expected to encounter a cage fashioned of gratuitous insults."

X

"Who said they're gratuitous?" chorused a cluster of voices around them. "Every one of 'em's well deserved."

"It will not work," Clothahump argued with the air. "You will never be able to hold us here, nor get us to fighting among ourselves. We are too intelligent and too diverse a group. Your best efforts have already failed." Mudge and Colin exchanged an embarrassed glance.

"Sinister, malign, and loquacious you may be," the wizard went on, "but you are also directed by an unbalanced personality and therefore can have no effect on those of us who are healthy."

"He calls us unbalanced," declared a voice. "Him, who's been senile for the past fifty years." This was followed by a roll of sardonic laughter. It faded away with frightening finality, like the door of a safe being slammed shut.

"This is ridiculous," Jon-Tom said. "There's nothing holding us here. All we have to do is walk away." He wasn't ready to grant that anything had actually stopped Sorbl. He started off to his left, striding deliberately toward the nearest trees.

"Think you're pretty smart, don't you, kid? You know nothing and understand everything. The turtle knows everything and understands nothing."

Jon-Tom bounced off *nothing*, as though he'd walked into a brick fireplace. *Nothing* was a good, solid, unyielding word. He reached out with both hands, found that the air in front of him had the consistency of transparent vinyl.

"Well, I'll be damned."

"I certainly hope so," said the voice, forcing him back a couple of steps.

"Words can be stronger barriers than metal," Clothahump told them all. "It has always been so, if not always recognized as such. This is one perturbation we cannot outwait. We must find a way to break through it. Insults can be as suffocating as any fire, for all that they smother the spirit instead of the body."

Jon-Tom grabbed up his cape and duar. "This is crazy, and we're getting out of here right now. Mudge and I have fought our way past djinn, monsters, swamps, evil magicians, and well-meaning muck, and I'm not going to let a few words stop me." He swung the duar around and began to sing.

But as soon as the music began, so did the voices. "A spellsinger, huh? You've got a lot to learn about music."

"Yeah. For openers, remarks aren't lyrics." Jon-Tom was knocked backward a step.

"He sings for the ages."

"Sure does," agreed another voice. "The ages between five and nine." Jon-Tom felt his fingers trembling. He began to miss notes.

"Obviously descended from a long line," said the first voice.

"Yep. A long line that his mother listened to."

Jon-Tom was forced to his knees, and the words caught in his throat.

"Actually," declared the first voice, "he hasn't any enemy in the world. And his friends don't like him, either."

At that point Jon-Tom gave up trying to play or sing. He swallowed hard, the insults catching in his throat, and rolled over onto his knees as he fought to catch his breath. It had been a long time since he'd faced magic as powerful and relentless as this, and never had he been confronted by anything quite as insidious. The strength of the perambulator, he knew. How could he counter it with simple songs, mere spellsinging? What could you sing to counter an insult?

Rock music was designed to make you feel good, to raise your spirits, not to knock down. But there was one kind of rock that was a reaction to that, just as it was a reaction against any kind of authority, against anything worthwhile. Knees shaky, fingers uncertain on the strings, he struggled to his feet. Yes, those were the only kind of lyrics that might have some effect on the cage of insults. He considered whom to begin with: Oxo, Sex Pistols, The Dead Kennedys, Black Flag, or some of the new groups. He began to feel some of his control returning along with his confidence.

You didn't need the haircut to sing punk.

Mudge put his paws to his ears, and Clothahump's expression reflected his thorough disgust with the lyrics Jon-Tom was singing. Excellent! It was proof that he was doing exactly what he intended to do. Like any good punk singer, he was doing his utmost to insult his audience.

"What do you think?" wondered the first voice. Jon-Tom tried not to rush his music. It seemed that the cage was tightening around them, restricting their range of movement even further. He staggered but didn't fall.

"Careful," said the other voice, "he might be dangerous after all."

"Not a chance. He's a sheep in sheep's clothing."

"He sings," rumbled the first voice, firing a serious salvo, "as if it were a painful duty."

Jon-Tom was forced backward. Delivered with precision and perfect timing, each insult struck him like a physical blow, as any good insult should. He felt like a boxer trying to go the full fifteen rounds, and his hands were tied to the duar. But he kept singing nonetheless. It was all he knew to do.

And still he was forced back. It wasn't that his punk anthems didn't possess an equal amount of vitriol, he thought, but the fact that they were blatant and straightforward that made them less effective. There was nothing subtle about them. He was a barbarian with a battle-ax, trying to fend off the attacks of half a dozen lightning-fast fencers. If he could just get in one solid blow with his music, one unparried stab, he felt certain it would shatter the verbal cage contracting around them.

But the insults continued to flow unabated, drawing their strength and power from some unseen well of acid, out-maneuvering him at every turn. A little jab here, a crude comment on his bodily functions there, a deprecatory nod in the direction of his ancestry slipping in to stick him from behind before his cruder counterjabs could have any effect.

"He is dull," claimed the first voice, "naturally dull, but it must have taken a great deal of work on his part for him to have become what we see now. Such excess is not in nature." Jon-Tom went to his knees.

"He's not all that bad," countered the second voice. "After all, he is capable of running the full gamut of musical emotion from A to B."

Now Jon-Tom was squirming helplessly on his back, still trying to play the duar, still trying to sing. He was finding it difficult to breathe.

Anxious faces peering down at him now; his friends, their concern reflected in their expressions.

"Take 'er easy now, mate." Mudge glanced up at

Clothahump. "You 'ave to do somethin', Your Wizardship. 'E's in a bad way."

"I have never encountered a distortion of reality of this nature before. It is difficult to know what to do or where to begin."

"Well, *I* know where to begin!" yelled Mudge, and he pulled the duar from Jon-Tom's weakened hands.

"Wait—no." Jon-Tom tried to sit up, failed. "You can't, Mudge! You don't know how to spellsing."

"Spellsingin' ain't wot's wanted 'ere," snapped the otter, "and neither is your bleedin' useless magic, Your Sorcererness." Mudge looked off-balance since the duar was nearly as tall as he was. Somehow he got it settled in front of him. He ran his fingers over the double set of strings, and notes, angry and atonal, floated out into the air.

"That's not music," said Dormas.

"Oh, yes, it is. 'Tis exactly the sort of music this monstrosity that's surroundin' us and tryin' to choke us off will appreciate."

"So he thinks he can sing," said the first voice as the contracting cage turned its attention away from Jon-Tom.

"Yes," said the second. "He doesn't realize that all he is doing is sitting in a sewer and getting ready to contribute to it."

"Is that a fact?" yelled the otter. "Well, 'ave a care an' listen to this, you invisible, impolite, perturbed arse'ole!"

The otter began to sing. The accompaniment the duar provided was nothing less than awful, but what mattered was not the ragged series of notes but rather the lyrics Mudge invented. For while Jon-Tom might be the spellsinger and Clothahump the wizard, when it came to concocting insults, Mudge had no equal in this world or in any other.

A kind of wave went through the atmosphere of the camp. A shudder, as though they had just passed through a cloud.

The oppression lifted from Jon-Tom, enabling him to sit up straight. The pain inside his skull began to fade.

The voices fought back furiously, though for the first time, Jon-Tom thought they sounded just the slightest bit hesitant.

"A foul mouth and getting fouler."

"The air around him is as he does."

"Is that the best you can do?" Mudge howled on, enjoying himself, letting his anger spill out of him. "An' you call yourselves insults? You wouldn't know shit if you were standin' in it!"

Jon-Tom found he could stand. He was wincing repeatedly, not from the insulting blows that had been rained on him previously but from the screeching, wailing sounds the abused duar was producing. Mudge might have fooled with a lyre or some other stringed instrument before, but the complexity of the duar was clearly beyond him. And yet the noise he was making, though bearing the same resemblance to music that a diamond does to a cowflop, seemed to be aiding instead of hindering his offensive efforts.

"Your master should 'ave great fortune," the otter sang. " 'E should become rich an' famous an' attractive, with all the world bowin' before 'im. An' 'e should learn at the same time that 'e 'as some 'orrible uncurable disease."

A blast of diseased wind rocked the camp, sending ashes flying from the fire. It was a last feeble attempt to whip them into submission, and it failed. Mudge was already beyond the original barrier, striding toward the trees as though stalking an unseen enemy. Which was exactly what he was doing.

"Go ahead, go ahead," squeaked the voice, desperately attempting to regain the offensive, "tell us everything you know. It won't take long."

Mudge sang back at it. "I'll tell you everythin' we both know—it won't take any longer!"

"If I had to listen to singing like yours much longer," moaned the remaining voice, "I'd poison you."

"If I 'ad to listen to *you* much longer," Mudge barked gleefully, "I'd take it!"

When the otter stopped strumming the duar, there was silence, save for the wind blowing through the trees. Nothing more, not a veiled comment, not a sound. The heavy, oppressive feeling that had crowded them into a smaller and smaller place was gone.

"Done already, you cowardly lot? You can dish it out, wot, but you can't take it. I'm just gettin' warmed up, I am." He plucked at the duar. "You think you've 'eard insults? You 'aven't 'eard any insults. I've got an insult for every day I've been alive and a few brought forward from prenatal eavesdroppin'."

"Mudge, it's over, you did it. You broke the cage and drove it off."

"Oh, right you are, lad." He handed over the duar. "I wanted to make sure. I did well, didn't I?"

Jon-Tom smiled down at his friend. "Mudge, it was positively inspiring."

"Aye." The otter drew himself up proudly. "Aye, it were, weren't it? A day to remember."

"And a lot of words to forget," said Clothahump. "It is wholly characteristic of this expedition that we should require rescue by a thersitical water rat. It is one more example of the unpredictability of the enemy we seek. We must be on guard for everything, including that which we cannot imagine. Had I more time, I would have managed to defeat this most recent adversary by more conventional and congenial means."

"Sure you would, Your Lordship," said Mudge. Jon-Tom hastened to step between them.

"I've listened to enough insults for one morning. Let's get our gear together and be on our way."

As they were packing to depart Jon-Tom strolled over to confront Mudge curiously. "Tell me something, Mudge. If what you'd sung, and I use the word hesitantly, hadn't done the trick, what else did you have in your repertoire? What's the worst insult you could have thrown against the cage?"

"Why, that's easy, mate."

Jon-Tom bent low. The otter cupped a paw to his lips and whispered in the man's ear. Jon-Tom listened intently, nodding from time to time, his expression twisting. Eventually the otter concluded his recitation and returned to his packing. As he did so there was a sudden rumble underfoot. Mudge jumped one way; Jon-Tom backpedaled and stumbled.

Fortunately the crevass, after splitting the earth between them for about a yard, ceased expanding. Man and otter crawled to the edge of the chasm and peered down into black depths that seemed to extend for miles. They could feel the heat rising from below, and the thick aroma of sulfur filled the air.

Mudge lifted his eyes to meet Jon-Tom's stare. "Crikey, mate, I 'ad no idea it were *that* insultin'." Rising, he retreated a couple of steps and, while Jon-Tom held his breath, sprinted forward and leapt across the bottomless gap. Mudge turned to look back at the rift he'd opened in the earth's crust.

"I don't understand, mate. I've mounted me share o' insults before and not one of 'em ever 'ad a result like this."

"The lingering power of the duar's music," Clothahump explained. "It will fade. You did well, though if any unusual ability might have been expected of you, the one you demonstrated was appropriate and unsurprising."

"Can't even give me a compliment when 'tis due, the old fart," Mudge grumbled. "I save 'is arse, save everyone's, and that's me reward. Well, 'e'll see. The next time trouble comes, you won't find old Mudge leapin' to the rescue. No, sir. Not by the thickness of a cat's whisker you won't.

"That's just Clothahump's way, Mudge." Jon-Tom tried to calm his friend. "You ought to know that by now."

"That's true, lad. That's 'is way—selfish, contemptuous, an' overbearin'. Me, I'm glad I'm no wizard if that's the personality that goes with it."

"Just don't utter any absolutes. We're not out of this yet, you know."

"Is that supposed to be a revelation, mate? I'm never out of it so long as I'm forced to 'ang around you and 'Is Snotness. Well"—he took a deep breath—"we 'andled 'is forest fire and we 'andled 'is farkin' insults. If that's the worst this 'ere madman can throw against us, we should 'ave a simple enough time of it settin' the perambulator free."

"I hope you're right, Mudge." Jon-Tom turned his gaze toward the northern mountains. "But we still have to worry about the perambulator itself. Somehow I have the feeling that everything we've experienced so far is just a foretaste of what it can do."

Sorbl had spotted a pass cutting through the first line of peaks, and they were climbing toward it. After weeks of marching through endless forest it was cheering to have a visible goal in sight. Having walked for more than a year, it was difficult to keep the excited Colin from sprinting out ahead of them.

"Slowly and carefully go," Clothahump warned him. "The nearer we get, the greater the danger. He knows now that we are coming for him. The cage of deadly insults he tried to trap us with is proof enough of that."

"I'm not afraid, Wise One. I don't care what form he takes or what obstacles he tries to put in our path. I've come long and far, and I can taste the moment when I put my sword through the throat of this crazed troublemaker. He's brought so much unpleasantness and discomfort upon the world."

"We are not yet certain our adversary is a 'he,' " Clothahump reminded the koala, "nor even if it inhabits a familiar form. There may be no throat to stick."

"You can bet I'll find an appropriate place to stick it, sorcerer." As he spoke, the turtle next to him was beginning to change. "Beware, friends! It's happening again!"

"The world looks the same," Sorbl argued.

"No, I can feel it coming too." Clothahump spread his arms wide. "Be at ease. No one panic. We have survived and overcome every perturbation to date, and we shall survive this one as well."

Had he known what was coming, it's doubtful the wizard would have voiced such confidence, for this was a perturbation so severe and unsettling, it seemed certain to drive them all mad before the world snapped back to reality again. All were affected. All save one.

Jon-Tom was not changed at all. Throughout the entire transformation he suffered nothing more than a momentary nausea. And while he could understand his companions' distress from a philosophical standpoint, it was hard for him to empathize with their metamorphosis.

"Oh, God," Dormas moaned, "this is too much! I—I don't think I can handle it."

"Easy, steady there." It was clear Clothahump himself, despite his brave and defiant words of a moment ago, was more than a little shaken by the change that overcame them. "I know it's bad, but we've come through worse."

"No, we haven't," cried Sorbl. "Master, this is terrible! I can't fly. I've lost my wings completely and I have *these* things instead."

Indeed there was something particularly heart-wrenching about an earthbound owl, though Sorbl was no more or less severely altered than any of the others.

"As 'eaven is me witness," Mudge was muttering disconsolately, "if I gets back me old self again, I'll never complain at wot fate 'as in store for me. I'm one with

Dormas on this, Your Sorcerership. I don't know 'ow long I can stand it.''

"We have no choice," Clothahump told them grimly. "We have to stand it—somehow." He stood there gritting his teeth, in itself a remarkable circumstance since turtles do not have teeth. But Clothahump had them now. So did Sorbl.

"Come on now." Jon-Tom tried his best to cheer them. "It's not all that bad. If you'll just try relaxing, you might find yourselves getting used to it."

"I'm gonna die for sure," Dormas moaned. Her toughness and resilience had deserted her in the face of this newest nightmare.

"Get used to this?" said Colin. "I'd sooner pluck out my eyes so I wouldn't have to look at myself."

"Yes, it's easy for you to stand there calmly and mouth platitudes," said a whimpering Sorbl. "You aren't suffering as we are suffering."

That much was true, Jon-Tom had to admit. Demonstrating an extraordinary and unprecedented selectivity, the perturbation had left him untouched, whereas his friends had been radically altered. Clothahump could now grit his teeth because for the first time in his life he had some. Sorbl was having to adjust to a body without wings. As for poor Dormas, she had to feel as if her whole skeleton had been wrenched sideways. It was a change they had been threatened with as children, and now they were experiencing it for real. Their worst nightmares had come true.

Each and every one of them had been turned into (it was almost too awful to say aloud) a human being.

There was Clothahump, holding his ground while furiously trying to recall some spell, any spell, that might restore them to their real selves. He had been transformed into a short old man with a long white beard, long hair, and a slightly smaller set of six-sided spectacles. He wore canvas pants and a tan safari jacket full of pockets. Only the eyes were the same, staring out from beneath a brow of hair instead of shell.

Next to him a strapping lady of fifty-five swayed awkwardly on her feet. She was six feet tall. Dormas hadn't been broken by her pack load because it, too, had been changed, shrunk down to a single backpack, which hung from shoulder straps. Her hair was short and black, and her handsome, if terrified, face was lined and deeply tanned.

Then there was a short, slim teenager whose eyes darted wildly in all directions. Once he turned and ran toward a nearby tree while flapping his arms, until he realized anew that he was incapable of flight. The look in his yellow eyes was piteous to behold. Colin tried to comfort the distraught Sorbl. The koala's attire was little changed from what he'd been wearing before the perturbation had struck. Black leather and metal studs, though altered to fit the body of a fullback. He stood five-nine and must have weighed a good two hundred and twenty pounds, Jon-Tom guessed, and all of it muscle. A perfect human analog of the little koala. He also had the face of a movie villain and eyes that glittered. It would have been an entirely intimidating personage if not for the retention, albeit furless, of grossly oversize ears.

And then there was Mudge. A man in his mid-thirties, thin and wiry. He wore his green cap and carried sword and longbow, both lengthened to fit his human form. Very impressive in his transformation, except for the fear in his face and the disgust in his voice.

"This is bloody awful, just bloody awful." He held out both arms and had to fight to keep from shaking uncontrollably. "Look at this sickening, naked flesh. Not a 'int o' fur anywheres." He twisted around to look behind him. "An' no proper tail, either. Nothin'. A void where an expression ought to be." He gazed pleadingly at Clothahump. "Tell us this ain't goin' to last much longer, sir."

"You are no more anxious for a return to normalcy than I,

water rat. If you feel naked and unprotected, consider for a moment the emotions I am experiencing.''

"It's indecent," Colin insisted. "Damn indecent. Enough to make a strong koala cry."

"We've got to do something," Dormas insisted. Her voice was clear, the phrasing elegant and little changed from her normal tone. "If I have to stay like this much longer, I'll go crackers. I keep wanting to sit down on all fours as is right and proper, and this body doesn't work like that. Look at these useless little things." She displayed first her right arm, then the left. "Put the slightest upper body pressure on them and they'll break, I know they will. The rest of you can go on about losing a little fur, but what about me? I can't even walk properly."

"What about me, what about these?" The teenager shook his arms at her. "Bats are naked, too, but at least they can fly. I'm grounded." He started to sob.

"Take it easy," Jon-Tom urged them. "We'll be changing back soon."

"Aye, an' wot if we don't?" Jon-Tom had to admit it was unsettling to find himself standing eye to eye with a swarthy older man and hear Mudge's familiar voice issuing from his throat. It was nothing but a man standing before him. There wasn't a hint of whisker or fur about the man's face, and yet he knew it was Mudge. In addition to that unmistakable voice, there were the eyes, blue and challenging. It was fascinating to watch him move. There were all of Mudge's little gestures and affectations, being played back at three-quarter speed.

"We can't stay like this much longer, mate. An intelligent mind can take only so much."

"I am trying," Clothahump said earnestly. "I have been trying for the past several minutes, but it is difficult to design the parameters of a spell with all of you moaning and blabbering at once."

"It doesn't bother me." Jon-Tom plucked idly, thoughtfully, at his duar.

Mudge hastened to put a restraining hand on his friend's wrist. "Be careful, lad. Don't screw this one up. Make this perturbation's effects permanent and you'll 'ave at least one death on your 'ands, because I'll surely kill meself if I'm forced to occupy this obscene guise forever."

"Don't worry, Mudge. Hey, I'm hot. Remember how I handled the fire?"

"Aye, and almost got yourself cooked in the bargain. Mess this spellsong up and I'll barbecue you meself." He removed his hand. "Bugger me though if I ain't curious to see wot sort o' song you can come up with to counter a catastrophe like this."

"Go ahead, my boy," Clothahump urged him. "You might as well make the attempt. I am as uncomfortable with the present circumstances as anyone else. With my thoughts as unsettled as they are, it is difficult to think clearly."

"I'll take care with the lyrics," he assured the wizard. So he would—if he could think of some. Mudge had a point. Their present situation was not one your average performer would think about when sitting down to compose a song.

Something he'd picked up while poking around the Department of Ethnic Music might work, but he'd taken that course years ago and didn't exactly practice African chants or Indonesian gamelan tunes daily. That wasn't the kind of music likely to put him on Billboard's Top 100. His rock repertoire was considerably more extensive and up-to-date, but for the life of him he couldn't recall anything that related even vaguely to changing humans into animals. Not that the lyrics had to be that precise. As he'd learned, it was the feel of the song, the driving emotion behind it that mattered most of all when one was spellsinging.

There was one song that might accomplish what the perambulator had already done. Suppose he sung the lyrics backward? Crazy—but no crazier than their present predicament. He knew the song well enough, cleared his throat, and began to play.

It didn't sound right, but neither was his friends' situation. Perhaps that was appropriate. Certainly something was, for as he passed the halfway point, there was a shudder in the air, that familiar queasiness in his belly, and a sudden haziness before his eyes, like waking up slowly on a Sunday morning. He kept singing, wanting to finish the song, and when he concluded with the opening stanza and emerged from that wonderful performer's trance, he saw with relief that it had worked exactly as he'd hoped. The perturbation had been reversed and everything had snapped back to normal. His friends were his friends once more.

"Me! I'm me again!" Mudge yelped as he jumped two feet into the air. He ran his fingers through his thick brown fur. "I'll never knock bein' meself ever again." He was prancing around like the kid who'd just discovered he'd won the special dessert at the school picnic.

Dormas had been restored to her powerful, four-legged form. "Disgusting experience. What did you sing, young one?"

"Rick Springfield song—'We All Need the Human Touch' —only I sang it backward. Worked as well as I could've hoped." He beamed at his restored companions.

Clothahump had his shell back. Sorbl was already in the air, driving through dives and barrel rolls. Colin flexed his short, muscular arms, wiggled his oversize ears, and rubbed his damp black nose.

"Much better, Spellsinger." He frowned at Jon-Tom. "Uh-oh. My friends, we've got ourselves another problem. I guess we ought to have expected it."

"Damn," said Mudge, staring in the same direction as the koala, "do you think we'll ever be free o' this thing's insidious effects, Your Wizardness?"

Clothahump, too, was gazing with interest at the center of attention. "Not until we find it and free it from its prison."

Jon-Tom tried to turn and look in the same direction as his friends, until it occurred to him that they were not staring past him but at him. At the same time he became aware that something was still not quite right. He swallowed. His spellsong had done everything he'd asked of it—and more.

Mudge studied him critically, lips pursed, hands on furry hips. "Well, Your Lordship, wot are we goin' to do about this?"

Standing there before them and looking very forlorn indeed was a tall, very slim howler monkey. It wore Jon-Tom's indigo shirt and lizardskin cape and boots, and it held tightly to the duar. Looking down at himself, Jon-Tom took note of his long arms and curving, prehensile tail. He flexed his mouth, feeling the thick curving lips and the sharp canines inside.

"That were some spellsong, mate," the otter told him sympathetically.

"Personally I think he looks better this way," said Colin. He stepped forward and drew his sword.

Jon-Tom retreated a step. "Hey, I can't look that bad, can I?"

"You deserve to see yourself as your friends see you." The koala held the highly polished blade upright.

Jon-Tom gazed into the narrow mirror thus presented for his use. His jaw dropped when he got a glimpse of himself. It dropped quite a ways, in fact, much farther than any human jaw could have fallen.

"Oh, my God. What have I done?"

"Right by us," Mudge said, "but maybe not so good by yourself."

Jon-Tom continued to stare at the reflection in the flat of Colin's sword. He'd gone and done it for sure this time. Until now the only one who'd ever been able to make a monkey out of him had been an attractive senior in his morning class on torts. She'd stood him up twice on successive weekends. Now he'd managed to better her efforts, physically as well as mentally.

"I've got to try to sing myself back."

"Wait a minim, mate. You can't use that same song again or you're liable to put the rest of us right back to where we were before."

"But that's the only appropriate song I know."

"Then you will have to try something else, my boy," Clothahump told him. "My powers are useless in this matter. I cannot help you. Only you can help you. But you must figure out a way to help yourself without harming us. That is only right."

"I know, but I've used so many songs. I'm tired, and I'm sick of these damn changes. I don't know what else to sing."

"You'll find somethin', mate." Mudge tried to encourage his friend. "You always do. Just try singin', maybe, and you'll likely 'it on the right tune."

"I don't know. It seems awfully haphazard."

But he didn't know what else to do. He didn't want to change his friends back into their unbearable human shapes any more than he wanted to remain a skinny simian with his knuckles dragging on the ground. There seemed no way out. Maybe Mudge was right. Maybe he should just sing whatever came to mind, whatever pleased him the most. He never felt more whole, more complete, than when he was singing. Maybe that was all it would take.

It was so damned unfair, though. Really, he was nothing but an ordinary and not too bright law student and would-be rock musician misplaced in time and space, and here these people kept expecting him to perform miracles. Which he'd done, time and time again, to help out this one or the other.

Now, when he was the one in need of assistance, what did they suggest? That he help himself. They couldn't do a damn thing for him. All right, then, he could damn well help himself, and to blazes with this whole unsettled, unnatural world!

He swung the duar around across his chest, clutching it to him with those impossibly long arms. His attenuated fingers easily spanned both sets of strings as he began to sing. So involved was he in his own pique, so mesmerized by his honest fury that he forgot just what he'd turned into.

There is nothing in the animal kingdom that has the proportionate lung power of a howler monkey. It has a voice that carries for miles, over mountains and across dense forest. Backed by the duar and combined with the anger Jon-Tom was feeling, the resultant explosion of sound was magnified and sharpened by the magic of his spellsinging.

So what emerged from his throat was not a passionate plea for restoration so much as it was a primal concussion, a sound so raw and powerful that Mudge and Clothahump, who happened to be standing in the line of lyrical fire, were blown off their feet. The wizard retreated into his shell. Dormas was knocked to her knees. Sorbl instinctively took to the air, only to find himself fighting for balance in the grasp of the small hurricane Jon-Tom was producing. It blew him up over the trees and out of sight down the far side of the hill.

None of this made any impression on Jon-Tom. As far as he was concerned, he was singing normally, generating the same volume as usual, because that was how his howler voice sounded to his howler ears. And as always, when concentrating on his spellsinging with particular intensity, he sang with his eyes closed. Mudge tried to let him know what was going on by shouting at him, but the otter couldn't make himself heard over the storm.

Dormas turned her back on the raging music while Colin and Mudge dug their claws into the ground and hung on for dear life. Sorbl sensibly stayed out of sight behind the hill while Clothahump remained bottle-up like a barrel. At least two landslides roared down the slope ahead of them, and one especially heartfelt refrain flattened a stand of trees for four hundred yards in a straight line in front of Jon-Tom's lips.

Finally there was nothing more to sing, no more musical pleading to do. Jon-Tom's throat was sore from the effort he'd put into his performance. Wiping dirt and leaves from their faces and clothes, Colin and Mudge slowly got to their feet. Sorbl peeped hesitantly through the trees while Clothahump stuck his head out of his shell.

Jon-Tom was himself again, and so were they. He looked a bit bewildered as he peered past his friends. "When did the wind come up?"

"When you opened your mouth, lad." Mudge clapped him on the shoulder, having to stand on tiptoes to do so. "The particular kind o' ape you were for a while there 'ad a voice that would've put a small volcano to shame. I should o' thought o' wot that might do when matched with your spellsingin' ability. When I did, it were too late. All the rest o' us could do was 'ang on an' 'ope you wouldn't sing us 'alfway back to Ospenspri. I think 'tis a mite safer 'avin' you just as you are, defurred an' 'uman 'an all."

Clothahump was trying to shake the dust out of his shell. "There can be such a thing as too much useful magic." He gazed past his companions, toward the pass that was their immediate destination. "One thing more we can be certain of. There can no longer be any doubt that our quarry is aware we are coming. All of the north woods must have heard that noise." The dust from the landslides was still settling on the flanks of the pass up ahead.

Jon-Tom was enjoying being himself once again. He looked down at his tanned bare arms and naked fingers, at the short, unfunctional nails. Turning them over, he inspected the pale, furless palms that had been callused by the time he'd spent in this world. Yes, he was glad to be human again.

And yet he couldn't help but wonder at the musical worlds

he might have conquered had he been able to change back while still retaining that incredible simian voice. He could have outsung an amplified choir. Then again, a voice that stimulated landslides instead of an audience might not be such a good idea. With such a voice, the old show business adage about bringing the house down might acquire a new and lethal meaning.

XI

Colin had to force himself to slow down. Excitement kept pushing him out ahead of the others. It was just that after more than a year of wandering, he was now close to his goal.

The character of the forest was changing, for which he was grateful. He was sick of evergreens and longed for the sweet, deciduous woods of home. The trees looming up just ahead were almost familiar. Instead of being thick and deeply scarred, their bark was thin and pale gray in color. Long strips of it peeled off the trunk and collected around the base of the tree. They had leaves, too, instead of the ubiquitous needles. Long, thin leaves shaded a pale green. The grove ahead even smelled different.

Then his eyes grew very wide. It *couldn't* be. It was impossible for such trees to live this far north. Yet there they stood, straight and beckoning. Their delicious, distinctive aroma could not be faked.

Aware that he'd moved out in front again, he shrugged off his knapsack and let it tumble indifferently to the ground. His companions would catch up to him soon enough, he knew. He added his saber and scabbard to the pile. Then he rushed forward as fast as his bandy legs would carry him.

Soon he was standing next to the nearest of the trees, caressing the trunk, the long strips of peeled bark splintering beneath his feet. Using his claws, he shimmied rapidly up the trunk, then walked out onto the lowest branch capable of supporting his weight. His hand was shaking as he pulled free a handful of the distinctive, narrow leaves and shoved them raw into his mouth.

As he chewed, a subtle sensation of heavenly peace and well-being began to spread through his body. His eyes shut halfway as he devoured the superlative mouthful, but he could still see the ranks of trees climbing the southern hillside, ranging far up toward the peaks themselves.

For a koala a single grove of such tall wonders was all anyone could hope to own in a lifetime. Here was an entire forest growing wild on unclaimed land. Paradise, and a fortune for the claiming. He plucked another handful, being more selective this time, extracting the dead or blighted leaves before stuffing the rest into his mouth. Crossing his legs, he sat down on the branch, put his hands behind his head, and leaned back against the trunk as he chewed while staring up at the blue, blue sky.

His dried-and-cubed eucalyptus had run out months ago. Since then he'd been forced to eat whatever greenery he'd been able to scrounge from the woods. His stomach had been constantly upset, and eating became a chore instead of a pleasure. Beans, nuts, and pine needles were little better than garbage.

And now he sat on a branch of the True Tree, nibbling its bounty and reminiscing. And planning. For all he had to do was package this produce and ship it back home. Within a year he'd be independently wealthy. A third handful of leaves followed close on the stems of the first two. For the first time in months he was able to relax.

The sweeping panorama of endless, rolling meadow struck Dormas like a solid blow as they turned a bend in the trail. There had been no warning. They had been marching through tall pine forest, tramping around bushes, and shoving aside low-hanging branches, only to emerge unexpectedly onto the open grassland.

No normal meadow this. You could tell that right away. There were no trees enclosing it, none at all, and in consequence it stretched endlessly in all directions, conceding not even the horizon to the lowering sky. More incredible still, it was composed not of sedge and other grasses but of multiple varieties of clover. There was red clover and blue-green, dandelion clover and seven-sided shaboum, which has a nutty taste when chewed slowly. The air was thick with green sweetness.

Most unbelievably of all, the consistency and height of the clover hinted that this was that rarest of all grasslands, a virgin meadow. No teeth had cropped at that rain-cleansed greenness. It was such a meadow as browsers and grazers only dream of.

She broke into a gallop, not slowing even when she plunged into the fragile growth itself. It parted around her like a green sea around the prow of a ship until she slowed, panting, and finally bent to use her teeth on the rich reward. The first taste was indescribably pure.

Here was a playground unthought of since colthood, a place to rest and regain the strength lost during the long journey from Ospenspri. She lay down in the clover, rolling and kicking her legs, drunk with the very smell of it. Every taste was cool-fresh, as though each blade had just been kissed by the first morning's dew. The occasional pungent clover flower only added spice to each exquisite mouthful.

The blossoms crushed underneath gave up their spring perfume to the air. Such a place could not be real, could not exist.

But it did, and she had it all to herself, a reward for a lifetime of hard work and ennobling sacrifice.

Flying scout duty, Sorbl couldn't quite believe what he was seeing. Below, the trees gave way suddenly to a wide expanse of golden-hued liquid. The lake lay just beyond the pass his poor land-bound companions were struggling through, nestled in the valley beyond.

At the far end it was a deep azure blue. But the southern third was no more than a foot deep, clear as glass above a bottom of smooth pebbles and pristine river sand. Swarming in incredible numbers above the gravel were more fish than he'd ever seen in one place in his life. The schools fought for swimming space, so thickly were they compacted. He picked out salmon and trout, bass and blue gill, their scales shining like metal in the midmorning sun.

There was no work involved, no strain. Precision was not required. You didn't even have to take aim as you folded your wings and plummeted toward the water. All you had to do was open your talons and touch down to be certain of coming away with a fresh meal of white meat.

Nor was that the only surprise the lake held. It puzzled him at first, then confused him, and when he hit the water and snatched his first fish, it astonished him.

The water splashed over him as he swept up the golden trout in his claws. It washed down over his face and feathers. That was when he knew it to be true. It explained the lake's golden hue.

Putting the trout aside for later eating, he hopped down to the water's edge. A single sip provided confirmation enough. Fields of wild grain lined the lakeshore. Some inexplicable fermenting process had transformed centuries of grain growth, and the result had been leaching into the lake waters ever since. How the fish could not only survive but thrive in the result he didn't know, but who was he to question such a wonder?

For the undeniable fact remained that the water was at least eighty-proof, and stronger in the shallows. Furthermore, different parts of the lake had different flavors, no doubt reflective of the particular grains growing along each section of shoreline. It was just like the master's cleansing rainstorm over Ospenspri, only here one didn't have to catch drops in one's open beak. Here one could sample and sip at leisure.

He drank until he thought he would burst, then returned to his fish. Settling down on his tail, he hefted the trout in both wingtips and began gnawing away. Time enough later for cooking, if he felt like some variety. The raw flesh was delicious, firm, and undiseased.

Why spend years of drudgery as a wizard's famulus when a fortune was staring him in the face? He would resign his service with Clothahump, fly back to Lynchbany or Ospenspri, and strike a deal with some major local brewer to bottle the lake and sell it all across the warmlands. As the discoverer, all he had to do was file a land claim with the nearest city recorder. He and his partners could supply every pub in the Bellwoods. He all but laughed himself silly as he thought of the anxiety and frustration that would infect the various municipal revenue agents as they wore themselves to a frazzle in a futile search to locate his hidden "distillery" so they could slap taxes on his produce.

And when he'd grown rich enough, he mused, he would hire Clothahump to work for *him*.

There was no way of telling how long the Library had been hidden from view, but it had obviously lain unvisited for a long time. Vines and creepers threaded their way over and through the ancient stone walls. Trees sent their roots through

the foundation stones, and their spreading canopies concealed
the building from above. It would have continued unnoticed
had not Clothahump chosen just the right moment to look up
to his left. He'd caught a glimpse of sunlight bouncing off
neatly trimmed gray stone.

Frowning, he turned and waddled toward it. He recognized
neither what remained of the architectural style nor the
designs carved over the still-intact door. The nature of the
structure remained a mystery until he managed to force his
way inside. Fortunately the aged doors were rotten.

The sight thus revealed took his breath away. A Library it
was, with row on row of shelves filled to the top with scrolls
and books and all kinds of unfamiliar records. There were
sheets and small round disks of plastic, each in its own
protective sleeve; knotted ropes; and inscribed stone tablets.
The more fragile materials had been preserved through the
extensive use of superlative preservatives.

What people had raised this Library and set it here alone
and by itself to be found by some fortunate passerby he could
not tell, but it was clear that they had built for the ages. He
wandered dazedly down one aisle after another, numbed by
the sight of so much knowledge. Unbroken cases of thick
glass lined the center of the floor, displaying beneath their
transparent curves tomes as ancient as time. Some of the
shelving was three stories high. Three separate mezzanines
wound their way completely around the interior of the building. Each was backed by iron railings worked in the form of
hieroglyphic writing. The building itself was so long, he
could not see to the far end.

How much knowledge was stored in this place? he wondered. How many secrets of the eons? Impossible to estimate,
foolish to guess. It would take years simply to count and
catalog the millions of volumes within. Where even to begin?

An index of some kind, perhaps set alongside a great
dictionary of languages and scripts. There must be something

like that here, he thought excitedly. He headed toward the first of the glass cases, trembling with anticipation. All he had to do was locate the Library catalog. Within its depths would lie the answers to all the questions he'd spent nearly three hundred years pondering. The mysteries of the universe waited patiently on the shelves surrounding him, waiting only for him to look them up.

Another lifetime's work lay spread out before him. The books and records had been awaiting his arrival for millennia. If he was fortunate he would be granted enough time to peruse a small part of the Library. It was a daunting prospect but one bursting with promise and excitement. He knew only that there was work to be done, and he fell to it with a will.

They'd gone and oversold the Coliseum, Jon-Tom mused as he strode out onto the stage to join his band. As he made his entrance a thunderous roar rose from the unseen crowd, from the milling mass out there beyond the footlights. The roar rose and fell, swollen by the hysteria barely kept in check out on the floor. It went on and on before changing into a deafening chant as thousands of fans began clapping in unison.

"J-T-M, J-T-M, J-T-M!" Jon-Tom's initials and those of his band. He let them scream themselves out, teasing them, in no hurry to begin, waiting for them to cool down enough to hear. Offstage right their manager grinned broadly and made a circle with his thumb and forefinger. Jon-Tom returned the smile indulgently.

This was the last performance of their year-and-a-half-long world tour, the last of eight consecutive sellout nights at the Forum in Los Angeles. Bobby, his drummer, eyed him with concern, and Jon-Tom gave him a single reassuring nod. The drummer could only shake his head in amazement. Friends, critics, and fans alike wondered where J. T. got his stamina from, just as they wondered at his ability to do the same songs over and over, night after night, without displaying any signs of boredom or burnout. The whole music industry stood in awe of him.

And really, the secret of his enthusiasm was plain for anyone to see. He no longer sang for the money. He had plenty of money. Nor for fame, for he was a famous as any performer could be. No, he kept singing because of the fans, the fans who had supported him and made him what he was today. Tonight was special, and not just because it was the final night of the tour. It was special because of the fans.

The Grammy awards had been handed out two weeks ago, and he'd won more individual awards than any other performer in history. The fans had done that for him. Now there was talk, nothing more than vague rumors, of course, that because of the penetrating and powerful social commentary contained in his lyrics, the Nobel committee in Stockholm was giving serious consideration to awarding him a special prize. It would be the first time a popular composer and performer had been so honored. The Pulitzer for music, he had been assured, was already in the bag. And, of course, the minority party was asking him, or rather pleading with him, to put his career aside long enough to run for the vacant junior senatorial seat from the state of California.

Yes, it might have seemed like enough to overwhelm any one man, but not Jonathan Thomas Meriweather. He handled success and adulation with the same ease as he handled his favorite guitar. Though he basked in his fame, he was still just the same regular guy as always, he'd explained to the hordes of eager reporters who kept pestering him for quotable quotes.

Ah, well, he supposed, he'd tantalized them long enough. He adjusted the Fender's strap, nodded toward his sidemen, and waited while Bobby started to work the crowd up all over again with his drums. A vast wave of adoration rolled forth from the audience to sweep over the stage in a great roar.

Yes, everything was going about as well as mortal man could expect, he told himself. He'd accomplished everything on this tour he could have hoped to do. No one knew yet, but tonight would be his last live performance. He was going to accept the offer to run for the vacant senatorial seat.

But something was not quite right. The strings of his guitar felt thin beneath his fingers. They seemed to stick, and there were more of them than there should have been. They ran the wrong way too. It didn't seem to bother the crowd, which continued bellowing and screaming louder than ever, but it unnerved Jon-Tom. He turned his back on them, letting Bobby and Julio carry the opening overture while he fought to sort himself out. Wrong, wrong, there was definitely something wrong!

As he turned away from the crowd the shouts of jubilation faded away, taking the people with them. The cavernous walls of the Forum disappeared and with it the overweening feeling of contentment.

It was the noise that drew Mudge to the cave, the laughing and sounds of carousing, along with the faint odor of liquor and pungent dope sticks. He knew that he should tell his companions, but surely he could check out this one anomaly by himself. Besides, he'd left them far behind, chattering mindlessly among themselves.

There was no one posted on watch at the entrance to the burrow. If he couldn't slip in, have a look-see around, and slip out again without being detected, of what use was he?

The tunnel was brightly illuminated by sweet-smelling torches instead of expensive spell-maintained glow bulbs. That suited him fine. He'd had enough of spelling and magicks. It led in and down before leveling off. The dirt floor gave way to smooth stone. A vein of malachite running through the pavement had been polished to a brilliant shine, the green-and-black waves undulating through the marble. He followed it toward the noise and smells.

A hundred yards on and the tunnel opened up onto a scene of sybaritic splendor. Ahead lay a chamber of epicurean delights. From the roof hung a massive chandelier ablaze with a thousand candles, each one fashioned of perfumed wax. He did not stop to consider how so enormous a fixture might have been brought into this place. He was too busy staring at the orchestra. It consisted of scantily clad females, each of whom was not only playing her instrument with consummate skill but clearing enjoying a personal and intimate relationship with it.

In fact, there wasn't a male in the entire assembly. There were females of many species, but the majority were otters: sleek and smooth of fur, long of whisker, and sharp of tooth. Thirty of them were dancing to the wild music of the orchestra, spinning and swirling like dervishes. He observed them transfixed, frozen to the spot. Faced with such an unexpected and astonishing abundance of feminine pulchritude, what else could he do?

Not stand there forever, however much he might want to preserve the moment. He had not come alone. With great reluctance he turned to race back out the tunnel to inform his friends of what he'd discovered when a sharp, startled scream split the air. The music ceased. The dancing halted. So did Mudge. Every one of those shining, voluptuous beauties was staring straight at him.

"Look," exclaimed one of the otterish houris into the lingering silence, "a *male*!"

Shrieks and giggles filled the chamber as they charged toward him.

"Now, lassies," he said uneasily, putting up both hands and assuming a defensive posture. "Let's not do anything drastic until we talk this over."

They swarmed over him, their perfume overpowering, each

fighting for the chance to touch and caress, to kiss and nip. Not struggling as hard as he might have, he found himself half pushed, half pulled into the chamber. The music resumed, freer and more undisciplined than before. They were inviting him to join them, he knew, in their celebration. To revel as he'd never reveled before. His friends were waiting, true but—they could wait. And if they couldn't, well, they'd just have to get along without good old Mudge.

He succumbed fully to euphoria.

Jon-Tom blinked, wiped at his eyes. He was gripping the duar so hard, his fingers hurt. Had he snapped out of it automatically or had he been fortunate enough to play a perturbation-canceling melody while still unconscious?

What had happened to the Forum, to the screaming crowd? Where there had been fans wild with delirium, fighting and reaching just to touch his boots, applauding and cheering every word that fell from his lips, now there was only rank upon rank of tall pine trees, of firs and spruces and an occasional young redwood. And their silence was deafening.

His companions surrounded him, but when he called out to them, they did not reply. They did not even seem to see him.

Colin sat up in a pine tree, munching away on pine needles and wearing the look of the exorbitantly stoned. Clothahump squatted beneath him, sheltered by two large roots. He was turning a flat rock over and over in his hands, a rapturous expression on his face. A sound made him turn to his left.

Dormas was rolling around in the dirt, her expression almost as beatific as Colin's. She had dumped her pack, and their supplies lay scattered all over the ground. Sorbl lay close by, facedown in a muddy puddle of rainwater. He was blowing bubbles and making swimming motions with his wings. He was further gone than any of them. And Mudge— Jon-Tom searched the clearing anxiously. Where was Mudge?

A noise that was part growl and part moan came from off

to his right. Holding his forehead (he had one hell of a headache), Jon-Tom stumbled off in that direction, trying to follow the sounds to their source.

They led him to a fallen log that the otter was embracing tightly, his face wreathed in a smile of languorous ecstasy. As soon as he saw what the otter was doing, Jon-Tom swallowed hard and turned away. During their travels Mudge had done absurd things, impractical things, even moderately disgusting things, but this—he tried to shut out the image that lingered in his mind as he considered what to do next.

Clothahump was the only one who looked half like himself. Jon-Tom walked up to the wizard and put a hand on his arm. He shook it hard.

"Wake up, sir! I don't know where you are now, but you aren't where you're at. Please, Clothahump, answer me."

The wizard ignored him. Trying to remember exactly how he'd returned to reality, Jon-Tom tried to reposition his fingers the same way on the duar. Taking a deep breath, he strummed a few chords without having the slightest idea what he might be playing.

It didn't sound very pleasant, but maybe that was part of it. The wizard blinked, much as Jon-Tom had blinked. A startled expression came over his face.

"What, who's that, what?" He finally focused on Jon-Tom, who was standing over him looking concerned. "Oh, it's you, my boy. What is it?"

"Clothahump, where are you? Right now, this instant?"

"Now? Why, I am in the Library, of course! The great Library. What a wonder it is! I am so glad you have found it, too, my boy. I shall require all the help I can get in the many years ahead." He displayed the weathered hunk of shale he was holding. "See, I have found the key already. Here is the first page of the index, clearly defined for any who cares to look, and easy even for the uninitiated to read." He started to wave it toward something in front of him. He paused halfway through the wave, staring straight ahead as if paralyzed.

"Clothahump? Sir, are you all right?"

Another moment of silence, followed by a whisper of resignation. "There is no Library here, is there?"

"No, sir." The wizard's expression was pitiful to behold. "I'm sorry, sir. It was an illusion. I experienced one myself. I still don't know if I came out of it because it had run its course or because I happened to hit the right notes on the duar."

"Not an illusion, my boy." The turtle swallowed hard. "A perturbation. Another cursed, damnable, cheating perturbation. You didn't see it, then? The Library?"

"No, sir. My illusion was different. I was standing on a stage, performing, at the summit of my profession. A beautiful dream. The fulfillment of all my most heartfelt desires. I had everything I'd ever wanted."

"And I as well. This time the perturbation drew on our innermost selves for its trickery." He looked down at the piece of shale, then irritably tossed it aside. "We are all fools."

"No, sir. Being fooled doesn't make us fools. The perambulator affects geniuses as well as idiots."

Clothahump smiled up at him. "You are trying to make me feel better, my boy. It isn't working, but it is appreciated. Give me a hand up." Jon-Tom did so. Then the wizard gave vent to as great a display of frustration as Jon-Tom had ever seen. Clothahump often grew incensed at others. Sorbl in particular. But never at himself. So Jon-Tom understood the depth of the wizard's disappointment when he kicked the shale hard, sending it bouncing down the trail.

"I feel better for that. My foot does not, but the rest of me does. I was in a Library, my boy. Such a library as has never existed. It contained within its shelves all the knowledge of everything that is, ever was, and ever would be. A Library of the past, the present, and the future. All the answers were contained within its walls. That's what I've dreamed about,

what I've wanted all my life, my boy. A little wisdom and a
few answers. It is not nice to be cheated by a phenomenon of
un-nature." He sighed deeply. "What of the others?"

Jon-Tom gestured to his left, then up toward Colin's
branch. "As you can see, sir, they're still all suffering from
their individual perturbations. Their respective illusions must
have a stronger hold on them than yours or mine did on us."

"Do not flatter yourself that your will or knowledge of
reality is any stronger. You needed the music to bring me
back to myself. I suspect you needed it to shock you back as
well."

Jon-Tom shrugged. "You're probably right, sir. A little
rock goes a long way."

The wizard growled. "Don't talk to me about rocks.
Come, we have work to do. You use your spellsinging and I
will employ my magic."

Jon-Tom chose to revive Dormas. She was deeply embarrassed
despite his assurances that she shouldn't feel that way. They
had all of them been equally bewitched. Nonetheless, she
insisted on trotting off to recover and to suffer in peace. She
also spent more than an hour walking back and forth through
the forest, searching for the emerald meadow of clover and
flowers and finding only dirt and scrub. Thus satisfied, she
located a small mountain pool and thoroughly doused herself.
From all the rolling about she'd done in her imaginary field,
she was filthy from forehead to fetlock. The dirt washed off,
but the anger and embarrassment did not.

Jon-Tom set about trying to put their supplies back into
some kind of order while Clothahump sought to magic some
reality into his famulus. When magic didn't quite do the trick,
the wizard began slapping the owl back and forth across his
muddy beak. Perhaps it was the lingering magic, perhaps the
slaps, or maybe the combination. In any case, Sorbl returned
to them. Returned to them as drunk as if his perturbation had

been real. Apparently certain mental effects were not as easily shaken off.

Finishing with the supplies, Jon-Tom climbed the big pine and got a firm grip on Colin. The koala was mumbling mantras to himself as he chewed on the pine needles, and Jon-Tom had to shake him hard while trying to play the right notes on the duar. Colin must have had a stronger grasp on reality than the rest of them because he snapped back immediately.

Unfortunately Jon-Tom had pushed a little too hard. The koala went over sideways right out of the tree and landed with a disquieting *thunk* on the hard ground below. He was also tougher than any of them, for he rolled over and was on his feet in seconds, looking around as though nothing had happened. The pose was an illusion itself. A moment later Colin staggered and sat down hard, put his face in his hands.

This was not because he had suffered a concussion from the fall, as Jon-Tom first feared. Just as Sorbl had retained the effects of his imaginary imbibing, so had Colin kept the by-product of chewing handfuls of eucalyptus leaves. As he explained to Jon-Tom, they were mildly narcotic. That was why koalas eating them full-time were always so sleepy and slow-moving. It would take awhile for the effect to wear off.

As for Mudge, once Clothahump got over the shock of his first sight of the otter, it took the two of them and Colin to pull him off his log. Whereupon they braced themselves for a confession of embarrassment that would put Dormas's to shame. The otter's response, however, was somewhat different. As soon as events had been explained to him, he let out a string of expletives and oaths and execrations such as this part of the world had never heard. The air trembled around them.

When he ran out of steam, not to mention insults and wind, he gave the remnants of the devastated log a swift kick, sending splinters flying, and stalked off to sulk by his lonesome.

"You'd think the degenerate water rat would be ashamed of himself," Colin commented.

"I don't think Mudge knows the meaning of the word. I think he's upset because we brought him out of his dream. He'll get over it, but it'll take awhile."

True to Jon-Tom's word, the otter pouted for another hour, then shambled back to help with the repacking of the supplies. Not a word was said until the last bedroll was back in place, the last container of food strapped down and secure. Then he glanced up at his tall friend.

"Did you 'ave to do it, mate? Bring me back, I mean?"

"What do you think, Mudge?" Jon-Tom checked the position of a sack of spare clothing on the hinny's back. "It was just a perturbation, an illusion. It wasn't real. I miss my own dream too. I had to bring you back."

"I know that. We 'ave a job to do an' we're all of us in this together. But did you 'ave to bring me back so *soon*?"

"There's no telling what might've happened if I'd waited any longer." He worked on another strap that looked a little loose. Dormas glanced back at him.

"Take it easy back there, man. That's not your shoe you're tying, you know."

"Sorry." He let the binding up a notch. "If I hadn't intervened when I did,, you might never come back to reality. Clothahump says you might've been stuck in that dreamworld forever."

"Now would that 'ave been so bloody awful?"

"Not for you, or for me, or for the rest of us, but it wouldn't have brought us any nearer to our goal, and there are others depending on us."

"That bleedin' altruistic streak of yours again! I've warned you about that, mate." He turned and stomped off in search of his longbow and sword, looking very unhappy.

Jon-Tom watched him go, considered what had happened to all of them. Each member of the group had seen their

wildest fantasy come true. Unlike Mudge, however, none of
the rest of them had any desire to succumb to that dreamworld for a lifetime. Eventually they would have given in to
boredom, for when one has accomplished everything, even in
a dream, there is nothing left to strive for. Clothahump
explained it very clearly. Trapped in an illusion of complete
fulfillment, unable to escape, the final result would have been
not nirvana but death.

Now, if he could only think of a way to call it up for an
hour or two at a time . . .

What might the perambulator be thinking? Did it think?
Clothahump wasn't sure if it possessed intelligence or not, or
even if it did, if it assumed a recognizable form. Did it
dream, and if so, what might something capable of traveling
between universes and dimensions dream of? Certainly it was
confused. Confused and nervous. The by-products of this
space-time traverser's anxiety were increasingly frequent perturbations. Interdimensional sweat.

There was no malice in them, save for those that the
perambulator's captor might be directing. The last one had
left them all feeling better, though relieved at its end. Perhaps
the perambulator suffered with each change just as they did.

As they climbed toward the pass he found that he no longer
wanted to free the perambulator simply to stop the disturbing
changes it was foisting on the world. He wanted to free it
because it was the right thing to do for the perambulator
itself, whether it was capable of emotion or feeling or not. As
a child, he'd once been locked in a trunk by some friends.
That caged feeling had never left him. He knew what it was
like to be trapped, unable to run, hardly able to move.
Nothing deserved a fate like that, not even something as
inexplicable and otherworldly as a perambulator.

We're not going to loosen a piece of frozen machinery, he
told himself. *We're on our way to perform a rescue.*

Clothahump called a halt just below the top of the pass.

They took shelter from the wind that blew steadily through the gap in the mountains.

"It would be useful to know what lies ahead and worth making the effort to find out. Would you be good enough to try, rune-caster?"

Colin sought out a protected spot beneath an overhanging granite ledge. "No promises now, friends. I'm willing to make the attempt, but don't expect too much."

"Anything you can tell us will be a great deal more than what we presently know about tomorrow, which is nothing," Clothahump pointed out.

"Right. So long as you don't expect too much."

The sun gleamed off the silver thread as the koala removed the rune pouch from his knapsack. Everyone gathered close as he untied it and spread the leather out flat on the hard ground. They waited quietly while he went through his preparations, finally picking up the runes and letting them fall onto the leather square. No one spoke; everyone stared.

Jon-Tom tried to find some recognizable pattern, to make some sense of the double handful of bone and stone and fabric spread out before him. He found nothing but the beginnings of a slight headache from concentrating too hard. Much as it bothered him to confess to ignorance, he had to admit that Mudge's description of the runes as so much garbage was as accurate as anything he could think of himself.

Clothahump was staring intently at the debris and nodding slowly to no one in particular. Whether the wizard actually understood any of what he was looking at or was just trying to keep up appearances, Jon-Tom couldn't tell, and thought it undiplomatic to inquire.

When he finally spoke, Colin's voice was unusually soft and thoughtful. "You were right, Old One. He knows we're coming."

"What can you see?" Clothahump asked anxiously. "Can

you tell anything of it at all? Size, strength, mental powers, anything that would be useful in compiling a profile? Any indication at all of whom we are up against?''

''First that 'he' is accurate. There are too many signs of maleness for it to be otherwise. And there are many suggestions of magic. A wizard or sorcerer of some kind, surely. The forest fire that almost engulfed us may not have been a perturbation after all. There is power at work here, enough to constitute a threat on its own, without the aid of a perambulator.''

Clothahump spoke quietly but firmly. ''Is his power greater than mine?'' He waited silently for the rune-reader to reply. They all did. Even the skeptical Mudge looked on anxiously.

''I cannot say that it is stronger,'' Colin finally declared. ''Different certainly, in a manner I can't describe or understand. I'm only a rune-caster, not a sorcerer myself.''

''What else do you see?'' Dormas asked him.

''He will not let the perambulator go without a fight. We will be strongly opposed. At that time one among us must take the lead. Only that one has the ability and strengths to see us through the final confrontation. At that time also, Wizard, your knowledge and experience will be of paramount importance to our survival. All of us may have to sacrifice, but one of us will be the key. Only he can counter what our opponent will throw against us.'' He looked up then to stare at Jon-Tom. So did the others.

Well, he'd half expected as much. He and Clothahump were the prime movers in this business. He was neither embarrassed nor intimidated by the stares of his companions. He'd been through similar situations often enough in the past to have gained a certain amount of confidence. And it was too much to expect that for once he'd be able to hang back and let bloodthirsty types like Mudge and Colin do the heavy work. He sighed.

''You're not telling me anything I didn't already suspect.

Are you sure you can't tell us anything more about what we're going to have to deal with?''

Again Colin turned his attention to the runes. ''I can see something but I can't define it. The runes are rarely precise. It isn't something I'd know how to handle myself. I can tell you that it will manifest itself in two ways. The first will take the form of a magic only you can counter.''

''More spellsinging.'' Jon-Tom grunted. ''Well, I had to fight it out with another spellsinger once before, and he and I ended up the best of friends. If I have to go up against another one . . .''

''The runes read in multiples.''

''All right, then, if I have to go up against several singers, maybe I can convert them the way I did the other one. They may end up as our allies instead of our enemies.''

''It'll be a wonder if you can turn these to friendships. I read no accommodating signs in the pattern. You will have a tough time combating them. The runes don't say if you'll survive the confrontation; so powerful, so evil and destructive is their particular brand of magic.''

Jon-Tom sat up a little straighter. ''I'll handle it. What form is the second manifestation going to take?''

''That much, at least, is clear.'' The koala stared at him appraisingly. ''The runes say that you will have to do battle with your own greatest desire.''

That set Jon-Tom back on his heels. He thought immediately of the dreamworld he'd been drifting through not long ago, of the thousands of fans cheering and screaming at him and the promise of a respected and venerated career in government.

''But I've already done that. It was part of the illusion I experienced earlier.''

Colin looked back down at the fragments of wood and stone. ''Maybe you'll have to deal with it again. It isn't clear here, but that's the closest description I can give. You must prepare to deal with that desire as best you're able.''

"Will we be successful in the end?" Dormas asked somberly.

"The runes don't say. Finality of any kind is the hardest pattern to interpret. The runes lead to a place and time of ultimate confrontation, but that's it. Beyond that point nothing is visible." He started gathering up the runes and the corners of the pouch.

"O' course, we don't know 'ow much o' wot you've said is certain an' 'ow much a product o' your fevered imagination, fuzzball."

Colin glared at the otter but his expression quickly softened. "I could take that for an insult, pilgrim, but I won't. Because it happens to be the truth. The reading felt unusually good here"—and he put one finger over his heart—"and here." He moved it to his forehead. "Sometimes the casting is bad and I can sense it, but this one was as accurate as they come." He glanced sideways at Jon-Tom. "I almost wish it were otherwise."

"No, I'm glad you did the reading," Jon-Tom told him thankfully. "I'd rather have some idea of what we're up against, even if your description did border on the nebulous."

Clothahump was peering through the pass ahead. "There is no point in putting off the inevitable. That is something that must always be coped with."

The attacks commenced soon after they started through the far end of the pass. Landslides repeatedly threatened to trap and crush them in the narrow defile. Each time the boulders came crashing down toward them Clothahump raised his arms and bellowed a single powerful phrase. And each time the rocks were blasted to fragments.

"Not the ideal solution," the wizard said, apologizing for the dust that soon covered all of them, "but I promise you a good cleansing spell as soon as we have done with this."

Eventually there were no more landslides. Instead the clouds opened up and they were drenched with a misplaced tropical downpour. It washed away the rock dust but also threatened to wash them right back down the pass.

Again Clothahump went to work, raising his hands and grumbling about the amount of overtime he was having to put in at his age. The flood rushing down upon them was transformed into a vast cloud of warm steam. For ten minutes the pass was turned into a giant sauna. Finally the steam dissipated enough for them to proceed.

"Look at this," Mudge complained, fingering one side of his vest. " 'Ow the 'ell am I supposed to get these bloomin' wrinkles out?"

"I am responsible for preserving your life, water rat," Clothahump told him sharply, "not your appearance. It would do you well to be more attentive to the terrain ahead and less narcissistic."

The otter regarded his filthy, damp fur and bedraggled attire. "As you say, Your Wizardship. I just 'ope we don't meet anyone I know."

"That's unlikely, pilgrim." The koala put a paw on the back of Clothahump's shell. "How you holding up, old-timer?"

"I am concerned with the simplicity of these attacks. There is little danger in any of them. That does not jibe with your reading."

"Like I've said, there are plenty of times when I'm not too accurate. I thought this last one was right on the money, but I'm not going to complain if I overstated the threat."

"You're underrating yourself, sir," Jon-Tom told him. "There aren't many individuals for whom multiple landslides and mountain floods hold little danger. I guess whoever we're up against doesn't realize who he's dealing with."

"Perhaps not, my boy. Or he may be attempting to lull us into overconfidence. The insane can be exceedingly subtle. Still, you may be right. The sorcery we have had to deal with thus far is of a most mundane kind. If we run into nothing more complex, we shall have no difficulty in reaching our goal."

"I can't believe that Colin's reading of the runes was that inaccurate."

"Neither can I, man," said the koala, "but there's nothing wrong with hoping that I was."

A voice shrilled down at them. Sorbl had returned from scouting a little way ahead. Now he circled low over his companions. "Just ahead, Master, friends! The pass reaches its end. Our destination is in sight!" He wheeled about, digging air, and glided out in front of them once more.

Increasing their pace, they puffed and panted the last few yards and finally found themselves looking down instead of up for the first time in weeks.

XII

Below lay a lovely little hanging valley, nestled between two towering peaks. The bottom was filled with a long blue lake. Evergreens lined both shores, though few rose higher than a dozen feet. The majority were gnarled and twisted, sure signs that powerful storms visited this valley frequently.

The tree line ended not far above the lake. A few isolated trees grew as much as halfway up the mountainside. Where they ceased to grow was sited the base of a monolithic, forbidding wall.

"The fortress of our enemy," Dormas declared. "It has to be."

Mudge squinted at it uncertainly. "That's a fortress?"

Truly, Jon-Tom mused, it was a most unimpressive structure. The single outer wall was composed of plain rock loosely cemented together. What they could see of an inner roof was made of thatch instead of some sturdy roofing material like slate or tile. Portions of the wall were crumbling and in a sad state of disrepair. The winding pathway leading up to the wall from the lake was in worse shape still. It was not even paved.

"What we can see has not been in existence for very long," Clothahump commented. They had started down toward the lake.

"How can that be?" Jon-Tom asked, confused. "It's falling down."

"In this instance that is not an indication of great age so much as it is of sloppy construction, my boy. It is poorly designed and ill built. Just like the series of attacks we had to deal with in the pass behind us. It indicates the presence of a lucky, haphazard opponent as opposed to a methodical and powerful one, although he may yet succeed in making lethal use of the perambulator's twistings and turnings. We must remain on guard. Remember the runes."

"I haven't forgotten, sir."

They walked along in silence for a while, each member of the party engrossed in his or her private thoughts. After a while Clothahump slid over until he was marching alongside Jon-Tom.

He finally gave the wizard a curious glance. "Something on your mind, Clothahump, sir?"

The sorcerer hesitated a moment, finally craned his neck to meet the tall young human eye to eye. "While I am confident, my boy, that we are dealing here with matters beyond the experience of most people, I cannot be certain of the outcome."

"Neither can Colin, despite his runes."

"Quite. Therefore, I mean to say a few things that perhaps should have been said before now."

"I don't follow you, sir."

"What I am trying to say, my boy, is that I have been brisk with you at times. As brisk as with Sorbl on occasion. Sometimes it may seem to you from my tone, if not from my words, that I only make use of your talents and care nothing for you personally. This is untrue. I have grown—quite fond of you. I wanted you to know in case anything—happens.''

Surprised and overcome by this wholly unexpected confession, Jon-Tom could think of nothing to say.

"Bringing you to this world was an accident and insofar as blame can be ascribed to it, it falls upon my shell. Your appearance here in response to my desperate request for sorcerous aid was not well received. I was most displeased and disappointed.''

"I remember," Jon-Tom said softly.

"Fate has a way of balancing the scales, however, and in your case, it has more than done so. Events have worked out better, I daresay, than either of us could have anticipated. Yet I fear I have been something less than a gracious host." He raised a hand to forestall Jon-Tom's protest. "No, let me finish. I am unused to personal expressions of humility, and if I do not finish now, I may never do so.

"You must try to understand that wizardry is a solitary profession. We who practice it have little time to develop social graces or refine interpersonal relationships. As the world's greatest wizard, I have had to endure the weight of reputation for more than a century. As a result I sometimes tend to forget that I am dealing with mortals less versed in life as well as in the intricacies of my art. I fear my impatience sometimes carries over into rudeness.

"What I am trying to say, and I fear doing a poor job of it, is that you have acquitted yourself admirably this past year. You have tolerated my personal peccadilloes gracefully, complained no more than could have been expected, and in general done everything that has been asked of you.

"I just wanted to tell you this so that you would know my true thoughts. I would not want either of us to pass on to a higher plane ignorant of these feelings. You give me hope for the youth of this world and have been a comfort to me in my old age.''

Before Jon-Tom could think of anything to say, the wizard had moved off to join Dormas in bringing up the rear. It didn't matter. Time did not provide him with a suitable reply. There was nothing to say. The turtle's speech was the nearest thing to an expression of genuine friendship he'd ever made. No, that wasn't right. It was more than an expression of friendship. It bordered on a confession of affection. No matter how long he lived, he doubted he'd hear the like again.

Replying in kind would only have embarrassed Clothahump. Jon-Tom had come to know the wizard well enough to know that much. So he kept his response to himself and let the warm glow the wizard's words had produced spread through his whole being.

Besides, there was no time to waste on sentiment. He had more important things to think about. There were useful songs to review in his mind, lyrics to recall. If Colin was half right, they would find themselves confronting something dangerous and unexpected anytime now, something only he was going to be able to deal with.

But he would never forget what the wizard had just told him, any more than he would let Clothahump forget those words the next time he flew into one of his rages and started bawling his young charge out for some imagined transgression.

They didn't have long to wait for the koala's predictions to begin to come true. The first attack came as they were leaving the scrub woods and beginning the long climb up the winding, dilapidated path to the structure clinging to the slope above. A cold wind sprang up, swirling around them, touching their faces and hands with all the forceful delicacy of a blind man. Such a wind was not to be unexpected at these altitudes, but the abruptness of it put all of them on their guard. This was not the time or place to take chances, even with a stray breeze. They huddled together and searched the land and sky surrounding them.

Colin had his sword out, clutched it tightly in his right

hand. The muscles bulged in his short but powerful arms. "Dormas, you have most of our supplies. You stay behind us. You're better built for fighting a rear-guard action, anyway. You, sir," he said to Clothahump, "stay in the middle where we can protect you. And you——"

"Just a minim, mate. Who are you to be givin' out orders? Maybe you forgot that we were the ones who 'ad to rescue you?"

"Defending folks is my other profession, otter. I'm taking care of defensive tactics because I'm the one best qualified to do so."

"Do tell." Mudge moved over until he was standing chest-to-chest with the koala. "As it 'appens, I've done a bit o' soldierin' in me time, too, and if there're any orders that 'ave to be 'anded out 'ere for defensive purposes, maybe we ought to——"

"Both of you shut up and concentrate on guarding your respective behinds." Clothahump's tone indicated that he wasn't in the mood to listen to a debate on the nature of childish macho prerogatives. "It does not matter how we approach this asylum or what flimsy weapons we brandish. We are likely to be confronted by something that steel cannot turn."

"You said that right, asshole."

Colin and Mudge turned from one another to confront this new threat. There were four of them. They stood side by side, blocking the pathway leading to the fortress above. In stature they resembled Colin, being no more than four feet in height and broad in proportion. Each was colored bright red. Looking at them, Jon-Tom didn't think they'd acquired their skin color from spending a lot of time vacationing in a sunny land, though from a southerly region they'd surely come.

Each boasted a pair of short, inward-curving black horns. Mouths seemed to stretch from ear to ear and were filled with short, pointed teeth. Their pupils were bright red on black irises. They were pointed like those of a lizard.

"He who brought us here sought far for us," the first imp declared. "He says you shall go no farther. You worry him by your presence, and he has no time for worry. He bids you depart from this place now or suffer the consequences."

"Sorry," Jon-Tom replied calmly. "We won't be just a minute. All we have to do is release his unwilling guest and then we'll be on our way." He took a step forward.

The second imp held up both clawed hands. "You shall not pass. Away with you!"

"You may be right, Old One," Colin murmured to Clothahump. "Steel may not be the right weapon to use here. But you'll forgive me if I find out for myself." So saying he lunged forward and brought his long saber down smack against the forehead of the imp with the raised hands.

The blade passed completely through the red-skinned homunculus to strike sparks from the ground. A shaken Colin backed cautiously away from the grinning creature.

"You don't listen so good," it told him.

"No," agreed the imp on his left. "Maybe a demonstration's in order."

Each imp reached behind itself. Mudge reacted to this threatening gesture by drawing his own sword while Clothahump hunkered down inside his shell and started retreating.

But it wasn't bows and arrows or swords and scimitars or pikes or knives or any other kind of traditional weapon that the imps produced. Instead each one brought forth a different kind of musical instrument. One held a bizarre flute that twisted and curved in on itself loosely in one hand. The second in line was clutching a flat wooden container with strings running over its top and bottom in a crazy-quilt pattern. The third displayed something akin to Jon-Tom's duar, save that it had only a single set of strings, and the last imp in line had swung a string of small drums around to rest on the upper curve of his belly. Or were they a part of the body itself? They might as easily have been a line of bulging, flat-topped tumors.

For that matter, all the instruments appeared to be growing out of the compact red bodies.

Mudge edged over close to Jon-Tom. "Spellsingers from 'ell, mate. That's wot they be." The otter threw Colin a quick glance. "Me apologies to you, fuzzball, for decryin' your rune-castin'. This much o' that prophecy seems to 'ave come true, though I wish it were otherwise."

"So do I." Despite its demonstrated ineffectiveness, the koala continued to hold his sword out in front of him, aware that it was no more a useful talisman than a weapon against this quartet.

"There's four of 'em, lad," Mudge whispered. "Can you 'andle four of 'em at once?"

"I don't know," his tall friend confessed. "Each of them carries a different instrument. Maybe they're only effective when working together. If that's the case, I'll only have to counter one spellsong at a time. We'll know soon enough." Slowly he brought the duar around to a playing position.

The second imp regarded him out of wide black-and-red eyes. It hardly looked alarmed, Jon-Tom thought. Amused, perhaps.

"Oh, ho, so," it chirped, "another singer! We were told we might encounter such. That's much better. Death and destruction is always tastier when rendered with a little spice. Make it interesting for us, man."

"I intend to," Jon-Tom told it grimly.

The imp regarded its companions. "Look to your tunes, to your chords and phrases, and beware your harmonizing!"

The first song was aimed not at Jon-Tom but at the member of the offending trespassers who'd dared to strike an opening blow. The words struck Colin hard. He dropped his sword, his eyes going wide, and he staggered backward with both hands clutched to his belly. Mudge instantly put his own weapon down and, moving as only a otter can move, just did manage to catch the koala before he collapsed to the ground. He held the wheezing, vomiting Colin under both arms. A single chorus had reduced him from a powerful, alert fighter to a physical and mental basket case.

The imps didn't bother to finish the song. A few bars and lyrics had lain the strongest of their opponents low. At the first notes Jon-Tom's jaw had dropped in astonishment, though the song had not affected him. But then, it hadn't been directed at him, either.

"You see"—the second imp sneered—"what we can do. Our master has given us the strength of spellsinging that arises from the deepest well of confusion, from the black pits where unpleasant songs of sorrow and despair mix together to form the most depressing soul-suffocating sludge. Our music moans of dark moments and wails of woeful weeping. No living creature is immune. None can ignore its effects."

"I'm afraid he's right, Mudge."

"You won't see me denying it." The otter gently lowered the still softly retching koala to the ground, trying to fight off the cold chills that were coursing through his own body. "Wot an 'orrible noise. 'Tis more sickenin' than I imagined music could be. But I saw your face when they started singin', mate. You recognize it."

"Yes, I recognize it, Mudge."

"Then you've got to try an' counter it, for all our sakes. If they sing much more o' that, they'll burn out our ears and then our 'earts. 'Tis worse than anything I've ever 'eard or ever 'oped to 'ear."

But Colin was not done. Breathing hard, he rolled over onto hands and knees, recovered his sword, and started crawling toward the quartet. Mudge tried to stop him, but the koala was still strong enough to shake the well-meaning otter off. The determination on his round gray face was something to behold.

Unimpressed, the imps put their voices together and began to sing again. A new song this time, one even more affecting and lugubrious than the first.

"Yourrr cheatin' hearttt . . . !"

Jon-Tom found he was sweating. Straightforward traditional country-western they were singing. Even though he was on the fringes of the music, it staggered him. He'd never expected anything so awful, so bright and brassy, so thick with saccharine lyrics and sickly chords. The imps sang on, harmonizing beautifully, their voices dense with despair and self-pity.

Colin couldn't take it. He had no experience of that degree of moroseness, and it knocked him flat. With a last burst of energy he threw his sword at the quartet's lead singer. A few strains of Hank Williams knocked the blade to the ground.

Then they turned to face the only one capable of standing against them. Jon-Tom held his ground, his fingers poised over the duar's strings, ready for whatever might come.

The simple Conway Twitty tune was a test, he knew, and he handled it easily enough, striking back with Springsteen's "Pink Cadillac." One imp gave ground, frowned, then returned to the lineup with a will. The hellish quartet segued instantly into serious solemnity with a typically maudlin Patsy Cline standard. Sweat broke out on Jon-Tom's brow as he countered with van Halen's effervescent "Jump."

As they traded songs the air itself seemed confused, uncertain of whether to give vent to rain or sunshine. Songs in four-part harsh harmony by Tammy Wynette, Johnny Cash, and Ronnie Milsap made it hard for the travelers even to breathe by turning the air into a cloying stew. Jon-Tom tried to lighten the atmosphere as best he could by responding with the more exuberant music he could think of, from Loggin's "Footloose" to a medley by Cyndi Lauper.

But there was no one to help him, and it was four against one. As always, his strongest ally was his own playing. The more he sang, the stronger his spellsinging became.

The imps began to retreat, falling back a step at a time as Jon-Tom advanced upon them. They were unable to deal with his exhilaration or the relentless vitality of his music. They drew closer and closer together until there was no space between them at all. Like four figures fashioned of Silly Putty, they began to merge, in body as well as in voice. When the convergence had concluded, Jon-Tom found himself facing a four-headed, eight-armed giant instead of the impish humanoid figures who'd first challenged him and his companions on the trail. It had the same four faces, played the same four instruments, but the body had grown swollen and distorted. Like a bloated four-headed slug it wove and danced before him, all the while continuing to sing, sing of a world in which work led only to poverty, beauty only to heartbreak, and love only to misery and loneliness.

As they sang on, something new became apparent. There was an air of desperation about their music. It carried over into the expressions on the four faces. Jon-Tom was winning. They knew it and he knew it, and worst of all, they knew he knew they knew it.

He pressed his attack with a vibrant, volcanic rendition of "Girls Just Wanna Have Fun" while letting Dormas take a temporary lead. The song seemed to invigorate the hinny as well, and she kicked and pawed at the stumbling, retreating monstrosity. The music flowed out of him. He felt good: strong; full of voice; his fingers a blur on the strings of the duar. It was an echo of his performance during the perturbation, when he'd played to that imaginary Forum crowd of thousands.

Utterly desperate now, the imp-monster counterattacked with the heaviest weapons in its arsenal—a string of greatest hits by Hank Williams himself. Taken aback by the overwhelming melancholy of the lyrics, Jon-Tom felt himself knocked back on his heels. Mudge was there to prop him up and to shout encouragement in his ear.

"Don't let 'em get you down, mate! You've got 'em on the run, you do. Stand up to it, fight back, let 'em have everything you've got!"

With the otter standing behind him and Dormas and Clothahump ranged to either side of him, Jon-Tom did just that, blasting out a string of platinum bullets by Stevie Wonder, the Stones, Tina Turner, and the Eurythmics. When the imp-monster sagged, he laid a little of its own medicine on it in the form of a soulful version of "Purple Rain." The imps' color began to run from red to lavender.

"You've got it, lad, you've got it now! Finish it off!"

Pulling itself together, the imp-monster tried to rally its former confidence and muster enough energy to attack with prosaic weapons like spears and swords. Mudge and Dormas made ready to defend Jon-Tom from this unmagical but possibly lethal attack.

Their defense was not required. Jon-Tom had his own, knew exactly what he was going to use for a lyrical coup de grâce. His fingers strummed faster than ever, and he felt as though the energy of the song would lift him off the ground.

Certainly the imps had never encountered anything with the relentless energy of the Pointer Sisters' "Neutron Dance." Momentarily transformed into a miniature particle-beam generator, the duar struck to heart of the monster. There was a small, very localized explosion. Everyone covered their faces, trying to shield themselves from the flash. Jon-Tom did his best to protect himself by flinging the duar up in front of his eyes, but he was still temporarily blinded.

When his vision finally returned, all that could be seen where the imp-monster had once stood was a ten-foot-high nonradiant mushroom cloud. It dissipated rapidly. The rocks and pathway were covered with bits of thin red flesh, as though a giant balloon had blown up in front of him.

"Cute." Dormas was eyeing the remnants of the cloud. "What do you call it?"

"Pure nastiness." He led them around the site of the explosion, giving the cloud a wide berth. It was impossible. There was no such thing as a thermonuclear explosion scaled down to midget size. Or was there such a thing as "no such thing" in this crazy world?

"There's the entrance!" Mudge pointed upward with his sword. "Nothin' to stop us now, mate."

Jon-Tom tried to keep up with the otter by lengthening his stride. "Don't be too sure, Mudge. Remember the rest of Colin's prophecy."

The otter forced himself to slow down so that the others could catch up. "Cor, I ain't worried no more, mate. Wotever 'tis, you can 'andle it. You just proved that, you did."

"Do not let confidence give way to cockiness, water rat." Clothahump was panting hard as he struggled up the steep path. "Though clumsy and not particularly skilled, there is much raw power at work here. I should not care to face it if its manipulator was better disciplined. I cannot believe we have penetrated his defenses so easily here, any more than I believed how quickly we made it through the pass." He cast an appraising eye at Jon-Tom. "Our spellsinger has yet to confront and deal with his heart's desire."

"I think I may already have done that, sir, but I'm ready in any case."

"Good," said Dormas sharply, "because here they come."

Pouring from the fortress gate was a ragtag army of heavily armed soldiers. Well, perhaps not an army, Jon-Tom told himself. Twenty to thirty troops, none of them demonic in shape or appearance. They were waving swords over their heads and screaming like banshees.

Colin steeled himself. "They think they've got us out-

numbered, but I've handled nearly that many by myself. And
we have the magic of both wizard and spellsinger to protect
us. They haven't got a chance.'' He sounded more curious
than uncertain. "One thing I don't understand, though. Why
would an evil sorcerer send only females against us, and only
human ones at that?''

Jon-Tom might have ventured a guess, but he couldn't
speak. He could only cling limply to the duar and stare up the
slope as the thirty redheads came charging toward him. They
had blood in their eyes and murder on their minds.

Mudge and Clothahump were also paralyzed by the sight,
but only momentarily. They were not as intimately affected by
the manifestation as the man in their midst, though they had
been afflicted with the same shock of recognition. Meanwhile
Jon-Tom made no move to defend himself from the onrushing
attack, not with his duar or with his ramwood staff. He just
stood and stared, a man struck dumb by the sudden realization of what it meant to confront his heart's desire.

An arrow whizzed past his head. He blinked but could not
bring himself to move, to dodge. He couldn't do anything
because each of the onrushing Valkyries looked exactly like
its sister, and that meant all of them looked like his beloved
Talea.

Talea of the bright spirit and long red hair. Talea of the
questionable occupation and brave heart. The same Talea he'd
proposed to and who had spurned him because she wasn't
ready to be tied to one man or one place but whom he'd never
ceased to love. A score and more of his heart's desire
running, racing toward him with something other than love in
their hearts. He hadn't seen her in over a year. He was totally
unprepared to see her now, here, in this place, far less in
multiple guises.

"What's wrong with the spellsinger?'' Colin wanted to
know. He held his saber ready to greet the first of the new
arrivals.

"I'll tell you wot's wrong, fuzzball," said Mudge. "This whoever 'e is don't fight fair. Every one o' them long-legged beauties is the splittin' image o' our friend's lady-luv."

Colin absorbed this revelation, nodded tersely. "We're dealing with a vile bastard for sure. What do you recommend?"

The mob of maddened Taleas solved the problem for them. All feelings of empathy aside, there are few options available when someone tries to split your skull with a battle-ax. Colin parried neatly and stepped aside as the first woman's rush carried her past him.

Mudge defended himself against a sword stroke, skittering backward and drawing his longbow. A spear splintered stone at his feet, and one fragment cut through his fur, almost reaching the skin. He looked toward Jon-Tom, and something in his voice made the tall man turn to face him. Something Jon-Tom had never heard there before.

Anguish.

"I 'ave to, mate," the otter wailed helplessly, "I 'ave to! We all 'ave to."

The otter's words and actions combined to make Jon-Tom move. He lurched toward his furry friend. "Mudge—no!" His feet didn't seem to be working. He felt as if he were trying to sprint through freshly laid asphalt. "Don't!"

But the otter let the arrow fly as the woman in front of him raised her sword for a killing blow. It struck her square in the left breast, directly over the heart.

Mortally wounded, the figure did not react as it should have. There was no gasp of pain, no collapsing body. Instead the female form began to writhe and contort. A whistling sound came from it as it shrank in upon itself, compacting and shrinking down into the shape of a fist-sized red-orange mass floating in the air before them. Then it exploded, sending tiny orange-and-red bits flying in all directions. There was a sweet, cloying, and yet somehow nauseating smell in the air. It was as though someone had just blown up a watermelon stuffed with freckles.

"Bugger me for a tart's tailor," Mudge muttered aloud, "the bloomin' broads ain't real." He glanced excitedly at his companion. "You see that, Jonny-Tom? They ain't real!" He notched a second arrow into his bow and fired. Another Talea metamorphosed into an exploding puffball.

Colin parried another ax swing and cut sideways. His blade passed completely through the body of his attacker, which promptly went the decorporalizing route of Mudge's two assailants. Displaying an agility that belied her age, Dormas pivoted and struck out with both powerful hind legs. Their supplies went flying. So did the Talea whose neck she'd broken. Change, compaction, poof—out of existence. The pattern repeated itself again and again.

And still Jon-Tom was unable to bring himself to raise his staff and fight.

Though the cluster of Taleas was fashioned of something other than flesh, there was nothing ephemeral about their weapons. One ax cut deeply into the flank of Clothahump's shell.

"C'mon, mate," Mudge urged him, even as he was defending himself against an assault by three redheads, "fight back. You 'ave to, and it ain't the loverly Talea you'll be fighting with." He struck with his sword. Shrink, whistle, *pah-boom*. He worked his way back to his friend, yelling at Colin as he did so. "Over this way, fuzzball! We 'ave to defend this twit. He ain't ready to defend 'imself."

The koala nodded, dispatched another opponent as he retreated to help protect the useless Jon-Tom. He was enjoying himself. For the first time since he'd begun his long journey, he had a chance to fight back against their unseen nemesis. It was a pleasure to be able to resort to good, solid swordplay for a change. He'd about had his fill of magic and mysticism.

Together he and Mudge, and to a lesser extent Dormas, greatly reduced the number of Talea-doppelgängers.

Sorbl was busy as well, swooping and diving while clutching a honeycomb dagger in each foot, the red hair making individual targets easy to hit. Mudge and Colin kept reminding the dazed Jon-Tom that their opponents were no more human than they were Talea and for him to fight back.

But how? His friends and his brain told him one thing, but his eyes were filled with contradictions.

"Put it out o' your mind, mate," the otter instructed him as he dodged a spear thrust and put an arrow in still another assailant. "You're too easy a target. We can't 'old 'em off you forever."

Even as he spoke the remaining Taleas had clustered around them and were trying to separate Jon-Tom from his stubborn bodyguards. Despite their valiant effort, Colin and Mudge were driven in opposite directions, away from Jon-Tom and from each other. Dormas and Sorbl were trying to protect Clothahump and had no time to spare for someone who wouldn't raise a hand to defend himself.

Then one of the Taleas burst through, charging down on Jon-Tom, holding her sword over her head. He could only stare. Talea, it was Talea, from her flowing hair to the tips of her toes. Yet he'd just watched while a dozen identical Taleas had turned into something small and brightly colored before exploding. They had been cloned by some devilry, called up by a sinister magic. They were not his beloved. His heart's desire was a phantom.

Then it was time for reflexes to take control from an unwilling mind. As the sword came down he brought up the front of the ramwood staff. The blade glanced off the nearly indestructible wood and slid harmlessly off to the side. He wasn't even nicked. Continuing the defensive motion, he brought the club end of the staff around to strike his attacker just above the temple, staggering her. The pain that shot through him had nothing to do with the recoil his arm muscles absorbed.

Recovering, she brought the sword around in a low arc, aiming for his legs and trying her best to cripple him. He had no choice but to thumb the concealed button on the side of the staff, releasing the six-inch-long blade hidden in the shaft. Closing his eyes as he did so, he stabbed swiftly. The point went right through his assailant's throat.

She let out a violent gurgle and fell away from him, but there was no blood, not a drop, not even when he withdrew the blade. Contraction, change, explosion, and she—or rather it—was gone.

"See, mate!" Mudge called over to him. "None of 'em is for real. They've been conjured up to confuse and bemuse us, and you most of all!"

Of course. When he'd defeated the impish spellsingers sent to stop them, he'd alerted the evil force within the fortress. Recognizing the danger Jon-Tom posed, the perambulator's captor had somehow conceived of and put into effect a defense specifically designed to take care of his most dangerous opponent. And it had nearly worked. Only his companion's ceaseless defense on his behalf had preserved him from a death by deception.

They'd carried the load for him long enough. It was time to strike a few blows on his own behalf.

"You're right, Mudge. I'm sorry." Angrily he waded into the thick of the fight, swinging the club end of the staff in great sweeping arcs. Now that he'd been jolted out of his reverie, he fought with twice the resolve of his friends, furious beyond measure at anything that would employ such insidious intimacy against an opponent. The ranks of identical attackers grew thin as one after another blew up and vanished into the clear mountain air.

Showing unexpected speed, Colin ducked, twisted, and struck with one booted foot at an unprotected knee. The

Talea on his left dropped her weapon, let out a loud moan, and fell to the ground. She knelt there, holding her leg and rocking back and forth. The koala brought the long saber up and around for a killing blow. At the same time it struck Jon-Tom forcefully that this was the first time anything like a lingering cry of pain had been produced by any of their attackers. But having progressed from one mental and emotional extreme to the other, he was loath to make a fool of himself again. So he hesitated.

"Son of a bitch," the injured Talea mumbled girlishly. Jon-Tom's eyes went wide.

"Colin, no!" He managed to interpose himself between the fallen woman and the falling sword just in time to block the decapitating blow. Colin gaped at him for a moment but, with no time to argue, turned to deal with another attacker.

It wasn't possible, of course. He held his staff out warily in front of him as he approached the figure that was rocking back and forth on the ground and clutching her injured knee. Lifting the spear end of the ramwood, he held it ready to thrust into the body beneath him. He was acutely conscious of the fact that the rapidly diminishing band of Taleas might be attempting to substitute craftiness for numbers. This might be a new ploy, designed to trap and bemuse him anew.

The figure seemed to see him for the first time, raised a hand in a feeble attempt to ward off the spear's point. "Please, Jon-Tom, don't you recognize me? It's me, Talea!"

While the battle raged around him there was another, no less furious, boiling within him. It looked like Talea, it sounded like Talea, but so had all the others, and when pricked, they had gone up in puffs of orange-red gas. He had time to hesitate, to consider, because Mudge and Colin were temporarily in control of his flanks.

"I—I have to do this. Forgive me." And he jabbed down with the point of the spear.

But only to puncture lightly, not to kill, tearing the slightest of cuts along one arm. The figure let out a little scream.

"You motherfucking bastard, you've ruined my blouse!" She started to sob.

Yes, it certainly sounded like Talea, but of more importance was the thin flow of blood that began to trickle down her arm. She grabbed at the wound and continued to curse him. It was difficult because she was crying so hard.

"She's bleeding, she's bleeding!" He whirled, shaking the ramwood staff joyfully over his head. "Did you hear me, Mudge, she's bleeding!"

"Right, mate, I 'eard you."

Colin spared a glance for the tall man, then commented to the otter fighting at his shoulder. "Sounds like these two have a wonderful relationship."

"Of course, I'm bleeding, you stupid imbecile! You stabbed me."

"I'm sorry, I'm sorry." He was so relieved and so happy, he could hardly speak. "I had to."

"You had to stab me?" She looked down at her arm. Blood continued to filter through her fingers. "If you wanted to tell me that you still love me, you could have given me flowers instead."

"You don't understand. Look. Look around you."

She did so, and blinked, several times. Jon-Tom had to catch her to keep her from falling. She was warm and familiar against him. Her anger vanished, to be replaced by fear and confusion.

"Where am I, Jon-Tom? What is this place? And—and why do all those women look like *me*?"

"You really have no idea?" She shook her head, wide-eyed, and suddenly looking very small and vulnerable.

He eased her gently down to the ground, left her sitting there, holding on to her still bleeding arm. "I'll explain it to you as best I can," he assured her softly, "as soon as the rest of you are all dead."

XIII

Thanks largely to the fighting skills of Mudge and Colin, the number of redheaded attackers was soon reduced to half a dozen. Acting under orders from an unseen master, these viragos retreated and prepared to roll heavy rocks down on the advancing intruders. They never had the chance to complete the planned ambush. Using his longbow, Mudge picked them off one by one. In so doing, he used the last of his arrows, but he was able to recover the majority of them from the surrounding rubble-strewn slope, where they had come to rest after passing completely through the spurious bodies of the Talea clones.

Jon-Tom and the others waited for the otter to conclude his collecting, a task in which he was greatly aided by Sorbl. Meanwhile the spellsinger held the hand of his heart's desire and tried to comfort her. Talea, however, was her usual self again, which meant that she was in no mood to be coddled. She did acquiesce to Clothahump's ministrations, allowing the wizard to bind the shallow cut in her arm. Actually

Colin's kick to the leg was giving her more trouble than Jon-Tom's revealing spear stroke. With his help she rose and tried walking. She found she could move well enough but with a definite limp.

Her shoulder-length red hair framed her delicate face, which at the moment was full of frustration and confusion. "I don't understand any of this. I was taking my ease with a friend in Darriantowne when the world turned inside out."

"Male or female? Your friend?" Jon-Tom couldn't keep himself from inquiring.

She managed a small smile. "Ever the hopeful lover, Jon-Tom?"

He smiled back and shrugged. "What else is there but hope when you're hopelessly in love."

"Female. Not that it matters. We were trying to acquire a necklace I'd admired for a long time."

"By stealing it," Clothahump said sourly as he repacked the medical supplies.

She stuck her tongue out at him, mitigated the charmingly girlish gesture by adding a finger. "Not all of us are as wealthy as you, master hard-shell."

"One gains riches by not having a hard head," he snapped back, but softly. He was in no mood for spurious argument. There were more important matters to be concerned with.

"Anyway," she continued, "I'd just picked up this beautiful loop of amber and blue pearls when my friend Eila screamed. Everything went cockaloop, and when I could see straight again, I found myself in a strange place. Eila was gone and so was the store." She turned, tilted back her head, and blinked. "I think I was in—that building."

"What did you see?" Jon-Tom made no effort to contain his excitement. Some irrefutable evidence at last! "Who was your captor? What was he like?"

"I can't remember. I can't remember much of anything that happened from the time the store disappeared until you were standing over me holding that damn spear of yours. But I remember—something else. Something like I'd never seen before."

Clothahump rejoined them quickly. "What was it like? Think, child!"

"I'm trying. It kept changing—I don't know." She rubbed at her eyes with both hands. "Everything kept changing. It's all a blur in my mind. I remember shadows. Shadows of myself being peeled away from me, like the layers of an onion. It didn't hurt. I didn't feel a thing. Then I remember running down this mountain, holding a sword, with all those shadows surrounding me. I knew they were shadows because none of them said anything."

"They looked real enough to us," Jon-Tom told her.

"I remember"— and she looked up into his eyes with such earnestness that it made his heart hurt—"seeing you, Jon-Tom. I knew it was you. And Mudge and Clothahump too. I wanted to cry out to you, to throw away the sword and run to you, but I couldn't, I couldn't!" She started to cry again. This time she let him put his arms around her.

"It was as if someone else, that someone up in that building, was controlling my muscles, my voice. I couldn't call out. And then I found myself trying to kill your friend." Colin and Dormas had moved over to join them.

"Lucky for us you didn't cut him first," Jon-Tom told her.

"No danger of that. Lucky for her I used a kick before the saber."

Jon-Tom ran the attack back through his mind, saw the koala striking out with his long sword first instead of his foot, the razor-sharp blade slicing through real flesh and bone. Saw the real Talea bleeding to death in his arms. Too close. It had been too close.

"Where are we?" She was trying to maintain her usual defiant pose, but to his surprise Jon-Tom could see that she was scared. She had a right to be. "What is this place? Has the whole world gone crazy?"

"Only at irregular intervals," Clothahump explained as he proceeded, with Jon-Tom's help, to tell her the tale of the perambulator and its captor and how the five of them had come to be there.

"And lastly," the wizard said, "being unable to defeat us by other means, our opponent sought a way of destroying the spellsinger among us. This he did by seeking out and bringing under his sway the spellsinger's true love, then copying her and sending all rushing down upon us. It would have worked if not for the soldierly poise of Mudge and Colin."

"True love?" Talea frowned as she used the back of one hand to wipe the dried tears from her cheeks. "Whose true love?"

Jon-Tom turned away from her. "I've always thought of you as that, Talea, from the night Mudge brought us together alongside that couple you hadn't finished mugging, to the day you told me you had to leave because you needed time to think our relationship through. You know that."

"I know what? Why should I know that?"

He turned back to her. "I told you often enough."

"Like hell you did, you great, gangling, impossible man! I thought all you wanted was to bed me. Every male I meet wants to bed me, including that obscene otter you hang around with, and he isn't even of the same species."

"Somebody mention me name?" Mudge looked up from his arrow-gathering.

"Never mind, Mudge." Talea turned angrily back to Jon-Tom. "You never said one word about my being your only true love."

"Couldn't you tell how I felt about you?"

She let out a sigh of exasperation. "You men! You expect every woman to be a mind reader. How am I expected to know how you really feel if you don't tell me?"

"Truthsayer," said Dormas sagely.

"I just thought—" he tried to say lamely, but she was in no mood for excuses.

" 'You just thought.' You men just think, and we poor women are supposed to divine what you're thinking about, and if we don't, then we're callous and uncaring and insensitive!"

"Now just a minute!" he roared. "If you think all you have to do after disappearing on me is . . ." And they went on in that vein, arguing loudly and incessantly, about just who had let whom down.

Colin was standing nearby, cleaning his saber. Mudge ambled over, nodded toward the pair of combative humans. "Charmin', wot? 'Ave you ever seen a prettier couple?" The koala nodded, turned his sword over, and commenced to polish the other side. It was thick with red-orange dust. "Listen to them squall. 'Tis true love for sure."

"Who's the woman?"

"Old acquaintance o' mine. Carries a sharp knife an' a sharp tongue an' is quick to use both. Introduced 'im to 'er when the two of us had occasion to 'elp 'er out o' a tight spot. They didn't 'it it off right away. She's a bit o' an independent, Talea is. Been awhile since they've seen each other. I imagine they've a bucket o' mutual insults to catch up on."

Mudge's sarcasm was grounded more in the otter's personality than in truth, for the argument soon gave way to recriminations and apologies. Before long, Jon-Tom and Talea were talking amiably and quietly. That was rapidly replaced by whispering, he doing a lot of smiling and she doing a lot of giggling.

"Bloody disgustin'," Mudge said, observing the congenial couple.

"I take it you're not looking for a permanent mate," Colin commented.

"Wot, me? Listen, mate, the only thing that would ever slow this otter down would be two broken legs, an' even then I'd do me damnedest to crawl out of any potential 'ouse'old.''

"I feel differently. Not married yet, but I hope to be someday. I just haven't found a lady with whom I'd feel comfortable for the rest of my life." He hesitated a moment. "I find talking about personal relationships with females difficult. I'm much more comfortable when the conversation has to do with casting the runes or the arts of war."

"Is that so? Well, then, if you'd like, I'd be 'appy to give you the benefit o' me extensive experience in that particular area in which you confess to a certain deficiency. If you can talk war, you can talk love, guv'nor."

"I know some folks consider the two not dissimilar." He eyed the otter warily. "It's just that I'm interested in the diplomatic angles, and I think you're more involved with subversion."

"Nonesense, mate!" Mudge put a comradely arm around the koala's broad shoulders. "Now the first thing you got to know is 'ow to . . ."

"I've been through several different kinds of hell this past year," Jon-Tom was telling Talea. "No matter where I was, in what danger, I was always thinking of you."

"I never stopped thinking of you, either, Jon-Tom. In fact, there was a time when I thought I'd made up my mind about us. I tried to seek you out, only to find out that you'd gone off on some fool errand clear across the Glittergeist Sea."

"Clothahump was deathly ill," he explained to her. "I went because he needed a certain medicine that was only available in a certain town. As it turned out, the whole expedition was unnecessary, but none of us knew that at the time. We didn't find that out until it was too late."

"There are so many things in life we don't find out until it is too late," she murmured, waxing uncharacteristically philosophic. "I'm beginning to learn that myself."

It required a tremendous effort of will for him not to press his affections on her, sitting there winsome and vulnerable as she was. But during their on-again, off-again relationship he'd learned one thing well about Talea: It was best not to push her, to insist on anything, because her natural reaction was not to acceed but to push back. Having found her again under the most unexpected circumstances, he was going to be as careful as possible not to drive her away again.

"It's all right. I understand. All of us need time to learn about ourselves. We have plenty of time."

She looked up at him sharply. "That's not what you said before. You wanted a permanent commitment right then and there."

"I'm not the same person I was before. I'm a full-fledged spellsinger"—that was only a small fib, he told himself— "I've been around, and I know a lot more about myself as well as about the world around us. Enough to know to let love or just friendship take its course." He reached out to caress her cheek with one hand. "Right now it's enough just to see you again, just to be near you. I just wish the immediate situation wasn't quite so desperate."

She nodded solemnly. "It's all so bizarre and crazy, but I keep telling myself it must be so because you and Clothahump both wouldn't lie to me."

"We wouldn't lie to you separately."

"So I have to accept it. The proof of it is that I'm here."

"I feel the same way."

She hesitated. "If this is a matter of magic, Clothahump could be the one to handle it. You and I could leave."

"I can't." He swallowed. The pressure of her hand in his sent fire racing up his arm. "I owe Clothahump too much. I have to help him see this business through to the finish, even if it means the end of me. Of us."

"That's what I wanted to hear," she said with relief.

"It is?"

"I was afraid that part of you, that bravery in the face of overwhelming odds, that committment to justice when confronted by indestructible evil, might have changed also. I wanted to make sure it hadn't. I couldn't love you if you'd gone sensible on me."

"Thanks—I think."

"I know from what you've told me that we have to free this perambulator thing from its captor up there." She indicated the fortress just above the place where they had paused prior to making the final assault. "I wouldn't leave now even if you agreed to. I've been used. I *feel* used. I want to make that unseen bastard pay. He almost had me killed, which isn't so bad. But he tried to make you do it. That's dirty. I don't like dirt, Jon-Tom. I like clean. There's something up there that needs cleaning up." She put both hands on his shoulders. Her lips were every close. He leaned forward.

"Maybe," she whispered lovingly to him, "if we're lucky, we'll have the chance to chop and slice and dismember him all by ourselves."

He licked his lips, sat back, and regarded the light in her eyes and the bloodthirsty grin on her exquisite face. This was his Talea, no mistake about it.

"Uh-yeah, maybe. Let's try that leg again, okay?"

"Okay." She let him help her up. When he let go, she took a few steps. The leg was stiff and it was hard going at first, but the rest had definitely helped her mobility. "Much better." She put her hands on her hips and tried jumping a few small rocks. "It'll get better still."

"I'm glad." He put his arms around her and this time had no second thoughts about kissing her. Finally they separated, and she pointed to her right.

"The hinny I've met, but I don't recognize your short fat friend."

"His name's Colin, and he's not fat, he's as solid as iron. He's a rune-caster, a reader of the future. Sometimes, anyway. His skill with the runes is about like my skill with the duar.''

"That bad, hmm?'' Seeing the look that came over him, she smiled and patted his cheek affectionately. "Just kidding, spellsinger. Speaking of which, you have your duar. Can I borrow your ramwood staff?''

"Lend 'er another staff o' yours, mate!'' Mudge howled gleefully.

"I should've split that otter years ago!'' she said through clenched teeth. Picking up one of the vanished clone's swords, she started chasing Mudge over the rocks. The cackling water rat eluded her with ease, taunting her each time she took a swing at him.

Colin strode by, intent on making certain their supplies were strapped tight to Dormas's back. "Glad to see your fiancée's leg's better.'' He glanced in the direction of the chase. "Sword arm seems okay too.''

"They're old friends,'' Jon-Tom told him.

"I know. I can see that.''

Eventually a winded Talea gave up and re-joined Jon-Tom. "One of these days I'll feed that foulmouthed otter his works.'' She reached up to push red hair out of her eyes. Then she put the sword aside to wrap both arms around him.

"Promise me something, Jon-Tom.''

"If I can.''

"When we find this evil one, let me be the one to slay him. I'll make him bleed slowly.''

"Talea, sometimes I think you enjoy fighting too much.''

She stepped back from him, pouting. "If it's a frothy petite woman you want, then you should never have fallen in love with me, Jon-Tom.''

"The woman I love is stronger than that, but she doesn't have to be a barbarian ax murderess, either.''

Silence between them. Then her pout gave way to a

scintillating smile. "They say that opposites attract, don't they? Didn't you tell me that once?"

"Yeah, and on reflection I think it was a pretty stupid thing to say. All I know is that I love you with all my heart, and if you want to carry a sword during the wedding, well, hell, that's all right with me, so long as it doesn't intimidate the wedding master."

"Wedding master." She looked uncertain. "You said you wouldn't push, Jon-Tom."

"No one is going to do any pushing except up this hillside." Clothahump regarded them sternly. "We have rested long enough. It is time now for us to make an end of this matter, lest it make an end of us. There is no telling what we may encounter inside these walls. Talea likely saw nothing because it was intended that she not. All of you must be prepared for an attack of the most outrageous possibilities.

"We have journey far but have the longest way yet to go. And there is no telling when the next severe perturbation will occur. Let us make haste to find the perambulator and set it free."

"I'm ready, by m'luv's legs," Mudge announced loudly. "Lead on, short, shelled, and stubborn! I'm with you for 'avin' an end to this business. There're ladies waitin' to be loved and liquor waitin' to be drunk, an' I'm sick an' tired o' livin' off the land when the land ain't very accommodatin'."

"You ain't the only one, water rat," said Dormas. "I'd hate to miss the opening trot of the social season."

With Clothahump and Jon-Tom in the lead they advanced toward the single doorway above.

Though they were ready for anything, and Colin and Mudge were spoiling for another fight, the actual assault on the falling-down fortress was more of an anticlimax than any of them could have foreseen. Mudge reached the doorway first. The double doors were fashioned of hand-hewn wood, and not very well seasoned wood at that. They were high but otherwise unimposing. There were no guards to challenge them, no perturbed monstrosities to confront them. Nothing, in fact, to object to their entrance.

Mudge put a paw on the latch, pushed down, and shoved hard. The door swung inward a foot, two feet—and there was a loud crack. Everyone tensed, and the otter jumped a yard straight backward, but it wasn't the sound of something attacking. The door had fallen from its top hinge. It swayed there, hanging precariously from the bottom loop of iron.

The otter slowly advanced to peer inside. "Well?" Clothahump prompted him.

"Scrag me for a Lynchbany tax collector, Your Sorcererness, if the bleedin' place ain't as deserted as a mausoleum!"

When they entered, they found the outer hall as silent and empty as a tomb, just as Mudge had indicated. But it hadn't been that way for very long. Benches lay overturned, chairs were smashed against walls, candle standards had been twisted like candy. A few decorative banners hung listlessly from the curved ceiling while others were scattered in shreds across the stone floor. Several had been piled in a corner to form a crude bed. A couple of matching couches were missing all their cushions. They found those a few yards farther on. All of them had had their stuffing torn out and thrown around the hallway.

There were gouges in the floor and on the walls. Half-eaten food and other debris was scattered over everything. Dark stains on some of the furniture and floor at first suggested grisly goings-on. They turned out to be from spilled wine, not blood.

"Well, this is encouraging." Jon-Tom studied the hallway ahead. It curved slightly to the right. Evidently Mudge didn't share his opinion. The otter let out a derisive snort.

"Why? Because it proves that the bastard we're fightin' is a lousy 'ousekeeper? Some'ow that don't reassure me." The otter's eyes kept darting from filthy corners to shadowed eaves high overhead as they advanced deeper into the fortress.

"No. Because it hints that he might have exhausted his resources trying to stop us outside," Jon-Tom replied. "Maybe he's thrown everything at us he could think of and he's run for cover."

"I do not think so." Clothahump indicated the destruction around them. "Look around you. Banners torn down to form makeshift bedding, chairs broken up to build fires in the middle of the floor: such a life-style would make sense only to a madman, and a madman would not have the sense to retreat. Nor do I think that after having defended his sanctuary so violently he would simply give up and run away. I admit that I did not expect us to enter so easily, but that is yet another indication that we are up against an unbalanced mind. What we see here is hardly the result of poor housekeeping."

"You can bet on that," Colin agreed. "It looks like there's been a war here." He pointed out places where a blade of some kind had cut not only into the furniture but into the stones of the wall itself. "Definite signs of fighting but no blood, no lingering aroma of death. I wonder who was fighting whom in here? You think others have preceded us and failed?" It was a sobering thought, one they hadn't considered until now.

"I doubt it," Clothahump murmured. "I know of no one skilled enough to detect this location and get here prior to us. That you arrived in the same territory at approximately the same time was due only to your unique ability to read some of the future."

The koala turned his gaze back to the devastation they were striding through. "Then who's been fighting here?"

"Our unknown opponent. I strongly suspect he has been doing battle with himself, as is not uncommon among the insane. I wonder how long he has been assailed by unseen demons and imaginary terrors?"

Sorbl fluttered along overhead, having to work hard to stay airborne in the confined space of the hallway. "Master, what kind of maniac opposes us for leagues and leagues, only to abandon the defense of his own home?"

"That is largely what we have come to find out, apprentice."

"Look there!" Dormas came to an abrupt halt.

"Where?" Jon-Tom joined the others in looking around anxiously.

"Road apples!" the hinny muttered. "Sometimes I regret not having any hands. It's hard to point with a hoof. Up there, off to the left ahead of us. I could swear I saw something move."

"Come on, then!" Mudge sprinted down the hallway, skidded to a sudden halt. "Wot the 'ell am I *doing*?" He waited for his companions to catch up to him before resuming, at a more prudent pace, his advance. And he permitted Jon-Tom and Colin to take the lead.

Clothahump noted that solid rock had replaced thatch and wood overhead. "We are inside the mountain proper now. This redoubt is much larger than it appears from outside. I wonder who raised it, and when. The exterior walls are of relatively recent construction, but this is old. Precalibriac, I should say. It wears the poorly constructed walls outside like a mask."

Sorbl backed air nervously. "Master, I hear something."

Weapons were readied, muscles tensed. "How many of 'em?" Mudge inquired of their aerial scout.

"It did not sound like people moving about." The owl sounded agitated. "It sounded like—like someone humming. Very loudly."

"Which way?" Jon-Tom asked him. The hallway forked ahead of them. The right-hand tunnel bent away, dark and downward. He didn't like the looks of it. The passageway on the left was weakly lit by a single torch. He was relieved when Sorbl suggested that they should go that way. Better to confront any opponent in the light than his own fears in the dark.

The instant they entered the branch tunnel, the sound that Sorbl had detected became audible to all of them. Even Jon-Tom and Talea, with their inferior human hearing, could sense it clearly. Sense it because it first manifested itself as a vibration rather than as true sound. He touched the near wall with his fingers. Yes, you could feel the thrum through the stone. Whatever was generating the noise was far more powerful than any individual.

Sorbl bounced from one wall to the other, crisscrossing the air above their heads. "It is near, Master, very near."

Another bend in the corridor. The vibration and humming were joined by a high-pitched whistling and a sound like amplified panpipes. It was a mournful, powerful lament. Jon-Tom thought of the multitude of tones a good snythesizer could generate as well as the extraordinary range of sound his duar was capable of reproducing, but never in his experience had he heard anything quite like this. It was as much a disturbance in the fabric of existence as it was music.

Without warning the corridor widened and they found themselves staring into a vast hexagonal chamber. The six walls enclosing them were paneled in lapis and jasper, while the domed ceiling was lined with cut crystal. It reflected back the aspect of the chamber's sole occupant.

So intense was the light that emanated from it, they could hardly look directly at it. It overwhelmed the torches that lined the walls as easily as it would have overwhelmed ten thousand such firebrands. As they shielded their faces their eyes tried to delineate its limits while their minds struggled to define it. The humming and vibrating it produced seemed to go straight through Jon-Tom's being. He could hear its song in the bones of his legs and the tendons of his wrists. It was not painful or unpleasant, merely deep and penetrating. It rose and fell, questing and inconsistent, like the waves on a

beach, and superimposed over the deeper rumble was that
eerie combination of whistling and panpipes.

It was, of course, the perambulator.

Jon-Tom had expected something full of power and majesty. That would be in keeping with something capable of
altering entire worlds by means of an interdimensional hic-
cough. He had expected it to be good-sized, and it was, for it
almost filled the chamber. It was substantial but also light and
airy. What he had not expected it to be was beautiful.

It hung there in the stagnant air of the chamber, and it was
never still. Changing, shifting, metamorphosing, altering its
structure from moment to moment, it looked like a series of
interlocking dodecahendrons one moment, an explosion of
colored fireworks the next. Each new shape was perfect and
tightly controlled, and each lasted no more than a few
seconds. Now it was an electrifying mass of sharp, fluores-
cent blades, now a series of infinitely concentric alternating
gold-and-silver spheres. The spheres gave way to a collage of
squares and triangles, which in turn were subsumed by an
exploding mass of tiny glowing tornadoes. It was translucent
and then it was opaque. It was a growling DNA-like helix
spinning at a thousand rpm and throwing off blue and green
sparks. The helix collapsed and left in its place a towering
cone of light within which multicolored bands traveled from
base to peak before bursting into the air at the crown as blobs
of pure color.

As it changed and contorted, rippled and glowed, it sang,
all whistles and panpipes and synthesizerlike dominant chords,
a living fugue of color and sound.

"Crikey," Mudge whispered as he joined his friends in gazing at the marvel, "you could bloody well charge admission."

"There are isolated descriptions in the ancient texts."
Clothahump was equally transfixed by the ever-changing
magnificence before them. "But they are based more on

supposition than on eyewitness knowledge. To actually see a perambulator . . ." His voice trailed away, lost in awe.

"Exquisite," said Dormas. "Wouldn't it look grand over the entrance to the stalls?"

"Pretty but dangerous." Colin had one arm over his eyes. "It doesn't belong here. You said as much, Wizard, and I can sense it."

"Seeing the future again?" Dormas asked him.

"No. Relying on my own inner convictions. It's been here much too long. It wants out."

"Is it intelligent?" Jon-Tom wanted to know.

"There are as many different definitions for intelligence as there are different varieties of intelligence, my boy." Clothahump was drowning in wonder but not to the point of having forgotten why they were there. "A more knowledgeable sorcerer than I would have to say. But I am of one mind with our fractious, furry friend. It needs to be freed, to be allowed to depart this cold prison so that it may continue its journey through the cosmos."

"Freed how?" Talea was brushing back her hair even as she was trying to shield her eyes. "I don't see any ropes or chains binding it."

Clothahump smiled as much as his relatively inflexible mouth would permit. "The ties that bind are not always visible, my girl. To tie down a perambulator in the manner you allude to would be as futile as trying to bottle a star. No, you require something else, at once barely perceptible and yet strong, like the forces that bind the building blocks of matter together. Something that even the perambulator cannot twist through." He was staring straight at the explosively metamorphosing mass now and no longer trying to protect his eyes. He was functioning at the pinnacle of wizardly perception, and he drank in the light as he drank in the beauty.

Jon-Tom tried to stare, too, but his eyes kept filling with

water, and to his chagrin he was forced to turn away from the brightness. "I don't see a thing, sir."

"Aye, if there's a cage 'ere, 'tis more than a mite insubstantial," Mudge added.

"So it is," Clothahump told them solemnly. "As insubstantial as an evil thought, as fragile as sanity, as tenuous as a nightmare, but as strong as life and death. This perambulator has been imprisoned in a cage of madness powered by hatred. I see it as clearly as if it were made of iron.

"Think! A perambulator is in constant motion, ever-changing, but there is nothing illogical or irrational about it. Each universe it speeds through is founded upon logic and consistency, no matter how alien or different from our own. But every universe is subject to aberrations, to unpredictable flare-ups of insanity and illogic. These the perambulator studiously avoids. Until now. Because someone here has managed to entrap it in a sphere of madness, which is the only thing it cannot penetrate. It has been walled in and pinned down.

"But it continues to change, and each time we see it change, a perturbation travels swiftly through the world and affects the fabric of existence. Most of the time the changes are infinitesimal and we notice them not. A red bug becomes a yellow bug. A leaf separates from a tree only to fall *up*. A human's tan deepens or the hairs fall from the tip of an otter's tail." Mudge glanced reflexively at his own.

"Normally a perambulator passes close by the world so infrequently that its presence is not remarked upon and its effects never noted. They move too fast to be detected, though sometimes their waste products can be measured by sorcerous means, even as it passes harmlessly through our own bodies."

Jon-Tom struggled to find an analogy for his own world, but the only thing he could come up with wasn't very pleasing. Could cosmic rays really be perambulator piss? Try laying that explanation on a particle physicist.

"That is what we have to deal with," the wizard was saying. "A cage of insanity. Somehow we must destroy it."

Jon-Tom found his attention wandering from the perambulator to the doorways that ringed the chamber. All stood empty—for the moment.

"Who could generate something like that?"

Clothahump, too, was studying the portals. "One of great power and utter madness. Both are required."

"A sorcerer off 'is nut. Great." Mudge moved a little closer to his tall friend. So did Talea.

"So you think I am crazy?"

Everyone turned. Instead of appearing at one of the other entrances, the questioning figure had snuck up behind them.

He was alone. Nor did he leave much room in the narrow corridor for anyone else. He was nearly as tall as Jon-Tom and much more heavily built. Mental condition aside, the owner of the challenging voice was not someone Jon-Tom would have cared to meet in a dark alley.

Colin held his long saber tightly in both hands. "Wolverine. Biggest one I ever saw."

"And quite mad," Clothahump murmured.

Even Jon-Tom could see the wildness in the wolverine's eyes, that faint burning light that was a mockery of the perambulator's own. It was staring straight at them without really seeing them, as though the animal's perception had become unfocused. He wore what originally must have been fine robes of silk and leather but which now hung about his massive body in rags.

In one huge paw he clutched a four-bladed battle-ax. Jon-Tom couldn't have lifted it, much less made use of it. But the wolverine made no move to attack. Instead he seemed to be searching the chamber beyond them. It was almost as though their very presence confused him.

"I am not crazy. I am Braglob, supreme among the wizards of the Northern Marches, and there is nothing wrong with me." He stretched his other arm out toward them. "Go away, get out, begone all of you! Leave me alone or it will go worse for you. I won't warn you a second time." He raised the immense battle-ax, holding it easily over his head.

Mudge slipped around behind Jon-Tom so he could notch an arrow into his longbow without being seen—and coincidentally take cover behind the human's lanky form.

Clothahump took a step forward. "I am Clothahump of the Tree, supreme among *all* wizards, and I tell you that we can't leave just yet. You know that we can't."

The wolverine's heavy brows drew together as he struggled to make sense out of this comment. It occurred to Jon-Tom that this Braglob was completely out of it. Not that it made him any less dangerous. If anything, the contrary was true.

"You have been warned!" Braglob waved the ax over his head. "I am master of the perambulator. I will cause it to turn all of you into pebbles. No, into tiny crawling things, into worms I can use for fishing. You will know your own slime."

"You will do nothing of the kind," Clothahump replied with impressive self-assurance, "or you would have done it already. You have repeatedly made attempts to prevent us from reaching this place, yet we stand here before you. There is nothing more you can do. I do not believe you control the perambulator. You can imprison it in a single sphere of space-time, but you cannot control it. Once I thought it might be possible. After seeing both it and you, I am convinced it is not, for it is more astonishing and awesome than I believed possible, and you are less so."

"Liars, intruders, trespassers, interlopers, all of you!" The wolverine hunkered down, and Jon-Tom tensed, trying to interpose himself between the huge creature and Talea. The redhead would have none of that and kept trying to edge around in front of him. Difficult to be chivalrous, he mused,

when the woman you are trying to protect is only worried
about whether or not she will have the opportunity to use her
sword.

Braglob again studied them without seeing them. Clothahump
was right, Jon-Tom thought. He is completely crazy. Despite
the near fatal encounters incurred during the long journey up
from Lynchbany, despite all the trouble caused by the perambulator, he found that he was still able to muster a soupçon of
sympathy for their opponent.

Physically he was more than impressive, but the torn
clothes, the dirty fur, mitigated that impression. Braglob
clearly hadn't bathed or groomed himself or had a decent
meal in no telling how long. Here was an antagonist more to
be pitied than feared. An individual at war with himself,
striking out at invisible opponents, fleeing from the tormentors that had invaded not his fortress but rather his own mind.

"Let the perambulator depart," Clothahump was saying
quietly, "and we will leave too. We need not fight. There is
no argument, no enmity between us: only an accident of
supernature. Let it go."

"*No*!" Braglob snarled, showing powerful teeth. "The
pretty stays. It makes me feel good. It warms me with its
company."

"See," the wizard whispered to his uneasy companions,
"he finds the perturbations reassuring. They convince him he
is no crazier than the rest of the world."

"*I am not insane*!" the wolverine shrieked in a shrill
voice. "It is *you* who are mad, who want me put away so I
cannot challenge the simpering, sickening status quo you find
so comforting. You and rest of the world." And he encompassed
it with a single sweeping gesture. "But the perambulator will
fix that." He adopted a sly expression, grinning at some
private thought. "I will keep it here close to me. The changes
will come more and more often. Soon they will be permanent."

"Being mad," said Clothahump slowly, "you can do one

of two things. You can make the rest of the world as mad as yourself or"—and he held out a hand in friendship—"you can make yourself unmad. If you would but let us, we might be able to help you. If your madness can be cured, you will no longer feel the need to live in an insane world. You won't be able to in any event, because before too long, the perambulator is going to perturb the sun itself. It will blow up and you will die, mad or sane, as quickly as the rest of us. Give it up, fellow practitioner of the art. Give it up."

"Prevaricator within a box, come no closer, I warn you!" The wolverine skittered back into the corridor a few steps and gestured threateningly with the battle-ax. Clothahump ignored the warning and continued his measured approach, reaching out now with both hands.

"Come now, since you still retain enough sense to execute spells, you must realize in some part of your brain that you are gravely ill. Why won't you let us help you?"

"No, please, stay away!" It was not a threat this time but a cry for help wearing the guise of an admonition, a desperate, pleading whine. The wolverine had backed himself up against a wall and held the ax out defensively in front of him. Jon-Tom was startled to see that the giant was trembling.

"Well, I'll be damned," Mudge muttered as Clothahump continued to talk to their nemesis in soothing, reassuring tones. "No wonder 'e's off 'is nut."

"What do you mean, Mudge?" Talea asked him.

"Cor, you mean you can't any of you see it? No, I expect you can't. 'Tis plain enough to me as the tail on me backside. This 'ere Braglob, for all 'is size an' sorcerous skill, 'e's a bloomin' coward. And I ought to know one when I sees one. No wonder 'e's crazy. As big as 'e is an' a wolverine to boot, why, if I 'ad that size and those muscles and that kind o' natural fightin' ability an' skill at magicking and was still a coward, I'd probably be a bit unbalanced meself."

"So *that's* what it is." Now that Mudge had pointed it out,

Jon-Tom wondered how he could have missed seeing it right away. The wolverine's whole posture and attitude since they'd encountered him was indicative not of defiance but of fear. *He* was afraid of *them*. All the threats he'd made since confronting them were just so much bluff.

That did not, however, mean that he was harmless. He flung the battle-ax aside and tried to crawl into the wall, wrapping his face in both arms as he turned away from them.

"No, don't come any closer, *get away*!"

How much of a wizard he was, they might never know, but madness can amplify magic as surely as it can physical strength. Insane people have been known to do extraordinary things, from bending the bars on hospital room windows to ripping off straitjackets while fighting a dozen men at a time.

Clothahump was blown backward by a blast of pure terrified madness, fueled by cowardice and powered by fear. He did have just enough time to draw in his head and limbs as he was thrown into a wall opposite. As he lay there rocking back and forth and trying to recover from the concussion, Braglob turned his paranoia on the rest of them.

"Go away, don't hurt me, leave me alone!" he sobbed.

The wind that struck them stank of madness. Dormas dug in and somehow managed to hold her ground. Colin had a low center of gravity to begin with. He immediately dropped to the ground and dug into the floor with his powerful claws.

But Mudge was lifted and tossed backward. Only his otterish acrobatic ability enabled him to tuck and roll. He was only slightly bruised as he reached out and grabbed onto one of Dormas's hind legs. He hung on as the insane gale tore at him, trying to blow him away, stretching him out behind the hinny like a furry flag rippling on a pole.

Jon-Tom had the duar around in front of him and was playing before the first storm-breath struck. The main force of the gale split and passed to either side of him. Talea stood at his back, shielded by his body and the aura of immobility in

which he'd wrapped himself. Her red hair streamed out
behind her. What wind did get through the spellsong ripped at
Jon-Tom's clothes and blew dust in his eyes. But it was not
strong enough to knock him off his feet.

Braglob slowly turned to stare at Jon-Tom, having at least
temporarily vanquished all other opponents. "You! Why
don't you go away too? I want you to go away!" He waved
both arms at Jon-Tom. A stronger gust of wind battered him,
but he was able to hold his ground. "Why don't you go
away?"

"Because I am not of your world, and so I do not respond
to your madness."

"What insanity is this?" roared the wolverine. "Another
lie!" His face twisted violently. "It will have to be something
special for you, then. Something unique. Something I have
never tried before. Something even more devastating than
your heart's desire."

"No, it won't. This madness has to stop. Not only for our
sake and for the rest of the world but for your own sake as
well, Braglob. It doesn't matter what you do from now on
because . . ."

And he began to sing, "We're not gonna take it. We're not
gonna take it. We're not gonna take it anymorrre . . . !"

Dee Snider and the rest of the gang would've been proud.

Braglob let out a tremulous howl. At the same time the
deep-throated hum and the song of the perambulator grew
louder still. Jon-Tom sang on, aware that Talea was tugging at
his shirt.

"Jon-Tom—look!"

There was something in the brilliantly lit chamber besides
the perambulator. Gneechees. Not just one or two this time
but a veritable snowstorm of them, each as bright and intense
as the perambulator itself. And for the first time outside of a
dream he found he could look at them directly instead of just
out of the corner of his eye.

They danced in the air, coalescing until they'd formed a laser-pure spiral that wove its way around the perambulator. They appeared to be tiptoeing on its fringes, tangent to but not quite touching the substance of the apparition that it was. They had been drawn to this place by Jon-Tom's spellsinging and remained to luxuriate in the instability generated by the perambulator.

Jon-Tom was growing hoarse trying to match his output to that of the otherworldly traveler. The sound battered at his body as much as at his ears. The music of the perambulator raged through his soul. He couldn't go on much longer.

So he threw the dice, took the chance, and tried to draw to an inside magical straight by changing his song in mid-refrain, switching abruptly (as abruptly as the perambulator, in fact) from a defiant ballad to the sweetest strong song he knew.

Braglob was ill-prepared for the sudden shift in tactics. The wolverine staggered away from his wailing wall, fought to draw himself upright. You could see the change come over him. His expression softened. His body relaxed as the tenseness drained out of his muscles. Most revealing of all, the wild, undisciplined stare began to fade from his eyes. Gone was the terrified, frozen glare; gone the hopeless, defensive posture.

He blinked once, twice, did Braglob the Mad, and smiled at Jon-Tom.

Behind him there came an explosion of light and sound. Even though he was looking away from it, the sudden pulse of energy temporarily blinded him. Gneechees fled the chamber like a million retreating miniature suns. The humming and whistling of the panpipes retreated before a single reverberating note like the lowest register of some gigantic organ.

Jon-Tom made himself turn, heedless of the consequences. The single devastating flash of light had faded, and he could see that the perambulator had been transformed a last time, into a crystalline geometric conglomerate so utterly perfect, so heart-stoppingly beautiful that he thought he would burst into tears.

He turned away just in time. A second energy pulse even more powerful than the first lit the walls. Jon-Tom felt himself lifted off his feet by the sheer pressure of light. He saw himself turning, tumbling, doing a slow somersault in the air, and bouncing gently off the far wall.

The organ pedal faded with the light, and so did his consciousness.

XIV

Calm. It was so calm, he thought as he regained his senses. It was quiet in the chamber, but in his mind he still heard that climactic final note, felt the photons lifting him off the ground and shoving him against the stones. Yet as he picked himself slowly off the floor and checked his bones, he discovered that there was no reminder of that hard contact, nothing broken, not so much as a bruise to indicate where he'd struck the wall. Even his clothing was undamaged.

A small shape lay crumpled nearly, lithe and familiar. It let out a sob. He stumbled over to kneel beside it. "Talea."

She was lying on her belly. He rolled her over, and she grabbed him tightly with both hands. He winced, having forgotten how strong she was. Then she recognized him and loosened her grip.

"Jon-Tom?"

"You're all right?"

She did not reply immediately, as though the question required some careful consideration. "I guess so. I shouldn't be. I think I bounced headfirst off the ceiling, like a ball in a game of whist.'' She sat up without his aid. ''But I feel okay. Just a little dazed. What happened?''

''The perambulator went away. It didn't go quietly, but I think it went joyfully. By breaking Braglob's madness we broke his control over it.'' He was looking past her, toward the center of the now-empty chamber. ''I think the perambulator, in its way, was saying good-bye to us as it departed. Or maybe it was nothing more than abstract noise. I guess we'll never know.''

Their companions were slowly picking themselves off the floor. Clothahump was examining the air beneath the dome. Protected and cushioned by his shell, he'd recovered first. Mudge was brushing himself off while Dormas was trying to untangle her legs from Colin, who'd been blown into her by the force of the perambulator's departure.

And there was one more who was recovering rapidly from the shock. Jon-Tom left Talea to cautiously confront their nemesis.

Braglob was flexing his muscles, testing first his legs and then his mighty arms. He appeared clear-eyed and alert.

''How do you feel?''

''Very strange, man.'' The wolverine lifted the hem of what once had been a fine piece of clothing. ''Why am I clad in rags like this? Wait—I remember now. Yes, I remember.'' He raised his eyes to meet Jon-Tom's. ''Something about changing the world. I was going to change the world so that I would feel comfortable with it.''

''But you don't have to do that anymore, do you? There's no longer any reason to live in a crazy world because you're no longer unbalanced yourself. You're cured, Braglob. Your madness departed with the perambulator. A little spellsinging goes a long way.''

Mudge had rejoined Colin, leaned close to whisper to the

koala. "Cured, 'e says. Look at 'em standin' there grinnin' at each other. If you ask me, the both of 'em are nuts."

Braglob listened, and as he listened, he was nodding slowly. "It is true. I don't remember exactly what I was doing or why. I remember only that I was afraid. I've always been afraid. Eventually my fears drove me from my family, my friends, my home. To this place, where I resolved to deal with my fears by changing the world. I had to do that, don't you see? It was the only way.

"My companions laughed at and tormented me until I fled to this remote region to escape their taunts. Even the smallest citizens, the rats and the mice and voles, threw things at me and chased me from their company. So I came here to practice my art. I studied hard. And I trapped the perambulator! Something the books said could not be done. I, Braglob, did this." He searched the chamber behind Jon-Tom. "And now it is gone isn't it?"

Jon-Tom nodded. "Gone like your madness and the fear that drove you mad. You couldn't live with your private terrors, could you? You couldn't deal with being a wolverine and a coward at the same time."

"You understand, then. But I am no longer fearful. I feel as I should. The fears are gone, every one of them, along with the pain and the hurt that was with me every day, here." He rubbed the back of his head and neck. "I feel—normal." His smile vanished.

"But I was going to change the world. I can't do that now. I was going to rule it. Tell me, man, is it better to live a sane but ordinary life or to be a mad emperor?" He reached for the massive battle-ax, which lay where he'd tossed it aside. "You have given me back my sanity but have stolen my dreams."

Jon-Tom took a step backward, his gaze shifting rapidly from the ax to Braglob's face. This was not turning out as he'd anticipated. Not only was the wolverine acting in a less than thankful manner, he seemed downright displeased about something.

"You could have left me alone to work out my problems on my own," Braglob growled.

"Left you alone? You mean, you were enjoying being a coward?"

"Of course not."

"Then you're saying you were happy as a madman?"

"No, but I didn't *know* that I was mad. I knew only that I was going to rule the world, or at least that I had the power to alter and affect it. Now I have no power at all." He held the battle-ax lightly in one paw.

"You don't need that now that you've had your sanity returned to you."

"A wolverine who has no need of power? What alien philosophy is that? I had power and you stole it from me. But you are right. You did cure me. I am quite myself now. Quite."

It suddenly struck Jon-Tom that having disposed of the perambulator and its perturbations, as well as having cured its captor, they now had to decide how to deal with an angry, intelligent, six-foot-tall wolverine with, so to speak, an ax to grind. Yes, Braglob was himself once more, with the temperament typical of a member of his species.

"Uh-oh, 'ere we go again." Mudge disengaged himself from Colin and made a dash to recover his sword and longbow. Dormas turned around so that her hind legs were facing the slowly advancing Braglob.

"Be reasonable. You're not thinking straight," Jon-Tom told the quietly furious wolverine. "There are six of us and only one of you."

Braglob was not impressed. "Six against one wolverine. Fair enough odds, man."

Jon-Tom didn't want a fight. It was crazy. There was no reason for a fight. The perambulator, the real cause of all the trouble and the reason they had made the long journey to this obscure mountain valley, had been sent on its merry way. It was ridiculous to think that they had accomplished all that they'd set out to do, only to be faced with an entirely new and unexpected danger in the form of this now-healthy, belligerent Braglob character. It made no sense, no sense at all. He wasn't going to stand for it!

However, he still had to convince Braglob of that.

"I could have lived with it," the wolverine was muttering angrily. "I could have coped. We wolverines live all our lives on the edge of madness as it is. But power is hard to get and harder to hold. You took it from me."

Jon-Tom was trying to think of what to say next when a small, squat shape stepped past him. "Your problem," Colin said as he fumbled with his pack, "is that you're not completely cured yet."

Holding the menacing ax high overhead, Braglob halted and turned his attention to this new arrival. "What do you mean, not cured?"

"It's obvious. You're still a coward."

The wolverine's eyes grew wide, and his nostrils flared. "Still a coward, am I? I'll show you who's a coward, fat-bear. I'll smash you like a bug."

Colin held up a hand. "You're still afraid. Not of me, or of any of the rest of us, but of the future. You don't know what it holds in store for you now that you've become yourself again, and it frightens you. When you were mad, you didn't give it a thought. Now you have to."

"Everyone is a little fearful of the future," Braglob snapped. "You as well as I. That is not cowardice, it is common sense. There is nothing that can be done about it."

"On the contrary." Colin extracted his familiar silver-and-black leather bag and stepped boldly forward. "I am a reader of runes. As a practitioner of the art, you know what that means. I can foretell the future. I can tell yours." He shook the bag so that Braglob could hear the pile of runes rattle within.

The wolverine hesitated. "No one can foretell the future. All rune-casters are charlatans and cheats."

"Not all. A few of us have the skill. None of us is perfect, but I'm pretty good."

"It's a trick. You're trying to shield yourselves from my wrath."

"Snakeshit. You can sit close and watch me. If I try anything that looks phony to you, I'll be in easy reach. Maybe if I tell your future and it looks good to you, you'll consider letting us leave without any bloodshed."

A long pause. Then the ax descended—to hang loosely at the wolverine's side. "Very well." He gestured past Colin with his free hand. "You see five tunnels leading from this chamber in addition to the one I am standing in. Only one other leads to freedom. The other four are dead ends." He sat down opposite Colin, blocking the hallway with his bulk.

"You can't slip out past me, and the odds against you finding the other exit on a first try are slight indeed. You will remain here as hostages to my disappointment until I have decided whether to reward this fat-bear or grind all of you underfoot."

"Fair enough." Colin sat down close to Braglob.

"Let's rush 'im, mate," Mudge whispered to Jon-Tom. " 'E's big an' tough and 'e might get one or two of us, but the rest would get away clean. An' if we 'it 'im fast enough, we might all of us make it. Let's 'ave at 'im while 'e's sittin' down an' preoccupied." His fingers began to slide slowly toward his sword.

Jon-Tom put a restraining hand on the otter's wrist. "No. Let's see what Colin can do first."

"Wot, an' wait while 'e entertains 'im at our expense? Better to 'ave a go now while we've 'alf a chance to surprise 'im."

"I said *wait*."

The otter whispered something particularly vile, and Jon-

Tom bridled, but he knew Mudge wouldn't attack on his own. Being the first into a fray was not the otter's idea of sensible strategy. So he fumed and kept his hand off his weapon.

For his part, Jon-Tom wondered what their best move would be should Colin's reading fail to assuage the wolverine's fury. Certainly he was big enough and fast enough to block the corridor he was occupying. Not even Sorbl would be able to slip past, for the roof was within reach of the wolverine's weapon.

"My future, then, and be quick about it," Braglob demanded, gesturing threateningly with the ax.

"You want this done right; it can't be rushed. First the ground must be prepared." Colin leaned forward and began smoothing the dust away from the polished stone beneath. "Everything must be just so, or the casting will be useless." Using the dust and dirt he'd gathered, he drew an ellipse on the floor. "Perfection in preparation is the key to a successful reading." He added several arcane symbols in the center of the ellipse. "See here. By concentrating the runes on this spot we'll have the best look at your immediate future."

Braglob leaned forward interestedly to study the symbols. "I have practiced the art, but I do not recognize these."

"They're not uncommon. It's just hard to delineate them properly when all you have to form them with is dirt and dust."

Braglob leaned forward until his nose was almost touching the symbols. "You are right. I believe I do recognize them."

"That's good, because it's almost time to cast." So saying, he grabbed the neck of the sack tightly with both hands and, with a swiftness even Mudge would have been hard-pressed to match, brought it down in a sweeping arc to land with a loud *whomp* on top of the wolverine's skull. Previously Jon-Tom had only considered their metaphysical weight.

Braglob's lower jaw dropped. Colin clobbered him with the bag of bone and stone a second time, and the wolverine keeled over to land chin first in the center of the circle as the sack exploded, sending the contents flying.

Mudge ran forward, bent to examine their opponent's face. "Out cold. Well struck, mate. That's what I calls predictin' the future."

"Yes, I thought a saw a period of extended rest in store for our combative friend here. It's not easy to read the runes through the leather." He eyed the shattered sack dolefully. "This will be hard to replace."

"I'll pay for the sewin'," said Mudge grandly. "Wot say we leave 'ere and find ourselves the nearest seamstress? Preferably one with talented 'ands." He gave the koala a hand in recovering the scattered runes.

"Should we finish him once and for all?" Dormas gave Jon-Tom's ramwood staff a nudge. He didn't like the idea of killing an unconscious opponent, but he looked to Clothahump for advice.

To his considerable relief the wizard agreed with his feelings. "My own prediction is that he will sleep for the rest of the day. This I base on my own reading of clever Colin's runes." There was a hint of a twinkle in the turtle's eye. "When he recovers, he will be mad again, only it will be a different and far less threatening kind of mad. If he is guilty of anything, it is of acting like one of his own kind. I know wolverines. Braglob will not come after us. They have short memories as well as short tempers, and this one has a great deal of reality to catch up with. When he comes 'round, he will have other things on his mind. Besides which, his species has no taste for an extended hunt and we will be well on our way.

"No, I think our misguided friend will be more interested in returning to his home and settling scores with his old tormentors rather than with us. Besides which, I am opposed to any unnecessary killing."

Mudge had tired of hunting for bits of bone and wood and

had been listening silently to the wizard's declamation. Now
he could no longer restrain himself.

"Unnecessary killin'? This oversized cowflop tries to destroy the whole world and then us in particular, an' you say
snuffin' 'im would amount to unnecessary killin'? Me, I never
saw a killin' so necessary!"

"You heard Clothahump," Jon-Tom warned his friend.
"There'll be no bloodshed here."

"Oh, who am I to argue with 'Is Sorcerership's ethics? I
ain't no grand master of magic. I'm just a simple gambler, I
am. I just like to cover me bets right is all, especially when
it's me life that's been pushed into the pot. 'No unnecessary
killing.' If I've 'eard that once, I've 'eard it a thousand times
from the both of you twits. I'm sick of it, you lot! Don't you
understand that there ain't no such thing as an unnecessary
killin'? It defines itself, it does. I calls it takin' out insurance,
is wot I calls it."

"Dormas, are you ready?" The hinny nodded. "Sorbl?"
The owl landed atop the pile of supplies and responded with
an agreeable hoot. "Let's go, then." He and Clothahump led
them up the hallway, past the wolverine's unconscious form.

"Oh, yes, let's go, by all means," Mudge grumbled as he
shoved both paws into the pockets of his shorts and stomped
off in their wake. "Nobody wants me advice, anyway." His
grousing echoed through the corridor as they retraced their
steps to the world outside.

Jon-Tom forced himself to sound casual as he spoke to
Talea. "You'll come back to Lynchbany with us, won't
you?" He held his breath while awaiting her reply.

She said nothing for several minutes, staring straight ahead
and looking solemn, but finally could contain the smile she'd
been holding back no longer. "Of course, I'm coming with
you, you silly spellsinger. Where else would I go in this bleak
and barren country?"

He swallowed. "Maybe—maybe you'll stick around a little

longer this time? Not," he added hastily, "that I'm trying to put any kind of restraints on you or anything. I know how much you value your independence."

Her smile seemed to shove the clouds back to the mountaintops as they emerged from the hallway onto the trail outside. "You know, Jon-Tom, anything can get old. Anything can become boring. Even independence."

He had composed a lengthy and carefully considered reply when he caught Clothahump grinning at him. He understood what the wizard was trying to tell him immediately. There were times when he talked too much and ended up talking himself into a predicament from which he couldn't extricate himself and in which he need not have foundered in the first place. So he just nodded down at Talea while adopting his most mature and farsighted expression.

"I understand."

She appeared to find this the ideal response because she rose on tiptoes, grabbed him firmly around the neck, and bent him forcefully to her. He held the kiss until his back began to hurt.

Finally he straightened, caught his breath, and turned to regard the poorly constructed fortress in which they'd encountered so much wonder and danger. His ears still rang faintly from the force of the perambulator's departure. It was a sight and sound he would never forget, a memory he would be able to call upon during times of darkness to rejuvenate and inspire his spirits. It had been his good fortune to look upon the majesty of the universe.

Hell, he'd jammed with it.

They made excellent progress as travelers always do when they are on their way home, and camped that evening on the far side of the mountain pass.

"Poor Braglob," Jon-Tom murmured. "May he finally find contentment and happiness within himself."

" 'Appiness 'e may find." Mudge scratched at one ear.

"But contentment? Not bloody likely. I never saw a contented wolverine. Those folks are always upset about somethin'. Even when they're makin' love, they're yellin' and screamin' at one another. Fortunately there ain't many of 'em around. Probably because they don't get along any better in bed than they do in society."

Jon-Tom turned to face Clothahump. The wizard was leaning against a log on the opposite side of the campfire. His eyes were half shut, and he appeared to be contemplating the night sky, a broad sweep of stars and constellations very different from those Jon-Tom had grown up with.

"What do you think happened to the perambulator, sir?"

"What?" The turtle glanced over at his young charge. "Went on its way, of course. Across the cosmos. Out of this universe and into another. I was just thinking: What if one could be controlled across such distances and brought back? What might we learn of reality? What images might we gaze upon, what mysteries might we solve?" He sighed deeply.

"That is a burden you will suffer under yourself one of these days, my boy. The pain of not knowing, the ache of ignorance, the compulsion to know what lies on the far side of the hill, while realizing that no matter how much you learn, there will always be another hill to surmount. That is the curse on a seeker of knowledge, the curse of never being satisfied.

"When I was very young and apprenticed to the famous sorcerer Jogachord, I would ask him new questions constantly until finally, tired of being pestered, he would say to me, 'Does there have to be an answer for everything?' And I would reply in utmost earnest, 'Yes!' Then he would smile at me and say, 'Apprentice, with that attitude you will go far—provided no one kills you first.' "

"The curse o' never bein' satisfied? I suffer from that meself," Mudge declared. "Only, it don't involve idiocies like 'too much knowledge'."

"We all know what it involves, Mudge," said Talea dryly. "You don't have to burden us with the details."

The otter looked hurt. "Now, 'ow do you know wot I was goin' to say, luv?"

"Because given the slightest opportunity, you always talk about the same thing, water rat. You have a one-track mind."

"Aye, but wot a pleasant track it is, especially when it leads to—"

"Mudge," Jon-Tom said exasperatedly.

The otter put up both paws defensively. "All right, mate. I can see that you lot don't share me favorite topic o' conversation. You'll just 'ave to suffer along for the rest o' the evenin' without 'earin' about me glorious exploits concernin'—oop, forgot. I ain't supposed to talk about that."

A sudden thought made Jon-Tom sit up straight. "Hey, if Colin can see into tomorrow, I wonder if he can predict if I'll ever get home or not?"

Clothahump shrugged as best he could without shoulders. "Anything is possible, my boy. It might be worthwhile to find out."

"It'd be a damned sight more than worthwhile." He let his gaze wander around the campsite. Dormas was sleeping soundly off to one side. Talea lay curled up next to him, her face a portrait of false innocence, the outline of her body a delicious sine curve against the ground. Mudge sat nearby, his paws behind his head and his cap pulled down over his eyes.

But where was their rune-reader? Come to think of it, where was Sorbl? He rose, nervously surveyed the encroaching night, and murmured to Clothahump. "Braglob? You think he's been tracking us after all?"

"No, no, my boy. It is most unlikely. In any case, he would have been detected by now. The wolverine scent is a strong one, and there are sensitive noses among us." He climbed to his feet and joined Jon-Tom in scanning the forest. "But your concern is not misplaced. I, too, wonder where our friend and my apprentice have taken themselves. Sorbl! You good-for-nothing famulus, where are you?''

Jon-Tom cupped his hands to his mouth. "Colin! Colin, answer us!''

"Now wot? I can't talk about love an' now I can't sleep.'' The otter jumped up. "The people I get mixed up with!''

They spread out but didn't have to search far. The two missing members of their party lay beneath the great spreading branches of a cocklegreen tree. They were singing softly to each other of their contentment and of life's disappointments. The almost-empty bottle that Sorbl was clutching in one flexible wingtip provided an explanation both for their disappearance as well as the impromptu concert.

Clothahump wrenched it from his apprentice's grasp and held it upside down. A few golden drops tumbled from the mouth. He shook it at the thoroughly inebriated owl.

"You useless bag of feathers, we accomplished what we set out to do! You were supposed to stop drinking. That was our agreement. Whatever was left was to be conserved for medicinal purposes only!''

"Thash whet''—the owl swallowed and appeared to having some difficulty speaking—"thash whet it was ushed for, Mashter.'' He promptly fell over backward. "You don't have to hit me, Mashter.''

"Disgusting.'' Clothahump threw the empty bottle into the bushes. "And *that* wants to become a wizard.'' He turned and marched angrily back toward the camp.

"I'll say 'tis disgustin'. It bloody well stinks.'' Mudge leaned close to the owl's face. "Why didn't you come and get me if you were goin' to 'ave yourselves a bleedin' party?''

"Didn't—didn't want to dishturb you.''

"And, besides,'' Colin said, his words grave and slow, "there really wasn't enough for three.''

Mudge glared over at the koala. "An' you call yourself a friend?'' He rose and stalked off in the wizard's wake, leaving Jon-Tom alone with the two revelers. He rose and walked over to kneel next to the koala.

"Colin?"

"Who?"

"Hey, that's my line," chortled Sorbl. He and Colin started cackling hysterically.

Jon-Tom waited a minute or two before putting a hand on the koala's shoulder and shaking him. "Colin, listen to me. This is serious. I need to know if you can read my future. I need to find out if I'll ever be able to go home again, back to my own world."

"Well, I might be able to," the koala replied with enforced solemnity. "I just might. Except for one thing."

"What one thing?" A hand came down on his shoulder, and he looked up into Talea's moonlit face. She was smiling down hopefully at him.

Colin raised himself up until his lips were close to Jon-Tom's ear. "I can't read runes tonight."

"You can't? But you've read them at night before."

"I know. But I can't read them tonight."

"Why not?"

The koala put a thick finger to his lips, leaned close again. "Because Mudge and I threw them in that river we passed this afternoon." His face contorted, and he and Sorbl fell to laughing uncontrollably again.

Jon-Tom gaped at him. "You did *what*?"

"Threw 'em in the river. Never did much care for rune-reading, anyways. Folks always bothering you, asking you the damnedest things, never leaving you alone. The hell with it. I'm going home and into my brother-in-law's eucalyptus-leaf pressing business, like my sister always wanted me to. That's a nice, sensible, respectable occupation."

"You couldn't have waited one more day, could you?" He sat heavily back on his heels. "I don't suppose you can read the future without runes?"

"What d'you think I am, some kind of magician?" The koala was rapidly falling asleep.

Talea reached over to run a hand through Jon-Tom's hair. Her presence made him feel very much better. "Hush and don't take it to heart, Jonny-Tom. For some of us the future is not to know." She put her lips to his ear. "But I can predict some very good things coming to you in the near future." Her voice dropped even lower, and Jon-Tom couldn't help but grin as she continued whispering to him.

He was still upset, though, and told Colin so. The koala frowned, struggling to retain consciousness.

"As a matter of fact, I did read the runes one last time before we cast 'em into the current of fate, so to speak. Sort of a farewell prediction."

Jon-Tom bent forward. "Whose future did you read? Not mine, or you would've said so already. Mudge's? Talea's?"

"Nope."

"Clothahump's?" The koala shook his head. "Sorbl's, then?"

"Nope. None of those. I was interested in where the perambulator was off to, after listening to you and the old one going on and on about how it can go anywhere and everywhere. I got curious, wondered if maybe it was going to come back to our world and start up the troubles all over again."

Jon-Tom shook his head. "That's nothing to worry about, unless by some unbelievable coincidence it lands in Braglob's vicinity again. Though since he isn't crazy anymore, even that isn't very threatening. We don't have anything to worry about anymore on that score."

"Maybe most of us don't, but *you* might."

"Me? Why me?"

"Because it's on its way to your world. It's going to stick around there for a while and do its dance. Things there are going to go a little crazy, maybe for a few years instead of a few months. I couldn't see a time line clearly. Why, it's probably there already, right now, even as we're sitting here talking about it. And I'm afraid it's gone and gotten itself stuck. That's what the runes said, anyway." He let his head back down on his hands, rolled over. "Now go away and let me sleep. All of a sudden I'm kind of tired."

"No, wait!" Jon-Tom shook him again. "I've got to know in case I do get back. Maybe it's stuck someplace where it can't do any real harm. You've got to tell me where it's going to go!"

Colin murmured something under his breath, blinked sleepily up at the insistent Jon-Tom. "Where? Oh, some little town called Columbia, in a district or state called Washington."

Jon-Tom let out a relieved sigh. "That sounds pretty harmless. Way up in the north woods somewhere."

"Or," Colin mumbled uncertainly as he drifted back to sleep, "was it someplace called Washington, in the district of Columbia?"

"Colin? Colin?" Jon-Tom finally stopped shaking the erstwhile rune-reader. He was sound asleep and snoring loudly. "I wish I knew which was right. It may be there already, undetected and unseen, twisting and turning, working its mischief."

"It doesn't matter. There's nothing you can do about it." Talea was easing him backward, planting small but intense kisses on his neck and chest as she did so.

Soon he was gazing thoughtfully up at the stars. "What the hell," he finally muttered, "they'd never notice the difference there, anyways."

Then he was staring up at Talea instead of the stars, and not an iota of beauty had been lost in the transition. . . .

THE SPELLSINGER SERIES
by Alan Dean Foster

___SPELLSINGER (E34-195, $3.50, U.S.A.)
(E34-196, $4.50, Canada)

John Thomas Meriweather—grad student, rock guitarist, peace lover—is magically transported to a wizard's world, a planet of disarming beauty and savage violence. Here he strives to save this new world as a crusader and a soldier battling with sword and song.

___SPELLSINGER II: (E34-181, $3.50, U.S.A.)
THE HOUR OF THE GATE (E34-182, $4.50, Canada)

The dreaded plated folk are coming, and it's up to the wizard and the Spellsinger to stop the invasion. In Foster's charmed universe of talking beasts, John Meriweather continues to follow his fate. Having stumbled into another world, the grad student and rock guitarist found himself to be a maker of musical magic, the powerful Spellsinger. Now, together with the wise Clothahump, the wizard and turtle, he must undertake a strange voyage into enemy territory in search of allies against an evil horde. It is a perilous journey few have attempted, and none have ever survived.

___SPELLSINGER III: THE DAY (E34-158, $3.50, U.S.A.)
OF THE DISSONANCE (E34-159, $4.50, Canada)

Confronting a forest of fungoid Frankensteins, a parrot pirate, cannibal fairies and the evil wizard of Malderpot, Jon-Tom journeys to a distant land on a mission of magic and danger!

WARNER BOOKS
P.O. Box 690
New York, N.Y. 10019

Please send me the books I have checked. I enclose a check or money order (not cash), plus 50¢ per order and 50¢ per copy to cover postage and handling.* (Allow 4 weeks for delivery.)

_____ Please send me your free mail order catalog. (If ordering only the catalog, include a large self-addressed, stamped envelope.)

Name _____

Address _____

City _____

State _____ Zip _____

*N.Y. State and California residents add applicable sales tax. 92